Compelling, breathtaking, and sometimes brutal, *Dawn of a Thousand Nights* pulled me into its WWII setting and kept me reading late into the night again and again. Ms. Goyer is a masterful storyteller who knows how to bring history to life.

—Robin Lee Hatcher, best-selling author of
The Victory Club and *Loving Libby*

A great story! A great writer! Historically accurate. I know. I was there.

—C. M. Graham, WWII veteran, Bataan survivor,
and author of *Under The Samurai Sword*

Heartbreaking and triumphant, *Dawn of a Thousand Nights* makes real the struggles and sacrifices of those men and women at home and abroad who fought to give us the freedoms we often take for granted today.

—DeAnna Julie Dodson, author of *In Honor Bound, By Love Redeemed* and *To Grace Surrendered*

It is rare to see a novel pay such attention to historical detail.

—Tony Banham, WWII Historian and
WWII Book Author

Tricia Goyer's *Dawn of a Thousand Nights* is a deeply emotional read, rich with historical detail and true to the heart of God.

—Lyn Cote, Author of *The W... of Ivy Manor*

Tricia Goyer h... searched and most accurate accou... ever read. She has woven her cha... Pearl Harbor, the Philippines, and ... that it is hard to remember that this is actually a book of fiction.

—Millie Dalrymple, Former WASP
(Women Air Force Service Pilot)

Having lived through WWII and actively participated in the military for the Air Force, I found *Dawn of a Thousand Nights* not only an easy read but an accurate portrayal. It brought to mind the suffering of those who had been captured and the realization of how man can be so cruel to man. Tricia Goyer is a very talented storyteller.

—Bernice Haydu, Woman Airforce Service Pilot of WWII, author of *Letters Home 1944–1945*

Dawn of a Thousand Nights gives the reader an amazing peek into history and into the human heart. This story is gripping and inspiring, written with grace and intelligence. The reader is in for a soaring flight of the mind, heart, and soul.

—Kathryn Mackel, author of *Outriders*

Tricia Goyer's masterful storytelling techniques will grip the reader with the magnificence of human emotions set in the midst of a tragic part of US history. Share in the victory and defeat, good and evil, and humility and pride as heroes are made within the pages of this unforgettable drama.

—DiAnn Mills, Christian Fiction Author

Tricia Goyer is a seamstress of fiction. She dares to weave designs full of suspense, history, humor, romance, and spiritual truth. In the same manner that Bodie Thoene's early novels brought new understanding, Tricia Goyer's stories never sugarcoat the horror, but always highlight God's workings in the midst of suffering.

—Eric Wilson, author of *Expiration Date* and *Dark to Mortal Eyes*

DAWN OF A *Thousand Nights*

A STORY OF HONOR

TRICIA GOYER

MOODY PUBLISHERS
CHICAGO

Library of Congress Cataloging-in-Publication Data

Goyer, Tricia.
Dawn of a thousand nights : a story of honor / Tricia Goyer.
p. cm.
ISBN-13: 978-0-8024-0855-6
1. World War, 1939–1945—Prisoners and prisons, Japanese—Fiction. 2. Bataan Death March, Philippines, 1942--Fiction. 3. Women Airforce Service Pilots (U.S.)—Fiction. 4. World War, 1939–1945—Philippines—Fiction. 5. Air pilots, Military—Fiction. 6. Prisoners of war—Fiction. I. Title.

PS3607.O94D39 2005
813'.6—dc22

2005011922

ISBN: 0-8024-0855-9
ISBN-13: 978-0-8024-0855-6

1 3 5 7 9 10 8 6 4 2

Printed in the United States of America

For Cory Joseph, my oldest son
Bravery and honor was proven
by the men I've interviewed.
I also see it every day in
the young man you've become.

PART ONE

"He has broken my teeth with gravel; he has trampled me in the dust.
I have been deprived of peace; I have forgotten what prosperity is.
So I say, 'My splendor is gone and all that I had hoped from the LORD.'"
Lamentations 3:16–18 NIV

Dishonor is like a scar on a tree,
which time, instead of effacing, only helps to enlarge.
–Samurai code

One

U.S. SENDING SCORES OF PILOTS
TO HAWAII AND PHILIPPINES

The latest transfer orders published by the War Department show that some 118 second lieutenants who have recently won their wings have been ordered to embark for the Pacific outposts in the next three weeks.

That necessity has in turn raised the problems of how to give young pilots actual army flying experience in high-speed, complex combat ships once they have completed their work with the slower trainers.

Until a pilot has had about a year of such experience he is not considered ready to engage in combat operations.

Excerpt from the *Washington Post,* June 5, 1941

Dan Lukens's leather-gloved hand rammed the throttle. The force of the screaming Allison V-12 engine shoved his body into the back of his seat. As the rumble from a half dozen fighters grew louder, Dan blinked sweat from his eyes. The metallic black "birds" came into view, distorting the air behind them into a fuzzy haze.

Grimacing, Dan shoved the stick full forward and rudder pedals full right and cranked his Curtiss P-40 into the Chennault maneuver. His nimble fighter spun into an outside barrel roll, jerking his body against his harness. He pulled out of the roll and converted his diving momentum to a high-speed climb, mentally preparing for the dogfight ahead.

"Come on, boys. Show me what you've got," Dan hissed through clenched teeth, his neck tensed and senses peaking.

But the attackers held back. They circled Dan's group cautiously. Finally, when minutes passed and they didn't strike, Dan took the initiative.

He broke left through a wispy cloud and targeted the lead plane. "You're mine now!" he yelled over the roaring engine. He pinpointed the enemy plane through his sights—a clear shot. He squeezed the trigger. "Got ya!" he yelled with excitement into his radio. "You're out of here, pal. Yes, I'm talking to you." When the plane fell away, he turned his attention to Gabriel Lincoln's plane—now being trailed by one of the attackers. Gabe attempted to shake him, to no avail.

"Keep it up, Gabe. Don't let him get you. I'm on my way."

Dan dropped into the sights of Gabe's attacker, hoping to draw his attention. The attacker pulled off Gabe, making a yard-wide turn and leaving a trail of exhaust behind him.

In their pilots' training, Dan's instructor had told him never to follow a Japanese Zero into a tight turn. Yet with adrenaline pumping, he turned after the plane in tigerish pursuit.

Dan pulled against his harness as if trying to urge every bit of power from the P-40. "That's the way, doll face. You've got it." He dove straight into the attacker's flight path, cutting him off. The attacker had no choice but to accelerate and pop up into Dan's line of vision, or slam into his plane. Dan was betting his life on the first option.

"Pull up. Come on." A loud roaring sound from beneath him drowned out his words.

Seconds seemed like hours as the long nose of Dan's P-40 blocked his view of the other fighter, but he held his position, worrying for the briefest instant whether he'd overdone it, cut the guy off too short.

Suddenly, the attacker increased his speed and altitude, popping into view not more than fifty yards in front of Dan. The pilot's sweaty, glaring face turned Dan's direction.

Dan grinned, spotting the plane in his sights. "Got ya!" he called into his radio, then waved to the pilot.

Dan noted his kill. The attacker dropped toward the ground, and though the temptation was strong to visually follow the plane's path to the harbor, Dan had better sense. Especially with other attackers around.

After picking off the rest of the "enemy" fighters, Dan headed back to once again claim the day's most kills. His heart still thumped as the harbor came into view, sparkling in the morning sunlight.

As long as I've got this plane, I can tackle anything thrown at me. He sucked in a calming breath as the Curtiss P-40 broke through thin clouds into the blue. A surge of confidence as strong as the plane's engine welled in his chest. Confidence in his flying and in his team. While others fretted that war was inevitable, Dan trusted that the U.S. Army Air Corps would hold its own . . . trusted that his leaders knew what they were doing.

As the P-40 continued its descent, Pearl Harbor greeted him, its blue waters spreading out in the shape of a cloverleaf—the stalk being the entrance to the channel and the leaves unfolding to the west, middle, east, and southeast lochs.

A four-leaf clover. Dan felt like the luckiest guy alive to be playing war games with fast planes in such a beautiful place. It reminded him of the toy battles he and his friends used to play in the sandlot at the end of the street. Only these weren't model planes, but rather the army's best, that he and his buddies maneuvered around the sky.

Between the east and southeast lochs, Ford Island bustled with activity. It was a compact airfield complete with tower and hangars, administrative buildings, and living quarters. The movement of people and machines on the island stirred in full gear.

Alongside the island, docked in the harbor, sat a fleet of battleships moored in pairs. Dan took note of their bows pointed toward the southwest channel. Intermingled among them, civilian ships dropped off tourist groups to be entertained on Waikiki Beach, lovingly referred to as the "Coney Island of the Pacific."

Dan had taken off from Ford Island numerous times, but today his maneuvers originated from another nearby air base, Hickam Field—due south of Ford Island and the Navy Yard—on the island of Oahu itself.

Within a matter of minutes, he had executed his landing at Hickam and parked his plane wingtip to wingtip next to the others. He joined the other pilots in leather flight jackets, who now formed a dozen-man circle on the tarmac. Dan slid off his flight helmet as he approached the group and ran his hand through his sweat-drenched blond hair. Perspiration had made a wet stain on his flight suit, ringing his underarms and making a dark spot on his chest.

A cheer rose from two or three of the guys as he approached. Others called out "Just lucky!" and "I'll get you next time!"

"I'm just glad you're on our side." His buddy Zeke Olson gave him a strong shoulder squeeze. "I guess that means you win the bet. I owe you a drink at the Black Cat."

"Nah. How about a football game on the beach?

I'm getting tired of all the commotion and noise in the honky-tonk district."

"You're on. UCLA paired up against Oregon State once again—Hawaiian style."

⁂

The aroma of tropical flowers wafted through the cool morning air as Libby Conners, dressed in a flight suit, strode across the tarmac of John Rodgers Airport to do a quick check of the Piper Cub. The plane wasn't as fancy as those she'd flown in the States, but it was simple and economical. And this newer Cub benefited from a wider front seat, allowing teacher and student to sit side by side rather than tandem. She considered the Piper safe and sturdy—until the trade winds blew in.

But to Libby, the best type of plane was any one she could fly. That's why she'd come to Hawaii and why she had stayed. Distanced from mainland prejudices against women, she had found a place where she could soar.

Satisfied the plane was in top shape, she patted its sleek metal belly.

"Mr. Conners?" said a youthful voice from behind her.

Libby turned, her tall frame causing her to meet the sailor eye-to-eye. *They're looking younger all the time.* She stretched out her hand. "Miss Conners, actually. Good to have you. This your first flying lesson?"

The boy's eyes widened as he studied her face and the medium brown locks she'd tucked into her flight helmet.

"Better close that jaw before you swallow a fly, kid." Libby took two long strides and pointed to the open door of the Cub. "The clock is ticking."

The sailor didn't budge. Libby glanced back.

"Uh, I didn't know I was gettin' lessons from a girl." His hands and shoulders moved as he spoke, as if he shrugged off his words as well as spoke them.

Libby crossed her arms, straightened her shoulders, and waited.

His eyes darted back toward the office, as if hoping someone would emerge and tell him there'd been a misunderstanding. When no one came to his rescue, he dug his hands into his pockets and offered a slight shrug. "Uh, okay, I guess. You're not gonna get me killed, are you?"

Been flying since you were still in elementary school learning how to read, Libby wanted to respond. Instead she reached over and patted the kid's shoulder. "Got my adequate teaching licenses all in order. Besides, during this first lesson I doubt you'll learn much anyway. Most guys are so excited by the sight of the island and ocean from the air that nothing sticks. So we'll sign you up for a lesson next weekend too. Saturday, if possible. Sunday's nearly always full."

The kid nodded and climbed into the small cockpit. His face reddened as Libby slid in next to him, their shoulders and hips pressed together in the tight space.

He'll get over that too. Libby quickly scanned the runway, checking for other planes before starting the engine. *Before long, he'll just think of me as one of the guys. A buddy, a pal. And a darn good instructor.*

❧ ❧ ❧

Sometimes, in the first waking heartbeat when dawn stirred Natsuo Hidki from his slumber, he believed he was there again. In the California town of modern living. In the country that could not comprehend the traditions of his homeland. At the college where friendships were made and soon abandoned.

It had been two years since he'd returned to Japan. His time at UCLA had been short. Why, then, did his mind keep taking him back? Perhaps as a curse. An aching reminder of his turning away from the Land of the Rising Sun.

Father had asked him to go. Believed that Western thinking and technology were important for the future of Japan. And though his mother dared not disagree, in the split second before she looked away Natsuo had seen fear in her gaze. She worried that her son would not come back. Just as his sister had not.

But Natsuo had returned. Smarter in the understanding of the world, and witnessing his homeland in a new light. Though still bound by his country's codes of honor, Natsuo's California teachers had succeeded in planting the sturdy oaks of Western thinking within the ancient soil of his soul.

America. Why couldn't it leave him alone?

As Natsuo lay on his mat and breathed in the scent of cherry blossoms through the open window, he wondered why he'd been transported back. It would be better to forget. Especially now, with his upcoming position as a soldier.

Through the thin walls of his childhood home, his mother's humming caused the corners of Natsuo's lips to flicker a slight smile. She was preparing his favorite breakfast, rice and miso soup. His call to service weighed on her heart too.

He rose from his mat and stretched in the morning rays, then padded across the cool wooden floor while his mind granted permission for East and West to coexist. Without hesitation, the words of the American poet Emily Dickinson joined his mother's tune:

He ate and drank the precious Words—
His Spirit grew robust—
He knew no more that he was poor,
Nor that his frame was Dust—

He danced along the dingy Days
And this Bequest of Wings
Was but a Book – What Liberty
A loosened spirit brings—

Natsuo had memorized the words long ago at UCLA, in a class his father had urged him not to take. How, after all, could American poetry ever make a difference to the future of Japan?

He only wished it would stop haunting his thoughts.

Two

WAR ON TWO FRONTS

Among many people there is a belief that the country should avoid any positive action in the Far East that might lead to war with Japan since this would interfere seriously with our aid to Great Britain. This may account in part for the fact that for three years we've been supplying war materials to Japan to enable her to defeat China, a nation whose preservation is essential to peace in the Far East. At the same time we have given moral support to China to encourage her to continue the war.

The amount of air force to give us supremacy is small compared to that required in Europe. Planes that are now held at Panama and Hawaii could be sent to the Philippines, where they could be of some use. Panama and Hawaii are entirely safe for some time to come.

Adm. H. E. Yarnell (U.S. Navy, Ret.)
Excerpt from the *Washington Post,* June 12, 1941

A row of palm trees greeted Libby with waving fronds as she took the concrete steps in front of her apartment two at a time. The short walk from the airstrip had been quiet except for the incessant cooing of pigeons in her favorite mango tree. She placed the ripe mango she'd plucked from its branches on her kitchen counter, then traded in her tailored slacks and sport shirt for a navy blue swimsuit and beach towel.

In the parking lot, her friend and fellow pilot Rose Wright waited in her parents' Buick convertible. Libby re-emerged with a wave, relishing the plumeria scents from the flowering trees dotting their complex, and hurried to the car. The Hawaiian sun hung high, glowing like a red-hot furnace in the midafternoon sky.

"Whew, it's hot! I have to get wet before my internal organs bake." Libby slipped into the front seat and tossed her towel to the back. "Hawaii's beautiful, but I miss the seasons back home. This heat would be easier to take if I knew we'd have cool weather or even snow coming in a few months."

"Aloha to you too." Rose backed up the car, tires squealing. "Did you say snow? I've never seen the stuff, but I imagine it's not half as fun as a mile of white sand . . . which is just what I've ordered up for you today."

Libby slipped a pink scarf from her handbag and

used it to wipe her face and neck. She glanced over at Rose. With her Hawaiian mother's thick, dark hair and rich complexion and her American father's blue eyes, Rose stood out, even among the locals. Her wide smile and outgoing personality made her a favorite at John Rodgers.

Libby, on the other hand, had medium brown hair that was harder to tame than the numerous sailors who roamed Waikiki, and her eyes were plain brown. She tied her hair into a loose ponytail with the scarf. "I take that back. White sand sounds perfect. Heading for our spot?"

"Where else? But I think I'll die if I hear one more pick-up line. The sailors seem to be multiplying by the day."

They traveled southwest, leaving the outskirts of Honolulu behind. The car paused at the train tracks. Tourists and sailors alike often rode the "Toonerville Trolley," the local train that carried them around Honolulu. Most of the *haoles,* or nonnatives, remained within close proximity to Honolulu. But since Rose was a native, their favorite spot was Ewa Beach.

The drive itself was worth the trip. Red and yellow hibiscus grew along the roadway, and papaya and guava trees grew wild, their fruit ripe for the picking. But Libby's favorites were the banyan trees, which sent shoots down from their branches to take root and become new trunks.

After twenty minutes of visually feasting on the island's vegetation, they arrived.

Libby grinned. "No one here; just how I like it."

"Me too." Rose quickly braided her hair, letting it fall like a thick rope over one bronzed shoulder.

Libby felt the tension slip away as she helped Rose scoop up the picnic basket and blanket. They strode onto the powdered-sugar sand, lined with swaying coconut palms, and spread out their things.

"A perfect getaway for sky-fliers, don't you think?" Rose lay down on her back and stretched her arms in the sunshine.

"Um-hum." Libby kicked off her sandals and headed toward the water's edge.

"Don't be out long," Rose called. "My mother packed us chicken *lau lau.*" She knew that the chicken and butterfish, wrapped in taro leaves, was Libby's favorite dish.

Libby breathed in the salt air and gazed at the deep turquoise blue ocean. She dove into a wave just before it broke, kicking as the cool water washed over her. The swimming was perfect, as long as one didn't venture out too far. The riptide had a nasty way of catching on and not letting go.

Coming to her feet on the other side, she shook off the water and trudged back to Rose. Diamond Head towered in the distance, deep green and jutting sharply into the sky. Libby had flown over the island hundreds of times and was always awed by the groves of banana trees, endless sugarcane fields, and the lush rain forests that were rumored to host wild orchids.

By the time Libby came dripping back to the blanket, Rose had laid out a feast of native dishes.

"*Li hing mui!* Your mom is a doll!" The sweet-and-sour dried plums were another of her favorites.

"Enjoy," Rose said, with an openhanded flourish.

Despite the fact that both women worked as flight instructors at John Rodgers Airport, it had taken months for them to become friends. Libby was an outsider, after all, but their shared interest in the zippy new military airplanes making their way to the island had created a bond between them. Now Libby was a frequent visitor to the Wright home and an "auntie" to the numerous waist-high neighbors and cousins she couldn't keep track of.

"I never thought I'd say it, but I'm tired of the attention of handsome sailors." Rose broke off a large bite of Hawaiian sweet bread. "Yesterday I received *six* invitations for dinner. I haven't been home one evening this week. My mom says it's inevitable. She married an American, and so did her three sisters. But I told her since I already have my U.S. citizenship, it's not like I *need* to marry military."

Libby popped a sour plum into her mouth. "Yeah, but it's not like there's many other choices. They're everywhere."

Rose stared into the cloudless sky. "All the poor sailors want to talk about is how much they miss their homes and their mamas. It's the same story told a thousand different ways." She sighed. "Can't we just hide here forever?"

Libby smiled and dug her toes deeper into the warm white sand. "Yes, let's do. I bet your mom will bring us food. Your dad can stop by to barbecue. After all, a girl needs to eat."

"Nah." Rose laughed. "We can live on coconuts." She pointed to the trees lining the beach and the many smooth, oblong coconuts that lay on the ground. "Only problem is, you don't know how to open them."

"Does any *haole?*" Libby grinned.

While they ate, Rose launched into a play-by-play of her most recent date. Libby kept quiet. Despite the ridiculous ratio of men to women, she hardly received one invitation a week. She blamed it on her busy schedule, or perhaps the baggy coveralls and denim cap she wore around the airfield.

Suddenly Libby cocked her head and moaned. "Please tell me I'm not hearing what I think I'm hearing."

Rose shielded her eyes with her hand. "Two guys in a convertible. Kinda cute, but, oh, yes, military haircuts. They've found us." She pressed the back of her hand to her forehead and plopped back to the ground in a Hollywood starlet's fainting spell.

Libby chuckled. "Maybe if we ignore them, they'll go away." She tied her scarf over her damp hair and attempted to tuck away the escaping strands.

"Here they come." Rose glanced out of the corner of her eye. "One of them looks like a young Clark Gable with blond hair, and . . ." She pressed a hand to her lips, speaking through her fingers. "There goes his shirt."

Libby refused to look, but she could clearly hear their voices and the sound of a football being tossed.

Rose slid her tortoiseshell sunglasses over her eyes. "As you said, maybe if we ignore them . . ."

Her words said one thing, but the soft grin on Rose's lips showed she meant something completely different.

For the next few minutes, Libby attempted to relax despite the sound of men's laughter bouncing across the sand. Was it just her imagination, or were the voices growing nearer? She dared to open her eyes, focusing on the lacy fronds of the palm trees that danced above her.

She leaned up on her elbow toward Rose, who was still "not looking" at the guys. "Have you noticed the harbor lately? The whole Pacific Fleet's been moved here from California. Has your dad heard anything?"

"Could be." Rose patted her damp hair with her towel. "You know I'm not at liberty to say."

"Of course not." Libby studied her stubby fingernails. "I don't think I could do his job. It would be too much for me to hold all that information inside. At least he knows you won't tell—"

The sound of a football thumping into the sand interrupted Libby's words. A spray of sand covered her legs. She brushed it away, ignoring the soft footfall of someone running up behind her. "My dad says the Japs are a bigger threat than we imagine and—"

A shadow fell over her. "Sorry, ladies."

Libby watched Rose's eyes lift.

"No harm." Rose gave a sweet glance from beneath her long eyelashes.

Despite her effort not to look, Libby found herself meeting the fellow's deep blue eyes with her own.

The footsteps receded, and Libby pretended to ignore the exchange. She also tried to ignore the memory of his dimpled cheeks and muscular chest.

"Anyway, Daddy wrote and asked me to come home. He's afraid the waters will be too dangerous to cross soon."

There it was again, the *whoosh* of the football and the sand splattering her legs. She sat up straighter and brushed it away. Again, the shadow and the apology. The sound of footsteps in the sand as he jogged away.

"Guys are so juvenile. Didn't they outgrow this in junior high?"

Rose nodded and mumbled an "mm-hmm," but her eyes continued to dart down the beach.

"Hello, are you with me?" Libby waved a hand in front of her friend's face.

"Of course. I'm listening. So what are you going to do? You're not heading back to the mainland, are you?"

Libby shook her head. "Not yet anyway. I mean, I'm getting more flight experience here than—"

Rose's eyes widened. "Watch out!"

Libby ducked just as she heard the *whoosh* of the ball pass her ear. It thudded on the blanket between them.

"That does it." She jumped to her feet and snatched up the ball, marching toward the water.

Rose leapt up, following. "What are you doing . . . Libby? Wait!"

Libby continued forward until the crashing waves broke at her feet. She cocked her arm and let the ball sail—through the air, over the surf, splashing down far out in the mounting waves.

"Libby!" Rose's jaw dropped.

Libby turned, finally giving the two men the benefit of a longer look. They both stared at the ball floating on the waves, then back at Libby in disbelief.

She clapped her hands together, brushed off the sand, and stalked back to her blanket. Then she plopped down, wrapped her arms around her legs, and lifted her chin in triumph. Libby expected Rose to follow, but instead her friend was approaching the soldiers. She was apologizing!

The dimpled, muscular man with blond hair rushed into the water. With a small dive he leapt into the waves, swimming with long strokes toward the ball.

Libby jumped to her feet and glanced to where the ball floated, remembering the riptide. *It's too far out. He'll get caught in the undertow.*

She took two steps forward. A knot formed in her stomach. He seemed to be doing okay. So far anyway. Within minutes the ball was in reach. Stretching his hand out, he grabbed it, then turned and kicked. Libby released a held breath. The soldier's awkward strokes, with ball in hand, easily carried his body across the water.

Show-off, Libby thought as she sank back onto the blanket. She had just begun to relax once more when Rose's cry pierced the air. Libby jumped to her feet and hurried over the sand. Her heart pounded, and her gaze swept across the face of the water, but the man was gone.

"Dan!" The second soldier's shout ripped through the air. He motioned to Libby and Rose for help. "I can't swim. You have to get him." He took two steps into the waves, then moved back up the beach.

"What happened?" Libby's eyes scanned the water.

"He was doing fine; then he just disappeared." Rose's chin quivered. "He seemed to go straight down. Surely he's just playing with us. Tell me he's just fooling."

Libby raced into the waves, the water reaching her knees, then waist. Just as she was about to dive, she saw a form surfacing not far beyond her. The man's face was red from exertion, his breathing labored. She could tell from the frantic darting of his eyes it was not a joke. He stretched his arm toward her, and Libby surged forward to grasp it and pull him toward her. Finally the man caught his footing. He struggled forward with one step, two steps, before straightening his shoulders.

She thought he was going to walk past her without speaking, but just as he reached her he leaned close and spoke into her ear.

"Nice spiral." She felt his winded breath on her cheek. "Not bad . . . for a girl."

"He asked about you." Rose brushed windblown locks back from her face. She lowered her sunglasses and glanced over at Libby as they drove back toward Honolulu.

"Who?"

"That guy you helped rescue. When I went back for my dropped sunglasses, he asked your name and where he could find you. All I told him was that you work for Honolulu's Flying Service at John Rodgers. I didn't say you were a pilot—or that you can whip any flier in the air, female or male."

Libby glared at her.

Rose adjusted her glasses. "What? Don't look at me like that. He wouldn't let me go till I told him."

"Yeah, he's probably looking for revenge—wants to throw me into the nearest whirlpool to see how well *I* can swim."

"Nah. I saw him glance over more than once. You know the football incident was just a stunt to get your attention."

"The sun must be getting to you." Libby reached over and pressed her palm to Rose's forehead. "Heatstroke."

"I'm not the one with heatstroke, my friend. It's your face turning a dozen shades of crimson."

Three

STRIKE ENDS IN HAWAIIAN DEFENSE BASES

The Hawaiian strike, which took place at Wheeler and Hickam Fields and Fort Kamehameha, involved carpenters, electricians, truck drivers, and laborers, the Associated Press reported. It was brought to an end last night when the men agreed to go back to work pending negotiations on their demands.

Dispatches say that the men were not unionized and that a demand for a flat $1.25 hourly wage was the sole issue of the walkout.

Alfred Friendly, Staff Writer
Excerpt from the *Washington Post,* June 18, 1941

Morning light tinted the airfield with a touch of pink as Libby arrived for work. It was only a twenty-minute walk from her apartment, and on the rare stormy or cold day she caught a ride with George Abel, the airport manager.

John Rodgers Airport was nothing fancy compared to Wheeler, Hickam, and some of the other military fields on the island. It was one of two developments set in a more rural area, sprouting up amidst fields of sugarcane and leafy green algarroba trees, which grew leathery pods producing a substance called carob. Not too many nights before, Libby had watched Rose's mother use the carob in a cake that rivaled any Libby had eaten.

The only other development along the strip was Joe's Hawaiian Grill. Libby smelled the familiar scents of bacon frying and coffee brewing as she passed.

"I'll be in later for a cup o' joe, Joe," she called through the open window. Her words were cut short, and she plugged her ears to block out the blare of a siren. The airfield had no tower, and the small planes, no radio. The siren was their sole warning for incoming aircraft.

A few minutes later a large silver plane descended, causing the mynah birds in the marsh south of the gravel runway to squawk.

Libby waved her own welcome to the large plane and then to the ground crew as she hurried past the hangars and past a naval officer on the tarmac. His arms were crossed tightly over his chest as he inspected her small Piper Cub the way a prizewinning jockey would eye a lame mule.

"Honey, I'm home!" Libby sidled up to the office counter covered with greasy wrenches, pilot sign-in sheets, and a large tube radio belting out "Green Eyes" by Jimmy Dorsey.

George stepped over to the counter, wiping his greasy hands on an equally greasy towel, then stuffing it back into the front pocket of his coveralls.

"What's he want?" She nodded toward the officer outside.

"Showed up for a flying lesson. He scheduled with Billy Jackson, but our instructor friend hasn't shown up this morn. Most likely sleeping away a hangover on Hotel Street." He picked up the clipboard with the day's flight schedule.

George's gray beard and hair reminded Libby of Santa. Only this Saint Nicholas sported a dark tan and a Hawaiian shirt under his bib overalls.

"I'd better tell the colonel there will be no lesson today."

"I can do the lesson." Libby zipped her coveralls up over her girlish frame and twisted her hair into a knot at the base of her neck. "Just give me a second to get myself together."

"Don't think it's a good idea, Libs. You know these officer types."

Libby waved a hand as if brushing away his worries, snatched up her logbook from the counter, and moved to the door.

"Libby! These guys are from the old school," George's voice called to her. "They don't understand—"

"I've got it under control, George. You worry too much."

Libby jogged up to the waiting colonel, who barely offered her a glance. "Hello, sir, ready for your lesson?"

"I've been waiting for ten minutes, young lady. And don't think your pretty face will smooth things over. Get on the phone and tell your instructor today's lesson will be free. And if he doesn't show up soon, I'm going to charge him for *my* time."

Libby ignored his comments and moved through the flight check. "Sorry about that, sir. Change of plans. I'm filling in. So if you'll climb into the passenger's seat, we can get started."

The colonel's eyes widened. "You? But I . . ."

Libby glanced at her watch. "I'm doing you a favor here. Time is money, sir."

The officer stood rooted in place. His eyes bore into Libby's. She glanced away and climbed into the cockpit, then patted the seat beside her.

His look of confusion turned to anger. "Now listen here, young lady. Just because you're one of these modern women who think they can do a man's job doesn't mean I'll have anything to do with it. Females are too . . . too scatterbrained to fly."

Libby shrugged and glanced at her watch.

"I've never heard of anything like this in my life." Face red, he stalked back to the office. Libby remained in the seat and fiddled her fingers on the throttle. A lump formed in her throat as she watched the colonel storm into the building, slamming the door behind him. As the minutes ticked past, she was sure she could hear his voice booming over the sound of a small aircraft coming in for a landing, and even over the chorus of Jimmy Dorsey replaying in her mind.

Why did every man who saw her judge her before she had a chance to prove herself? In her training, she had to work harder than any of the others. The instructors looked for every little excuse to dock her points. And now that she'd made instructor, she had to prove herself again with every student.

She glanced toward the harbor, then northwest toward Wheeler Field where army pilots took off and landed in their fancy planes. She blinked, refusing to allow a single tear of self-pity to escape. Still, if she were a man, she'd be up there in army pursuits, leading the pack. She'd be the one giving orders.

"Penny for your thoughts."

The male voice made her jump. She watched as the man hoisted himself up into the Cub and plopped into the seat beside her.

"The old fool doesn't know what he's missing. I've heard you're the best instructor on the island. Since you obviously have an empty spot, will you sign me up?" A boyish grin spread across the speaker's face.

Libby's jaw dropped. "Aren't you the guy from the beach?" She reached her hand toward the Cub's door handle, preparing to make a quick escape.

"What? You don't recognize me when I'm not dripping wet and panting? If you're talking about the dummy that almost drowned, yup, that would be me."

"Rose said you'd track me down. I told her you were probably seeking revenge. But I have to say, I wasn't in my right mind, really. I mean, with the whole football thing. I just snapped—"

"Libby, please." He held up his hands, halting her words. "It was *our* fault. My buddy and I were interrupting. I'm the one who needs to apologize."

"How do you know my name?" A warm, giddy feeling flowed through her in a way she hadn't expected. She brushed her hair back from her face, feeling a few wayward strands escape the hair clip at the base of her neck. "Never mind. Rose told you."

He combed his fingers through his hair, then buckled his seat belt. "Like I said. You're supposed to be the best instructor on the island. I'd heard of you even before our little incident. Can you take me up?"

"On one condition. I need to know the name of the man I almost killed."

"Dan. Dan Lukens." He reached out and took her hand in his strong grip. "Nice to meet you."

"And you trust me? In the air, I mean." She slid her flight helmet onto her head.

"Wouldn't be here if I didn't."

Libby gave him a quick overview of the various roles of the controls and switches in the cockpit.

"Some people think that piloting is just like driving a car, but what they don't realize is the additional need for lateral control. An automobile must be steered left or right. A plane climbs, dives, and turns. It can also tilt from one side to another." She laughed. "Drivers don't have to worry about keeping their wheels on the ground, but pilots must also keep their wings level."

Dan's eyes were fixed on Libby as he listened intently.

She felt her face heat up again as she took the stick in her hands. "Now this is the level that makes the plane go up or down. It also tips the wings. When you push to the left, the left wing is depressed, and the same to the right. Are you with me so far?"

Dan rubbed his chin. "I think so."

Libby adjusted her flight helmet. "Some guys get a little sick when we first go up, but I'm a pilot, not a maid. If you lose your lunch in my plane, you'll be the one cleaning it up."

"Understood." Dan smirked.

Libby was about to start the engine when George jogged out of the office, waving his arms to get her attention. She climbed down from the Cub and met him halfway across the gravel tarmac.

"Sorry to stop you, Libs." He ran a hand over his gray beard. "But a call came in for Sergeant Lukens. They need him back at Wheeler."

"The airfield? Don't you mean the harbor? Isn't he a sailor?"

"No, the airfield. Lukens is one of those hotshot pursuit pilots. They say the labor strike is off, and they need him back. He's got some maneuvers to lead."

Libby pressed her hands to her hips and cocked an eyebrow. "Hotshot pilot? You don't say." She glanced back to where Dan sat in the passenger's seat and gave him a thumbs-up. "Yeah, George. I'll be happy to give him the word."

⁂

Dan strode onto the asphalt tarmac on Wheeler Field, passing the rows of army fighter planes now lined up where Amelia Earhart had taken off for her first solo flight between Hawaii and California only six years before. The once-quiet airfield had come alive since then, as rumors of possible Japanese conquests in the South Pacific forced the U.S. to take a military stand in the Pacific. He breathed in the intoxicating aroma of exhaust intermingled with saltwater air.

The army's massive Schofield Barracks bordered the field to the northwest, but the buildings weren't visible due to the large hangars that lined the runway. A grin filled Dan's face as he scanned the bustling airfield. The sun's hot rays beat down on the men, as on foot or by jeep they moved around the warehouses, radar hut, fuel tanks, and ammo dumps with purpose.

With a quick stride, making sure to step over the hot oil puddles on the pavement, Dan approached Gabriel Lincoln, who was zipping up his flight jacket. He grasped his friend's shoulder with a firm grip.

Gabe turned with a grin. "Aloha, Daniel. Where have you been? The captain has been looking for you."

"Ah, just trying to spend some time with the woman I'm going to marry."

"What are you talking about? I just saw you twenty-four hours ago, and you didn't even have a girl, let alone a fiancée." He winked. "Did you make it to the Black Cat with Zeke after all? Maybe got a date with one of those girls in hula skirts that all the sailors pay to get their picture taken with?"

"Nah, it's someone you haven't met." He gave Gabe a friendly punch in the shoulder.

"One of those girls from the beach last week? Zeke told me about the dark-haired one." Gabe let out a low whistle.

"No, the other one. I—"

"The one who almost killed you?" Gabe interrupted. "Are you nuts?"

"Maybe. But she's a pilot. An instructor. And she's even prettier and feistier than I remembered."

"And was she glad to see you again? I hope she held her temper this time."

"Are you kidding? I signed up for a flying lesson. Unfortunately, she found out I was a pilot."

"And she wasn't too happy?"

"Let's just say I received one of the worst tongue-lashings of my life."

"Sounds like true love to me."

Dan shrugged. "Give it time. Come on. Let's see that new machine."

* * *

A group of pilots stood outside the hangar closest to the runway, eyeing the new plane.

"Men, I'd like to introduce you to the P-40B." Captain Davis stood, shoulders straight, and pointed to a pursuit plane that appeared to be the stronger big brother to the one Dan was used to flying.

"It's basically the same as the P-40," the captain continued, "but it has become evident to our government that more powerful weaponry may soon be called for."

"Does the president know something he's not telling us?" one pilot called out.

Captain Davis clasped his hands behind his back and continued on without a response. "This B model has four wing-mounted .30-caliber and two nose-mounted .40-caliber machine guns. It also introduces cockpit armor, which is good news for you. A dozen of these fighters are going to be arriving soon. This is just a sample. News from the top says we'll soon be taking a whole fleet of P-40Bs down to the Philippines to build up our defenses."

"But how does it fly?" Gabe climbed up the footholds to the cockpit and leaned out to get a better view of the wings. "I mean, with all that extra weight, will we be able to maneuver the thing?"

"That's why I've called in Sergeant Lukens to give us a demonstration. It seems no one's too certain how it will handle, especially under the fancy maneuvers necessary in dogfights. I hate to say it, but we don't even have a flight manual for this thing yet."

"Are you gonna do it?" Gabe looked to Dan; his eyes flicked with foreboding. "If body armor weighs it down too much, it could—"

Dan turned to the captain. "Do you feel it's safe, sir?"

The officer took a wide-legged stance and nodded.

"I believe it is. I can't imagine them sending over anything that isn't worthy of our men. For you, Lukens, it will be simple."

"Okay, I'll do it." Dan pressed his flight helmet onto his head.

"Are you crazy?" Gabe tapped his finger to the side of his head. "At least wait a few days till we get a manual."

Dan smiled and winked. "I'm just an old football player, pal. Gotta trust the coach if you wanna win the game."

❧ ❧ ❧

Libby gazed out from her second-story apartment window and spotted the last gray puffs of smoke dissipating in the air. The day's work at the harbor was complete; the smoke was from practice shots from the antiaircraft guns on Battleship Row. The first time she'd seen it, she'd thought the harbor was under attack.

"Gray smoke means nothing. Them's just practice shots," George Abel had informed her. "But if you see black smoke, run for your life. Black is the real stuff."

Libby tilted the slatted windows, opening them wider to let in the cooler trade winds. She loved the lightly falling afternoon rains and breezes the sea brought in. They stirred up floral scents so strong she could almost taste them. And it wasn't only the flowers outside that were so fragrant. She traced her fingers over the petals of the large purple blossoms in a windowsill vase that her Chinese maid had filled that morning.

She'd grown accustomed to simple comforts like household help and bouquets of flowers—things that hadn't fit into her world in northern California. There, the small house she shared with her dad was weathered, and not in a charming way. It was a simple dwelling with a sagging roof and dingy curtains. The house faded into the dry brown hills around it, not worth a second look.

Here, household help was inexpensive; everyone working on the air base had a maid. And flowers were so abundant, it seemed wasteful not to bring some inside to enjoy.

Still, living in the midst of a full-scale military boomtown had its quirks. Once a week the power would go out, and darkness covered every inch of the island. After a few moments, the radio stations would announce that another blackout drill had been completed. It hadn't happened yet this week, which most likely meant tonight was the night.

Libby thought about walking to town for dinner, yet sailors who were away on shipboard maneuvers during the week hit the beaches, bars, and restaurants on the weekends. She wasn't desperate enough for companionship to venture into that mob. Instead, she strode from the window and wished she knew where Rose was. No doubt her friend was on the arm of some handsome sailor . . . or pilot.

A flush rose to her cheeks as she thought about Dan Lukens. The man had lied to her. Or at least, tried to fool her. And, boy, had she let him have it.

But somehow the poor guy had seemed to shrug away her words. The more she thought about it, the more ashamed she felt. After all, what had been the point of his little charade? She ought to be flattered.

Why do I always blow it? She opened her pantry, then closed it again, realizing she wasn't hungry. Another Friday night with nothing to do.

❧ ❧ ❧

Natsuo glanced around at the faces of the men who lounged around the grassy lawn in front of the military barracks. He knew many of them—Haro, Kin, Yashiku, Akio, and a dozen others. And while today they were simply neighbor boys thousands of miles away from home, tomorrow they would all be soldiers.

Growing up in Kobe, Natsuo's favorite game had been the game of war. He and the others would gather driftwood sticks washed up on the shore and play soldiers. He had never imagined himself as a real one. As children, war had meant *kendō,* Japanese fencing.

In *kendō* it didn't matter that Natsuo was smaller than other boys. He was taught by his father to wait patiently, reading the eyes of his opponent until the enemy brandished a sword high above his head and took aim at his forehead. Waiting until the last second, Natsuo would then dodge, thrusting the play sword into his opponent's chest, while his foe's sword hit the ground where he'd been standing.

"It is the spirit of *kendō*. You have done well," his

father had boasted after witnessing one of these play matches. "The mind is as important as the body." He rumpled Natsuo's hair. "No, more important."

Haro and Kin played the same game today. Their bamboo sticks cracking against each other almost sounded like the beat of a drum punctuating the evening air. Kin won the match, and Haro waved him away.

"You may be better at *kendō,* but you'll never beat me as a first baseman." Haro swung the bamboo stick, mimicking the arch of a baseball player's bat. "Too bad Babe Ruth wasn't Japanese. Did I tell you I met him once when he visited Japan?"

"Yes," a dozen voices called in unison.

Haro tramped over to Natsuo. He lifted his bamboo stick as if preparing to whack Natsuo's head; then he grinned and dropped it to the grass with a *thump*. "What about you, Noodle Boy? Do you like baseball?"

Natsuo cocked his hand back as if pretending to make a long pass. "I prefer football, actually."

"Oh, yes, I forgot. Noodle Boy is too good for Japan and for *kendō*. That's why he left us and went to the United States."

Kin joined in. "I bet he wishes he were still there. Wishes he lived with his sister and fought for their army."

Natsuo jumped to his feet. His fists made tight balls at his side. "I do not. I will live and die for my country. The emperor is my god!"

"Calm down." Kin placed a hand on Natsuo's shoulder. “We will live and die together.” He settled onto the ground beside Haro. “We are friends, remember?”

Natsuo didn’t answer. He thought back to those childhood days. Whenever he could, Natsuo would escape from the heat and aroma of his house over the shop where his father made noodles to explore the neighborhood with the other boys, especially Haro. But he could never escape the scent of hot oil and dough that had permeated his skin since birth. He hated that nickname, Noodle Boy, but he tried not to let it show. Certainly, he never let them see him cry like his sister, Hoshiko—like all girls.

They lived on the road that traveled between the sea and the Takatori train station. Locomotives belched smoke and steam as they crossed over the nearby Myohoji River. And looming above it all was beautiful Mount Takatori, four kilometers to the north. Natsuo’s favorite place was the sandy beach to the south where he and his friends swam on summer days in their loincloths, shooting through the waves like skinny, dark fish. As they swam, he forgot he was a simple, poor boy who stank of oil and dough.

Natsuo shook away the memories. He rose and moved back into the coolness of the cement barracks. The last time he had received a letter from Hoshiko was right before passing his medical health inspection. He didn’t have a chance to return home. The army needed him immediately, as the threat of war in the South Pacific mounted.

So instead of returning home for a victory dinner,

Natsuo had cabled his family with a simple message: CLASS A BANZAI! He was sure the news brought warm pride to his father, yet sprouted tears from his tender mother. He could imagine her face swollen from crying. Still, losing him to his military wasn't as bad as losing him to an enemy country.

He was a servant of the emperor, after all.

Four

WORLD'S BEST PLANE
LOCATOR CREDITED TO U.S.

The United States is credited with possessing aircraft detection apparatus superior to any in use abroad. The aircraft spotting devices adopted by the army, members of Congress have been told, are effective at well over 100 miles, piercing fog and darkness to give defending fighters at least 15 minutes' warning of the approach of hostile aircraft.

Congress included $6,929,000 in defense funds for detectors to be installed in warning stations on the Atlantic, Gulf, and Pacific Coasts, and in Hawaii, Alaska, Puerto Rico, and the Canal Zone.

Excerpt from the *Washington Post*, June 20, 1941

Libby's swivel chair creaked with her every move as she sat behind the gray front desk in the airport office. She flipped through papers on a clipboard, looking for the day's flight schedule. Early morning was her favorite time for flying. At dawn, the cooled land created an onshore breeze that counteracted the trade winds. The air was calm and quiet, and if it weren't for the rumbling of the plane's engine, she might think she was floating over the lush land, the boats, the harbor.

Later in the day, sightseeing became tricky and flight lessons impossible. The land warmed up and the trade winds resumed, flowing briskly from the northeast. The wind tossed small planes around like autumn leaves caught in an updraft.

The bell on the front door jingled, and Libby lifted her face to see Rose approaching in her flight suit. "Hey there." She offered a small wave. "Another wild night on the town?"

Rose yawned and stretched her arms. "Went dancing again. I keep thinking I should gain weight after eating all those fancy foods every night. A good steak is only a dollar, you know, and the fellas like to treat. But I don't have a chance to worry. There are enough soldiers to keep me on my feet dancing all night. You should join me sometime."

"Or maybe you should join me," said a male voice.

Libby whirled around to see Dan Lukens walk into the office, dressed in his Army Air Corps uniform. Dan's hair looked even lighter next to the pressed blue suit. A true California boy.

Heat rose to Libby's cheeks, and she glanced away, irritated that her girlish blushing displayed her emotions for all to see. "Come back for more, Mr. Lukens? Do you enjoy being abused?"

Dan approached the counter, reached over, and gently took the flight schedule from her hands. Then he took a pencil from the desktop, wrote something on the page, and handed it back to her.

Dinner with Dan. 8:00 p.m.

"But I—"

Rose's throat-clearing interrupted Libby's refusal. She glanced over to see her friend subtly nodding.

Libby slowly mimicked the motion, looking up into Dan's face. "If this isn't a trick, and you still want to talk to me after yesterday's tirade, then sure."

"Great. I'll pick you up at your place at six. How do I get there?"

Libby scribbled down the address and handed it to him, her fingers brushing his as she did. "I'm upstairs. First set of stairs on the left. And if you see someone watching you from below, don't worry. It's just Mr. Atkins. He's sure that everyone not wearing a uniform is a spy."

"I won't be in uniform, but I'll try not to look too suspicious. See you tonight."

It wasn't until Dan had left the office, striding to a waiting jeep, that Libby noticed George, who had apparently been watching the transaction with quiet amusement.

"What was that all about?" Libby demanded. "Why'd *he* stop by?"

George pushed the bill of his cap up from his face and leaned against the wall. "Seems obvious to me." The corner of his mouth lifted in a sly smile. "He *said* he wanted to show me the new P-40B that just arrived at Wheeler Field. It has some pretty fancy additions over the older model."

"Right," Rose said with a grin. "Do a lot of pilots stop by to show you their new planes, George?"

George shook his head and crossed his arms over his heavy paunch. "Nope. Can't say that they do."

After work Rose came over to Libby's apartment and made her try on every outfit in her closet. They finally settled on a light blue two-piece dress with a dart-fitted waist and a flared skirt. White pearl buttons trailed from collar to hem.

"You're going to be turning heads on the strip tonight, girl. You're adorable."

"Hardly, Rose. But fortunately, 'adorable' isn't a prerequisite for flying planes."

"Here, sit down. Let's get your face on."

Libby rolled her eyes, then snatched up a brush and tugged it through her hair.

"Hey, now, don't make that face." Rose's voice was stern. "The makeup will be so light you'll hardly notice. Just a little color to highlight those pretty brown eyes." She patted the mattress beside her and opened her handbag.

Libby took a deep breath and settled next to Rose.

"You'll be gorgeous, girl. Why don't you ever wear makeup, anyway?"

"Because, I've never been around girlie-girls. Until you, that is."

When her friend was finished, Libby stood in front of the mirror and had to admit she was pleased with the results. She threw her arms around her friend. "Thank you so much."

"Don't mention it." Rose pressed her cheek to Libby's. "Just go out there and knock him dead. It can be your second attempt."

Both women laughed.

"Or . . . just knock his socks off. You might want to keep that guy around awhile."

"You're right." Libby heard a knock on the front door. "I just might."

❧ ❧ ❧

A twenty-five-cent cab ride took the pair downtown. They drove past the army and navy YMCA, past the tattoo parlors and the popular Black Cat Café where a soldier could get a hot dog for a nickel and spend all the money he'd saved for dinner on slots. White-uniformed sailors roamed the streets with Pacific tans and handsome good looks, money jingling in their pockets.

The cab pulled over in front of an open-air fruit stand. Dan climbed out, then turned to offer his hand to Libby.

"Let me guess . . . will it be the Kau Kau Korner or Chinatown's Wo Fat? From the looks of you, I'd say you're a Kau Kau Korner type of guy." Libby watched the cab pull away, joining the mass of vehicles typical of a Friday night in Honolulu.

"Do you think so?" Dan jutted out his elbow.

Libby obliged but made sure there was space between them.

"And what about you?"

"Oh, I'm Wo Fat all the way." She patted her stomach and grinned. "No, seriously, I've had a fascination with China ever since I was little. My favorite schoolteacher had a little treasure chest on her desk for us to put coins into. The money went to support Christian missionaries in China."

As they walked, Dan and Libby weaved through the crowds of sailors. To Libby's surprise, they strode past both the restaurants she'd named.

"I bet there's not too many of those missionaries who've stuck around." Dan scooted her around two soldiers who carried their buddy, smelling of beer, between them.

"I know. I've read about Japan's invasion of China. Millions of men, women, and children murdered for no reason. I'm just waiting for the U.S. to do something about it. It's enough for me to want to join the army and fight for China myself."

"You'd be an asset, all right. But I don't think our country will ever let women in its military ranks."

Libby was about to comment when Dan patted her

hand and pointed to a side door near the marketplace. "This is it. Hold on right here for one minute."

Libby watched as he hurried to the door and knocked twice. When the door opened, a Hawaiian woman, about as wide as she was tall, stepped out and handed him two picnic baskets. She smiled and waved at Libby.

"What do you have up your sleeve? A moonlight picnic on the beach?"

"Well, we could do that. But I thought you might like to see the new plane at Wheeler Field."

"Are you joking? Is that where we're going? But why two baskets? If we eat all that, I really will be *wo fat.*"

"Yes, ma'am. That's where we're going. And as for the extra basket . . ."

With perfect timing, a car pulled up to the curb and gave a short honk. Libby looked over to see Rose in the driver's seat with a ridiculous hat pulled down over her forehead like a chauffeur's cap. A large guy in a sailor's suit sat next to her, with an equally wide grin.

"Sir. Ma'am. Your ride awaits." Rose gave another short beep of the horn, causing numerous heads to turn their direction.

Dan and Libby slid into the backseat.

Rose pointed a thumb at her passenger. "His name is Jack Webster. I picked him up down the road because I thought he was cute. Hope you don't mind."

Libby glanced at the sailor with his white uniform and circular cap tilted to the side. This guy was huge—he had to be at least six foot four, and sitting next to

Rose's petite frame, he made her look like a little kid barely able to peek over the steering wheel.

"Not at all." Dan stretched out his hand. "Jack, nice to meet you."

Dan slid the basket next to the door and scooted closer to Libby. "It's good our chauffeur has a date. I have a feeling love is in the air tonight."

"Actually, that's the smell of roasted pig." Libby pointed to a small restaurant with a long line out front. "Pig and stale beer."

Dan chuckled, then squeezed her shoulder. "That's what I like about you, Libby. You bring me back to earth. But, no, this time I believe you're wrong. I'm sure that fragrance is pure romance."

Rose and Jack decided to picnic in the moonlit car as Dan and Libby made their way to the hangar housing the P-40B. Libby had been to Wheeler Field a few times before, yet everything seemed larger and more mysterious at night. Pursuit planes lined the asphalt runway wingtip to wingtip. Machine guns were mounted on their wings. She let her finger glide across one of the planes as they walked by. They seemed so official and dangerous compared to the simple two-seaters she was used to flying.

Yet Libby knew that even the power of these planes was limited in comparison to the large bombers located at Hickam. Libby longed to fly one of those bombers someday. Or at least one of these pursuits.

Dan led her to a far hangar, picnic basket swinging in his hand, and flipped on the lights just inside the door. The large Quonset hut flooded with a warm, golden glow, and Libby eyed the newest pursuit from the assembly line, taking in the sleek gray machine with a large air scoop under the engine cowling. She pressed a hand to her pounding heart and let out a low whistle.

Dan placed the picnic basket on the concrete floor. "What are you waiting for? Climb in."

"Really?" Libby didn't wait for him to offer twice. She kicked off her heels and scampered into the cockpit the best she could in a dress and stockings, sliding into the firm leather seat. She reveled in the smell of new parts and oil as she scanned the operational controls. She figured out what most of them were, but some of the new devices were a mystery. Dan climbed up, standing on the footholds on the wing.

"What's this for?" Libby pointed toward a row of switches near the throttle.

"That would be the control to drop the 700 pounds of external bombs." He smiled. "It seems the instructor is now the one receiving a lesson."

After thirty minutes of pilot talk, Dan jumped to the ground, his boots slapping the concrete. "How about some dinner?"

He spread a torn parachute on the concrete floor, then laid out a variety of Hawaiian dishes similar to those Rose's mother usually packed.

Libby eased herself onto the silky white parachute

and pressed her skirt around her legs. "This is by far the best date I've ever been on."

She picked up a piece of smoked poi, then gazed into Dan's face. His boyish excitement was easy to read.

"Me too." Dan took a large bite of pineapple and wiped the juice dribbling down his chin with the back of his hand.

Libby took a neatly folded white napkin from the picnic basket and handed it to him. "Except for Rose, I've never had a friend who understood about flying. I mean, my dad supported me and all, but to him, flying was just a job. Nothing more."

Dan shook his head in disbelief, then nodded toward the pursuit. "Taking that baby up and checking out what the V-1710 engine can do—that could never be just a job. Speed. Weightlessness. And soaring through the air as though I'm part of the machine."

The evening passed quickly, and Libby smiled to herself and the giggly Rose who drove them home. *Maybe this pilot's a keeper.* And when Dan walked Libby up the stairs to her apartment, they lingered a few minutes at the door.

"You're a very pretty girl, Libby Conners," he said. "But that's not what made me interested in you that afternoon on the beach."

"What, then?" Libby demanded. "I suppose you could tell I was a pilot just by looking at me?"

"Actually," Dan said with a wicked grin, "it was the spiral. I've never seen a football thrown so perfectly by a girl."

❧ ❧ ❧

Natsuo and his friends from Kobe, who were now official soldiers, had been transferred to a training camp in the jungle on Japan's southernmost coast. It was a part of his country Natsuo had never seen before, and it felt like a different world. His days once again consisted of war games with his friends, but on a much grander scale.

Cuckoos lived among the tropical coconut trees. A fine drizzle fell continually on the fresh green leaves. And it was among this beauty that Natsuo first witnessed death.

Like many of the others, Natsuo had known Akio Satosan since boyhood. He knew Akio did not want to return home to his family as a failure—his sickly father whose hopes all rested on him, his screeching mother who was impossible to please.

Akio worked hard to succeed, but he struggled with both the physical and mental demands of the training. When he finished the first obstacle course far behind the others, he was called to step out of the straight line of recruits. Natsuo and the others were forced to watch as the bamboo cane crashed against Akio's flesh again and again.

"We *will* indoctrinate you with the military man's spirit. *Nippon seishin.* You will be made worthy to wear the uniform of an imperial soldier!" their trainer declared.

As the trainer beat Akio again and again, Natsuo's

eyes widened. He noted the strained smile on Akio's face—teeth clenched, cheeks drawn back, eyes narrow.

It wasn't the first time Natsuo had seen that look. Akio had always been slower, dim-witted; yet when his anger released, it was with the fury of an uncaged tiger.

With a loud shout, the wire in Akio blew. He snatched the cane and turned with fury on the officer doling out his fair punishment.

With a rush of screams, the other trainers attacked Akio with leather straps, canes, and even their leather shoes, slapping against Akio's skin with horrible thuds.

The recruits in line stood frozen. Natsuo didn't even dare turn to those on his right or left to catch their expressions. Surely they were as horrified as he.

"How dare you turn a hand on the emperor's chosen!" one officer screamed. "You will receive your just due!"

Ten minutes later, the officers stepped back, panting and weak from their spent energy. Akio lay like a human puddle on the ground, his swollen face not even recognizable to those who'd known him for years.

"This is an example of the cost of disobedience, of dishonor!" One officer shook his leather strap toward the other recruits. It extended from his hand like another appendage, trembling, daring them to say a word or make a move.

They remained there, standing erect in line, Akio's body before them, until they were released for dinner. Natsuo forced his food down, feeling as if it would come back up at any moment.

After dinner Haro, Kin, and Yashiku joked around, wrestling on the manicured lawn in front of their bamboo barracks. Natsuo didn't know how they could joke and play after what they'd just witnessed.

The next morning, as they gathered after reveille, one officer stepped forward. "As a result of yesterday's display of dishonor, Akio Satosan's parents were notified that their son was a traitor to his emperor, and his name is forever to be a disgrace to their family. As for you, if the thought ever crosses your mind to commit an act of disobedience against one of the emperor's chosen, remember the cost to your family. Think of their disgrace!"

When Natsuo wrote home that evening, he kept his thoughts to himself. He knew to speak of it would cause his own disgrace.

Besides, in the end, what did it matter? Akio was now in a better place. A place of peaceful slumber. Akio would become like a god, protecting their nation. Protecting his friends who still remained.

May he ever have peaceful repose.

Five

U.S. DESTINY IS TO THE WEST, MAAS ASSERTS

Honolulu. August 5. Representative Maas (Republican) of Minnesota, House Naval Affairs Committee member on active duty as a Marine Corps colonel, said today, "We are either going to be an empire or we are going to be part of somebody else's empire.

"There's only one defense against modern warfare, and that is to strike first and hardest, otherwise you are licked before you have started."

Excerpt from the *Washington Post,* August 6, 1941

Libby led Dan by the hand as she made her way through John Rodgers Airport, gazing at the new dawn that wrestled to replace the darkness. For the past month, they'd spent every evening together. They walked the beach at sunset and took rides around the island with friends. Mostly they spent their time talking about planes, flying, and the threat of war from both sides of the ocean.

But today was different. Today Libby had Dan to herself all day.

"Sorry, kiddo. No lessons today," she muttered as she walked past the Piper Cub.

Dan lifted her hand to his lips and kissed it. "That's right, little Piper. She's all mine today."

While Libby enjoyed giving flight lessons, her favorite part of her job was taking customers up on sunrise tours. She usually flew them in open-cockpit biplanes, making a ninety-minute loop to the west side of Oahu. Today, Dan would be Libby's honored guest, and instead of the biplane she'd chosen George's new Interstate Cadet with enclosed side-by-side seating.

"Get in and buckle up, sir," she said in her best tour guide voice. "Today you will get a view of Hawaii from the air, something every tourist dreams of."

After taxiing the Cadet to the runway, Libby pushed the throttle forward, the engine revved, and the Cadet lifted effortlessly into the sky. "As we lift off, Mr. Lukens, if you look to the west, opposite the rising sun, you'll see Pearl Harbor. It's a bit crowded this morning, and I'm sure you know the reason why even more than I—military secrets and all."

Dan leaned forward to peer out the window. "No comment." He grinned.

"As we turn, you'll spot an industrial area to the north, then forest. Beyond that the Ko'olau Mountains."

"Oh, I like the way that rolls off your tongue."

Libby tried to ignore his comment, but she couldn't help but smile. "To the south is the Pacific, of course. And to the east, with the rising sun, are Waikiki, Diamond Head, and downtown Honolulu."

"My least favorite part of the island, if I may say so."

"I agree." Libby turned the plane toward the tropical side of the island. "Now comes the good part. Prepare for a beautiful flight over gray green pineapple fields and banana trees. We'll reach our destination in about twenty minutes."

They rode in comfortable silence the rest of the way. The landmass below sparkled green and alive as dew-covered vegetation reflected the sun's first rays.

Libby sighed contentedly as they neared the farthest shore. "We'll be landing today near the Haleiwa, an old hotel right at the edge of the ocean. It's a beautiful place and . . . well, just wait."

As Libby neared, she tilted the plane in a forty-five-degree angle and wagged her wings at the hotel. Then she set the plane down on the grass landing strip. A minute later a young boy could be seen hurrying down the runway with a two-wheeled banana wagon, his jet-black hair flapping against his forehead as he ran.

Libby jumped down from the plane and turned to Dan. "Hungry?"

The boy waved. "Aloha!"

"Aloha," Libby and Dan responded in unison.

The wagon was filled with all types of breakfast items, and Libby's stomach rumbled. The boy spread out a picnic blanket for them, offering a variety of fresh fruits and homemade breads.

"You sure know how to treat a guy." Dan attacked the fruit placed before him, smiling as he bit into a slice of fresh mango. "The flight, the food—"

Libby slid off her white flight turban and tossed her hair. "They say the way to a man's heart is through his stomach."

After refueling at the airstrip, she flew the plane in the direction of Maui, a short hop from Oahu. "Have you see Haleakala yet? From the sky?"

"No, but I hope the volcano is extinct."

"It's only been two hundred years since the last eruption."

Libby resumed the tour. "The Hawaiian name for the volcano is *Hale-a-ka-la*, which means 'House of the Sun.' According to legend, Maui kidnapped the sun god *La* from the top of Haleakala. Maui only released La once he agreed to move more slowly through the sky, giving these islands sunshine and warmth. There it is." She pointed.

The summit stretched as far as her eyes could see with black and red rock. There was no vegetation in sight.

"Amazing. It seems like another planet, an alien desert or something."

"And look some more." Libby took the plane in a wide turn and pointed to the slope leading to the blue Pacific. "More pineapple fields where the lava fields stop. Don't they look as though they're tumbling down the slope into the ocean?"

On the way back to Oahu, she turned the controls over to Dan and sat back to enjoy the ride.

"So why did you sign up? For the military, I mean." She was mindlessly counting the dozens of battleships and aircraft carriers that moved between the islands of Oahu and Maui, leaving foaming white trails in their wake.

Dan laughed. "It's stupid, really. My friend showed up at football practice one day furious, waving a copy of *Reader's Digest*. The article said that our generation —I think they called us war babies—were incapable of taking on responsibility. Said we were aimless, soft, and immature. So my buddy and I signed up the next day, to the horror of our parents—and our coach."

"You played football?"

"UCLA first-string."

Libby tapped her finger on her chin. "Hmm. So if you're a college player, why did you have so much trouble controlling the football that day on the beach? You couldn't have been doing it on purpose, could you?"

Dan wrinkled his brow. "What? You think so?"

Libby crossed her arms over her chest and made no attempt to hide her grin. "So you joined up to try to prove something to a writer who had never heard of you, had no idea of your resolve, and most likely wrote those words to sell more copies? That's about the silliest thing I've ever heard."

"Oh, look who's talking, Miss 'No-Man-Can-Outfly-Me.' Like you've never felt you had something to prove?"

Dan dropped his altitude as the island of Oahu neared, then circled John Rodgers Airport in preparation for landing. Libby watched as his hands skillfully maneuvered the plane's controls. His eyes were quick as they took in everything around him. And although he was undoubtedly handsome and kind, nothing attracted her more than to see the passion in his gaze as he flew.

He set the plane down without a bump, taxied, parked, then turned to her. "Okay, enough with the flying and spinning a yarn. Are you ready for some sand and sun?"

"Please, Dan, you're wearing me out. It's not like we have to do it all in one day."

Dan released the controls and grasped Libby's fingers, lifting them to his lips. "Yes, but I don't want to waste any time that we can have together. You never know what the future holds."

A few minutes later, after they'd refueled and prepared the plane for its next pilot, Dan took Libby's hand, and they started back to the office.

"I have one more thing to show you before we head to the beach," Libby announced, pulling him toward the largest hangar—a big Quonset held up with metal struts. "This, my friend, is one of the biggest radio antennas in the world. If you put your ear in the right spot, you can hear one of the Honolulu stations."

They approached the big hut, and each placed an ear against the warm metal—their faces only inches apart. Libby felt Dan's warm breath on her cheek as he sang along to Glenn Miller.

"You and I know . . . why love will grow from the first hello until the last good-bye. So to sweet romance, there is just one answer, you and I." Dan straightened and wrapped his arms around her, pulling her close. "Libby, I believe that's our song."

❧ ❧ ❧

Libby and Rose sat in the convertible outside the Schofield Barracks, waiting for Dan. The whitewashed stone barracks supposedly were the largest in the country, set behind massive gates with a beautiful lawn stretching out in front. Soldiers hustled to and fro in jeeps, on foot, or on bicycles. The summer sun cast a warm glow over the busy scene.

Yet it was quiet compared to the rest of Honolulu. The traffic in the expanding city was frightful, and automobile accidents were more the norm than the exception. The roads bustled with soldiers, delivery drivers, and official cars that ferried around the officers and their families. Sometimes Libby watched them wistfully, wondering what it would be like to live their lives. Women in dresses, white gloves, and hats. Children in pressed suits or frocks, heading to the Royal Hawaiian Club for four o'clock tea.

While she watched, an attractive young woman emerged from the barracks. Two small blond boys trailed behind her, their arms stretched out from their sides, swaying from side to side as if mimicking the planes that filled the sky. Maybe someday she'd have little boys like those. . . .

"Hello, are you listening?" Rose tapped her shoulder. "I've asked you a question twice, but your mind is someplace else."

Libby turned to her friend, taking in the wide-brimmed hat that Rose had recently received by mail order from Sears and Roebuck. "Hmm?"

"I was just asking about Mr. Atkins downstairs. Has he done anything outrageous lately?"

Libby gave a low sigh. "Unfortunately, yes. A few days ago he called the police concerning my maid. It appears that she was drying the sheets on the balcony, and Mr. Atkins thought they were signals to Japanese spies on the island."

"Isn't your maid Chinese?"

"Yeah, but the old man won't believe me."

Rose laughed, and Libby sat up straighter, recognizing Dan's familiar stride as he hurried across the lawn toward them. It was a half-jog, half-march, and reminded Libby of a junior high boy just let loose after a long day at school.

"Not fair." Rose threw her hands up with a pout. "Here I am the chauffer again for you two lovebirds, while Jack has to spend all week cooped up in that little ship."

"I know, poor Jack." Libby blew a kiss to Dan as he climbed in next to her. "You should have dated a flier."

"Tell me about it. Jack's sick and tired of having to stay below deck in the engine rooms, working on maintenance all day. He's almost aching for some action to get them out to sea. Except for the fact that he'd miss me like crazy." She glanced over to Libby as she started the engine. "Where to?"

"How about Ewa Beach?" Libby pulled out her trusty scarf and tied it over her hair. "We haven't been there in a while."

"Oh, shucks," Dan moaned. "And I didn't bring my football. Want to turn around so I can get it?"

"No, thanks." Libby wagged a finger at him. "I might kill you next time."

They pulled onto the main highway leaving Honolulu. Rose drove with one hand on the steering wheel and the other on her hat to keep it from blowing away.

"Dan." The wind whipped her words. "What happened to your friend, the one who was at the beach with you? I haven't seen him in a while."

"Zeke Olson? Ah, he's homesick like crazy. Spends most of the time in the barracks writing letters to his wife back home."

"He's married?" Rose sighed. "It must be so hard to be apart. I'd love to be married. In fact, Jack and I are talking about it."

"Are you serious? You just met the guy." Libby didn't mean for her voice to sound so harsh.

"When you find *the one,* it doesn't have to take a long time to know it," Rose declared. "Jack is sweet and fun to be around, and he adores me."

Libby didn't know what to say. She waited for Dan

to respond, but he must have been waiting for her, because neither said a word.

Libby liked being with Dan. In fact, she was quite sure she loved him. But marriage? She wasn't ready to talk about that.

Apparently, neither was he.

Six

ARMY STUDIES
COCHRAN CORPS OF EAGLETTES

Fresh from firsthand knowledge of bomber ferrying and the role English women are playing in the Royal Air Force, Jacqueline Cochran has presented a workable plan to the War Department on the use of women in wartime. The American sorority of lady fliers would be trained to fly bombers and other planes from aircraft plants to operation bases, pilot transports, and supply planes. After ferrying an American-made bomber to Britain, Miss Cochran spent several days with the Women's Auxiliary Air Force and made detailed notes of the outfit in action before flying back to America.

Of the 2,469 girls who have received instruction and passed their solo tests, only a handful have reached the high rating status demanded of bomber and transport pilots.

Lee Carson, International News Service
Excerpt from the *Washington Post,* July 15, 1941

The scents of ginger and curry punctuated the air, and a Benny Goodman wannabe played in the background as the two couples circled the table at Lau Yee Chai's, Waikiki's hottest nightspot and their new regular hangout. Dan bumped his head on a fuchsia-colored paper lantern as he pushed Libby's chair in for her. Settling in, Rose and Jack chatted while Dan and Libby listened to the band made up of musicians in brightly colored aloha shirts. Dan wondered what Benny would think of this South Seas interpretation of his songs.

Dan took Libby's hand in his, resting them both on the wicker-edged tabletop, fingers entwined. Libby looked beautiful in her Hawaiian print dress. Her skin glowed from a summer tan. A white orchid was tucked in her carefree waves of brown hair.

They had been dating barely two months, and to Dan it seemed she'd always been a part of his life. Yet he worried. The war in Europe mounted as Germany gobbled up nations and opened up an eastern front on the Russian steppes. The U.S. continued to receive pleas from its allies to join the fight. And with the British cutting off all supplies of rubber to Japan, and the U.S. government freezing all Japanese assets due to Japan's continued attacks on China, he knew it wouldn't be long until his country was sucked into war on one side of the world or the other.

Dan felt trained and ready to do his part, but he hated the thought of leaving. His captain had mentioned a possible transfer to the Philippines. If he were shipped out, the last place he wanted to leave Libby was in the middle of the Pacific. He'd rather see her home with her father in northern California. Because if he guessed right, the Japs would strike hard and fast. Japan wanted control of every island in the Pacific, mainly for resources and supplies, and there was only one nation that stood in their way of doing so—the United States.

The young waitress arrived and placed a large porterhouse before each of them. Dan looked at it and lifted an eyebrow. "As much as I enjoy steak, do you know what I'd really like right now?"

"Hmm, what's that?" Libby was cutting into her steak with gusto. She often put away as much food as any of Dan's buddies, and it was one of the things Dan loved about her. She didn't worry about being "proper" or trying to impress him.

"Creamed beef on toast," he said wistfully.

Libby paused and tugged on her ear, leaning closer. "The music's too loud; I'm not sure I heard you right. You didn't say creamed beef on toast?"

"Yeah, just the way my mom makes it. I'd trade in this steak in a heartbeat." He laughed and leaned back in his bamboo chair, making it creak.

"Men." Rose glanced at Jack with a grin. "They're always comparing everything to how their mother makes it. Jack was drooling a few days ago just talking about his mother's chocolate cake."

Dan put down his fork and took a long swallow of his sparkling mango-guava drink. "Uh, actually, Libby and my mom have nothin' in common. You shoulda seen her reply when I wrote that I was in love with a female flight instructor. Mom figured Libby was from some rich family back East."

Libby smirked. "Nothing could be further from the truth."

"And how did you respond?" Rose delicately cut her steak into small pieces.

"Told her not to worry. Libby's smart, but she'd happily don an apron and join Mom in the kitchen . . . to help with dishes, that is." Dan grinned. "She's let me know she doesn't cook."

"My poor father," Libby agreed with a laugh. "With my mother gone, and me in the kitchen, he was skin and bones."

Jack gazed at Rose. "You girls prove you're tough in the air. And Rose here can whip up a mighty fine meal. The question is . . . how can you manage to do all that and be so darn beautiful too?"

Rose squeezed Jack's arm. "Now do you see why I love this man so much?" She placed her hands on his cheeks, then leaned forward and planted a firm smack on his lips.

Dan leaned his forearms on the table. "Actually, I was hoping this topic would come up."

"Flying, cooking, or kissing?" Libby wagged her eyebrows.

"Just wait a sec." Dan pulled a few newspaper clippings from his pocket and spread them on the table. "You gals might be interested in this." He also handed Libby a white slip of paper with an address. "There's a congresswoman from Massachusetts who's met with the army's chief of staff to discuss a new bill. Guess what it's about."

"Outlawing men from comparing their mothers' cooking to their girlfriends'?"

"Don't you wish, darlin'. Actually, it seems she's trying to start an army women's corps that would be separate and distinct from the existing Army Nurse Corps. I guess in the Great War, female civilians who worked overseas with the army or as volunteers didn't have official status. They had to get their own food and living quarters."

"Yeah, I've read about that." Libby scanned the article from the *New York Times*. "And after the war they weren't even entitled to disability benefits or pensions. Can you imagine, working so hard for your country and then being left high and dry?"

Dan nodded. "While the army claims they don't want women in their ranks, I heard they might be moving toward a compromise. They're starting up the Women's Army Auxiliary Corps to work *with* the army. They might get some status and benefits, but women wouldn't have men serving under them."

Rose snapped her fingers. "Oh, shucks." She winked at Jack.

"The bill was introduced in May, but it failed to get full support." He gave a wry smile. "But if we get sucked more into the European war, and the Japs keep rattling their swords . . . ya never know."

Libby tucked her hair behind her ears—a quirk that Dan had learned meant she was deep in thought. "That's interesting, but what does it have to do with us? I don't type, and I'd never be satisfied being a switchboard operator."

"Well, ladies." Dan leaned back, crossed his arms, and cocked an eyebrow. "I've heard rumors they might need pilots."

⁂

A pounding sound stirred Libby from her dreams. She shook off sleep and rose from her bed, noticing through the window that the sickle moon was still out. Surely it wasn't Mr. Atkins again, waking her to report some new warning against the Japanese.

She slid into her robe and wrapped it tight around her. The knocking at her door continued.

"Libby, wake up! It's me." It was Rose's voice.

Libby swung the door open and grabbed her friend's arms, yanking her into the living room. "Are you crazy? What's going on?"

Rose's eyes were bright, and a smile filled her face. "I just need you to cover for me for the next few days. I have a few sunrise flights and a lesson or two. Can you do it?"

"Hold on." Libby attempted to wipe the sleepiness from her eyes. "Is something wrong? Your mom's okay, isn't she?"

"Perfect, silly. I just need to spend a few days away . . . with my husband. We're heading to the other side of the island for our honeymoon."

"Your *husband*? Rose, please. Slow down."

Rose lifted her hand, and a gold ring glimmered in the moonlight. "I did it. *We* did it. Jack and I were at dinner last night at my parents' house, and we decided to take the plunge before he has to leave for maneuvers again. Our neighbor is a minister, and we had an impromptu wedding right there. Dad made a personal call to Jack's CO to get approval for the marriage license."

Libby didn't know what to say.

"Oh, Libby, I'm sorry you couldn't have been there. It's just this talk of war. It makes lovers want to do crazy things. So can you do it? Can you take over my flights?"

Libby grasped her friend's arms and found her voice. "Sure. Of course. And yes, I would've liked to be there . . . but never mind." She nodded toward the door. "You just go and be with Jack. You're perfect for each other. You did the right thing, of course."

Rose offered a quick hug before disappearing as quickly as she'd arrived.

Libby stepped onto the landing and watched her friend rush down the outside stairs, across the green lawn, and into the borrowed convertible. Jack sat at the wheel; he offered an excited wave, and Libby waved back.

Libby watched the car's taillights as they drove away. Why wasn't she driving off into the night with Dan? She didn't know whether to feel relief or envy.

Libby rubbed her eyes, hoping some extra energy would kick in once she made it into the air. After Rose's announcement, she hadn't been able to sleep, thinking about the ins and outs of marriage—and from what she experienced with her own parents, mostly the outs.

The airfield was quiet this morning, as if all the mynah birds had also been up late and decided to sleep in. She slid her coveralls over her slacks and blouse, then zipped them up to her neck, eyeing the plane in front of her. She was about to tell Rose's student, Otis, to go ahead and board the plane, when George waved to her from across the airstrip. Dan was at his side.

Libby grinned, waved, and turned to Otis. "I'll be back in a minute."

She jogged across the gravel runway, then came to a stop in front of the men and placed her hands on her hips. "Let me guess. A new plane has arrived, and we're invited for a look? Did they add new bombs to—?"

Libby stopped short when she noticed the dark circles under Dan's eyes. His lips were drawn into a tight line.

George placed a hand on her arm. "I've called in another pilot to take over this lesson for you. He'll be here in a few minutes."

"Sure, George, but—"

George walked away, and Libby turned back to Dan. "What's going on? Is it your family? I'm supposed to be filling in for Rose—"

"Libby, we need to talk; that's all." He attempted a carefree tone. "I was thinking we could head to the beach." He took her arm and guided her toward the office.

"Dan, I can tell something's wrong. Did George tell you about Rose? She and Jack were married last night."

Dan scratched his forehead. "Married. That's nice. We can take a taxi to Waikiki. Maybe stop by your place for a swimsuit?"

Libby pulled her arm from Dan's grasp. "Head to the beach in the middle of our workday? Did you just hear me say that our best friends had an impromptu wedding? Dan, something's wrong, and I want you to tell me *now*." She crossed her arms over her chest.

A few of the mechanics in the nearby hangar turned their head at the sound of Libby's raised voice, but she didn't care. "George doesn't pull me from my schedule for no reason, and you just don't leave the base, unless . . ." Her hand trembled as she covered her mouth, her eyes searching his face. "Unless you're getting transferred."

Libby had seen it enough times with her students to know the procedure. The orders came, and within twenty-four hours they were gone.

Dan lowered his gaze. "Really, I'd like to discuss it at the beach. Someplace quieter."

Libby reached for his chin, forcing him to look at her. "That's it. Isn't it? You're leaving."

Dan nodded slowly, then took Libby's hand and placed her palm against his lips. "I'm so sorry. I wanted more time. I . . ." His eyes moistened with tears. He blinked them away and then pulled back from her slightly.

Libby watched as he took in a deep breath, then lowered himself onto one uniformed knee on the graveled runway.

"Dan?"

He reached into his pocket and pulled out a small velvet box, then took Libby's hand. "I wanted someplace romantic to do this. I've been thinking about it for weeks." He gazed into the cloudless sky behind Libby, as if the right words were written there; then he looked at her again.

Libby's heart pounded. "Dan, are you leaving? Please tell me it's not for good."

"Wait, just listen. Maybe this is the perfect place after all. This place is *us*." He flipped open the box with his thumb and held it up for her to see. A gold band glinted in the sun.

"They're shipping me out. I'm heading for the Philippines. But before I go, I need you to know how much I love you, Libby. And I want to know you'll be waiting for me."

She squeezed his hand. "Dan, are you asking what I think? Do you want me to marry you before you leave?" She thought about Jack and Rose's rushed marriage. The one thing Libby needed was time. It was what she'd prayed for before drifting back to sleep.

"Well, we could, but we don't have to. I want you to wait until you know for sure." Dan's blond hair fluttered in the light breeze. "Just say you'll marry me when I return." He released her hand and took the ring from the box.

"Yes." Libby nodded and stretched out her hand, allowing Dan to slip the ring on her finger. This was a step she could take.

She lifted her hand and looked at the ring. "It's beautiful." She met Dan's gaze, and he pulled her into his embrace. Her cheek pressed against his uniformed chest.

"Dan." She took a deep breath. "When are you leaving?"

"Tomorrow, Libby. I'll be gone tomorrow."

Seven

TOP HATS AND TIARAS

Washington—used to its roving citizens returning to the capital with tales of danger, destruction, and tragedy—should be gratified to hear the lyric praises of Mrs. Golden Bell for her recent two years in Manila.

With the wives and daughters of army and navy officers ordered home, the traditionally gay Army-Navy Club, around which much of the occidental social life in Manila circulates, is somber in tone. "It's amazing and rather gratifying to see how dejected the husbands look," laughs Mrs. Bell.

Though admitting the hot stickiness of the islands, where you constantly feel as if you've been "bathed in honey," Mrs. Bell finds the spontaneous hospitality of the people and the beauty of the surroundings more than adequate compensation.

Patricia Grady
Excerpt from the *Washington Post,* September 28, 1941

Natsuo's mind filled with the words of a poem as he awoke. A few months ago it had been an English poem stirring his thoughts. Now it was the words of Minamoto Sanetomo.

Seven hundred years ago, Minamoto had been the third Kamakura Shogun and the last head of his family's clan. Not wanting to meet the same fate as his brother, who was assassinated for plotting against the throne, Minamoto put all of his time and energy into writing poetry.

As Natsuo rose and prepared for the day's training, one stanza of Minamoto's poem ran through his head—he'd known the words since he was a boy, and they echoed over and over in one long refrain.

When mountains are split
And the seas run dry—
Should such a world be born,
I would not show a double heart
In the service of my lord.

The shadow of a cherry tree swaying in the morning's slight breeze danced over Natsuo's face. He knew in his heart the words to the poem had special meaning—perhaps sent as a message from the Lord Emperor himself, the true god. Natsuo had read ancient tales about men who had been given a high appeal to service in such a manner. He'd heard stories of those who heard voices in their minds.

Now during the day, despite the tedious drills, the sharp commands of the trainers, and even the occasional snap of a bamboo stick over his head, Natsuo felt renewed vigor. He'd been called for a purpose. He had thought his fate in joining the army had simply been part of a government requirement; now he knew otherwise.

War was coming.

A greater war than the one witnessed in China. The mountains would split and the seas run dry, yet Natsuo would not show a double heart. He would give life and service to his lord, the emperor.

His time in the United States had been part of this overall plan, he concluded. What he'd learned in the States would help him defeat the enemy. He'd touched the American souls and understood their weaknesses. He'd been trained in their ways.

⁂

"Should I have said yes, George? I'm not good enough. I don't even know how a successful marriage works." Libby fingered the gold band that looked oddly out of place on her hand.

She was sitting across from George in the airport office, watching the planes take off and land. Billy Jackson, despite his ever-present hangover, had taken Libby's lessons for the day.

George leaned back in his chair, which gave a loud squeak of protest. "It sounds like you're trying to talk yourself out of it. You could give the ring back until Dan returns." George leaned forward again. "But if I were you, Libby, I'd hang on to this guy . . ."

"Maybe I'm uncertain, but I'm not stupid. I mean, really, George. Dan is the kindest, most wonderful man I've ever met."

A mechanic peeked his head inside the door. "Hey, George, got a minute?"

"Sure thing, Larry." George rose, then paused before Libby. "Do you believe in the good Lord, Libby? Do you believe He's in control, even in this crazy, mixed-up world we live in?"

Libby studied George's eyes. She knew she couldn't fool him. "I believe there is a God. But to be honest, it's been a long time since I've thought about Him. I used to pray sometimes, but then . . ." Libby lowered her gaze. "Then I began to wonder if the praying did any good."

George's voice was gentle. "Whenever I get all worried, the thing I focus on is what I know to be true. First God, then His love for me. Next, I think about the truth of whatever situation I'm in. Once I know the truth . . ." George patted her back. "Well, things tend to fall in place from there."

Libby nodded. "Thanks, George. I'll think about that."

He moved to the door. "You're a bright girl. Don't

let fear stand in your way of happiness. Just start with what you know for sure."

❧ ❧ ❧

Start with what you know. George's words replayed in Libby's mind as she walked toward the Schofield Barracks. What did she know? She knew that since meeting Dan, she wasn't lonely or sad. Dan also had a way of calming her anger. Of making her smile and not take life so seriously.

For the last few months, she had half-expected him to wake up one day and change his mind about her. Expected that he'd get tired of her or find someone else. But that hadn't happened. He'd wanted to see her as often as he could. In fact, Mr. Atkins had complained about Dan's frequent visits and their long chats on the stairwell under the light of the moon.

Yes, she knew he loved her.

But how did she feel about him? She laughed out loud. No question about that. Being with Dan gave her an even greater rush than the moment of liftoff.

Libby paused as she stood before the barracks. She glanced toward the sky and noticed afternoon clouds forming. Now that she was here, she wondered if she'd even be allowed to go in. She was about to take a chance and stride up the front steps, when she noticed a familiar face.

"Excuse me, Zeke. Do you know where Dan is?"

"Libby! He's looking for you. He went to your apartment and couldn't find you."

"I thought he was packing. We're getting together tonight, but I just—"

"No time to blabber, girlie. There's word that some Jap ships are causing trouble in the middle of the ocean. Dan's group has to leave right away, or they lose their window for safe passage. The planes are being taken by aircraft carrier, and the pilots are hopping a ride too. He's already at the docks, but if you hurry you can make it."

Zeke's words tumbled over each other, and Libby attempted to take them all in. *No, not yet. I'm not ready. . . .* A few soft raindrops fell on her face, and Libby brushed them away.

"Wish I could help." Zeke removed his cap and scratched his head. "But I've got no wheels. I'd take a taxi if I were you."

Libby didn't realize until her legs were sticking to the vinyl seats of the cab that she hadn't even thanked Zeke for his help. When she arrived at the harbor, things were even crazier than she'd imagined. Pilots and sailors, wives, children, and girlfriends were intermingled in a mob of movement, frantically trying to find their loved ones for a final good-bye.

"Excuse me; I have to get through." Libby pushed through the crowd, getting as close to the aircraft carrier as possible. Bigger raindrops were falling now. She brushed wet strands of hair back from her face.

Dan couldn't leave without knowing. Without her

telling him once more that she loved him and that she would wait as long as it took.

Libby made her way to the gangplank connecting the carrier to the dock. Her eyes scanned the high deck, hoping for a sign of him. But it was too far away, and there was too much motion aboard as the crew prepared for the journey ahead.

Bodies pressed against Libby as they moved past her, and tears filled her eyes. Then a gentle hand touched her shoulder, and her heart leapt as she turned and saw him.

"Dan!" She wrapped her arms around his wet shoulders and planted a kiss on his chin. "I thought you were gone."

He looked down at her with those blue eyes full of love. "No way, lady. I would have held up the whole ship just to say good-bye."

Libby took a deep breath and let the words spill out. "I want you to know that when I said yes, I meant it. You'll come back, and we'll be together. I promise."

"It won't be long." Dan brushed her hair from her face, wiping raindrops from her cheeks. "Wait for me, and I'll think of you. I love you, Libby."

Libby heard a knock at the door, and fear clawed at her chest. No one came by at this hour unless something was wrong. Maybe something had happened to Dan's transport. Perhaps his convoy had already hit trouble out at sea.

She slid from beneath her sheet and quickly donned her bathrobe, hurrying to the door. "Who is it?"

"Libby, it's me. Rose."

Libby opened the door, and her friend hurried in.

All day Libby had been strong. She'd shed no tears as the aircraft carrier slipped out of the harbor. No tears as she'd walked home alone. But now, with one look at the concern and compassion on Rose's face, a river of hot tears began to flow.

"Oh, Libby. I'm so sorry." Rose wrapped an arm around her shoulder.

"What are you doing here? You were on the other side of the island on your honeymoon, remember?"

Rose clicked on the table lamp and led Libby toward the sofa. "We came back as soon as we heard. Jack said he'll have me forever, but you need me now."

Libby clung to her friend. "Thank you. I can't believe it, but thank you."

Rose set a small satchel down on the floor.

"What's that for?" Libby managed between sniffles.

"It's my things. I'm going to stay with you a few days, just to keep you company."

Libby wiped tears from her face and neck. "You don't have to. I'll be fine, really. You need to be with your husband."

Rose smiled. "Your mouth's saying one thing, but the way you're clinging to my hand says another."

"But you're a married woman now. I mean, you should be with Jack."

"I wish I could be. He goes out on maneuvers during the week, remember? Don't worry. I'll be back with him by the weekend." She picked up a throw pillow and hugged it to her chest. "You have two beds. I thought I'd bunk here for a few nights."

Libby showed Rose through the dark hallway to the extra bed.

Rose slid off her long, tan raincoat that belted at the waist, and Libby saw that she was wearing baby doll pajamas underneath. She wanted to ask a hundred questions about her wedding, about what it was like to be married. But now wasn't the time. Libby couldn't bear to know how really wonderful it was being with the man you loved.

Rose pushed back the covers and snuggled in. "It's a sleepover!"

Libby climbed in between her sheets. "Good night, Rose. And thank you."

"No problem, sweetie. Just glad to be here."

The moon hung heavy in the window between the two beds, casting a gentle glow.

How many nights will it be until I see Dan again?

A few minutes passed, and Libby could hear Rose tossing and turning beneath the thin blanket. She wondered if her friend regretted coming, regretted not sleeping by her husband's side one more night before he went back to sea.

"Wow, the moon sure is bright." Rose turned again. "My parents' house is on the edge of a plantation, and the trees block most of the moonlight. Here I feel like I'm trying to sleep in the middle of the day."

Libby rolled onto her stomach. "It's perfect for me." She glanced out to the full orb in the sky. "Even on cold nights I push open the drapes to let the moonlight in. I don't like the dark . . ."

Rose didn't reply, but Libby could tell that she wasn't sleeping. Sure enough, when Libby glanced over, Rose lay on her side, propped up on one elbow, waiting.

Libby returned to her back and pulled her blanket to her chin. "I was only five when my mom left." She stared at the pattern the windowpanes made on the ceiling. "She came and stood in my doorway in the dark, and I could hear her breathing. I didn't say anything, and neither did she."

"Oh, Libby, I didn't know."

"She stood there, and I thought she was going to apologize for the fight she and Daddy had gotten into. She always did that. After their blowups, she'd come up to my room and say, 'Don't worry, little girl; the sun will come up in the morning, and all will be forgiven. Do you want pancakes for breakfast?' "

Libby felt the tears come again, as the pain of her losses, one fresh and one long buried, rose to the surface.

"You didn't see her again after that?"

"No." Libby rolled to her side. "The sun did come up the next morning, but there were no pancakes, no mother."

Rose climbed out of bed and sank down by her side.

"How come they always leave? Why did I let this happen to me again?"

She didn't expect an answer, and Rose didn't give one. She just held Libby and cried with her.

Why didn't I tell Dan about my mother? Libby wondered. *There is so much of me he doesn't know.* She promised herself that next time they were together, she would tell him everything. *No holding back. My whole heart, I promise.*

And it was somewhere in those words that Libby realized her plea had turned into a prayer. *Start with what you know,* George had said. Here was another thing she knew for sure: She needed God's strength to hold herself together until Dan returned.

Eight

U.S. FORCES IN PHILIPPINES
MUCH LARGER THAN REALIZED

The size of the air force under MacArthur's command is a military secret, but it admittedly has been greatly strengthened in recent months. . . . A few years ago, many military experts held that the Philippines could not be held against a Japanese attack. Today, few such assertions are heard.

An invasion could not even be attempted without withdrawing large numbers of troops from China, and even then, the army being whipped into shape in the Philippines might well make an invasion too costly to be profitable.

The American Far East forces, it is believed, would be a "hard nut to crack."

John G. Norris, Staff Writer
Excerpt from the *Washington Post,* November 19, 1941

The Japanese recruits lounged around their cement barracks, happy to be given a day without training. The popular song "Kantar of Ina" carried on the noonday air, escaping from the open windows of the officers' quarters. Natsuo listened as his bunkmate sang along, "I may look like a crook and a ruffian. But witness, O Moon, the splendor of my heart."

In his mind, Natsuo joined in with the next refrain. *O Moon of my homeland, I am newly reborn. Mirror the brightness of my soul tonight.*

Many men spent their free time writing letters home, but Natsuo knew his father would consider it foolishness. Natsuo was here to train, to become a fine soldier and make his family proud.

His notes from his week's classes were spread before him on his mat. The lectures were meant to sharpen the fighting spirit of the warrior, just as physical drills honed the body. On the battlefield, only one thing mattered—to fight for the emperor, their great one who watched over his children. Fight for him or, most honorably of all, die for him.

They'd been reminded in class today that any soldier taken prisoner, who later managed to return to Japan, was subject to court-martial and a possible death penalty. Even if the penalty was not carried out, anyone who returned would be so thoroughly ostracized he might as well be dead.

The teacher's words had imprinted themselves in Natsuo's mind: "Soldiers are supposed to give their lives for the cause, not grovel in enemy prison camps."

On one hand, the words were no different from the patriotic training he'd received in his primary school near Kobe. Yet later teachings—false guidance—conflicted inside him. In America, professors had spoken of "life, liberty, and the pursuit of happiness." What foolishness such notions were. Yet disloyal memories of those lectures made his mind wander into forbidden places.

Saburo, another of Natsuo's childhood friends, strolled over to his mat. "A few of us are heading to town. I hear there's a pretty girl who works at the movie house. We're catching a ride with one of the delivery drivers in exchange for a promised bottle of *sake*. Will you come?"

Natsuo noted his friend's shirttail hanging out and diverted his gaze. "I'm finishing my studies, then turning in early. Besides, it's a long trip, and there's a chance you might miss the nightly inspection." Natsuo set his chin in determination, knowing his hard work would be rewarded, and remembering that disobedience brought a slap in the face, a hard whack over the head with a bamboo stick, or sometimes worse.

Saburo nodded and smiled. "Once a noodle boy, always a noodle boy. You have a weak spine, Natsuo." His round face contorted into a smirk. "Grow up. Stop worrying about Mama and Papa's approval."

Natsuo knew Saburo's words deserved no response. But his friend was right; Natsuo did view his instructors as his parents now. And the emperor as his great father, who asked for only one thing: *Hakko Ichiu,* "the whole world under one roof." Peace would only come to their nation, to their lives, once their enemies bent on weakened knees, submitting under imperial domination. But in order for that to happen, the emperor's children must commit unswervingly to his cause.

Saburo strode out of the barracks onto the dusty road where he and a few other recruits would hitch a ride from the transport truck. It grated on Natsuo's nerves that his friend could care so little about their duty. Their rank as soldiers was one they held for life . . . or until their death. *Gyokusai,* the soldier's mandate, held that they were required to fight to the end for the emperor. *Gyokusai* meant "the breaking of a jewel" —a crushing of what was most valuable for a greater cause. The thought both frightened and excited him.

Music played on in the background, yet as Natsuo attempted to focus his mind on his country, on Father Emperor, on *gyokusai,* the music reminded him of Saburo's offer and of the fun he used to have near the UCLA campus. He remembered school dances and pretty American girls with swishing skirts, bared calves, and high-heeled shoes. And despite the training manual open before him, Natsuo's mind recalled the female laughter that tittered along with American jazz tunes. And one young woman in particular, who didn't seem to mind that he was Japanese. Clara was her name, and they'd danced the night away more than once.

Thoughts like these angered Natsuo, but he kept that, too, bottled up inside. Yet no matter how mad it made him, he couldn't help but wander amongst the memories, strolling back to lazy days before cultural burdens weighed him down. Before death was the focal point of all his thoughts.

❧ ❧ ❧

Dan's trip to the Philippines from Hawaii had been boring and lonely. He'd heard rumors of Japanese warships following off the port side—at least that would've broken up the monotony, yet nothing had come of it.

The ship they piggybacked on had been designed as a floating runway for planes like the Douglas SBD-2 Dauntless bombers. Instead, their P-40s were loaded up, heading for their new home. The ship sailed safely past the Marshall Islands, Cook Islands, Guam, and then on toward the sunset to the Philippines.

On the way, the sailor in the bunk next to Dan, a fresh-faced country boy who admitted to being only sixteen, had become so stricken with anxiety over possible attack that any sudden noise made him hit the deck. Then there was the kid on the bunk above Dan—the bunk inches away from the ceiling—who struggled with seasickness. Dan didn't savor the nights he awoke to the sound of puke hitting a pan.

Instead, he often found himself on the deck, watching the roiling sea. The whipping winds threatened to carry him overboard, but the loneliness thrashed him even harder. He wrote Libby numerous letters signed "Somewhere at Sea" and planned to mail them upon landing.

The ground swayed as he disembarked, and humidity

wrapped around him like a thick blanket. Also, he discovered, the sun was even more direct than it had been in Hawaii. Beads of perspiration trickled down his temples as he and the other pilots loaded their belongings into the waiting jeeps. Their first stop, before heading to Clark Field, was Manila.

"I've heard that because of the heat, we don't work in the afternoons." Gabe ran a hand down his cheek. "Short days. Long nights. Which would be fine with me, if only my wife were here."

"Ah, I'm not thinking about work yet. Just trying to let the beauty sink in." Dan eyed the unique landscape, making mental notes to relate to Libby. "So lush—even more beautiful than Hawaii."

On the ride into town, the countryside looked calm and primitive. Birds chattered in towering acacia trees. Native women beat their brightly colored sarongs on the rocks at the muddy river. Naked little boys dangled their fingers in the cool water as they floated on rafts of coconuts.

But within the city limits of Manila, the movement of the crowds surprised Dan. Their driver found a space along a crowded street and pulled over to park. Dan, Gabe, and the others climbed out.

"Captain said you all can spend a day in town before heading up to the base." The driver sank into the seat and lit a cigarette. "I'll stay here and watch your things. I think you'll like it—land of coconut palms and violet sunsets." He nodded to the narrow dirt streets that bustled with even more congestion than Honolulu.

“No soldier should miss the pleasure of seeing Manila.”

They walked along, and Dan smiled as he scanned the crowds. Instead of soldiers and sailors striding around in matching uniforms, varieties of native dress brought color and interest. Turbaned men hurried in majestic strides among the crowds of Japanese, Chinese, and Filipinos. Blind beggars huddled against the old Spanish walls. Gabe stopped at the first one he saw, offering him a few coins and a firm handshake. The man’s unseeing eyes peered up at them, and he nodded his thanks.

Ponies wearing tinkling bells pulled two-wheel carriages and were the most used form of transportation. The whole town reeked of barnyard scents, and the men learned to watch their step. Taxis also filled the streets; their bumpers, hoods, and windshields so decorated with flags, banners, and crucifixes that excited drivers had to crane their heads out side windows in order to see the road in front of them.

“I wonder where everyone’s going.” Dan watched a young boy leading a pony cart piled with packages. The boy was cheerfully singing a tune to match his steps.

“I’ve heard for three pesos you can get a Filipino-made knife, and twenty will buy you a suit.” Gabe glanced into a store window as they passed.

Dan paused before a vendor on the street selling orchids. The scent reminded him of Libby. “I’ll take some.” He fished a peso from his pocket, and then he lifted the flowers to his face and imagined her weaving the flowers through her hair.

Dan smiled at the memory and stroked his finger

over the satin petals. As they crossed the busy street, an American soldier walked by with a beautiful Filipino girl on his arm. They both glanced at the flowers in Dan's hand, giving him a knowing look. Despite the cars that honked, urging them to hurry their crossing, Dan wanted to stop them and explain. To tell them his girl was actually back in Hawaii, and he'd bought the flowers because they reminded him of her. But they'd already passed, their arms wrapped around each other, their laughter intermingling with the noise of the street.

Then Dan spotted her. She looked like any other young Filipino girl except for her large eyes that were the softest shade of blue. She waited at the street corner for her turn to cross. Dan hurried toward her. He lowered himself on one knee, bringing him eye-to-eye with the youngster. "Here, these are for you."

The girl looked over her shoulder, as if believing his words were intended for someone else. "Thank you," she said in clear English. "You nice GI."

Dan rose and patted her shoulder, then caught up with his friend.

"We have one more place we need to visit before meeting back at the jeeps." Dan pulled out a hand-drawn map that the driver had given him. "These are directions to Intramuros, the famed Walled City and showpiece of Manila."

Thankfully, the jeep had dropped them off less than a mile from its entrance, and they arrived by foot in a matter of minutes.

"Look at this, will ya?" Dan pointed to the walls,

chiseled out of some type of polished stone. They appeared to be nearly twenty feet high with a base twice as wide. Watchtowers stood at the corners, and massive wooden gates with carved lintels faced the four points of the compass.

Gabe stopped to read a plaque inside the entryway. "Says the Spaniards built this part of the city back in the sixteenth century. Guess they occupied it for a while." He caught up with Dan, and they walked through the streets in silent reverence. In the center of the walled city they discovered a grand cathedral. Voices from inside sang hymns in the Spanish-sounding native language, Tagalog. Though he couldn't understand the words, the emotions they released washed a soft peace over Dan, something he hadn't felt since leaving Hawaii.

Gabe paused in front of the massive steps. "Do you want to go in?"

"Go ahead." Dan motioned with a nod of his chin. "I'll wait here." Though he felt drawn to the music flowing through the doors, something inside him felt uneasy. Perhaps it was the murals on the walls that too often illustrated a suffering Savior. Or the large crucifixes that portrayed a weak and dying man.

Though Dan had attended church for years as a child, the pieces of the spiritual struggle never seemed to fit together in his mind. How could a God of love allow such horrible things to happen to His own Son? The suffering, the pain. It wasn't something Dan could connect with—or wanted to. He settled onto a stone step and pushed the thoughts of the pierced Jesus out of his mind.

Dan eyed the Filipinos who bustled within the walled city as they had done for hundreds of years. Colorful long skirts swooshed around the women's ankles. Fancy cotton blouses were buttoned to their necks, and their lips wore warm smiles. The Filipino men wore baggy trousers and sandals, and every man or woman who passed Dan offered a wide grin and a wave. Their eyes also held a special twinkle as if relating, *All is well. The Americans are here to protect us.*

Dan returned their smiles, feeling a sense of peace knowing that inside the church building Gabriel was offering up prayers for their unit's safety, in addition to prayers for his family back home. He hoped Gabe also prayed for those left behind in Hawaii.

❧ ❧ ❧

The tent city to which Dan and his friends were assigned seemed to have sprouted overnight on the perimeter of Clark Field. Just a few days earlier it had been a large parade ground. Now it was an ocean of white canvas spread out as far as his eye could see.

Each structure looked like a tent house with a wooden floor and supports. Canvas stretched over the frame, with a door and two window openings on each side. Three metal cots were lined up against each of two walls, and Dan and five others now called this place home.

"Bayanai, here, is our houseboy." Irvin, one of Dan's

roommates, pointed to the young Filipino who sat in the corner. "He takes care of our shoes and clothes and keeps the tent shipshape. He also washes and presses our uniforms twice a day. We change often because of the humidity."

The new bunkmate continued in what Dan assumed to be a southern drawl. "The best part is our siesta from one to four. It's too dang hot to work around this place, so we just nap or write letters home."

Another soldier strode into the room, removed his cap, and tossed it onto the large rectangle of trunks in the middle of the room. The trunks held their gear and doubled as tables or extra seating space.

"Did y'all arrive with the new shipment of planes?"

Dan could see he was a pilot by the uniform. Tall and slender, he placed a booted foot on top of one of the trunks and fanned himself with an oriental-looking fan. "I'm Oliver, by the way. But everyone just calls me Tex." He stretched out his hand, and Dan shook it vigorously.

"Yeah, we arrived with them just this morning." Dan nodded toward the others. "I hear we've been pulled in to make defending this island possible."

"That's the plan, I guess." Oliver swatted at a pesky fly with his fan. "Someone told me that with this newest shipment, we now have the largest concentration of U.S. Army aircraft outside the U.S. And the best planes to boot. Over a hundred P-40 fighters and a couple dozen bombers by last count."

"Only problem is we don't have any air-raid plan,

or antiaircraft guns to protect them." Irvin pulled out a cigarette from his shirt pocket, lit it, and took a long drag. "And I heard some of your P-40s aren't even flyable. The army's gone and shipped them without cooling fluid. Dumb move. Our only hope is that we strike 'em first." He tapped the ashes from his cigarette onto the floor. "If I were running this joint, I'd take our current state of alert seriously and get down to business."

"Ah, come on, you really know how to sour things, don't you?" Tex sank onto his bunk. "Who says the Japs are gonna strike at all? The squint eyes would be nuts. I mean, how can runts from such a tiny island think of pairing up against the good ol' U.S. of A.?"

"Just stating the facts." Irvin spoke slowly. "Trying to bring a little reality to the sit-u-a-tion."

Soldiers are the same everywhere, Dan realized as he unpacked. *Each with his own opinion, his own preconceived ideas of how the army should be run.* But it didn't bother him. *Let them think what they want to.*

As for Dan, he only had two desires. First, spending more time in the air than on land. And second, getting back to his girl as soon as possible.

Nine

JAPAN RATTLES SWORD BUT ECHO IS PIANISSIMO

Over in Japan the sword rattling goes on with all sorts of threats and dire predictions of what will happen if the United States tries to tell Tokyo what to do; yet the echo in Washington does not hurt the eardrums. The Japanese spokesmen in the American capital wish to continue the negotiations with the United States.

Obviously, one may argue that Tokyo is seeking to gain time in which to get into better shape for the threatened war. One may also argue, however, that Japan does not wish the war.

In a difficult and ticklish position, it appears that the State Department and President Roosevelt have handled the Japanese well up to the present. They have not been impressed by the Japanese threats.

Edwin L. James
Excerpt from the *New York Times*, December 7, 1941

Dan had already been gone nearly two months when Libby received his first batch of letters. She loved opening the thin red, white, and blue-trimmed envelopes marked "Air Mail." The first dozen were those he'd written while out at sea. After that, she received long, detailed reports about the beauty of the island and Dan's daily routines, which included flying planes in the mornings and taking long naps in the afternoons.

As she read each letter over and over, Libby smiled at how Dan's handwriting changed by location. She'd notice a food stain on the page and know he was writing during mealtime. His writing slanted to the left when he was on the bunk, and to the right when he was in a hammock under one of the trees on base. By the size of the print, she could even tell which letters had been written by flashlight, while his roommates slept, in comparison to those written in daylight or by electric bulb.

It took about fifteen days for a letter to travel to her. Fifteen days seemed like a wide chasm separating Dan's thoughts and hers. But at least the letters came often enough to keep her from worrying too much. She looked outside to the predawn morning at Pearl Harbor and reread the latest one.

Dear Libby,

I'm missing you and lovin' you, of course.

Another bunch of letters arrived yesterday. I love reading your words. It's almost as if you're right here talking to me, sharing your latest antics. Did you follow up on the possible new units for women pilots? You'd be one sharp tack, Libby gal, blowing them all away. Of course, you'd most likely have to head back to the States and away from the beauty of the islands if an opportunity like that ever arose.

I've spent more time in the air lately, bending the throttle on some of the new planes to see what they're made of. The sky over Manila is nearly as pretty as the one over Hawaii. But it would be even prettier if you were my co-pilot.

I suppose tearing through the skies beats being a blisterfoot. Those infantrymen are arriving in record numbers too, except the army doesn't seem to know what to do with them all just yet. I guess the brass realizes more defenses here are in order. But translating that into a workable plan is a different matter. The foot soldiers have even more free time than us dopes who have our machines to fly.

This note will be a short one tonight as the guys are urging me to turn out the lights in preparation for the blanket drill. That's "sleeping" in nonmilitary terms, or in my case, dreaming of my doll face back home. Think of me in the sky, as I think of you the same.

All my love,
Dan

A flock of seagulls flew by Libby's window, unsettled by something in the harbor. She slid the letter into the envelope and thought about his words. Dan believed in her, believed she could be part of something greater. Maybe she should check in and see what these women air pilots were all about . . . sometime in the future. For now the peace of the island soothed her. Her friendships with Rose, George, and the others at the airfield made it feel like home. Besides, Hawaii was the closest to Dan she could get right now. Here, it only took fifteen days for their thoughts to cross, and Libby wasn't willing to give that up just yet.

She stood and slipped on her flight suit, then headed out the door for John Rodgers. It was Sunday, and she had a full schedule.

It's going to be one busy day.

❧ ❧ ❧

"Okay, once that plane passes, let's take her in for a landing," Libby said to her Sunday morning student. Pride swelled inside her as she observed her apprentice in action. She'd done her job well.

The morning sky was slightly overcast—not cloudy enough to hinder vision—yet a military aircraft continued toward them. Didn't he see her yellow Cub?

At first Libby thought it might be one of the B-17s due in from California, but the plane was too small, too quick.

"Hold on!" Libby wrenched the controls from her

student's grip and jammed the throttle wide open. The plane lurched upward just in time.

"What the heck?"

The plane passed close beneath, causing the Cub's celluloid windows to quiver. Libby watched as it sliced through the sky, toward the sea, toward the harbor. The morning sun reflected two red circles against a white flag on the wings—the Rising Sun.

Leveling off, Libby made a sharp turn to the west and sighted, beyond the solo plane, formations of silver bombers bearing down on Pearl Harbor. Her hands felt clammy as she watched the rogue plane join the formation. Then, as though caught in a bad dream, she watched something detach from the plane's underbelly and plunge toward the harbor. She'd seen bombs attached to aircraft, seen them loaded onto ships, but she had never seen them dropped. And never against her own people. She tensed her jaw in horror and anger.

Antiaircraft guns from the ships spit shells in return, and puffs of black smoke rose from the decks. But it wasn't enough. Their efforts didn't even make a dent in the waves of planes. *Why aren't they doing more?*

Libby swept her plane by John Rodgers, preparing to land. Then she spotted sleeker, faster Japanese pursuits that amazingly resembled the P-40. They swooped like angry hornets, spitting bullets at the surprised sailors on the docked naval vessels, causing fingers of smoke to billow up from the entire fleet of ships docked at the harbor.

Libby's Cub bounded down the runway in a hard

landing and stalled. She glanced at the sky and motioned toward her student, who sat frozen in the seat, his face white. "Get out! Take cover!"

The man did as he was told, and together they sprinted off the runway. Libby pushed her body harder, not daring to glance at the sky. She focused her eyes on the cement office building ahead. Her legs pumped as hard as they could, but she couldn't keep up with the long-legged student.

She felt the presence of the fighter plane bearing down, like a demon breathing down her neck. Then the ripping of metal, as bullets tore into her tiny plane left behind.

As the fighter's shadow swept over her, a bullet smacked the tarmac behind Libby. It ricocheted, buzzing past and pelting her with chunks of gravel.

"Dear God, no!" she screamed.

George opened the office door and yelled something at her as the fighter roared over. His wide eyes scanned the sky; then his bulky frame lumbered toward her. "Libby, hurry!"

She pushed her legs faster. "Get back inside!"

George's disbelieving gaze was transfixed on the sky.

Libby motioned to him as she scrambled past. "George, get inside!" Whether it was the same fighter returning for the kill or a different one, Libby couldn't tell. But machine-gun fire picked up again. Bullets whizzed past her, embedding in the cement blocks as she dashed through the side door.

Her feet crunched broken glass from the window.

"Do you think we're okay here?" Libby leaned down, hands on knees, panting. She turned, expecting to see George behind her. The doorway was empty, and now a louder roar of planes drowned out the blaring radio on the counter. "George?"

Libby hurried back to the door. George lay on the ground exactly where she had passed him. "George!" Libby screamed, running back to him. His eyes were open as if still staring up in disbelief.

She fell onto her knees and shook him; then she spotted the two bullet holes in his chest. "No!"

Strong hands grabbed Libby's shoulders. "Come back inside, Libby. He's gone. There are more Japs coming!" It was Billy Jackson.

"But it's my fault." Libby succumbed to Billy's strong arms. "I led the bullets straight toward him."

"No time to think of that," he shouted in her ear. "Get inside! Here they come again!"

Ground-shaking explosions punctuated Billy's words. She looked around for her student and assumed he'd taken cover in one of the hangars.

Inside, Libby stared out the window, her eyes fixed on George's lifeless body. Tears streamed down her face. "Do you see that?" She turned to Billy. "They just keep coming. I can't believe the Japs are attacking us. It's really happening."

Another group of fighters swarmed the airfield, machine-gunning anything that moved. Their fixed landing gear looked like the talons of giant birds of prey screaming down.

"Get away from the window! I told you, there's nothing we can do for George now." Billy tugged on her arm.

Libby couldn't pull her gaze away from the fighters. They moved through the air as if part of some ancient ritual dance among the backlit clouds, circling around the airfield.

The radio on the counter behind her still emanated soothing Hawaiian music, adding to the surreal quality of the scene. The music had played during the night as Libby had lain in bed thinking of Dan. It had played while she rose, bathed, and dressed. It had played during her early morning drive to the airport. And she knew the reason . . . *the B-17s*. The radio was a homing beacon for the large American bombers on their way to the islands from California. Unwittingly, it had also been the perfect beacon for enemy attackers.

Then, as if finally catching up with the attack, the music cut short and the radio buzzed with news bulletins —torpedoes had been launched against the ships anchored in Pearl Harbor. Planes had been spotted in the north, south, and west.

The ground shook again. Libby covered her ears against the explosion. A hangar to the right of the office exploded into flames. *The hangars . . . they're bombing all the hangars.*

Suddenly a deeper droning filled Libby's ears, different from the high-pitched whine of the Japanese planes. She glanced out the window in time to see Japanese Zeros opening fire on one of the B-17s, finally arriving after its long journey. The silver mammoth circled the field, preparing to land. Flames leaped from one of the bomber's right engines; bullets riddled its side. The bomber swept low, but Libby's abandoned and bullet-riddled Piper Cub blocked its path.

Please, God. Please help them land.

With an earth-shattering explosion, the B-17 crash-landed on the runway, its fuselage split open like an overripe watermelon. One of its wings skidded across the runway toward the office. Libby and Billy vaulted behind the desk just as the ripped wing crashed into the wall and pierced through the already-destroyed window. The wing's impact sent the desk, along with Libby and Billy, sliding across the floor. They hit the counter, knocking over the still-screeching radio.

Libby squirmed out from under the desk and made her way to the door. Hit squarely by the bomber, her Cub had been tossed aside like a child's broken toy.

But there was no time to think of that. Flames leapt from the B-17. *The crew!*

Covering her head with her hands, Libby raced toward the B-17. Men's cries filled the air. As she neared, half a dozen men staggered from the gaping hole.

"The pilot is trapped!" one man yelled above the drone of planes and the pop of bullets on the asphalt. "I'm too big. I can't get to him."

"Get in the office. Take cover!" Libby jumped through an opening of twisted metal. Flames engulfed the back portion of the wreckage. The fuel tank was back there—she'd have to hurry. The front half shifted and shuddered with a deep metallic groan.

The left side of the plane had caved inward. Libby squeezed through a narrow opening toward the cockpit. The pilot, soaked in his own blood from a gash in his forehead, slumped in the seat. As Libby leaned close, the man moaned.

"Hold on, buddy; I'll get you out." She tilted the man toward her and reached around his back, under his arms, interlocking her fingers around his chest. Thick smoke assaulted her eyes. She pulled, but the pilot didn't budge. Libby held her breath and tugged even harder.

The man cried out but remained stuck. His legs were pinned. Heat radiated from behind her, and she knew it was only a matter of time before they would be engulfed in smoke and fire.

Libby secured her feet and prepared to give another tug when she felt someone else squeeze into the tight space.

"You work his legs, I'll pull!" It was Billy Jackson's voice.

"'Bout time you showed up!" Libby shouted as another explosion rocked the airfield. She crawled under the controls. "On the count of three!" She rocked the man's legs. "One, two . . ."

"Now!" came out as a grunt, and Libby pushed the legs free. Billy wasn't about to stop. He pulled the man toward the gaping hole, and Libby scrambled out behind him and gulped fresh air.

Everywhere she looked, hangars and fuel trucks were ablaze, belching smoke. The airport office was still standing.

With his neck craned toward the office, Billy pulled the man across the airfield. The pilot was limp, and his legs snagged against the gravel like draglines.

Catching her breath, Libby caught up and tucked the pilot's legs under her arms. Soot streaked Billy's face, and blood dripped from a deep cut on his chin. Was this the same man who always showed up hungover, if at all?

"We're gonna make it!" Billy yelled. "We're gonna make it." Then his words were lost in another explosion.

⁂

CLARK FIELD, PHILIPPINES
MONDAY, DECEMBER 8, 1941

The American flag whipped and snapped on the flagpole as Dan hurried past in the first light of morning. The cool humidity nudged him awake along with the strong scent of jasmine. They'd been summoned to the briefing room, and Dan knew the news wasn't going to be good.

Dan and his squad's footsteps beat on the wooden floor of the command tent as they passed through the reception room into the briefing room. Dan took his place at the metal table inside and looked around. The pilot on his left was wiping the sleep from his eyes. Dan noticed he'd missed a button on his uniform shirt. Gabe sat across the table, combing his fingers through his hair in an attempt to tame the bed-head.

The colonel stood at the end of the table with a wide-legged stance, his arms crossed over his chest. He nodded to a soldier to turn down the excited voice of Don Bell—the local American radio broadcaster who gave the day's news. Dan thought he'd heard Bell say something about Hawaii. His throat constricted, and his heart pounded a double beat.

"Men, I have hard news to share. I've just heard over commercial radio that Pearl Harbor has been attacked by the Japanese."

An audible gasp passed through the room, and the pilots exchanged glances.

The officer's report seemed to buzz in Dan's ears as he remembered his last glimpse of Libby—standing at the dock, fading away as the carrier nudged toward the open sea. He clenched his fist and inhaled, trying to focus on the colonel's words.

"Minutes ago we received word from Iba Field that a formation of planes is about seventy-five miles offshore, heading for Corregidor. I'm sending out the P-40s to intercept. Dan, Gabe, boys, you'll be heading out as soon as you're ready."

Dan glanced down at his hands, attempting to hide their shaking. He spread his fingers over the metal table and glanced at the worried, angry faces around him. Each of the men had been transferred from Hawaii in the previous months.

"What about the bombers?" One of the B-17 crew members rose from the metal chair and paced the room. "Shouldn't we be doing something too? I'm sure this means we're in a state of war. We have to hit the Japs before they hit us."

"How come we've gotta hear the news from commercial radio?" another pilot demanded. "Are they gonna let the Japs sneak up on us too?"

"Well, what do you expect?" Gabe asked. "In the middle of being bombed, do you think they're going to stop, pick up the line, and spread the word?"

"Is that too much to ask when we're most likely next in line?"

Gabe raised his hands in a gesture of truce. "Hey, man, I am not the enemy here."

"Settle down, men." The colonel raised his voice. "Good news is that we haven't been attacked, and we'll most likely be able to intercept any attempts. This will also give us time to figure out what's next."

"We can't just stay here like sitting ducks," the bomber pilot said. "Please, sir, may we have permission to load the bombers? I'm certain we can take out the enemy on Formosa. If we can get there now, we could direct a severe blow. It's what, six hundred miles? Maybe even stop them before they hit us."

"Sorry, Lyle. You know I'm in no position to order something like that. We hafta wait for orders. Besides, just what are we going to attack? We can't just go drop bombs for the sake of dropping them."

"Well, forget Formosa. Maybe we should just head

out and see if there happen to be any aircraft carriers nearby. If the Japs have already struck Hawaii, we're sure to be next."

"Can't do that. Orders say—"

"Orders." Lyle swung a fist in the air. "I'd like to ask our buddies at Pearl Harbor what they thought about their orders not to strike until they've been hit upon—" He slammed his fist on the doorjamb and stalked out of the room.

Gabe leaned close, clearing his throat. "Lyle has a brother at Pearl."

Dan swallowed hard. He didn't want to think about the extent of the damage to Oahu.

The group quickly dismissed, and he grabbed his gear on his way out to his P-40. Anger surged through him, vibrating his very core. Anger that the Japs would attack without an official declaration of war. Anger that he had no idea if Libby was okay. Anger that he had no way of finding out any time soon.

Ten

BIG FORCES ARE MASSED
FOR SHOWDOWN IN THE PACIFIC

Men stood to arms along the shores and upon the islands of the Western Pacific yesterday as the storm of war, roaring eastward out of Europe, clouded the skies of the Orient.

The Philippines have been heavily strengthened, both with land and air forces, and Lieut. General Douglas MacArthur has now assumed direct command of United States armed forces in the Far East, with regular army troops and 150,000 Filipinos under his orders.

In a full-blown war, Japan's task is immediately spread all over the map. She may have to attack Siberia or defend herself from Russian attacks; hold the Chinese in check; smash Singapore by air, if not by land; reduce Hong Kong; perhaps attack or neutralize the

Philippines; hold off the harassing air and sea attacks by Britain and the United States; and eventually—if she is to reap anything from her hostilities—she must move either into Malaysia and Burma, or into the Netherlands Indies, any one of them a major, risky, and unpredictable operation.

Hanson W. Baldwin
Excerpt from the *New York Times,* December 7, 1941

It was 11:30 a.m. Six hours had passed since they'd received news that the Japanese had attacked Oahu, but so far they'd seen no action in the blue skies over the Philippines. Six hours was a long time to be alone in an aircraft with one's thoughts.

Dan circled Clark Field, preparing to land. Beneath him the airfield spread like a lake of compacted dirt in the midst of a thick jungle. Along the edges were the recently built tent barracks, large wooden hangars, and beyond those, Philippine homes on stilts that cascaded down the treed hillsides surrounding the base like wooden waterfalls. And past those hills, barren mountains, which looked like large anthills from the air.

Dan noticed a long line of men stretched in front of the door to the thatch-and-bamboo chapel, and he wondered if their prayers centered on those they'd left behind in Hawaii or on their own fate. Though no one said it, everyone knew the Philippines would be a key asset for Japan's control over the South Pacific. Their question wasn't if the Nips would strike, but when.

Dan landed his plane, opened the canopy, and taxied the plane down the dirt runway. The blazing Filipino sun scorched his gray flight suit. No wind today. Not even an ocean breeze to cool him off. He lined up his Curtiss P-40 Warhawk with the others and waved to the maintenance workers busy with refueling.

As he strode across the length of the airfield toward the thatched mess hall, he scanned the skies for enemy planes. He let his mind wander to past flights over Pearl Harbor with Libby at the controls.

Dan pictured her face, heard her laughter, remembered the way she scrunched her nose when he told a bad joke and the way she bounded over the hot Hawaiian sand in large leaps all the way down to the waves.

He knew that her Sunday schedule meant a full day of student flights. With weekends off, soldier and sailor alike hoped that polishing flying skills would mean future advancement. She would have been up in the air as the first Japanese planes approached. What had she seen from her vantage point? The first bombs dropping in the harbor? A swarm of enemy fliers surrounding her small plane? The Piper Cub posed no threat; surely the Japs would've realized she wasn't part of the Army Air Corps. But would they have cared?

Dan strode by the B-17s, also known as "Flying Fortresses," lined up in a long row on the side of the runway. A flurry of activity surrounded them; twenty-pound, fifty-pound, and hundred-pound bombs were being loaded into their bays, like huge silver bullets being shoved into a gun cartridge.

Dan approached one of the planes. "Heading out?"

"Yup. They gave us the thumbs-up. We're heading to Formosa to send our yellow friends a message." Sweat mixed with dirt and grease glistened on the worker's biceps as he continued to load.

Dan patted the hard surface of a fifty-pounder as it was set gingerly in its cradle. "Do your job, big guy. Show those Japs who they're dealing with."

A red-haired bomber pilot approached, checking out the crew's work. He slapped his sweaty hands together, then rested them on his hips. "Just a quick lunch, and we're outta here."

"Same for us." Dan patted his stomach. "Quick is the word. Drives me crazy being grounded too long."

"Yeah, the Japs snuck in on Hawaii, but there's no way we're going to let that happen here." The bomber pilot walked with Dan toward the mess hall in the distance. "We'll show them, all right. I—" His words caught in his throat.

Dan glanced over and noticed the pilot's forehead tensed into hard creases.

"Sorry. My best friend is stationed there. On the *Arizona.*"

The sinking feeling in Dan's stomach grew larger. "No need to explain."

He heard the same talk, the same declarations of revenge, spoken all around the lunchroom.

"My girl was stationed as a nurse at Hickam. I swear, if any Japs' hands touch her . . ." The soldier's fist struck the table, causing the water to slosh in their tin cups.

Dan patted his shirt pocket where he carried Libby's photo. Still, he refused to voice his concerns. Somehow mentioning her name and stating his worry would make it all the more real.

Suddenly, vibrating over the noise of voices and forks scraping against dishes, they heard the drone of planes overhead. Dan cocked his ear toward the doorway.

A young soldier sitting at his table shoved another spoonful of corned beef hash into his mouth. "Sounds like our guys are back up keeping watch."

"Can't be. Our guys are right here!" Dan's stomach lurched as he jumped from his seat and sprinted to the door. Before he even made it to the threshold, he heard the whistling of bombs falling from the sky. The explosions, sounding like thousands of firecrackers going off at the same time, were punctuated by the tremor of the floor beneath his feet.

"Japs! Attack!" a voice behind him called.

"Well, it's here," a soldier to his left said almost casually as he strode up to the doorway. "This is what we came for, I guess."

"Okay, let's get it over with, and then maybe we can go home," another soldier answered, strapping his helmet to his head and running out the door toward a line of waiting tanks. Within seconds everyone on hand had moved into action.

The planes! We've got to get to the planes. Dan felt helpless on the ground, especially remembering that their aircraft sat side by side on the runway. Perfect targets.

As he sprinted toward the airfield, he cocked his

head to watch the V formation of Japanese planes, black against the sky. They were flying in from over the mountains, up from the China Sea. The bombs dropped with huge explosions, moving ever closer down the line.

Dan's eyes darted to the pursuits as he pushed through a group of soldiers. His feet pounded on the asphalt as he moved to the P-40 nearest the chow hall. But he couldn't move fast enough. The silver bombers dropped their loads on the silent aircraft, picking them off one by one the way Dan and his friend used to hit tin cans lined along their backyard fence.

Dan was within thirty feet of the closest P-40 when a silver streak slid through the air and landed directly in the center of the plane. The explosion knocked him to his face, and cries of injured men rose above the ringing in his ears. He tasted blood in his mouth and felt the sting from biting his tongue. He spit out bits of rock and held his scraped cheek. Heat slapped his face, and he shielded his eyes from the wall of fire that had consumed the plane.

Got to find another. Got to get up in the air. The ground continued to rock under him, shaking as if it had a life of its own.

A voice rose over the din. "Machine guns open fire!" The chattering began as golden strands of tracer fire shot up to greet the visitors.

As far as he could tell, the only retaliation against the Japs came from those .30- and .50-caliber machine guns mounted on tanks and half-tracks placed there to protect the field. The sounds of their *rat-a-tat-tat* now joined in the commotion. But they did little good as the bombs continued to whistle, whanging their way to earth.

Soldiers poured out from the tents surrounding the field, hurrying to their tanks and machine-gun nests. Others ran from the field in terrified screams. Already, wounded men littered the field, their pained cries for the most part ignored.

Regaining his resolve, Dan jumped to his feet and moved to where more planes waited in the distance. He'd almost made it to the next waiting plane when the last of the bombers dropped their payload. As the drone of the bombers eased, the cries of the injured grew more prevalent. Dan heard one man's voice as he ran. "Captain, Captain, Captain!" At first he thought the man was calling for help, then noticed it was a private, a deep wound to his shoulder, lying over the chest of another man, Capt. Richard Tyler. His dead eyes stared into the busy sky.

"My captain," the private cried again.

Dan wanted to stop, to urge the private to leave the field, but he didn't have time. He had to get to a plane.

Just as it seemed they'd receive a bit of respite, dozens of small, one-man Japanese Zeros swarmed in from all directions, raking the confusion on the ground. They dived shallow, at forty-five-degree angles, spitting bullets all the way. As the planes swooped, the red orbs seemed to glow from under their wings. Then the Zeros peeled off one by one, diving at separate targets. One hummed down toward the battery. Another turned off and flew toward the fuel dumps.

One swooped so low that Dan felt the wind current from the plane's wings, and he cursed at the wide smile of the goggled pilot.

"Over here!" Dan heard the familiar voice and turned to see Gabe Lincoln waving toward two P-40s still untouched.

Dan ran toward the waiting plane. Gabe reached the other and scurried into the cockpit. Dan climbed in the second, hoping that it had been refueled.

Then again, one direct hit . . .

He couldn't worry about that now. Instead, he climbed into the cockpit, lowered the hatch, and with the flips of knobs and dials, the engine roared to life.

Now to find a way out of here.

Another bright light flashed out of the corner of his eye. There was no time to think. His airplane taxied forward—as if by instinct—dodging bits of plane parts, human corpses, and bomb craters that littered the airstrip. An intense heat and a second explosion told Dan two more planes had been hit—he could only hope one wasn't Gabe's.

Within a minute Dan's plane lifted, joining the Japs in the air. He'd never felt so alone.

"Just find one and pick it off. That's all you can do," he told himself. Dan banked the aircraft in a wide turn toward the enemy planes. Then he saw it, a lone Zero trailing the others. Getting it in his sights, Dan worked as one with the military machine. He imagined the look of surprise on the Jap pilot's face as the P-40 sneaked up behind him.

When the Zero was in range, Dan's thumbs hit the trigger buttons for the wing-mounted machine guns. "Say bye-bye." He held his breath.

"Bull's-eye!" he shouted seconds later as the bullets hit their mark. Like a wounded bird, the Zero shuddered and then plummeted to the ground. Everything in Dan wanted to keep his eyes fixed on the target, to witness the kill, but he knew dozens more fighters swarmed the skies. He directed his gaze toward his next victim.

❧ ❧ ❧

Darkness had fallen, and Libby stood in the bell tower of the small schoolhouse, watching thick black smoke roll across the harbor.

Rumors spread that the Japanese would be coming back to invade Honolulu. Antiaircraft guns were aimed at an enemy that was surely out there somewhere.

Yet the darkness was far from silent.

Shells from the burning ships continued to explode, sending flashes across the dark sky. And when Libby looked across the harbor, she could clearly make out the American flag still waving from the sunken U.S.S. *California*—the pole mostly submerged, the flag tattered.

"The rockets' red glare, the bombs bursting in air," she said under her breath with a trembling voice.

After the first wave of bombing, just when they

thought the worst was over, a second wave of Jap fighters swooped in to finish them off. When all finally died down, word had reached the John Rodgers airfield that help was needed with the wounded. As fast as they could, Libby and Billy Jackson made their way to the nearest hospital. The blood, the broken bodies, the cries for Mom . . .

Hours later, the commotion still hadn't died down. All available nurses had found their way to the hospital, and Libby had joined other volunteers at a local school that was quickly organized into a temporary emergency room. Classrooms still decorated with children's paintings and clay models had rapidly filled with injured men, most of whom had been brought in by rescue crafts from the harbor. The injured sailors were covered with oil from the sinking ships, if they were lucky. Those not so lucky were covered with burns.

The school cafeteria had been transformed into an operating room, and the kitchen into a center for sterilizing instruments. There was a shortage of bandages and medicine. Too many needs and not enough help. It took everything within Libby not to turn and run from the scene, but then she thought of Dan. If he were injured, she hoped there'd be someone there to help him.

She'd washed bloodied bandages in the large enamel kitchen sink, looking out the window at long lines of soldiers who still waited for care. She'd scrubbed oil from the skin of many soldiers. Many just lay there, as if in a daze. She'd swabbed wounds and wiped tears from trembling chins, caring for each man as if he were Dan.

Now Libby turned her back to the glow of the harbor once more and took in a deep breath. With slow steps she moved down the winding staircase of the bell tower, knowing more young soldiers were in need of care.

❧ ❧ ❧

Dan had managed to cause damage to quite a few Japanese Zeros, and counted two sure kills, before the Japanese planes returned over the mountains to the sea, where their carriers waited. He returned to Clark Field, and his initial relief that the Japanese were gone was replaced by horror at the destruction left in their wake.

The ground beneath his feet was tinted red with the blood of the dead and dying. He wiped his hand along the stubble on his chin and looked around. Hangars still burned, and ammunition sporadically ignited, causing the eyes of weary men to grow wild once more. As he strode by one hangar, a chunk of metal slid from the roof; he jumped to the side, barely skirting it.

Scattered trucks, jeeps, and planes were burning. The jeep he'd ridden in just the day before was wrecked and still smoldering. The wounded had been taken away, but the dead still lay where they fell. Dan attempted to step over the bodies without looking into their faces, but it was impossible. They were young men. Strong men like him, who just this morning had no idea that today would be their last. As he walked past, Dan shooed away the blue flies that covered the bodies like death shrouds.

He paused before a whole B-17 crew lying dead next to their burning ship. They'd been preparing to leave for Formosa and had been hit by a bomb before they could reach cover. But that wasn't the only B-17 hit. The largest four-engine bombing force in the world—boasting twenty-two planes—was demolished.

"We only got four ships off the ground." Gabe strode up to Dan. His sleeves were rolled up to his elbows, showing off his brown, muscular arms. Blood streaked those arms; as soon as Gabe had landed his plane, he'd been out there in the wreckage searching for survivors. They hadn't pulled one man out alive.

Dan tried to remember what Clark Field had looked like the previous day. A runway that stretched like a neat line down the center of the jungle with planes lined up. Buildings filled with happy-go-lucky soldiers, chatting about their dates with local girls or army nurses, or showing off the souvenirs they were packing up to send home.

"I heard Don Bell report that they struck Iba Field too. All but two of the 3rd Squadron's P-40s were destroyed." Gabe ran a hand down his face. "The planes were riddled before the engines could get started, just like here." Gabe pointed to a smoldering plane closest to the tent city. "Hansen was burned alive. Can you believe it? Hansen was always the cocky one."

Dan continued on with quivering legs toward the charred buildings. His mind raced, searching for the right thing to say, but no words seemed adequate. They walked past a large black crater where a gasoline shed had sat. Dan was sure he smelled the scent of burned human flesh.

"A gang of maintenance workers ran inside when the bombing started." Gabe glanced Dan's direction. "The whole place was blown up about a minute after they got inside."

Dan swore under his breath. "The Japs didn't miss. Every bomb hit its target—a gasoline storage tank or an airplane. How could this happen? I mean, we'd been up in the air just minutes prior. We could have got them good if we'd refueled earlier, or—"

"Dan, no." Gabe placed a charcoal-smudged hand on Dan's shoulder, halting his steps. "There's no way we could have known."

Dan nodded and wiped his face. "That's just about the worst luck I've ever heard. Just thirty minutes sooner or later, and the outcome of this battle would've changed."

As Dan leaned over to pick up a bloody pilot's cap lying on the tarmac, he felt the crumple of paper in his pocket and pulled out a crushed envelope, remembering how he'd stashed it there the previous night with the intention of finishing his letter to Libby this morning. He unfolded the sheet of paper and reread the news he planned to share—news that was surely null and void.

Dear Libby,

All is well in Paradise. And good news—I'm higher than a Georgia pine knowing that in less than a month's time, I'll be heading back to Hawaii to train more pilots. That's right, I'm heading back!

More P-40s arrived safely, and the military is bulking up against the threat of war that supposedly could be around the corner, but the bigwig says planes aren't any good without pilots. They need someone back at Hickam to train the new crop. That someone will be me, and I'm hoping that a lady I know can give me pointers on how to train them good.

Dan had ended the letter there, and reading his words now caused a wave of foolishness to flood over him. What had he been thinking? All the signs pointing to war had been glaring at them like neon billboards. Although they talked as though war could happen, none of them really understood what it would be like when it did. No one figured that the greatest nation on earth would be caught with its pants down . . . twice, unable to defend itself against a weaker Japanese army.

Dan looked at the paper again. Then he crumpled it in his hand and threw it into a smoldering pile of debris. Personal mail would be the least of the army's concerns. Sending out death notices would be top priority now.

Dan watched as a corner of the letter caught fire; then he hurried to catch up with Gabe.

"So one day of war, and just like that we lost half our airpower." Gabe slowed his pace.

"Half? You do try to look at the positive side of things, don't you? I'd say *most.*"

Gabe rubbed his temples. "Come on. Let's pack up

our things. I've got word from headquarters. We're being bivouacked away from the base about a half mile out."

"In the boonies?"

"Heck, as long as there's a field kitchen with hot food and a place to sleep, I don't care where they put us." Gabe ran a filthy hand through his equally dirty hair. "Don't worry; we'll get the rest of our things later. We just need to survive a night or two."

Survive. Dan let his friend's choice of words replay in his mind. How quickly things had changed.

Eleven

JAPAN SEEN TRYING FOR AIR "KNOCKOUT"

Washington, Dec. 8 (U.P.)—Japan was trying to deliver a knockout blow against American airpower in the Pacific to stall the bombing of Tokyo and other major centers, authority military quarters said tonight.

The Japanese hoped to sever air communications between Hawaii and the Philippines, and then to concentrate on the destruction of the Philippines' military establishments either by aerial bombardment or direct invasion, the informant said.

Excerpt from the *New York Times,* December 9, 1941

The sound of the "Battleship March" reverberated in Natsuo's ears.

"News special. News special." The announcer's voice quivered with excitement. "Beginning this morning at dawn, war has been declared against the Americans and British!"

Cheers arose from the small classroom where Natsuo sat.

"We did it!"

"Wonderful!"

"Banzai!"

Natsuo joined in the chants, lifting his arms into the air with each cry. It seemed they'd been doing a great deal of celebrating lately.

Yesterday Prime Minister Hideki Tojo had reminded them that in the 2,600 years since their nation was founded, the empire had never known a defeat.

"I am resolved to dedicate myself, body and soul," Tojo had said over the radio. "And I believe every one of you, my fellow countrymen, will not care for your life but gladly share in the honor to make of yourself His Majesty's humble shield."

Like pieces in a chess game, their forces were succeeding in positioning themselves for the checkmate to come. Soon the entire Pacific Theatre would be in their control. Natsuo's training was coming to the end, and he wondered what part he'd play. Would he be sent to invade Hawaii? the Philippines? or one of the lesser islands? Energy surged through his veins as he witnessed the celebrations around him.

"America is evil! Britain is wrong! For the sake of His Imperial Highness!" Natsuo called out. "May I forever be His Majesty's humble shield!"

Libby kept the radio on throughout her waking hours. For two days after the attack, the airwaves remained silent. Every once in a while an excited announcer would break through with news updates, including reports that barges crammed with thousands of Japanese troops had landed on the north side of the island—reports that later proved false.

The newspapers also continued to churn out print, especially putting blame on the numerous Japanese—one-third of the population—who lived on the island. Just this morning, the headline read "Caps on Japanese Tomato Plants Point to Air Base."

As far as Libby was concerned, the whole island had gone mad. Surely the Orientals all weren't spies. And if some were, did the newspapers really think tomato plants could be reliable secret signals?

On Monday, December 8, Congress had declared war on Japan. During his speech President Roosevelt had informed the world that Oahu wasn't the only island attacked. Malaya, Hong Kong, Guam, Wake Island, Midway Island . . . the Philippine Islands. *Were the Philippine Islands as bad off as Hawaii? Were they worse?*

Libby paced the room. She knew that Dan would be right in the thick of battle. Fear scratched at her chest. *As long as Dan was in the sky he'd be okay,* she told herself.

But with Oahu in chaos, she couldn't just sit home

and worry. She tucked her gas mask inside her purse and ventured into Honolulu in search of fabric for blackout curtains. The streets were nearly empty. Memorials to both military and civilian personnel hung in store windows. Some buildings lay crumbled, heavily damaged by the navy's antiaircraft fire.

She stepped over crumbled bricks and hurried from store to store, with no luck. The same disbelieving gazes from storeowners stared back at her, and she ached for their warm Hawaiian smiles. She ached for the hustle and bustle, the friendly soldiers, the carefree days.

Gas stations were also shut down, and most people took to foot or bicycle. Thankfully, the Toonerville Trolley continued to run. Libby climbed back on with empty arms, then rode the trolley to the one place she knew she could serve.

Libby had already spent two nights at the school, and it looked as if another one stretched ahead. Sirens sounded at dusk, and all citizens were ordered to stay put until the *all clear* came the next morning.

With weary steps, she fetched bandages and sterilized supplies. She rewrapped bandages and comforted injured soldiers until the clock ticked past midnight. Unable to stand up for one more minute, she collapsed onto a now-vacant cot, ignoring the scent of petrol that clung to the sheets, trying not to think of the soldier who no longer needed a bed.

"Lady, you're not hurt, are you? Do you think you can help me?"

Libby sat up on the cot. It seemed as if she'd just lain down, but now the sun was bright in the sky. She rubbed her eyes and turned toward the young navy officer, who held a stack of postcards in his hand.

"Of course. What do you need?"

"The navy needs the survivors to write home. Their folks need to know they're doing okay."

Libby jutted her chin into the air. "Do you really think any of these men are 'doing okay'?"

He lowered his head, fumbling with the postcards in his hands. "Well, at least their folks need to know they're still breathing. With so many dead—"

"But the postcards will take months to get there. What about cables?"

"About 350,000 are trying to get out. The wires are jammed."

Libby softened. "Of course I'll help. I'll fill them out for those who can't. But first, can you tell me . . . how are we doing in the harbor?"

The sailor lowered his voice and leaned in close. "Three battleships were sunk. The *Oklahoma* was capsized. A dozen others are heavily damaged."

Libby shuddered and wondered to herself if those on the air bases had fared any better. "And the deaths? Do we know how many men?"

"We have no clear number, but we're guessing over two thousand, maybe as many as three thousand." The sailor handed over the stack. "Just make sure not to describe the attack."

"Of course." Libby grabbed up a pen and turned

her attention to the nearest sailor. His body was bandaged from head to toe.

"It's not as though we can change anything," she added to herself as the sailor strode away. "Don't they realize? Not knowing is the hardest part."

Later that day, Libby found herself at Hickam Field. It was even worse than she'd imagined. The roofs of the military barracks had crumbled into the structures, leaving only outer walls. Burned-out hulks of bombed aircraft littered parking aprons and hangars.

Libby didn't even want to think what John Rodgers looked like. She remembered her last view of it. As they drove away, her mind had fixed on the fragments that had formerly been her Piper Cub. She hadn't been back. She couldn't face the others, knowing she was responsible for George's death.

Not that she was needed there. Nonmilitary air traffic had been shut down completely.

Libby stood at the metal gate of Hickam Field and looked in. Civilians armed with '03 Enfield rifles—officially titled the Hawaiian Air Depot Volunteer Corps—patrolled the airfield. They didn't wear military uniforms or carry military identification, but Libby knew they took their job seriously.

Sending up a prayer for favor, Libby zipped her flight suit to her chin and tucked her hair into her pilot's helmet. She slid on a pair of sunglasses, then moved through the gate. The guard put up a hand and motioned for her to stop. She handed him her pilot's clearance pass, hoping he didn't recognize the difference between the military and civilian forms. The guard returned it and nodded her through. She hurried across the airfield as fast as her legs would take her. She moved from hangar to hangar, scanning the faces of the pilots and flight crews, throwing a salute to any patrol volunteer she came across.

Then she spotted him. Dan's friend Zeke Olson was sprawled on the ground looking at the underside of a P-38.

"Zeke!" Libby called out and instantly realized her mistake.

A patrol volunteer hurried over and grasped her by the arms. He was a native Hawaiian—at least a foot taller and double her weight.

"Hey, now, what do you think you're doing?" He pulled her back toward the gate.

Libby tugged against his grasp and cocked her head in an effort to see around him. "Zeke, it's me! Libby Conners, Dan's girlfriend . . . uh, fiancée!" Her voice echoed in the cavernous interior, and the warm air smelled strongly of gasoline fumes and oil from the disemboweled planes parked inside.

Zeke rose from the ground, hurrying over. "It's okay—she's with me."

Reluctantly the large man released his grip and glanced to Zeke. "Don't know what this is about." He crossed meaty arms over his chest. "But this is no place for a lady. Especially one who tries to sneak around. You sure she's okay?"

"Yeah, she's harmless." Zeke smirked. "Complicated but harmless."

Libby slid off her sunglasses and smiled at the patrol volunteer.

When he had stalked out of earshot, Zeke turned his attention to Libby. "I'm glad to see you're okay. I heard John Rodgers was badly hit. But what are you doing here?"

"Did you also hear that George Abel was killed?" Libby tried to keep her voice from trembling.

"No, sorry to hear it. A lot of good men were lost. Some of my buddies . . ."

"I'm so sorry." Libby glanced to the patrol guard, then back to Zeke. "Speaking of buddies, have you heard from any of the guys in the Philippines?"

Her eyes attempted to scan his face, but Zeke lowered his gaze and shook his head. "Sorry, doll. There's been no word. Things are so crazy here that communication has been nonexistent. I've been wondering too."

"But they were part of your unit. Surely you've heard something. Anything." Libby took Zeke's hand between both of hers, squeezing. She forced firmness into her tone. "Zeke, look me in the eye and tell me you've heard *nothing*."

Zeke lifted his gaze. His brown eyes were filled with sorrow. "Fact is, Captain heard that nearly the whole fleet was wiped out. I don't think they have ten flyable planes left, and we're still not sure about the pilots. It seems the Japs were as successful in that campaign as they were here."

Libby felt her legs weaken. She reached for the wall behind her and slid down it onto the concrete floor.

Zeke squatted down before her. "I'm sorry. Maybe I shouldn't have told you. I mean, we really don't know. Dan could be just fine."

Libby offered Zeke a weak smile. "No, I needed to hear it. Needed to know . . . I can handle it, I mean, until we know for sure." Libby's voice wavered, and suddenly she was tired of being strong. She wrapped her arms around her legs and pulled them to her chest, letting her forehead fall to her knees.

Zeke placed his hands on her trembling shoulders.

I shouldn't be doing this to him, Libby thought. *Zeke has enough to worry about.* But no matter how she attempted to pull herself together, Libby couldn't get up from that hangar floor.

"I'm so sorry," she finally commented. "I didn't plan on this, I—"

"Nah, don't worry, doll. If the places were reversed, I know Dan would try to be there for my wife."

Zeke settled on the floor next to her and wrapped a strong arm around her shoulder. "Go ahead and cry it out. You're not the only one on this island letting the tears flow. I'd be more concerned if you didn't cry for the man you love."

❧ ❧ ❧

Since each house and business on the island was required to be blacked out at night, Libby spent the remainder of the afternoon again moving from store to store, to no avail. There was no fabric to be had. Unable to turn on her lights, she now sat in her apartment in the dark, feeling sorry for herself. She thought about the possibility of Dan's death and the fact that she was stranded on the island, unable to fly. What did she have left? She couldn't even get a message to her father to let him know she was okay. Her stomach churned, considering his worry.

The open window let in a warm evening breeze. She sat there listening to the defense workers as they walked up and down the streets ensuring compliance. Mr. Atkins had been one of the first to apply for the job, and more than once Libby had heard his booming voice yelling at one of their neighbors to put out a cigarette—as if the small, red glow would draw in the next Japanese bombing raid. He even convinced her neighbors to stop drinking milk because it was home delivered—often by people of Japanese extraction. She guessed they believed his rumors that poison was injected through the cardboard caps.

As Libby watched out the window, she spotted a car moving slowly down the road, its headlights covered with blue cellophane. It parked in front of her building, and in the moonlight Libby made out the form of a woman hurrying toward her apartment.

"Rose." She moved to the door. Libby had no idea how her friend had made it out past curfew, but she was thankful she had. She opened the door, but before she could get a word out, Rose fell into Libby's embrace.

"Oh, Libby." Rose wept. "Jack is gone."

The news hit Libby like a brick to the stomach. All the time she'd been volunteering at the school, she'd been searching the sailors' faces, looking for Rose's Jack. She'd assumed that not seeing him was a good thing.

"Rose, no. What happened? I mean, do you know for certain? There are people showing up all the time, injured but—"

Rose pulled back and moved to Libby's sofa, sinking into the cushions. Even in the moonlight, Libby could see her friend's puffy eyes. Her dark hair fell in tangled clumps around her face as if it had been days since she'd brushed it.

"I know it for sure." Rose ran a trembling hand down her face. "They told me. They saw him go down with the ship. But if it weren't for Jack . . ."

Libby sat on the couch beside her. "Start from the beginning. Who are 'they'? His crewmates?"

Rose nodded. "I spent the last two days searching the hospitals. Finally, at one of them, a sailor stopped me. One of Jack's friends. He was so badly burned that I hardly recognized him. He said . . ." A solitary cry burst forth, and Rose shook her head, unable to continue.

Libby didn't press, and after a few minutes Rose sucked in a deep breath, wiping away her tears. "He was on the *Oklahoma,* you know. He worked on the engines way down in the hull. There was a group of guys stuck in a compartment. A small porthole was the only way out. They say that Jack got the porthole opened and began pushing them through. He wasn't even going to try it himself, but the guys convinced him. Those on the outside tried to pull him through. He was about halfway when he got stuck. My big guy. He was so broad. They tried to pull him, but it was no use. When others came up behind them, Jack asked to be pushed back through. Then he helped push the rest out. And with each guy he pushed through he said the same thing: 'Tell Rose that I love her. Don't forget to tell her.' "

"Oh, Rose." Libby wrapped her arms around her friend.

"This stupid war." Rose stood and paced to the window. "I'm just so mad. Why my Jack?"

Libby had no response, but in her mind she asked the same questions. *Why Dan? Of all people . . . why did he have to go?*

Twelve

LARGE U.S. LOSSES CLAIMED BY JAPAN

Tokyo, Tuesday, Dec. 9 (From Official Broadcasts, Distributed by the Associated Press)—Japanese Imperial Headquarters announced last night the sinking of two United States battleships and a minesweeper, severe damage to four other American capital ships and four cruisers, and the destruction of about 100 American planes in Japan's surprise blows at Hawaii, the Philippines, and Guam.

Japanese Army headquarters announced that fifty or sixty American planes were shot down in air combats over Clark Field in the Philippines and forty more over Iba, eighty miles northeast of Manila, Domei said. The Japanese acknowledge the loss of only two planes in Philippine actions.

Emperor Hirohito in an imperial rescript broadcast

by Domei called on "the hallowed spirits of our imperial ancestors" and "the loyalty and courage of our subjects" to achieve victory, and repeated Japan's argument that the United States and Britain prolonged the war in China by aiding Chungking, leaving Japan "no other recourse but to appeal to arms."

Excerpt from the *New York Times,* December 9, 1941

Dan sat in the cockpit of his P-40 waiting for his turn for takeoff. Oliver "Tex" Watkins's P-40 taxied down the runway ahead of him. The airstrip, still littered with debris, was a mess. With only a narrow strip cleared, Dan hoped they'd have enough room to make it out safely, especially since trying to see the runway beyond the nose of the P-40 was nearly impossible.

A sinking feeling came over him as he watched Oliver's plane. "You're too close," he said to himself.

He grabbed his radio and called into it, "Pull left! You're too close to the edge!" But before he could finish his warning, the right wing of Oliver's plane snagged one of the smoldering B-17s and spun into the wreckage. Dan gritted his teeth and winced, looking aside as his friend's P-40 burst into flames.

No one could have survived that ball of fire.

But Dan could do nothing. He remained in his stifling cockpit and fought back tears of rage and sadness.

Within ten minutes, ground crews had pushed the burning wreckage of Tex's plane to the side and signaled Dan clear for takeoff. He had no choice but to follow through with his mission. Japanese ground troops were landing on the island. He had to find out what they were up to—while avoiding getting shot down.

Dan lined up his P-40 on the runway. He wiped the sweat from his eyes—telling himself it was the heat that was getting to him. He pushed his throttle forward to the wall, standing on his brakes until his Allison's power built to its maximum. His chest quivered, but his gloved hands held his control stick steady. Taking a deep breath, he released his brakes, and the pursuit picked up speed. He pushed thoughts of Tex out of his mind as he hurled past the burning wreckage. It wasn't until the wheels lifted that Dan realized he was still holding his breath. He let out a slow, trembling whistle and steered north.

He yawned and attempted to focus on the 550-mile round trip despite his weariness. For the last few nights, he and the others had tried to sleep in the jungle—literally using the waxy, elephant-ear-sized leaves of the Gobi plants as blankets. Thankfully, during the night most of the birds—noisy parrots and hornbills—stopped their jabbering.

Since showers hadn't been reinstalled, he'd attempted to bathe in a muddy river. It had done little good. The cockpit reeked of his own body odor, and he was thankful his plane wasn't a two-seater. Not that he wouldn't have appreciated support.

News of recent assaults around the island had reached them even as they tried to rest. Some reported that Jap strikes had demolished Nicholas Field near

Manila. Others said that the enemy had invaded three separate points of the island. Dan believed these reports, since things hadn't let up at Clark. The runways, fuel dumps, even storage buildings continued to be bombed every day at noon.

When he wasn't out on a mission, Dan and the other men hid in the jungles as Japanese planes arrived on schedule, circling like giant hawks in search of prey. The Japs wanted to wipe out the U.S. air support. And they'd come close. While ground forces of both Filipinos and Americans seemed to be fairly well equipped in their stations around the island, by last report only twenty-three P-40s and eight P-35s remained on all the airfields. Then Dan remembered the fiery blast of Oliver's plane. His hands gripped even tighter on the control stick, and he blinked back tears. *Make that twenty-two P-40s.*

Yesterday he had bumped into a B-17 crew who, along with another, had decimated four Japanese tanker ships off-loading at Gonzaga. Dan and a few other P-40s had been busy themselves, providing fighter escort for bombers attacking the Japanese landings at Vigan. As gratifying as it was to watch two Japanese transports go up in flames and a minesweeper disappear into the sea, he knew these air attacks couldn't significantly delay the Japanese assault. Sometimes as many as 150 Zeros accompanied the Japanese bombers on their daily visits to Clark Field.

"As futile as trying to knock out a swarm of yellow jackets with a BB gun," Gabe had said last night.

All they could do was hide their remaining planes and take them out only for vital missions.

Dan scanned the clouds that now hid the island of Luzon below him. He was to provide reconnaissance for landings at Aparri—225 miles to the north of Clark Field. The overcast sky forced him to rely on his compass to make it there.

Finally, as his plane neared the location, he descended through the clouds.

"Here goes nothing," he said aloud, wishing Oliver were around to back him up.

As he broke through, Dan sucked in a breath. Below him were two enemy destroyers escorting the invasion fleet.

"Golly gee. Look what we got here!" He let out a shout as antiaircraft guns opened fire on him. Dan quickly made a sharp turn out of their range. "You think you can shoot *me*?" His heartbeat pounded in his temples. "Just try, you crazy Japs!"

As if moving on their own, Dan's hands pushed the plane into a deep dive, and he headed back toward the destroyers. Closing in, he laid hold of the triggers and strafed one of the ships. Then he pulled skyward, satisfied he'd done at least minor damage.

Dan broke up through the clouds again only to discover five Zeros on his tail. *How'd they get up here so fast?*

He didn't have time to wonder. Rolling the plane over, he dove back toward the sea, hoping to lose them in the clouds. The quick maneuver worked, and when

Dan punched back through, he noted only two remaining. Yet these two were gaining on him, one on each wing.

Dan chopped his power and pulled back on his stick, nearly stalling his plane. The Zeros roared past, and with a single move he shoved his throttle, pushed the nose back down, and kicked his rudder hard right and then left, as he fired the machine guns. Within seconds both Zeros burst into flames, and he took a second to catch his breath.

Moving to finish his recon mission, he flew toward the island and dove back through the cloud cover. Below him, he discovered that the Japanese *had* infiltrated the island. They'd even set up a new dirt runway where twelve Zeros sat parked in a straight line. And although Dan's presence was already known, the targets seemed too good to resist.

"I'll take this as a parting gift." Dan bulleted his plane toward the ground, raking the enemy planes with gunfire. Before flying completely out of view, he noted that three Zeros had already burst into flames. A smile curved on his sweat-drenched face, and he turned south toward Clark Field. *This* was what he was here for.

❧ ❧ ❧

Noontime sun beat through Libby's bedroom window as she rummaged through her bureau drawer, pulling out the letters from Dan, the seashells they'd collected on their trips to Ewa Beach, and a photo of the two of them lounging on the lawn in front of her apartment. She laid each of those things aside on the threadbare brown carpet, then dug back into the drawer, finally finding the folded slip of paper she'd stashed there. Folded within the paper were the news articles Dan had given her.

She plopped onto her unmade bed and looked at them again. Although mere months had passed, it seemed like another lifetime since her dinner with Dan, Jack, and Rose. A light smile touched her face. *That band.* She rested her chin on her hand. *Those silly paper lanterns. Jack's guava-mango drink with the paper umbrella . . . poor Jack.* He and Rose were just getting to know each other then. As for Dan . . . his strong arm had encircled her shoulder, and Libby had known she was falling in love.

Months ago, when Dan gave her the news clippings, the idea of women pilots working in conjunction with the military seemed far-fetched. But overnight things had changed.

Libby unfolded the slip of paper and read the name *Jackie Cochran.* Under the name, Jackie's address had been written in Dan's neat script.

Except for Amelia Earhart, the missing aviatrix, Jackie Cochran was the most famous woman pilot in the world. In 1937, she earned the award for the best female flier of the year. Then three years ago, in 1938, Jackie was the first woman to win the Bendix Trophy Race. And earlier this year, she'd been the first woman to fly a bomber "across the pond" as a delivery for the British military.

Jackie was giving her all for the cause she believed in. Surely there was something Libby could do too.

Earlier that morning, Libby had gone with Rose to the ceremonies commemorating the dead from the battleship *Oklahoma*. As clouds rolled into the cool, clear morning sky, hundreds had gathered at the military cemetery. Rows of plain wooden boxes, draped in flags, had been lined up in a shallow mass grave.

Libby's heart had ached as she watched the grieving families around her. A young girl, not more than four years old, had worn a crisp, white dress and clung to her mother's hand. No tears had fallen down her soft cheeks, but her eyes were the saddest Libby had ever seen. "Bye-bye, Daddy," she had said. "Bye-bye."

And one of the boxes held the remains of Jack—Rose's Jack. His body had been found among the wreckage of the ship. Now he'd never leave the island, forever buried in the Hawaiian soil he loved. Sobs had racked Rose's body as the bugler played taps, followed by a twenty-one-gun salute. Libby had held her close.

Seeing and feeling her friend's pain, and knowing the desperate frustration she felt herself, Libby decided she must do something—anything—to help with the war effort.

She wondered how long a letter would take to reach Mrs. Cochran. Rumor had it she'd ventured back over the Atlantic with a group of American women ready to join a British women's pilot group. Still, it was worth a try.

Libby moved to her small desk and pulled out a piece of paper and pen.

Dear Mrs. Cochran, I am a female pilot. . . .

Dan had received a hero's welcome upon his return, but now, days later, it seemed that shooting up five Zeros had done little more than give him a minor sense of satisfaction. During today's run, more pilots had managed to make it up into the air, but only a few returned. Most had been shot out of the sky. They'd all managed to bail out, and Dan hoped that, with the help of locals, they'd find their way back to the base.

Weary from their futile efforts, Dan and the remaining pilots returned to the jungle to hide out for yet another night. He bunked down with the others in a small clearing. Exhaustion caused his body to sink to the ground.

The flame of a cigarette lighter trembled in the hand of the man next to him, and from his vantage point Dan could see much larger fires continuing to burn at Clark. "Hafta admit, those fires are kinda purdy," the soldier said, as if reading Dan's thoughts.

"Yeah." Dan rubbed his tired eyes. "Too bad, though."

In the moonlight, Dan glanced at the wording of a telegram his CO had promised to send out the next day.

DEAR FOLKS DON'T DESPAIR STOP ALIVE

AND UNINJURED STOP NOTIFY LIBBY STOP LET HER KNOW I WILL COME BACK STOP WITH LOVE DAN STOP

He slid it back into his shirt pocket. *I wonder if these words will still be true by the time the message makes it there. How long can one remain "alive and uninjured" under these circumstances?* He quickly banished the idea from his mind. He had to make it back. Had to get home to Libby.

Tomorrow they'd be packing up and heading to the coast of Luzon in a final effort to keep the Japs from completely taking over the island. In preparation, earlier that day, he'd returned to the nearly leveled tent city to scrounge for whatever remained of his personal items. Finding his small trunk, Dan had taken out his most cherished possessions and spread them across his disheveled bunk. Photos of Libby, family pictures, a few seashells, his binoculars, camera, civilian clothing—not all of it would be able to go. He selected one photo of a smiling Libby and tucked it into a canvas bag with an extra set of clothes.

Now Dan used the bag as a pillow. He snuggled closer to the ground and pushed his hair off his damp forehead, wishing it was as easy to push away the urge to run back and find the rest of the photos of him and Libby together. To look at them one last time before descending deep into the jungle.

Other pilots also sprawled on the ground, attempting to catch a few winks—all except one young soldier who'd been hanging around with their unit after he was unable to find his own group. At first the kid had tried to play tough, but Dan soon learned he was only sixteen. He had lied to get into the army with hopes of seeing the world. Now the only thing he whimpered for in his dreams was to make it home to his mother.

The boy sat erect in the center of the clearing. His heavy helmet, shaped like a metal bowl, rested on his head. It flopped loosely as the boy turned his head from side to side, scanning the trees that surrounded their group.

"Hey, kid, why don't ya settle down and get some shut-eye?" one pilot said.

The pimply teen shook his head. "I'll just wait up. Watch for a while."

"Kid, just because the Japs have invaded the island doesn't mean they're anywhere near us," Dan offered.

His stomach rumbled. It had been days since he'd eaten anything besides a chunk of half-rotten beef and a cup of coffee. "You haven't eaten, haven't slept," he said to the boy. "You're going to wear yourself out."

The kid didn't budge.

"Whatever, kid. You keep watch, and let us know if you see anything." Dan curled onto his side, too tired to worry. Too tired to care.

Thirteen

HONG KONG STILL HOLDING OUT:
STAND IS PRAISED BY JAPANESE

London, Dec. 20—British Imperial Forces in hard-pressed Hong Kong were still holding out today against the Japanese invaders, according to reports received in London up to a late hour tonight. These reports, although meager, were greeted with some surprise because they came on the heels of undenied Japanese claims yesterday that the main island had been captured.

Domei said British troops had retreated to points around Victoria Peak and Victoria Park and to the Stanley Peninsula in the south. This agency admitted that the "expected imminent fall of the colony has been staved off by the stubborn defense," adding that British

Imperial Troops had "fought desperately in a manner even to win the respect of the tough Japanese."

James MacDonald
Excerpt from the *New York Times,* December 21, 1941

The crowds outside the train windows continued their heated chants. Old men, women, and even small children lifted their hands in unison. "*Banzai! Banzai!* Congratulations!"

Through the train windows Natsuo waved, then eyed the banners they lifted high.

Congratulations on Being Called to Fight! one read.

Prayers for Your Eternal Success at Arms, said another.

The frenzy outside the window was a ritual Natsuo had experienced many times growing up during the Manchuria and China affairs. As soldiers left for war, it was a tradition for citizens from nearby villages to gather with triumphant cheers. Natsuo knew more celebrations would be taking place back home. This very evening, Mother would serve sea bream and prepared red rice, demonstrating—on the surface at least—what an auspicious occasion it was to have a son in service of the emperor. Natsuo gazed down at the "thousand-stitch belt" she'd sent him. Like all traditional Japanese, Mother thought that if he wore the *sen'ninbari,* bullets would not hit him.

Father had also displayed his pride. In the tallest cedar near their home, Natsuo knew a sun disk had been hung for him. As it swung with the evening breeze, it showed proof of a son's dedicated service.

Please do not worry after you leave, Natsuo's father had written. *If you fall in action, we will enshrine you in Yasukuni.*

Natsuo had visited the greatest shrine in Tokyo only once, and within its gates, morning and night, citizens worshiped the spirits of those who'd fallen in defense of the emperor. Yet that offered little consolation for Natsuo.

Although he'd received adequate training—learned *Yamato damashii,* the spirit of Japan—he felt more like an actor on a stage, merely playing the part of the Japanese fighting man, full of courage and dedication. And perhaps his performance hadn't been as convincing as he'd believed.

The last soldier took his seat, and Natsuo felt the train lurch. There was no turning back. The voices of the crowd faded, and the sounds of the engine grew. They'd travel by train and then by ship to a new land that would soon be theirs.

Around him, the voices of the soldiers rose, singing "What It Means to Be an Infantryman."

Ten thousand clusters of cherry flowers
Blossom on your collars—
Storm winds blow the blossoms in Yoshino,
And you, who have been born sons of Yamato,
Will scatter like blossoms in skirmish formation.

Natsuo sang along, remembering that only one week ago, on December 8, the Japanese Air Force had attacked Kai Tak airfield—the Royal Air Force Base on the British Crown Colony of Hong Kong. As with Pearl Harbor, the Philippines, and Midway, their attack had been a success.

Yet even as his countrymen rejoiced over their numerous victories, Natsuo's thoughts were on Hong Kong alone. As of yesterday, bombings of the island had begun in preparation for an amphibious assault.

Their trainer had gathered them around before they loaded the ship. "You have chosen to fight for the emperor with loyalty and sincerity. You left your homes as boys, but now arrive at this place as soldiers in the army of Jimmu, our first emperor. And today, even the humblest soldier among you is prepared to smite and destroy the enemy in this time of great need. It is a holy war. Look around at the faces of the brave soldiers who fight with you, and together make a solemn pledge that you will not return if not victorious."

"We will not return"—their voices had shaken the air—"if not victorious!"

Natsuo's voice rang out with the rest, but what the other soldiers didn't know was that he wouldn't be joining in fighting for this great and eternal cause. As of last night, he'd been given a new assignment—as an interpreter for the English-speaking prisoners of war. His path to sacrifice had been stripped from him. Unlike the others, the will of the gods did not include his cheerfully venturing into the jaws of death.

This journey to Hong Kong marked his last days with the men who had trained with him. As Natsuo looked around, a thought pushed to the forefront of his mind. *What will these men think when I do not fight with them? What will my parents think?*

After all, everyone knew it was a good thing to fight, die, and be enshrined in Yasukuni—forever worshiped as a god.

❧ ❧ ❧

Dan circled the P-40 over Lingayen Gulf, scrutinizing the landing party below. For weeks his CO had believed the other, smaller invasions had been mere distractions. Now Dan knew it was true. From the looks of it, tens of thousands of troops poured into the gulf only a hundred miles north of Manila. Twenty thousand. Thirty thousand. Perhaps even more than forty thousand Japanese soldiers bent on taking over the island.

Yesterday, Dan strafed enemy soldiers who had landed on San Miguel Bay, but it had done little good. They were doing their best to hold back invaders, but he knew they'd get nowhere without the supplies and troops sure to arrive any day. *Our boys from the States should have been here by now.*

His eyes scanned the distant sea beyond the nearly one hundred Japanese ships, searching for any sign of American defenders. He'd heard rumors that American battleships bore down on the islands, prepared to fight for those stranded. Dan just hoped they would hurry. Morale was falling faster than a monsoon rain. Hunger and weariness had put them all on edge. And, he quickly discovered, untrained comrades were to be feared as much as the enemy. Friendly fire had taken more than one of his buddies.

All I want for Christmas is to see American battleships filling the harbor, Dan thought, remembering the holiday was only days away. Since he couldn't have Libby in his arms, it was the next best thing.

❧ ❧ ❧

Natsuo stepped out of the jeep and adjusted the bayonet in his hand. His unit had missed out on the battles of the last few weeks. Not that they were needed. The imperial army had found success. As of this afternoon, the British army had surrendered Hong Kong, and most of the island was under imperial control.

Natsuo's eyes had taken in scenes of destruction when they first landed, and he knew the fighting hadn't been pretty. The crumbling buildings, cratered streets, and dead bodies were his first view of war. It was hard for him to believe that only weeks ago the streets had surged with crowds of men and women going to work, taking leisurely rides in rickshaws, or being driven around in fast limousines.

Now the job given to Natsuo and others was to intern the prisoners. There would be no more teatime or afternoons at the racetrack for these British chaps, nor for the Dutch, Australians, or Canadians who also called the island home.

Natsuo hurried his steps and scanned the countryside surrounding the village of Stanley. Picturesque cottages dotted the island's hillsides. An odd mix of European settlers and Chinese scurried up the dirt road, seeking refuge from the advancing imperial army. But it was too late. There would be no more running.

A bad taste rose in Natsuo's mouth as he spied the British flag waving in the distance. The West had dominated the East long enough. Within minutes, the flag of his fatherland would wave proudly in its stead.

Ten days of fighting. That was all it took to twist the reins of control away from British hands. Natsuo stiffened his shoulders and walked toward the British soldiers' quarters. His jaw tensed when he considered the British surrender. Only those without honor would give up so easily. Anyone in the imperial army knew it was better to die fighting than to surrender in shame. The fools. Weak and timid fools.

Natsuo paused as a woman's cries carried over the rumble of approaching jeeps. With a quick turn of his head, he noticed two children hovering outside the nearest cottage door. The screams echoed from inside.

He moved in the direction of the children. The young boy and girl cowered by the door but did not run. With a quick kick, Natsuo struck the door with his booted foot. It swung open, falling halfway off the hinges. He moved inside.

Two young imperial army soldiers stood over a woman cowering in the corner. She was English and beautiful. The men screamed at her in Japanese, asking where she kept her valuables. It was obvious that she couldn't understand a word they were saying. One soldier slapped the woman, whipping the blows back and forth across her face with all the strength he possessed while yelling in Japanese. Sudden anger radiated through Natsuo's frame. Their mission was to intern the people, not to plunder them.

With his right hand, Natsuo grabbed the collar of the soldier. He twisted the fabric in his fist, cinching the man's neck. The man gasped and clawed at Natsuo's hand. Natsuo pushed him outside and released his grip. The second soldier scurried out too.

"Stay here!" Natsuo called back to the woman. Somehow the children had made it through the door past him. They now hovered at the woman's side.

Natsuo slammed the broken door behind him and approached the men. Although he was no higher rank than these others, they waited. Fear filled their gazes as they glanced at his interpreter's uniform. The man on the left quivered like a girl. *Weakling*. Natsuo inched closer until his face bore down on them both.

"Never," he hissed in Japanese, "dishonor a woman like that. Now go!" Both men scurried away, joining the groups of soldiers who hurried up the road.

Honor. Did these soldiers not understand?

He marched back into the room. The children had vanished. The woman now stood, eyes wide, and wiped the blood that flowed from her split lip. Then she attempted to straighten her dress that had been torn at the collar. At the sight of her creamy white shoulder,

Natsuo's thoughts took him back to American girls who'd walked the campus in their short-sleeved spring dresses. He quickly glanced away.

"Those soldiers will never touch you again."

The strength in the woman's voice surprised him. "You—you speak English? American English?"

Natsuo nodded but refused to meet her gaze. "I studied in United States." He would say no more. "You stay here. I will guard your door until it is time to leave."

He moved toward the door but not before catching a glimpse of disbelief in the British woman's gaze.

Natsuo squared his shoulders, tightened his hand around the bayonet, and willed himself to wash all thoughts of those beautiful American students, of this equally beautiful British woman, out of his mind. He had a duty to fulfill. For his country and his people.

PART TWO

"I remember my affliction and my wandering, the bitterness and the gall.

I well remember them, and my soul is downcast within me.

Yet this I call to mind and therefore I have hope."

Lamentations 3:19–21 NIV

Fourteen

MACARTHUR IN THE FIELD

Manila, Thursday, Dec. 25 (AP)—United States Army forces with Gen. Douglas MacArthur personally in the field staved off Japanese advances toward Manila from both the north and south this Christmas Day, but the invaders continued to land in such numbers that it was obvious the battle for the Philippine capital was under way. Consistent Japanese aerial activity in the provinces obviously was designed to disrupt communications and prevent American and Filipino reinforcements from reaching the battle zones.

Excerpt from the *New York Times,* December 25, 1941

After a week without a bath, a grin filled Dan's face when he discovered a small creek running along the outskirts of their new jungle camp. The sun had just begun to set, yet the air was warm, and the water even warmer. If not for the constant booming of the enemy's big guns, the scene would have been tranquil. Dan slid out of his clothes and pounded them on a nearby boulder just as he'd seen local women do. Yet his eyes remained alert on the jungle around him. Despite the warm water, a shiver ran up his spine.

The dirty clothes clouded the murky water even more, and when they finally looked clean, he scrubbed his body with his hands, dipping his hair into the cool water and running his callused fingers through it as best he could.

"What I'd give for soap and a soft, fluffy towel," he commented to one of the soldiers who'd joined him.

"Ask them. Maybe they got some." The soldier nodded toward a clump of trees.

Dan spotted the eyes first, then the smiles hiding behind dark-skinned hands. The native women's shoulders shook in laughter as they watched the white-skinned men.

"What are they doing here? Don't they realize how close we are to the front lines?" Dan climbed from the creek and slid into his wet clothes, attempting to ignore his audience. With his pocketknife, he poked a new hole in his belt and cinched it even tighter.

"They're escaping the cities and villages that the Nips have taken over. I guess many of their husbands were rounded up and tortured for helping the Americans."

"They look as bad off as we are." Dan placed a

hand over his stomach, but he had no hope of the pain easing any time soon.

"I hear our guys are having a Christmas service over in that clearing." The young soldier pointed. "There's no Christmas dinner, no presents, but at least I feel better to have cleaned up for the celebration."

Dan nodded a good-bye to the soldier and headed back. The dirt around the camp was compacted and hard, with spiderweb cracks running through it. He found what appeared to be the softest spot under a large tree and sat down to watch a large crowd of soldiers circled around the army chaplain. The padre's white tropical robe appeared like a spot of purity amongst the bedraggled soldiers.

The men's voices lifted in harmony. "O Little Town of Bethlehem," "Joy to the World," and "Silent Night" rang out, filtering through the jungle trees in sweet melody. But this night, like the others before it, was anything but silent. The distant boom of artillery sounded, even over the unified voices.

The last song faded, and the chaplain raised his hands high to get the soldiers' attention. For such a small man, his large voice carried over the entire camp.

"If any of you have not looked past the babe in the manger to accept Jesus as the Savior of the world, tonight is the night," his voice rang out. "While it is true a physical enemy desires to destroy us, let us not forget the Enemy of our souls. If you would like someone to pray with you, come forward. Jesus is knocking at the door of your hearts. Won't you let Him in?"

I've heard that a hundred times. Can you come up with something new? Dan watched as a large number of soldiers moved toward the priest. Others kneeled where they were. Groups of twos and threes bowed their heads in prayer. Dan both longed to join them and despised himself for feeling so needy.

He thought back to Gabe's prayers in that Manila cathedral just a few months ago, and he wondered if the ornate building still stood. In the past week, Japanese bombers had circled Manila nearly every hour, bombing at leisure. Then, just this morning, it had been declared an open city. The Americans had barely exited the city limits when the Japanese swarmed in like fire ants over a dead carcass.

Instead of the Stars and Stripes, a white flag with a red orb waved on the high pole in the city center. Dan recalled his last view of Manila from the air. The tangled steel of gutted buildings jutted upward. Hastily thrown-up boards covered glassless windows, and the once-busy streets seemed like those of a ghost town—the residents hiding away in their homes, fearful of what would happen without the Americans to protect them.

News had arrived from MacArthur that as of tomorrow, only the peninsula of Bataan and the island of Corregidor—which lay just across the north channel of Manila Bay, a few miles south of Bataan—would be defended. Thousands of Americans and Filipinos were ordered to retreat to these areas. Yet managing to follow these orders proved to be the tough part. Bataan was mountainous and heavily forested. Only a few clearings and trails wound through the thick jungle. And a single road ran along the east side of the peninsula. Rivers and streams were plentiful, but bridges were not. Each soldier had to get to safety on his own.

Thankfully, Dan had arrived in a P-40, landing on one of the makeshift airstrips prepared for the pilots. Others had journeyed here on inter-island steamers. And some hadn't made it at all—killed during bombing raids, or shot down from the strafing of Japanese planes. Their corpses had been left behind to rot in the jungles with no one to cry over them, let alone take time to bury them.

Dan glanced once more toward the soldiers in the clearing. Thin, filthy, some injured, and all so far from home. *Is this the way God answers prayers?*

Bataan had been divided up into sectors, with Filipino soldiers holding the front lines. Dan wondered how long they'd hold out.

With only seven planes remaining, there was little need for airmen. The air corps, including Dan's outfit, had been reassigned as infantry. Most of the fighter pilots had been given old rifles from the last war and told to defend the front lines. Dan was one of the lucky ones and was put in charge of the few remaining planes. He'd do whatever it took to keep them flying. The alternative—being grounded and unable to rise above the ground warfare, with thousands of Japs streaming onto the island—scared him to death.

Dan watched as more men staggered into camp, joining the large Christmas gathering. A group of twenty

Filipino soldiers emerged from a narrow jungle path. They were covered in sticky sludge—most likely from an attempt to cross a muddy river. With weary faces, they knelt before the priest and made the sign of the cross almost in unison.

Dan leaned back against a fallen log and laced his fingers behind his head. Climbing red bougainvillea ran through the trees like fire. It was the closest thing to a Christmas tree. *What's Libby doing this Christmas? Spending it with Rose and Jack? How does she celebrate the holidays? What are her traditions?*

He imagined what his mother would be cooking up in her small kitchen. Most likely a goose purchased from old Farmer Landing down the street. Mashed potatoes. Pumpkin pie. His stomach growled again as he realized he hadn't eaten anything since earlier that morning. He didn't expect much for dinner either.

But even greater than his desire for a Christmas meal was his wish for a Christmas miracle—to keep the planes flying. Seven planes were all that remained. Seven that must hold out until help arrived.

❧ ❧ ❧

Natsuo remained outside the English woman's home as long as he was able, but soon he was called to the auxiliary hospital at Stanley for his assistance as a translator. When he arrived, he was surprised to find bitter fighting still going on.

St. Stephen's College Emergency Relief Hospital had

somehow ended up on the front lines at Stanley. On the way there, Natsuo was updated on the progress of overcoming the defensive lines. The first line conquered was just north of the college. The second ran through it, to just south of the hospital.

When he arrived he noted a football field at the base of the high hill. A thousand memories flooded Natsuo's mind as he noted the goalposts and wooden stands—he pushed them all away. At the top of the hill stood St. Stephen's College. Nearby was a small cemetery where pine trees stood an eternal guard.

Natuso's eyes widened at the sight of the bodies of Japanese soldiers littering the hillside seemingly by the thousands. It was as if wave after wave had stormed the college, soldiers using their dead comrades' backs as stepping-stones. He wondered if any of his friends lay among them.

Even now there was a large crew quickly removing the dead soldiers in order to have them cremated. Then, in little white boxes, their remains would be shipped back to the shrines in Japan.

An officer approached with quickened steps. "Our troops have ruptured the first line. Now we need the hospital cleared out. You must go inside and tell all those who can walk to move to the top level of the building."

"And those who can't walk?" Natsuo adjusted the collar of his uniform, peering at the officer.

The officer looked at Natsuo, and his lips curled into a smile. "Do not worry. They will be taken care of."

They arrived at the building, and although the hospital had a red cross painted on its roof, a bloody battle raged outside its doors.

Natsuo watched as the Japanese commander ordered a group of soldiers to storm the building. They rushed headlong, with fixed bayonets, breaking through the door. The officer then motioned Natsuo to join them.

Natsuo marched up the steps, and just as he reached the landing a British medical officer was thrown past him—out the front door onto the lawn. The Englishman's eyes were wild with fear, and before he had time to lift himself from the ground, half a dozen soldiers plunged bayonets into his stomach, as they'd been trained. Other medical personnel inside were dealt the same fate, and their bodies now littered the narrow hallway.

"Upstairs. Everybody who is able. Upstairs now!" Natsuo called in English, stepping over their bodies and moving from room to room. Many struggled from the beds, but a few remained too weak to move. Natsuo paused before one young soldier. His red face burned with fever. His hair was blond and fell across his forehead in sweaty clumps.

At first Natsuo thought he knew the young man. Yet, it was impossible. Natsuo's friend had been American, not British. Still, the resemblance was remarkable.

"Somebody. Help this boy upstairs." Natsuo motioned to two British soldiers. "Do not leave him! Take him with you." They complied, struggling to carry the young man between them.

"The island of Hong Kong is now controlled by imperial command!" Natsuo shouted as he strode up the stairs behind the staggering prisoners. Nurses and doctors had also joined the sick in the small rooms. The collection of humanity smelled of disinfectant and filth.

The commander arrived, and Natsuo's eyes darted from person to person, refusing to look into a frightened face for too long.

"You are now considered prisoners of the emperor! Your needs as prisoners will be taken care of shortly. You will remain here until instructed otherwise!" Natsuo turned with movements precise enough for a drill instructor and followed the commander out of the building.

Outside, to the south, the battle-weary warriors conquered the third line of defense. Now the whole area would be under complete imperial control. Hong Kong was theirs.

Hours later, over two thousand men, women, and children were herded into a small group of buildings on the hospital campus. They'd come from the village of Stanley, the hospital, and the housing around the college. Japanese soldiers barked orders. Lowly gendarmes joined in, pricking the prisoners with their bayonets.

As Natsuo continued to shout commands to the new arrivals, his CO approached with quickened steps. "Tell the nurses they will be shown preferential treatment. Three to a room. My men will be in to check on them later."

"Yes, sir!"

Natsuo accepted the instructions without a blink of an eye, but inwardly he remembered the English woman assaulted in her cottage earlier that morning. Would these nurses be treated the same? Was that their "preferential treatment"?

He pushed those thoughts from his mind, then marched to the nurses. After relating the news, he watched as soldiers herded them into one wing of the hospital. Soon female screams filled the air. Outside, the cries of children being hustled into nearby buildings joined the chaos.

Hearing their cries made Natsuo think of his sister's young son and daughter. He'd gotten to know them well while living in California. Thankfully, they were safe. No armies threatened their coast. Most likely they were spending the day preparing for their Christmas celebration. Although his sister continued in the Shinto religion, she'd raised her children as Americanized as possible, celebrating the Christian holiday with fervor.

As he strode back to the commander, eager for his next orders, Natsuo passed a young boy, obviously lost. Tears streamed down the child's face, and he cried out for his father. Natsuo took two steps toward him, then paused, biting his lip. He watched helplessly as the boy caught his foot on a tree root, tripped, and fell. The boy's chin knocked against the ground, splitting it open. With an angry shout, a Japanese guard lifted the boy by his hair and pushed him forward with a booted kick.

Natsuo looked away. He clenched his fists and continued forward. This was not what he had imagined war would be like.

❧ ❧ ❧

Dan realized he'd dozed off when a man's voice spoke through his foggy dreams. "What about you? Do you need prayers tonight, son?"

He opened his eyes and was surprised to see the white-robed padre sitting by his side.

Dan rubbed the sleep from his face and scooted into a sitting position. "Don't know if they'd do much good."

The chaplain didn't speak but instead peered into Dan's eyes as if he could read a story inside them. It was no use trying to hide the truth from this man. Dan shrugged and spoke the words he'd bottled up for so long.

"I trusted the army. I obeyed each order given. I flew every plane they deemed safe and left those I love for this cause. So where are they?" Dan jutted his chin in the direction of the harbor. "We heard that more forces were due to arrive. More food and medicine. That was weeks ago." He slumped back against the tree. "Nah, I don't need prayers. Don't think about God much."

"So because men you respected and trusted have let you down, you have no need for God?" The priest's words were sterner than Dan expected. He even noted a flash of challenge in the man's gaze.

"Obviously, if God is who He claims, then we wouldn't be in this situation."

"And how much do you know about God, son?"

"Well, my girlfriend, Libby, and I have discussed that before. She was raised going to church, and she prays sometimes. She has a friend, George, who works at the airfield. He talks to her about God. Hey, I was raised in church too, but it doesn't seem very relevant today. Do you think 'loving your enemies' applies to our situation? Should we throw a welcoming party for the Japs? That religion was for another time, another place."

The priest lifted a single eyebrow. "Amazing. For someone who doesn't think about God, you seem to have it all figured out."

Dan couldn't help but soften to this man. "So what's your answer? If I don't have it right, what am I missing?"

The priest glanced in the direction of the men still circled up. Many still kneeled with heads bowed. Others had united their voices, singing another hymn.

"Sometimes it's in the darkest places that Christ's love can truly shine. And during circumstances like these, even the most rock-solid hearts soften to Jesus." He gave a sad smile. "I can preach a hundred sermons, but nothing gets a guy thinking about God faster than having an artillery shell land a few feet in front of him."

Dan crossed his arms over his chest. "So you're saying God put us here so more guys would seek Him? He put us in this horrible spot so we'd pray more? That doesn't sound like a very loving God to me."

The priest rose and laid a gentle hand on Dan's shoulder. "No, son. Men put us here. But God will never shy away from a good opportunity."

Fifteen

SOUTH PACIFIC WAR DEPENDS ON FLIERS

London, Jan. 2 (AP)—A British spokesman declared today that British and American fleets cannot be expected to operate effectively in the South Pacific until they can obtain adequate air support.

"Without an umbrella of protecting planes from carriers or land bases," the spokesman said, "warships would be at the mercy of Japanese aircraft from dozens of bases in the Philippines, Indo-China, and Malaya."

Excerpt from the *New York Times,* January 3, 1942

Dan strode along the airstrip they called Little Pilar, the morning sunlight already warm on the top of his head. Along the strip rice-straw had been arranged in windrows to hide its true purpose. The planes themselves were hidden in wooded areas to the north and south. He rubbed his sleepy eyes and headed back to his palm-log and sandbag dugout. Last night it had been his turn watering the strip to keep the dust down. At least it was something to do. Even worse were those nights when he lay awake with the endless ants and lizards crawling over him, sure that every sound was that of Jap soldiers closing in.

Suddenly, the air around him began to vibrate as the ominous sound of dive-bombers carried over the hill from the west. He sprinted to the dugout less than a hundred feet away, his feet getting sucked down by the recently watered-down dirt.

Three Jap dive-bombers crested the hill, and Dan prayed they didn't see him. He passed the camouflaged kitchen hut as he ran, noting that the foxhole nearby was already packed full of men.

The whistle of bombs made him run faster. He heard them falling, and the ground under his feet quaked like the footsteps of a giant gaining on him. For each bomb that hit, his body bounced, lifting him from the ground.

Then the pounding moved in front of him. One explosion, then two. Dan shielded his eyes and gasped. He staggered forward to his dugout, pressing his hands to his ears, sure he'd lost his hearing.

He'd barely reached the hole when a large banyan tree snapped, slamming into the ground where he'd stood just seconds before. Dan hunkered down next to Gabe. Somehow it made him feel better to be with someone on God's good side.

After a few minutes the pounding stopped. Dan placed a hand to his chest, attempting to calm his thumping heart. Then he laughed, sucking in a breath and leaning back against the dugout wall.

"That is about the most nervous laugh I have ever heard." Gabe couldn't hide the quaver in his voice. "Looks like they found us. Thankfully, we're heading out." Then it was Gabe's turn to laugh. "I came here to find you, to tell you the news—but it looks as if you found me."

"New assignment?" Dan shook his head, causing clumps of dirt to tumble onto the floor of the dugout. "The day's hardly begun, and for some reason I'm ready for it to be over."

"They need us to head to northern Bataan to check out the movement of Jap troops."

"Is recon all we're good for?" Dan stood and brushed off his fatigues. "Isn't there anything we can blow up?"

Gabe shook his head. "Too dangerous. They need our planes to last awhile."

Dan closed his eyes, his body suddenly weary at the thought of taking his plane up. Weary from being on constant alert. Tired of not being able to walk a few steps without fear of being blown into pieces.

"Just think, I used to be friends with a Jap." Dan ran a hand down his face, scratching his scraggly beard grown from necessity.

"Oh, yeah?" Gabe climbed out, then offered Dan a hand and pulled him up. "I didn't know that. When you were a kid?"

"Nah. Just a few years ago, at college. He was in a few of my classes, and we teamed up together to do a poetry presentation." Dan smiled. "He was okay. Loved the U.S. and playing football with us. Wonder where he is today."

Dan stepped over the fallen tree. The fury of the bombing was evident everywhere he looked. Trees had been stripped from the bomb blasts. A shell crater steamed not fifty yards from their dugout. In the distance, wrecked equipment was strewn over the airfield. "Who knows? Maybe he's one of those jerks bombing us right now."

"If he is, I'd like to meet up with him—in the air. I'm with you—recon is for the birds. I need a little excitement to make me alive again." Gabe cocked his head and dug his hands deep in his trouser pockets. "Besides, when I get home I want to be able to tell my boys that their daddy was a hero. He didn't just sit around in some foxhole." Gabe grasped Dan's shoulder. "I'd rather die than not go home a hero, wouldn't you?"

❧ ❧ ❧

As he stared at the Murray Parade Grounds, Natsuo was glad they'd left the carnage of St. Stephen's College behind them. It was bad enough witnessing the wandering women and children, who seemed fearful of their new positions as prisoners. Soldiers rounded them up, taking them to former brothels and squalid tenements —their new homes. Some women were dressed in simple clothes, others in gowns and fur coats. The latter were the colonial elite—wives of businessmen, government officials, and military personnel. Overnight they'd become captives, caged like animals.

Japan had been at war with America and Britain less than a month, and it had been only weeks since the Japanese attack on Hong Kong. Now look at what had become of her residents.

Natsuo's gaze continued to search the parade grounds until he caught sight of the woman from the cottage. She looked taller than she had that day, stronger too, as she strode through the hysteria, attempting to bring order to the chaos.

"Line up. Older boys back there. Women and children to the front of the line," she called.

He wished he could approach her. Speak to her in her native tongue. He wondered if she would thank him for helping her that day. As he watched her every move, Natsuo noted that her blonde hair, which had been coiled on her head the first time he saw her, now hung around her shoulders in dirty curls. Still, she looked beautiful.

"What are you doing here? They need you at headquarters!" The voice of the officer interrupted Natsuo's thoughts.

Natsuo turned and bowed low. "Yes, sir. Right away." He turned to hurry toward the headquarters.

"Natsuo!"

He paused and turned, gazing upon the officer's shiny shoes, not daring to look into his face.

"They are vermin. Remember that. Do not let an ounce of mercy into your heart."

"No, sir." Natsuo bowed low again. "Never, sir."

❧ ❧ ❧

Six P-40s took off from Little Pilar Field for observation. Dan led them, his head pounding from lack of food and sleep.

"Hey, Dan. You see that?" It was Gabe's voice coming through the radio. "To your left."

Dan glanced over and spotted the six-plane formation of enemy twin-engine bombers flying over Manila Bay. They were heading toward the peninsula. He let out a moan. "Haven't they done enough damage for one day?"

"What do you think? Should we swing around and take a bite out of them?"

"Hey, you were the one talking about the importance of keeping our planes safe for recon. Remember our orders?"

Gabe's voice crackled through the radio. "I was also the one talking about returning home a hero."

Suddenly Gabe's plane broke from formation, swinging around to the direction of the bombers.

"Gabe, what are you doing?"

"Going to shoot down your Jap friend. Whadja think?"

Dan cursed under his breath. Sure, he too had gone against orders more than once, strafing when he should just be observing, but this didn't seem like the right time to be goofing around. Hadn't they come close enough to death for one day?

As Dan craned his neck and locked his vision on the distant formation, common sense told him to leave Gabe to his own devices.

Yet if anything happened to his friend . . .

"Let him go, Dan. We've got a job to do." Mike Wright, one of the other pilots, spoke through the radio.

"Sorry, can't do that. You guys go ahead. I'm going to babysit Gabe." Dan swung his plane in a wide turn, just as Gabe neared the Japanese formation. Then, as if watching it in slow motion, fire burst from the Jap's tail gun, hitting its mark. Fire erupted on Gabe's right wing.

Dan held his breath. *Bail out! Bail out!*

The plane plummeted toward the ocean, and just when he thought there was no hope, he watched Gabe's body separate from the diving craft. In an instant, the parachute filled with air, like a large dandelion puff in the cloudless sky.

Dan moved his plane in the direction of the parachute and circled, keeping his eyes open for any sign of the bombers returning. It seemed as if hours, not minutes, passed as he watched Gabe float downward. And as he circled, every horror story of parachuting pilots being shot out of the sky filled his head.

"Curse you, Gabe. This was not your day to die." Dan circled one more time, finally seeing Gabe hit the water a few hundred yards off the coastal village of Orani. Thankfully, Orani was still in American hands.

Dan continued to watch as a small boat was launched and Gabe was pulled aboard. When he turned his plane toward the direction of the others, they were already returning.

"So nice of you to be around to lead us back," Mike's voice said through the radio static. "Where's Gabe's plane?"

"The plane is now in the bay. Gabe decided to take a little swim. Thankfully, he was fished out."

As they headed for Little Pilar, Dan spotted smoke and fire rising from the airfield.

"Abort landing. Abort landing. The field's under attack!" Dan shouted into his radio.

No wonder the bombers hadn't bothered finishing off the parachuting pilot. They had a more important mission. From a distance, Dan watched as the Japanese planes circled, bombing at leisure. He thought of all his buddies who remained on the ground. Remembered them huddled in the foxholes next to the open-air kitchen. The first bombing raid had been just an appetizer for what was to come. There was no way those men could survive this.

Dan's stomach knotted, knowing that if it weren't for this short assignment he would have been there with them.

"Abort landing. Head back to Orani! There's a small field there. Mike, you lead the landing."

"Will do. Follow me in, boys."

The radio was quiet for the remainder of the flight to Orani, and Dan knew each of them was considering how close they'd been to losing their planes . . . and their lives.

Orani. It looked as if he'd be meeting up with Gabe tonight after all.

Sixteen

OVER RADIO TO BATAAN TRAVELED A SONG OF "OLD DOUG MACARTHUR JUST FIGHTIN' ALONG"

Schenectady, N.Y., Feb. 21—A new General MacArthur song which will be a feature of the annual dinner March 7 of the Inner Circle, New York political writers' organization, was sent by shortwave this morning at 3:15 Pacific war time (6:15 Eastern war time) to General MacArthur's forces from KGEI, the General Electric radio station in San Francisco.

Fightin' out there in the Bataan jungle
Fightin' out there in the green hell's heart
Shootin' down Japs from the dawn till sunset.
Makin' 'em die if they don't retreat.
. . . With his men he sweat and strain
Bodies all weary and wracked with pain

Ships get sunk and planes get downed
But Sam he wouldn't give an inch of ground.

Excerpt from the *New York Times,* February 22, 1942

The envelope in Libby's hands trembled as she slid her finger under the flap to open it. The return address read *Mr. and Mrs. Alexander Lukens*—Dan's parents. Before he'd left, Dan had mentioned that if he couldn't contact her directly, news would arrive from his mother. Libby had chided him at the time. Of course he'd write. Unless . . .

She unfolded the letter and slumped onto the sofa.

Dear Libby,

I wish it were under better circumstances that I write this letter. Daniel wrote home about you often, and both his father and I were eager to meet you and welcome you into our family. That was before his assignment in the Philippines, of course.

I heard of the bombing of Pearl Harbor while in church. I immediately thanked God that my boy was no longer there, only to hear a few hours later that bases all around the Philippines had been bombed. The worst is not knowing.

Our thoughts also turned to you, and we wonder how you fared during the attack at Pearl Harbor. We both hope this letter finds you well.

My Alex contacted the War Department, but they have little information. Communication from the Philippines is sparse, and letters or postcards sent by soldiers haven't been able to get through. The War Department cannot tell us which soldiers are dead or injured. My husband is not a religious man, but I pray daily that Daniel is alive.

If you come to California, please look us up. We have a humble home and lead a simple life, but we would welcome you with open arms.

I hope this letter arrives in a timely fashion, although it seems all I have to offer is more uncertainty. I pray the good Lord will also give you peace that passes all understanding. Somehow my mother's-heart believes my son is still alive. I only hope it is so.

With much care,
Ima Jean Lukens

Libby read the letter a few more times. It was written by was someone who also loved Dan. Someone who prayed for him, and for Libby too.

Libby refolded the letter and stuffed it into the envelope, trying to imagine Ima Jean. Did she have blue eyes and blonde hair like Dan? Libby was certain Dan had her tender heart; she could sense it in the letter.

When Libby returned stateside, she would look this woman up. And perhaps find out just what a "mother's-heart" was all about.

Libby placed the letter in the drawer next to Dan's, and a peace settled over her. No news was better than bad news, after all.

She strode to her desk and sat with pen and paper in front of her.

February 23, 1942

Dear Mrs. Lukens,

Thank you for your letter. I'm hoping next time your note will have news that Dan is alive and well. I pray for this too.

If Dan told you of our love, I'm sure you might question how two people who knew each other for such a short time could have such a deep heart-connection. I can assure you that our love is true. I can also tell you that I will wait for him. No matter how many dark nights must pass between us, I will wait until your son returns to me.

"Libby. Libby Conners, come to the window!"

Libby sighed and placed her pen on the desk.

Mr. Atkins's voice called again, louder. What could be the matter now? Perhaps he'd heard rumor of another invasion.

Libby leaned out the window, peering to the sidewalk, where the thin, older man stood. "Yes, Mr. Atkins?"

"Turn your radio on! The president is discussing the situation in the Philippines. He said—"

Libby didn't wait to hear the rest. She hurried to the radio on her bedroom dresser and clicked it on. President Roosevelt's voice filled the room.

"Immediately after this war started, Japanese forces moved down on either side of the Philippines to numerous points south of them—thereby completely encircling the Philippines from north and south and east and west.

"It is that complete encirclement, with control of the air by Japanese land-based aircraft, that has prevented us from sending substantial reinforcements of men and material to the gallant defenders of the Philippines. For forty years it has always been our strategy—a strategy born of necessity—that in the event of a full-scale attack on the islands by Japan, we should fight a delaying action, attempting to retire slowly into Bataan Peninsula and Corregidor."

The president went on to speak about MacArthur's army of Filipinos and Americans, and their brave fight. Then Libby's ears perked again as he mentioned Pearl Harbor. She glanced to the harbor out her side window. After two months, Pearl was still a mess. Cranes and other machinery filled the shore, attempting to resurrect some of the damaged ships. Others would never be moved—a watery graveyard for those still entombed inside.

Libby hung on the president's every word.

"It has been said that Japanese gains in the Philippines were made possible only by the success of their surprise attack on Pearl Harbor. I tell you that this is not so," the voice through the radio continued. "Even if the attack had not been made, your map will show that it would have been a hopeless operation for us to send the fleet to the Philippines through thousands of miles of ocean, while all those island bases were under the sole control of the Japanese."

He continued on, speaking of the official losses at Pearl Harbor, of the weakening of Germany, Italy, and Japan, and the strengthening of the Allies through production of arms, ships, and planes. He also spoke of the work and sacrifice that would be required of their nation in the months to come.

Still Libby waited to hear the promise. For him to tell the country that although reinforcements to the Philippines would be a challenge, they'd do all they could to assist those fighting on Bataan and Corregidor. But the words never came.

Instead, he ended with these words: "Tyranny, like hell, is not easily conquered, yet we have this consolation with us, that the harder the sacrifice, the more glorious the triumph."

Libby couldn't hold back the tears as his voice faded.

Sacrifice? Lord, I can't do it. I'm not willing to let go.

The tune of "God Bless America" filled the room. Libby reached over and unplugged the radio. Then she curled on her bed, unable to stop the shaking that had overcome her.

"Don't abandon them, Mr. President, please." She wiped her moist cheeks with the back of her hand.

Please, Lord. Don't let them sacrifice Dan.

❧ ❧ ❧

Natsuo strode through the internment camp, noting that the haggardness of the women seemed to increase with each passing day. There was a distinct bite to the morning air, and he cinched the belt of his jacket tighter around his waist.

The English-speaking citizens captured on Hong Kong now resided in new billets, yet Natsuo wouldn't board a dog in such a place, much less children.

Outside the compound, the beauty of Hong Kong—Fragrant Harbor—took Natsuo's breath away. Ferries crisscrossed the clear, blue water. Chinese junks with frail-looking batwing sails also filled the space between the white, sandy beach and the small islands in the harbor. But beyond these things, it was the shattered buildings, the mounds of rubble, the equally broken people that drew Natsuo's eyes.

As he walked, he noted no cooking facilities, no furniture, no crockery, no cutlery. The toilet facilities were far from adequate, and there was no water except for what young Chinese boys brought in every day—barely enough to keep the prisoners alive. The list of insufficiencies continued to click through his head.

His feet stirred dust from the barren compound as he walked, and he inwardly questioned why he must do this—why he must serve here while battles raged on distant shores. Battles he could fight for his emperor.

His duties as a translator were called upon often. To translate for the camp commander, and to provide a line of communication between the captives and their captors. His most difficult duty, though, was keeping silent.

Even worse than what the English women didn't have was what others desired to take from them. Just this morning the male internees had complained about sharing rations.

"We'd have more food and water if it weren't for those bloody women and kids," one British soldier had complained. "If they'd left for Australia as they'd been ordered to, we'd not be in such a bind."

Then there was the drunkenness amongst guards, and their sexual hunger that longed to be satisfied. They prowled like predators, looking through windows of the women's billets. Or worse, taking for themselves what they wanted.

As he neared the center of the compound, a line of young women shuffled past, some with small children on their hips. They collected their meager bowls of soup from the kitchen.

"You! How dare you look me in the eye!" a guard shouted in Japanese, stepping in the path of a young woman. Her proper English dress was smudged and dirty, and although it appeared she had tried to fix her long hair, it straggled around her shoulders. She couldn't understand his words, yet Natsuo saw a tremble travel through her body. Her child struggled and cried in her mother's arms.

The guard laughed, then kicked his booted foot against the woman's leg, tripping her. She fell forward, and in an attempt to protect both her meal and her child, her face hit the ground with a thud. Blood spurted from her nose and lip. The child screamed.

An older boy rushed forward and lifted the small girl from the ground. "It's okay, Penelope. Shhhh, don't cry."

"What are you looking at?" The laughing guard

strode up to Natsuo and stared down at him nose to nose. "Do you wish to help her up? To comfort her with English words?"

"Never," Natsuo answered nonchalantly. "Just watching the show. Now if you'll step aside, please, I have been called to the commander's office."

The guard did so, but not without casting a challenging glare.

Natsuo knew he'd have to try harder to hide his disapproval. Try harder not to let his mind find comfort at the sound of English voices spoken around him.

He glanced at the woman once more as he continued on. The boy had calmed the toddler, but another child with blonde curls, who couldn't have been older than three, stood next to the woman wailing, clutching an empty bowl to her chest, realizing there would be no dinner tonight.

Would those he loved soon be living like this? Just two days ago Natsuo had heard a troubling report. An imperial radio broadcast stated that all citizens of Japanese descent living on the west coast of California were being placed into internment camps—that meant his sister and her family.

Somehow, he'd find a way to hurt the Americans who'd dare do his sister harm.

❧ ❧ ❧

"Here they come!" The roar of planes drowned out Dan's voice. Three Jap bombers flew overhead in a triangular configuration. When they turned Dan's direction and started to glide, he knew what was coming.

He sprinted for shelter in the banyan trees and dove under the large, solid tree roots. As the whistle of bombs came, the four to five inches of protection the roots gave him seemed worthless.

After the whistle came the tremble of the ground. One after another—a continuous quake. Finally, minutes later, the explosions ceased and the sounds of the planes faded. Feeling a slight headache, but otherwise intact, Dan climbed from the hole, dusted himself off, and turned back to the work at hand. Bombings had become a way of life—a disruption to their newfound work of sabotage.

"Do you think our weapons will convince the Japs?" Dan returned to the stripped logs painted black.

"I think from the sky they would look like cannon barrels. At least they'll make nice targets for the circling bombers and keep them away from our planes," said José Martinez, a soldier of Mexican descent from Arizona, who was applying a final layer of paint that they'd scrounged from a nearby village.

It had been Gabe's idea to take logs from the abandoned timber mill and create mock cannons, just as it had been his plan to make antipersonnel mines using bamboo shells, dynamite, and nails. He'd even fashioned detonating devices that would activate when stepped upon.

"We did find some dynamite, didn't we?" Dan scanned the treetops, looking for the perfect spot to set up their artillery. "When the Jap bombers approach we'll set off a few sticks. That'll send up a loud bang and a cloud of dust and smoke. Dumb Japs, they'll fall for our ground artillery, for sure."

Now all they needed was to elevate the logs on hand-fashioned sawhorses and place them under the banyan trees with their dark ends sticking out.

"Hey, have you seen Gabe?" Dan wiped the sweat from his brow. "I haven't seen him since the last bombing."

"Oh, he's most likely listening to the radio broadcasts from Tokyo. I told him not to. It's anti-American propaganda, to be sure." José chuckled. "But hey. When the Japs announce to their country the number of artillery pieces blown up on Bataan, we can laugh to ourselves, can't we?"

Dan felt a sinking feeling. "Nah, I don't hear the radio. I'll be right back."

It took twenty minutes of searching before he finally stumbled across Gabe, leaning against a fallen tree sheared off from the latest bombing. Blood dripped from his forehead. Dan hurried toward him, but as he grew closer he realized it was only a small gash.

"Hey, I've been calling. Are you okay?"

"Just leave me alone." Gabe evaded his eyes and hunkered down with his arms wrapped over his head.

"What do you mean? We have work to do. The Japs'll be back soon, and we've gotta make a new plan. Should we try to rebuild that plane that crash-landed yesterday or just leave it?"

"Did you hear me?" Gabe swatted a hand in Dan's direction. "Figure it out yourself. I'm tired of fighting this thing. Tired of waiting. It's hopeless. There's a couple dozen guys that can help you. Just tell my sons . . . if you make it, tell them that being their dad was the greatest accomplishment of my life."

Dan squatted beside his friend. "Snap out of it, Gabe. We can't give up, as long as we have planes . . ."

Gabe let out a harsh laugh. "Are you kidding? What do we have left? A few P-40s with homemade mounts? There's hardly any ammo for them. Not to mention our dwindling gas reservoirs."

"What about the others we've picked up? There's the biplane, the Beechcraft, and a few of the guys salvaged a Navy Duck from the waters near the coast."

Even as Dan spoke the words, they sounded foolish to him. How were they to fight a war with that?

"Oh, yes, your Bamboo Fleet. I forgot." Gabe lifted his gaze. His voice softened. "Dan, please tell me that you are tired too, and I'm not just a wimp. I mean, we're spending as much time finding food as trying to trick the Japs, and for what? I'm sick of eating monkeys and lizards. I'm tired of the bombings and news that Japs are breaking through, pushing back our lines. Aren't you tired?"

Dan placed a hand on Gabe's shoulder, grabbing more bone than flesh. "Yeah, I'm tired, but we haven't lost yet. We can't give up. Just think of all the stories we'll have to share back home."

Dan lowered his voice and used his fist for a microphone. "This is Yan Jinsuo on Radio Tokyo, reporting live from Manila with a Monday Night Special. Live Bombing by Sake-Crazed Soldiers. Sure to bring chills and thrills." He leaned forward and placed one hand over his ear. "On the opposite side is MacArthur, who tries to fool us with stage props. Do not miss the thrilling event."

Gabe cracked the faintest smile. "Come along and bring a friend," he added. "Sponsored by the Morale Office. Admission is free."

"Oh, it's not free." Dan rose and dusted off his trousers. "It might just cost us our ground artillery . . . which still smells of fresh paint." He patted Gabe's shoulder. "I'm not ready to quit yet. Not as long as we still have planes and bullets. In fact, I have a plan."

⁂

Dan walked for over an hour down the jungle road before hitching a ride with a jeep to make it back to headquarters. It was a small hut, and the phones seemed to ring continuously as Dan approached. Inside, bits of paper and other garbage littered the ground.

The colonel stretched out his hand. "Good to see you, Lukens. Your men have been doing well on the front. But I have to admit it's a surprise to see you. What brings you here?"

Dan twisted his cap in hand. "As you know, sir, the Japs are landing in Subic Bay on the northwest coast. We have some 500-pound bombs left and some .50-caliber slugs. I know we can't do much, but we can show them a little opposition. My P-40s are in top shape. And there are a few other fighter pilots who can tangle with the Zeros while I hit my mark. We can do this. It will help, I think. Build up morale."

The colonel smiled and tipped his hat at Dan. "Go for it, son. What've we got to lose?"

Seventeen

GENERAL FLIES OUT

Washington, March 17—General Douglas MacArthur today became Supreme Commander of the United Nations forces in the Southwestern Pacific.

A few hours after announcement of the action, President Roosevelt told a press conference that he was "sure that every American" agreed with his decision to take General MacArthur out of the Philippines.

He recognized, he said, that Axis propaganda agents would see in this move abandonment of the Philippines, but this is not the case. General MacArthur will command everything, including sea and air forces, east of Singapore in the Southwestern Pacific, the President added, and will be more useful in Australia than on Bataan Peninsula.

Charles Hurd
Excerpt from the *New York Times,* March 18, 1942

The bombing raid at Subic Bay was a success. And although the commander couldn't offer Dan more fuel or planes, he did give him a field promotion, putting Dan in charge of even more men—just what he needed.

Dan sat observing a small Filipino soldier as he loaded bullets into his rifle. While MacArthur's army of Filipino soldiers seemed sufficient on paper, boasting over a hundred thousand men, Dan knew better. The Filipinos were as weak and ill prepared for fighting as this young man, and many couldn't even communicate with each other due to their dozens of different dialects.

More Filipinos joined Dan's unit by the day, retreating from the ever-nearing front lines. As they staggered into camp, they reminded Dan of pictures he'd seen of ragged soldiers from Valley Forge—only these soldiers wore blue fatigue uniforms and tennis shoes held together by scraps of fabric and string.

The soldier, who was at least a head shorter than Dan and even skinnier, finally lifted the Enfield rifle to his shoulder, aimed at a monkey in the tree, and pulled the trigger. The gun kicked back like a frightened mule, knocking the little guy onto his butt.

"Ayyee!" he yelped. "I do that every time."

"Need some help?" Dan rose from the ground, his body weakened from minimal rations and overexposure to the elements.

Most mornings he bathed in the murky creek waters, but it did little good. When the sun rose, his clothes became drenched with perspiration, and dust caked his face and hands. He felt more like an animal than a man, hiding in the covering of trees until the sun faded so he could scour the jungle for dinner.

The Filipinos were experts at foraging. Most of Dan's American soldiers would be dead if it weren't for the Filipinos pointing out edible plants and roots.

Dan stretched out a hand and helped the soldier off the ground.

"My name is Paulo." He made the sign of the cross. "Like the famous apostle."

"Well, Paulo, it seems that gun is giving you trouble." Dan strode to the hollowed log where he stored his supplies and pulled out a .25-caliber rifle that someone had recovered from the body of a Japanese infantryman.

Dan ran his hand over the Mauser bolt action, then handed it over. "Here. This might be easier. Lighter, anyway. No use holding on to a souvenir when it could be put to good use."

"Thank you very much." Paulo nodded his head vigorously.

Suddenly the sounds of Jap fire and shouts of advancing soldiers rose like a distant roar. *Getting closer.*

Their new assignment was to defend the sector between Manila Bay on the right and the foothills of the central mountains on the left. The sturdy mountain range in the center created a natural line of defense.

I'm up. Might as well get back to work.

With weary steps, Dan moved to the pile of old Enfields, grenades, and crates filled with air-cooled machine guns. The machine guns had been recently discovered in an abandoned transport truck and were designed for

Douglas Dauntless dive-bombers. They were currently being used for a more practical purpose.

He scanned the faces of his unit. Intermingled with the Filipinos were skilled men who'd previously worked with bombsights, radios, and delicate cockpit instruments. Now they attempted to hit ground targets with .30-caliber rifles that jammed more often than they fired.

Dan watched as Paulo aimed at the target and pulled the trigger. The Jap gun had much less of a kick, and Paulo gave Dan a thumbs-up.

More noise filtered through the jungle. This time it sounded like a single voice.

Paulo lifted the rifle to try again, but Dan shook his head and placed a finger over his lips. Paulo motioned for the others to also be quiet.

"Did you hear that?" Dan cupped his hand around his ear. "I'm certain it's a Jap voice."

Paulo nodded his head. "It is. I know some Japanese words. He's injured and has been sent into the woods. He cries out for his emperor to find favor with him."

"Injured? Why don't his comrades help him? Should we call a medic?" Gabe neared, his rifle in hand.

"No!" the shout from the Filipino surprised Dan. "Do you not know? We saw it many times on front lines. The Japanese kill their hurting. They make weak the group." Paulo pressed his rifle to his shoulder and hunkered down behind a log, as if he expected the enemy to burst through the woods any moment. "And those they do not kill, they give grenade."

“For them to commit suicide?” Dan also lowered himself behind the log.

“And to take out a few Americanos. The injured soldiers cry for help. When the Americans arrive, they blow them up.”

Despite the heat, Dan felt a shiver creep up the base of his neck. “Kill someone who’s trying to save your life?”

Paulo lowered his gaze and lifted the crucifix that hung around his neck, pressing it to his lips. “The priest, he helped me understand. They do it for love. For their country and emperor. They are his children.”

“Maybe love.” Dan’s thoughts moved to the Jap friend he knew once. “Or maybe fear of dishonor.” He slid his finger over the barrel of his rifle, and more Japanese voices joined the first. “Either way, it’s not right to hurt someone who wants to save you.”

Libby looked around the bare apartment. It was the last night she would sleep on the island. Mr. Atkins had used his connection with a distant cousin—a congressman in California—to secure her passage to San Francisco. But it had come too late. By the time she’d arrive home in mid-March, her chance to fly with Jackie Cochran would already be gone. Libby pulled the telegram from her pocket and reread it again.

MRS. JACQUELINE COCHRAN REQUESTS MISS LIBBY CONNERS LEAVE FOR ENGLAND

FIRST OF MARCH TO JOIN WOMEN'S FERRYING UNIT STOP PLEASE RESPOND IMMEDIATELY STOP TRULY YOURS JACQUELINE STOP

A knock sounded at the door, and Libby slid the telegram into her pocket. She opened the door to find Rose.

Her friend's eyebrows were knotted in worry. "I just heard the news." Rose swept in the door with the fragrance of spring trailing her. "And it's true—you're leaving."

"I've been trying to reach you for days. I'm going home after all."

With nowhere to sit, Rose paced the bare living room, her yellow skirt swishing around her legs. "Are you sure? I really don't think you should leave. Didn't your dad want you to stay put until things calm a bit?"

"I'll be fine. My father's a worrywart. He didn't want me to be a flight instructor or to come here in the first place."

"But I heard on the radio just last night that the Japs are sinking commercial ships." Rose gave Libby a hug. "I just can't lose you too."

"All good things must come to an end, and I have to go home now," Libby whispered into Rose's ear. "The weather here is fabulous, the students were pleasant, the planes wonderful . . . and our friendship the best. But really, if I can't fly, I'm of no use."

She pulled away and turned to the window, glancing

toward the distant harbor. "And it doesn't seem as if Dan will be returning any time soon."

"It's amazing how fast things change. You in that plane, coming so close to losing your life. And at the same time Jack . . ." Rose bit her lip.

Libby placed her fists on her hips. The last thing she wanted was the two of them to spend their remaining moments together in tears. "Yeah, speaking of which, I need to send a bill to the Imperial Japanese Army." Libby tensed her jaw. "After their little fiasco, my student ran off. The guy never did pay."

Rose laughed. "I don't know how you do it, but I'll miss the way you make me smile."

"Here's hoping you won't miss me for long." She slid the telegram out of her pocket and held it out to Rose. "I'm going to try for a job with the WAACs, and I'll recommend you too. It's too late for this assignment, but I'm sure something else will come up. It just has to."

"You received a telegram from *the* Jackie Cochran? The one and only? Humdinger." Rose punched an arm into the air. "Well, now, this is a different story. This just might be something worth traveling Jap-infested waters for."

* * *

Dan felt as if someone had punched him in the gut, as he sat with his unit in the cover of darkness, listening to the broadcast from Tokyo on Gabe's battery-operated radio. He would have thought it was a hoax, a ploy to weaken their moral, if it weren't for General MacArthur's own voice speaking over the airwaves.

"Men of Bataan and Corregidor. After declining to leave you twice before, I have now received orders from our commander in chief to proceed to Australia and take command there. Men, I must leave you now, but you have my solemn oath that if God spares me, I will be back to stay. Have faith, men! God bless you!"

It gave little consolation that the general's voice trembled with sadness and sincerity. They had been abandoned.

"Hey, turn that thing off. I think I hear something." José spoke in a fearful whisper.

Gabe obliged, and soon the sound of their heavy breathing was the only noise that filled Dan's ears.

"Are you sure?" Dan whispered.

"Shhhhh." The soldier placed a finger over his lips.

The sound came first as a shuffle of foliage. Then the clear sound of footsteps.

José lifted his rifle to the edge of the foxhole and pointed it in the direction of the noise. "Who's there?" he called out. "Reveal yourself!"

"It's me, Paulo! Don't shoot! Mr. Dan, are you in there?"

Dan placed his hand on José's rifle. "It's okay. He's one of us. Yes, Paulo," he answered. "We're here. To your left. In the foxhole behind the log."

Within seconds the small Filipino slid into the hole, joining them. "I found papers in the jungle. The Japs send messages. They dropped them from the sky."

Gabe pulled out his lighter. Its small flame danced before the bated breath of a dozen men. Dan held up the leaflet and read the text.

"PROCLAMATION. Bataan Peninsula is about swept away: important points of southern Luzon between Ternate and Nasugbu are in the hands of Japanese forces and mouth of Manila Bay is under complete control of the Japanese Navy. Hopes for the arrival of reinforcements are quite in vain. The fate of Corregidor Island is sealed."

Dan swore under his breath and then continued.

"If you continue to resist, the Japanese Forces will by every possible means destroy and annihilate your forces relentlessly to the last man. This is your final chance to cease resistance. Further resistance is completely useless. Your commander will sacrifice every man, and in the end will surrender in order to save his life. You, dear soldiers, take it into consideration and give up your arms and stop resistance at once. Commander in Chief of the Imperial Japanese Forces."

No one spoke at first; then Gabe threw down the lighter and snatched the leaflet from Dan's hand. "Give me that."

He climbed out of the foxhole, his boots flicking clumps of dirt on their heads.

"What are you doing?" Dan stood. "You think you can take on the Jap army yourself? Or are you planning to march to headquarters and give Wainwright a piece of your mind?"

Gabe blew out a harsh laugh. "No, Dan, I've given

up trying to be the hero. But if you must know, I'm going to the slit trench to take a dump. I just needed some paper."

ॐ ॐ ॐ

It was dusk when they arrived. City lights were just beginning to sparkle as Libby's ship steamed under the Golden Gate Bridge into the San Francisco Bay. Oahu had been under blackout conditions so long she'd forgotten the beauty of lights reflecting on water. The air here was cold and crisp. Libby pulled her jacket tighter to her chin as the cool, salty breeze played with her hair.

The ground seemed to sway under her as she disembarked, and she hurried down the pier. A woman and a photographer waited near the end of docks, making Libby wonder if there'd been an official or celebrity on board. The two waved as she approached, and Libby turned to see who was behind her. Except for a few sailors unloading the luggage and cargo, there was no one.

"Miss Conners! Miss Conners! Please, may we have a word with you?"

Libby pointed to herself, and the reporter nodded vigorously, her red-lipped smile filling her face.

"I'm Lee Donnelly with the Associated Press. This is my photographer, Lou Davis. We were wondering if we could interview you?"

Libby folded her arms tight to her chest. "What's this about?"

Lee slid a pencil from the tight bun at the base of her neck. "Your experiences on Pearl Harbor, of course. I think the world will be fascinated to learn about a woman pilot who was soaring the skies of Oahu when the Japs swooped in, and who helped pull an injured pilot from a burning plane. The senator who issued your travel permit gave me the scoop."

"Okay, but can we do this over a cup of hot tea? I'm sorry, but I'm used to much warmer weather."

"Sure thing." Lee pressed her hand to Libby's back and guided her through the complex of docks. "But just make sure you start from the beginning. I want the whole story."

❧ ❧ ❧

Libby gazed out the window as she rode in the truck's passenger seat next to her dad.

The little town of Olive City in northern California seemed smaller than she remembered, as if someone simply decided to plop a few buildings in the middle of olive orchards.

"Alvin Tourney was killed at Pearl Harbor, you know." Her dad pointed to the Towne Pump gas station where Alvin used to work. "Didn't you go to school with him?"

Just like Dad. Libby reached over and took his hand. *It always takes twenty minutes of small talk to warm him up. I'm bursting inside to see him, and he's always even-keeled.*

"Alvin was a year behind me. Real sweet kid. If I'd known he was on the island, I could have looked him up."

"Been meaning to head to the store." He turned their old truck onto the main highway, heading out of town. "Don't have much for meat. No sugar for coffee neither. The rationing, you know. Doesn't look like things will let up anytime soon. Radio says the German army is deep in Russia. Fighting's intense in North Africa and the Pacific too." He pushed his hat back farther off his forehead. "Times like these a man's happy to have a girl child instead of a boy. At least I know you'll be safe. Not off fighting on some distant shore." He glanced at her with a bright twinkle in his eye. "You always were my little olive pit."

Libby scooted closer. She wrapped her arms around her father's shoulders, then planted a large kiss on his whiskered cheek. "Oh, Daddy, you sure know the way to warm a girl's heart. I don't care about meat, or coffee and sugar, for that matter. You know what I'm itching for?"

"The sky, of course." He cast a grin, then scratched his bearded cheek. "I told old Charlie to fuel up the jalopy—he owed me a favor. That plane's been mighty bored just spraying trees. It misses you."

Libby squeezed tighter and rested her cheek on her father's shoulder. "I missed you too, Daddy. And you know what?" She sat up again, realizing for the first time how frail her dad appeared, how much he'd aged. "I missed the first boat with those lady pilots, but I'm hoping to catch the next ride. Do they still have that Link trainer at the airport in Sacramento? I'd be interested in taking those instruments courses. I hear the new trainer even pitches and yaws in sync with the pilot's actions."

"Sure, but I doubt you'll get much time to yourself. Everyone's eager to meet the lady pilot who escaped the Japs by the skin of her teeth." He reached under the seat and pulled out a copy of the *New York Herald.* Libby, fresh from the ship with her dark hair puffing around her face, smiled from the front page.

"The *New York Herald.* You can't be serious! Do you think other papers have picked up the story too?"

"I think they just might have, from the constant ringing of my telephone. The thing's rung more the last ten hours than it did all last year." He patted her knee. "But let's not worry about that now. The jalopy's waiting, and some dad-and-daughter time is in order."

Libby smiled and turned the paper over in her hand. Then something caught her eye. *One-man Scourge of the Japs.*

Pilot Dan Lukens claims that as long as there's a plane to fly on Bataan, he'll be in the air. On March 3, news reached Lukens that the Japs had landed on Bataan. Attaching a bomb to his still-flyable P-40, Lukens took to the sky. On his first mission he missed with his bomb, but sprayed the ships and barges with .50-caliber slugs.

Loading up again, Lukens dive-bombed a freighter from 10,000 feet. Pulling out at 2,000, he hit it squarely.

Debris and smoke mushroomed gloriously. Again the P-40 strafed the area.

On his third mission, Lukens hit an enormous supply dump on an island in the middle of the bay. Then, with his six machine guns, he attacked a transport slipping out of Subic Bay. Incredibly, this ship caught fire, and it too blew up. The bay was a holocaust. Later the Japanese claimed it had been raided by three flights of four-engine bombers.

The other fighter pilots had been carrying the fight to the enemy too, but by the end of the day, Lukens's plane was the only P-40 left on Bataan. With men like Lukens in our ranks, how could we not win this war?

A shrill of joyful laughter escaped her lips. No picture accompanied the story, but Libby's eyes scanned the text a second time. "He's alive. Dan's alive!"

Her father craned his neck toward the paper. "Who's alive? What this about?"

"My fiancé, Dan. And he's giving the Japs a run for their money. Daddy, my Dan is alive!"

"You don't say."

Libby glanced at her father. It wasn't joy that she saw in his eyes, but worry—concern that his little girl would once again lose someone she loved and get hurt all over again.

Eighteen

SERVICE ON BATAAN MOST IMPRESSIVE:
MEN ATTEND EASTER RITES
WHILE ENEMY BOMBERS THREATEN

With General Wainwright's forces in the Philippines, April 5 (Delayed) (AP)—They came with revolvers or automatic pistols slung on their belts. Many of them carried rifles. There wasn't a necktie or a pressed uniform in the lot. But it was a most impressive Easter service.

Many soldiers, sailors, and marines—all part of this gallant band defending this tiny strip of land—admitted it was the first time they had attended a church service in years.

Excerpt from the *New York Times*, April 7, 1942

Dan didn't realize it was his own voice crying out in the night until he felt Gabe's hands shaking him.

"Wake up. Are you nuts? You're going to lead the Japs straight to us!"

Dan opened his eyes to view what looked like an apparition of the man he used to know. Heavy, dark circles hung under Gabe's eyes. His cheekbones protruded, giving him an eerie appearance in the pre-dawn glow.

Dan grabbed his hand. "You're alive. You're okay." He breathed his words out with a sigh of relief.

"For the time being, at least. But I have to admit, things aren't looking that great."

Dan nodded and sucked in heavy breaths as he eyed the nearby acadia trees for signs of his parachute. The form of an owl in its branches was the only thing he could make out. It had only been a dream. He ran a hand over his scraggly beard, remembering.

In the dream, he'd been forced to bail out of his plane, his body drifting to the earth but never arriving. As he hovered, he watched Jap planes bomb his buddies. Finally, as he neared the ground, his parachute tangled in tree limbs. He'd swung there, unable to move as the responsibility for all those deaths pressed on his shoulders. *If I'd stayed with my plane, I could've stopped the bombing* . . . He searched his dream over and over, forgetting the reason he'd bailed in the first place.

Gabe placed a cool hand on Dan's forehead. "Gee, man, you're burning up. I'm gonna see if I can get a medic to check you." He scrambled out of their dugout. "Try to rest. We may be heading out soon."

Heading out?

Then Dan remembered. The Japanese had opened their attack against the Bagac-Orion line yesterday, and the whole southern half of Bataan had shaken with great clouds of dust. Yet they could do little to help. Their orders had been to remain here, to hold this line of defense no matter what came their way.

But only stragglers came. Injured soldiers hoping to make it to the hospitals in the rear. Since gasoline was depleted, there were no longer rides to take them back.

"It is the anniversary of the beginning rule of Emperor Jimmu, the first emperor," Paulo had informed the group. "I used to work for a Japanese man. He always celebrated this holy day."

Dan considered the holy days celebrated back home. Soon it would be Easter. Memories flooded him of egg hunts at the local park, pressed suits with itchy collars, and spit-shined oxfords. He also thought of childhood Sunday school stories. Of the thin and frail Jesus hanging on the tree, carrying the sins of the world.

Hanging on a tree . . . how did He ever bear it?

Dan pressed his fingertips to his throbbing temples. He stood and peeked over the edge of the dugout, hoping the fighting had settled in the night. He placed his hands on the edge and tried to pull himself out.

Where's Gabe? I need to tell him about the dream . . .

His arms refused to hold his weight, and he slid back into the hole, scattering more dirt on top of him.

Two months still remained until the rainy season, and all moisture had evaporated. The jungle floor was ankle-deep with fine silt. Silt that now covered him and everything else like a blanket.

In the distance a giant flare burst, and the ghostly glow of magnesium filled the sky. Closer, a machine gun opened up, shooting small streaks of red tracers through the air. He pressed his hands to his ears, willing the noise to stop. Lately, there hadn't been a moment without the crash of bombs and shells. And he couldn't remember how many days they'd hovered in foxholes with little food. Mainly, it was their nervous energy keeping them going.

Dan leaned his head against the wall of the foxhole, his last reserves of strength giving out. He tried to catch his breath, but the phosphoric odor of smoke burned his nose and throat. Fear rumbled in his stomach at the thought of the battle bearing down. He'd heard rumors of Japanese bayonets and samurai swords.

Dan must have drifted to sleep, because when he awoke Gabe had returned, and the morning sun now hung bright in the sky.

"Morning, sleepyhead. Looks like that quinine's doing some good. I think you have malaria."

"Medicine?" Dan rubbed his eyes, and the haziness from earlier that morning dissipated.

"Don't you remember? I begged some off one of the other guys in a nearby foxhole. He didn't want to give it up, but I told him if our best flier was down, all of us would be in trouble."

"I'm not much of a flier without a plane, and I'm afraid to see if the one we have left is still in one piece."

"Here." Gabe handed Dan a small cloth bag. Dan opened it to discover something that looked like oyster crackers mixed with small balls of white sugar. He tossed a handful into his mouth.

"Where'd you find this?" It was sweet to his tongue, and he hungrily tilted the bag to his lips, shaking more into his mouth.

"I found it on a dead Jap. Must've been his rations. Also found some sticks that looked like resin. It was solidified fish soup. I mixed it with water and ate that while you slept."

Dan held out the bag to Gabe. "Want some?"

"Nah, you go ahead. I'm good."

In less than a minute, the contents of the bag were gone. Dan turned it inside out and licked the remaining crumbs, then sat back with a smile. It hadn't filled his stomach, but it gave him the boost he needed.

He watched Gabe clean his rifle with a piece of oiled gauze. The scent of oil permeated the dugout.

"Stupid thing keeps jamming on me. These dang weapons must have belonged to the Confederate army." Gabe worked the gauze, plunging it up and down the barrel of the gun. "Our other weapons aren't much better. The grenades are old and damp. Only one out of the last three worked. From what I hear down the line, the antiaircraft shells are so ancient their timers have worn out. They fly into the air and then just fall back. One guy was killed when it exploded right above his head. Boy, am I sick of this. I'm sick of praying and not seeing any hope."

Dan closed his eyes and leaned his head back against the dugout wall. "Me too. But what if our saviors are pulling into the harbor as we speak? I bet MacArthur's message was just a hoax to catch the Japs unaware. Maybe he's rounding up the best battleships and planes to rescue us."

"Yeah, right."

Despite their sarcasm Dan knew they had to keep faith. The alternative was unthinkable.

He remembered his short interview with a war correspondent, Frank something, after the bombing in Subic Bay. Frank had shared a poem that spread through the units like wildfire:

We are the Battling Bastards of Bataan,
No Mama, no Papa, no Uncle Sam!
No Aunts, no Uncles, no Cousins, no Nieces,
No Planes, no Pills, no Artillery Pieces!
And nobody gives a Damn!

Yet Dan had to have hope that someone still cared. That his mother still prayed, and Libby still loved him. He had to cling to that.

❧ ❧ ❧

Two lines of men made their way through the darkness, each one putting his hands on the guy in front of him. Their pace quickened as the booming behind them increased. They'd been given the orders to retreat. It was no use trying to hold back the Japs. No use sacrificing more men for a lost cause.

Dan panted, still feeling weak from the malaria. He squeezed Gabe's shoulder. "Hold up. I need to catch my breath."

Immediately the group of twenty men halted—Filipino soldiers, infantrymen, and a few remaining pilots. Men that only a few months ago were strangers now had an odd bond of understanding between them.

Dan glanced back over his shoulder. Flashes of artillery fire splashed in the inky sky.

They'd found a dry riverbed and decided to follow it. Dan was pleased with the decision, because he knew it led them toward the last plane, his plane, hidden under a pile of brush near one of their abandoned airfields.

He held his side where a sharp pain cramped up and felt like a fool for stopping their retreat. Who was he kidding? Even if the plane were still flyable, he was in no condition to take it up.

Suddenly the ground shook and the stones in the river began to roll, tumbling over their booted feet.

"The Japs!" José held his helmet tight to his head.

"Not Japs. An earthquake!" Paulo, the young Filipino, made the sign of the cross and fell to his knees. "God has come to our rescue!"

Dan's heart pounded, and he wondered if such a thing were possible.

The tremor grew in intensity, and José joined Paulo on the ground. The rest followed suit. Dan didn't know if it was the force of the quake or Paulo's words that brought them to their knees.

When the trembling stopped, the fighting too ceased for a brief moment. Except for the excited chattering of monkeys in the trees, the night air was silent.

The rocks from the riverbed cut into Dan's knees, and he wondered what it all meant.

Paulo pulled rosary beads from his pocket and rubbed them between his fingers. "Do you know? Today is Good Friday. Easter is in two days. All those years ago—the ground shook then too."

They pondered Paulo's words, then somberly rose from the ground and continued on in silence. This time, Dan and Paulo led the way.

The men again stumbled through the darkness side by side. And although Dan noted he stood at least six inches taller than Paulo, he somehow didn't feel as big as the man walking beside him.

⁂

They walked along the roadway, their 1918 mess tins and canteens clanking at their sides. Dan's legs felt like rubber stilts, shaky and detached from him, as if those two thin sticks were not his own. His dirty shirt clung to his back, damp with sweat.

He felt disassociated with their movement somehow, as if he wasn't really part of this. The real Dan

Lukens was back in Hawaii, tossing a football on the beach, training new pilots, and going out to dinner with his girl.

Sometime during the morning, word had come that they'd surrendered. Major General King had thrown in the towel, not wanting to sacrifice any more lives. The word had come down the line that they were to walk to a staging center at Mariveles.

Others had joined their small group, and as they trudged along, Paulo shared how the Israelites had been led through the wilderness by a pillar of fire. But for this group of haggard pilgrims, the only guide was a narrow road and the sun reflecting off the green crest of the Mariveles Mountains, beating down on them with sweltering intensity.

Yet staring at that mountain was far better than taking note of what littered the roadway. There lay American soldiers, some just boys, their bodies cast aside like refuse. Some still alive, but just barely.

During the months of training, surrender to the enemy had been discussed, yet no one believed it would happen. One fought to win, not to give up. Rich and poor, officers and reserves, old men and those straight out of high school—they were all identical now.

Dan couldn't help but be drawn to a young soldier who lay on the side of the road with a wound to his stomach. It looked as if he'd been bandaged, then left to fend for himself. Dan paused, lowering himself to the ground beside the lad.

"I'm afraid to die." The soldier's tears streaked the

dirt on his bloodless, white face. His lips trembled. "I'm too young to die. My legs feel cold," he wheezed.

"It's okay, kid. Who says you're going to die? I'm right here with you." But the boy didn't seem to hear him. One last breath shuddered from his body, and Dan's fingers closed the sightless eyes.

He stood and continued on, feeling as if he, too, had died inside. "Things like this shouldn't happen. That guy should have been home, finishing high school. He should be attending the prom and worrying if Betty Sue likes him as much as he likes her." Dan's words piled up, weighing on his chest. "He shouldn't be dying on some godforsaken island halfway around the world."

Gabe placed an arm around Dan's shoulder as they walked. "I agree. It's a horrible way to die. Alone, without those who love you the best."

Dan wiped at his eyes and noted the smell of gasoline on his hands. He'd done it. As soon as the word of surrender came, he'd spilled the fuel from his P-40 on the ground and lit it himself. They'd been ordered to destroy everything they left behind. There was no way they were going to let the Japs use their supplies. And if the last P-40 were to be destroyed, he would do it himself.

He wrapped his arms around his aching stomach, lowered his head, and let the tears fall. Not only for the boy, but for everything he'd lost that morning, including his ability to fly.

Gabe's jaw was also tight with emotion. The men around Dan spoke in hushed tones. Weak, tired, unsure about this next step, they tried to convince themselves that captivity would be better. At least they'd have food.

The road that wound along the foothills of the Bataan Mountains was also scattered with Jap souvenirs that had been thrown out. Money, guns, scarves with Japanese lettering—anything that they could be accused of taking from a dead soldier. Or anything else the Japs would want for themselves.

Dan glanced at his wristwatch. It had been his great-grandfather's, passed down from father to son for generations. He'd received it after his first year at UCLA.

He hurriedly pulled it from his wrist, then cocked his arm back as far as possible and chucked it into the trees lining the roadway.

Gabe turned to him with a single eyebrow raised.

"I won't let some Jap have it."

Gabe removed his wristwatch and did the same. Many of the others joined in.

Dan's chest ached as he realized that the watch had been the last connection with his family. In fact, only one small memento from home remained. He pulled his leather wallet from his pocket and slid out the photo inside. Libby smiled at him with twinkling eyes, wearing her flight suit. Her hair was tucked up in a pilot's cap, with dark curls poking out, framing her face. There were other photos he'd been forced to leave behind, but this was his favorite. The joy in her eyes as she stood beside her plane was unmistakable.

Dan caressed the image with his thumb, then tucked it into the lining of the metal helmet that Paulo had insisted he wear.

"You'll need it," the Filipino soldier had said, placing the helmet upon his head and buckling the strap tight. "To protect from the sun."

As long as Dan had this photo, he had hope.

High-pitched yelling caught Dan's attention even before the sound of the jeeps. Up the roadway, the line of men slowed as a Japanese tank rolled around the corner. Armed infantrymen rode on the outside. Dan didn't know what he expected Japanese soldiers to look like, but their olive green uniforms were tattered. Their caps had a little star above the bill, and flaps hung over their ears and the back of their necks. They looked nearly as thin as those marching—yet the razor-sharp bayonets in their hands reminded everyone who was in charge.

One officer, in a pristine uniform, stood inside the tank. He regarded them over the turret, his lips curling upward in a smile.

Dan leaned in close to Gabe. "Don't look a Jap officer in the eye. At best it's impolite. At worst, a direct challenge."

More Japanese followed in a truck behind the tank. An interpreter's voice barked instructions in English through a loudspeaker.

"Attention! All American personnel are ordered to report at the airfield at Mariveles. I repeat, proceed immediately to the runway at Mariveles and await further orders!"

Gabe leaned close. "Where did they think we were headed? Out for an afternoon stroll?"

As they trudged on, a soldier on Dan's right panicked. "They'll kill us all!" His eyes were wild. "We need to run now while we still have the chance!" He turned, his stick legs barely able to carry him. Two others joined him, taking long strides into the jungle.

Suddenly, the sound of a half dozen machine guns erupted. Dan covered his head and threw himself to the ground. He pressed his face into the dirt road. Once the chaos quieted, he dared to open his eyes only to find one of the soldiers hung up on the roots of an acadia tree not far from the roadway. Dan couldn't see the other two, but he assumed they'd also been mowed down. The officer in the tank began shouting in Japanese.

"Get up. Now. Hurry." Dan lifted himself off the ground. "We need to get moving before they decide to use us for target practice too." Dan reached down and helped Gabe to his feet. Then he turned and helped a few other soldiers.

"I don't understand." The young soldier's whole body trembled. "When we were on the front lines, Japanese aircraft flew overhead blaring promises that they'd stick to the Geneva Convention. They said if we surrendered we'd be back home in a few months."

"Yeah," said another soldier who stood even taller

than Dan. "It's part of their Bushido code—no needless bloodshed."

Dan placed a hand on each shoulder, glancing between the two. "I've talked Bushido, with a Japanese guy, in fact. Things have changed. The new soldiers are taking what they want from the code and throwing out the rest. In fact, my friend told me that for a Japanese to surrender is to create a great dishonor. His family must forget him completely."

"Like he's dead?" José glanced back over his shoulder at the tanks that continued down the road.

"No, more like he never existed."

"I believe it." The tall soldier nodded. "We captured some enemy soldiers on the front lines. And when the Japs broke through, we thought they'd be happy to get their men back." The shuffling of their feet on the road accented the man's words.

"What happened?" Dan studied the man's face, realizing how quickly strangers became friends under circumstances like these.

The man lowered his voice. "Those sake-crazed Nips marched their own soldiers into a clearing, offered each a cigarette, then shot them. Not only that, but they left them there, unburied."

"They're nothing more than animals." Gabe stumbled, then reached a hand to Dan.

Dan reached over and righted him. "Actually, that's what they think of us. And if that's how they treated their own, what do you think we can expect?"

Just then, a single Jap stepped out from behind a

tree with cigarette in hand. He leaned back against the trunk, watching them pass.

Dan watched as Gabe clenched his fist, then scanned the road both before and behind them. "Doesn't that guy realize there is only one of him and a lot of us? We could rush him if we want, strangle him with our bare hands."

"I guarantee there's more than one of him." Dan refused to look at the Jap, but he was certain he saw movement in the brush to the man's immediate left.

The Jap soldier whistled, and as they glanced over, he waved and smiled.

Then he approached Dan. "Nem?"

"Pardon?"

"Nem. Nem!" He pushed a finger into Dan's chest.

"Dan. Daniel Lukens."

"No worries, Daniel Lukens." He spoke in English. "Japan treats prisoners well. You may even see our country in cherry blossom time, a beautiful sight!" Then he fell back, letting them pass.

"Japan? Did you hear that? They're taking us to Japan?" Gabe hissed under his breath. "Maybe those guys had the right idea. We can slip off this road and take off for Corregidor. Or maybe we can see how long we can survive in the jungle. Surely it's better than giving up so easily."

"If we were healthy and fit, I'd consider it." Dan lowered his gaze.

As if knowing the nature of their discussion, the Jap soldier fell in behind their group, his rifle pointing at their backs. "You walk so proud, you Americans. Show me that you understand that we are now in control of your lives."

Dan lifted his arms in the air in surrender; yet it was an outward sign only. They maybe had control of his freedom, but they would not take his soul.

Nineteen

BATAAN FALLS AFTER EPIC STRUGGLE

Bataan, Bay of Bengal, Burma—these were names that spelled bad news last week.

The magnificent stand of the American-Filipino army on Bataan was broken. Smashing through Gen. Jonathan M. Wainwright's left flank, the vastly stronger Japanese troops swarmed over the peninsula and threw a sack around some 36,853 heroes who had held them at bay for three months and six days.

From a numerical standpoint it was "the most severe reverse ever suffered by an American force in a single engagement with a foreign foe."

But Bataan also was one of the most glorious pages in America's military history, a symbol of courage and fighting skill against impossible odds, and a portent of the fury that is to strike Japan one day when the tide of battle turns.

Edward T. Folliard, Staff Writer
Excerpt from the *Washington Post,* April 12, 1942

Dan sucked in a mouthful of dusty air and wiped a filthy hand across his forehead. As they trudged along, their group caught up with other stragglers. Comrades carried injured men, blood-soaked rags covering their wounds. Dan could smell the gangrene of sores as they passed.

Yet even those considered to be in the best health were thin and haggard. Their olive fatigues hung on emaciated frames. Thin, sore-covered legs moved forward, ever forward, afraid to stop. Worried eyes glanced behind, anticipating the enemy at any moment.

Dan kept pace with his friends, thankful for their companionship, even though conversation had been dropped along the way.

As they moved forward, in step with some and passing others, Dan thought he recognized the walk of one husky soldier. The man ran his hand down the back of his neck and glanced over his shoulder, as if feeling Dan's gaze.

"Colonel!" Dan's voice rose above the shuffling boots and low moans.

Colonel Preston paused, and a crooked grin lifted a dirt-smudged lip. "Daniel. It's good to see you."

Colonel Preston was a large fellow, at least six inches taller than Dan and probably weighing over 250 pounds. Though his face looked slightly thinner, Dan wondered how the man had been able to maintain his girth with such meager rations. Then Dan noticed the heavy barracks bag slung over the colonel's shoulder. He walked awkwardly under its weight.

"Do you need help with that, sir?"

The colonel shot Dan a wary glance, and Dan could see his hands tightening their hold around the drawstrings.

"No, thanks. I've got it."

"Can I ask what you've got in there?"

"Extra shoes, uniforms. Just supplies I may need."

He didn't mention food, though Dan was sure he could make out the shape of K-ration cans through the bulging fabric.

"Well, if I may have the liberty, it might be a mistake to carry that much. We don't know how long this will last. Perhaps you should reserve your strength."

"Oh, no." The colonel shook his head. "I might need this gear."

Dan shrugged and hurried to catch up with José and Gabe, who had already passed.

"See you around, sir," Dan called back over his shoulder. Yet something in the pit of his stomach doubted his own words.

"I'm not sure why he hasn't been looted already, but I've got a bad feeling that when the Japs catch up to him, things will not go well."

Dan's companions barely lifted their heads to acknowledge his words.

"It's old-fashioned thinking." José shrugged. "Colonel's been around awhile. He trusts the system and believes their promises."

"And you don't?"

"Not enough to walk one step without prayer. I have an awful feelin' we've seen nothing yet."

❧ ❧ ❧

A Jap soldier walked through the milling crowd and stuck a pole into the ground. From it hung a flag of the Rising Sun. Dan ignored the flag and instead glanced back, noting how far they'd come. Mount Bataan with its cool crater stretched behind them, jutting into the blue sky. In the distance, it seemed untouched by the tiny men who had fought on its sides. His group made it to Mariveles. It was official. Every hope of freedom had been left behind.

Japanese enlisted men, dressed in patched and ragged uniforms, circled Dan's group. One corporal, who had a thin moustache reminiscent of Adolf Hitler's, strode up to Dan, moved his hand to his mouth, and inhaled.

"No cigarettes. Sorry." Dan shrugged his shoulders.

It wasn't the answer the Jap was looking for. Before Dan could react, the butt of the gun slammed into his forehead, and a warm wetness flowed from the spot.

Everything within him told him to raise his hands, to defend himself. He refused, simply lowering his eyes in submission. *Do it for Libby. You're living for her now.*

Other Japs circled his buddies. For no apparent reason, one pounded José's head with a bamboo stick filled with sand. Another motioned for them to raise their hands, then proceeded to frisk them for valuables. A cry arose from one man down the line. Dan glanced over from the corner of his eye, noting the sergeant stripes on his uniform.

During the fighting, many officers and noncommissioned officers had removed their ranks for fear of becoming targets for the numerous Japanese snipers. After the surrender, some had put their rank back on, believing they would receive better treatment as dictated by the Geneva Convention. It appeared this wasn't the case, and instead the sergeant was dragged off into a nearby clearing. Dan was thankful he'd left his stripes off.

Other men were being called out of line too, and after studying their faces, Dan knew why. Their gazes peered off in what some called a thousand-yard stare. They looked into the horizon without seeing. Some trembled with spasms. One man not far from Dan yelled, "Boom, boom, boom" over and over again, his arm punctuating the air with each eruption of his voice.

When they dragged those fellows off, Dan considered the act merciful. Until he remembered the mothers of those poor soldiers. To think one would invest so much in a life, only to have it end like this.

They stood for what seemed like hours, and Dan shivered despite the sun that beat down on them like a furnace.

"You have the chills, and your face is the color of dishwater." Gabe wiped Dan's forehead with a filthy handkerchief. "Malaria does that. Here." He opened his canteen, gulping down the last of its contents. Then he shook it, and something rattled inside. A small bottle fell from the opening. "There is only a little quinine left, but it should help."

Dan took the bottle and drank it dry, wanting more than anything to curl up on the ground in a ball and fall asleep.

"I don't know what I would do without you." Dan handed back the empty bottle.

"I feel the same." Gabe put it back in the canteen. "Just in case we can refill it later."

Gabe switched the shoulder strap of the canteen to the other side. His shirt drew tight across this chest, but instead of the outline of toned muscles, protruding ribs stuck out.

"Looks like we're heading out." Gabe nodded to a line of jeeps moving forward. "Without even a break."

"I just wish I knew where to."

Gabe readjusted his helmet. "Sometimes, friend, it's better not to know."

Libby wiped last night's crumbs off the flower-embroidered tablecloth her mom had made and placed a plate of eggs and toast on the table before her father. He'd never gotten rid of the feminine touches around the house after Mom left. He probably hadn't thought to. Or perhaps he'd hoped she'd return someday.

For the last three meals, Libby had served eggs. Her father called them her specialty, but actually it was the only thing she knew how to fix that they could choke down. In Hawaii, cooking hadn't been a problem. There were always fresh fruits and vegetables available. And smoked meats were cheap to pick up from the numerous barbecue pits around town.

She wrinkled her nose at the smell of cooked eggs and thought longingly of pig roasts and mango groves.

Her father folded his hands to pray, but instead of bowing his head, he immediately rose from the table and strode to the wood-paneled radio that sat on the armoire in the den.

"Daddy, please, can't we have one meal without that thing on?" She poured herself a glass of water, also remembering the fresh pineapple juice she used to enjoy.

Her father flipped on the radio, then pointed out the kitchen window. "See that? It's a sign from Evelyn Mead."

Sure enough, their widowed neighbor was leaning out the kitchen window, waving a white dish towel over her daffodil-filled flower box.

"She listens to the thing nonstop, then lets me know when there's something important."

Her dad fiddled with the tuner, and within seconds the excited, high-pitched voice of the radio announcer filled the air.

"That's right, ladies and gents, the Japs continue their swarming of the Pacific nations, hitting hard and overwhelming our gallant men. It's been reported that yet another of our strongholds has fallen under the hand of the Imperial Japanese Army. Just this morning word arrived that General King, in an attempt to save the lives of his remaining men, has surrendered his American-Filipino army to the Japanese. That's right, ladies and gents, surrendered."

Libby set down her glass, but it caught the edge of the plate, spilling all over the table. She covered her mouth with her hand and glanced at her father.

"Thousands of men have died in recent months of fighting: infantrymen, tank drivers, pilots . . . all giving their lives in hopes of stopping the Japs. But to no avail. Here they are, MacArthur's very words, rebroadcast so you can hear his response to the situation yourself."

MacArthur's saddened voice filled the airwaves: "The Bataan force went out as it would have wished, fighting to the end of its flickering forlorn hope. No army has ever done so much with so little, and nothing became it more than its lasting hour of trial and agony.

"To the weeping mothers of its dead, I can only say that the sacrifice and halo of Jesus of Nazareth has descended upon their sons, and that God will take them unto Himself."

Libby began wiping up the water on the table. Then she pushed the plate of eggs in front of her father. "You better eat before they get cold."

He took her hand between his.

"They weren't talking about Dan." She looked away. "He's not dead. You saw the newspaper article yourself. They're speaking of others."

He caressed her hand with his thumb. She looked at him, and he only nodded.

"Of course, you're right. I'm sure you'll hear something. They'll notify the government with the names of their prisoners soon."

The word *prisoner* stabbed like a knife to her heart. Even if Dan were alive . . . what was he facing now?

Libby pushed back from the table and stood. "I'm not hungry. I think I'll head to the airfield for a while."

Her father took a sip of his coffee. "You do that, but remember: There will come a time when you'll have to face your emotions. Not every problem is solved by getting in the cockpit."

"Yes, but at least I can escape for a while. You know the cardinal rule for pilots—don't take your problems up in the air."

Day and night seemed to blur as their column trudged on. American generals and privates walked alongside Filipino soldiers and civilians. On the road lit by a huge orb of a moon, Dan even noticed a few American nurses who'd joined them.

With every mile it seemed a new rumor was circulating. The current one stated that an agreement had been made between the United States and Japan. There were no details, but some believed they were being marched to a nearby harbor where American transport ships awaited, ready to make a prisoner trade.

As they trudged forward, a heavy stench filled Dan's nostrils. The slit trenches that had been dug along the roadside now overflowed. Many prisoners suffered from dysentery brought on by exhaustion and the lack of sufficient food and water.

Those who took too long at the trenches soon found themselves the targets of numerous blows, and before long the roadway consisted of a thick sludge of fecal waste and mud from those fearful of leaving the path.

Yet despite the stench, Dan was thankful for the cool of darkness.

When he didn't think he could take another step, they were corralled into a small field and given a ladleful of water each. Dan slurped it down greedily and thanked the Japanese soldier who'd brought it with a bow of his head.

As they rested, Jap soldiers moved among them. They held their rifles flat and prepared for the smallest outburst. Even in the dim light, Dan noted their suspicious gaze, their glaring eyes.

Before long the GIs were on their feet again, as the warm glow of dawn cast ribbons of light on the mountains. The only water they were allowed to fill their canteens with was green muck from a caribou wallow. Dan did the best he could to strain out the solid sludge with his shirttails.

In addition to the foot soldiers, Japanese officers

strode back and forth in the road, their samurai swords in bamboo cases clacking against their black boots.

The cool of dawn gradually turned into a hot morning; and the more they marched, the hotter it grew. The roadway had changed, becoming wider and paved with crushed rock. Dan didn't know what was worse, the sludge they'd just tromped through or the white clouds of dust now kicked up by their shuffling steps. It made breathing difficult and blinded their view of what lay ahead.

The men began to falter. Some cried for water. Others stumbled and never rose. All suffered from hunger.

Memories of combat haunted them. Dan thought of soldiers strewn over the airfield after the bombing raids. The numbers of bodies along the sides of the road that increased by the hour. Oliver's plane bursting into flames.

About midday, José gradually dropped back. Dan and the others slowed in an attempt to encourage him. When that didn't work, they took turns supporting him, dragging him along.

Cries from approaching Japs changed all that. With quick jabs of their gun butts, Dan was prodded forward. He had no choice but to release José and continue on. After they'd taken twenty steps, the young man's cries could be heard.

Dan paused slightly, but Gabe grabbed his arm and urged him on. "Don't stop. Don't look back. There's nothing we can do for him now."

A single shot rang out. Dan cursed under his breath,

but he heeded Gabe's advice and continued forward. *José had faith. Where is the God he believed in now?*

As noon approached, Dan lifted his head, certain he again heard the rumble of vehicles on the roadway ahead. A Japanese guard ran up and motioned them to the side of the road.

The first to pass were Japanese horse artillery. The Japs hurriedly moved by, eager to get the weapons to Corregidor where American soldiers still fought to hold that small bit of land. Behind them a 1942 Cadillac drove down the road. A wooden platform had been attached to the roof.

"What the heck is that?" Gabe scratched his forehead.

Before Dan had a chance to respond, the car stopped, and the driver and single Japanese passenger jumped out. The passenger scrambled onto the platform while the driver scurried to the car's trunk and pulled out a tripod and camera, handing them up.

The cameraman waved his hands, motioning the prisoners to move close together. They complied, and he nodded his approval. The cameraman snapped a few photos and then climbed down and returned to the car. It sped off in search of the next photo opportunity.

Dan ran a hand down his face. "Looks like we might be in all the Jap papers soon. They should've warned us. We could've shaved first."

A slam of a rifle butt brought shooting pain down Dan's spine, and he woke with a scream, then hurried to his feet.

"I think they want us up," he gasped, sputtering out the gob of dust that had settled in his mouth as he slept. He bent over and reached for Gabe. His whole body ached, and it seemed as if they'd just lain down. And maybe they had; the sky was still dark. "Come on. You gotta get up."

"Don't think I can make it. My leg." Gabe's voice was raspy. "The Jap hit me in the leg!"

Dan glanced over his shoulder, anticipating the next blow. Instead, the Jap was occupied in cutting a wedding band off a soldier who'd succumbed during the night.

"Hurry. There's no time."

Dan pulled Gabe to his feet, and they limped along, staying as close to the center of the road as possible. The banyan trees along the sides of the road were black against the morning sky as their small group of men joined a milling mob, an endless line, its staggering members moving ever forward.

The road they marched on was about twenty feet wide and constructed of rock covered with crushed stone. Their footsteps stirred up a heavy white dust, which settled on them and made the half-dead soldiers look like ghosts in the headlights of Japanese trucks.

After an hour passed, Dan scanned up and down the road. There were no Japs in sight. He turned to Gabe. "Would it help if we rested a few minutes? We should be safe."

Pain distorted Gabe's features, and Dan noticed thick blood weeping from his leg wound. Gabe nodded with a violent shock, as if not caring whether they moved forward or remained at this spot forever.

Dan eased his friend's hand from around his shoulders and lowered him to the ground. Suddenly the rumble of a truck filled the air; and before he could react, a metal object crashed upon Dan's head, knocking off his helmet.

He wrapped his arms over the back of his neck, recognizing the cold, hard metal of a rifle. More cries filled his ears. *Gabe.* Dan moved toward his friend, attempting to block the blows; but before he could reach Gabe, strong arms thrust him back on his feet and pushed him back into line.

"Wait, Gabe!" Dan craned his neck to get a view of his buddy. He was huddled on the ground in the fetal position. His cries grew weaker with each blow.

"Let me go!" Dan pulled against the arms that held him and amazingly felt them release. Staggering back, he dropped to Gabe's side.

"You want help your friend? You think you save him?" The Jap lowered his voice several notches to make it sound deeper, harsher.

Dan glanced up at the Japanese soldier, who spoke in English.

"Go ahead, GI Joe. You want to help. You carry."

Without hesitation, Dan bent over and scooped up Gabe's thin frame into his arms. Though now limp, heavy breathing shuddered from Gabe's frame.

"You go now, GI. Don't stop. Don't put down. You take your man with you." With a laugh, the Jap returned Dan's helmet to his head.

Dan spoke steadily in Gabe's ear. "It's okay now, buddy. I've got you." He took a step forward.

Gabe's body hung limp, his feet dragging along the ground. Ten steps later, Dan knew he'd made a mistake. The days on the road without food or water made it hard enough to carry himself, let alone Gabe.

"I need you to work with me here. Walk with me. Move your feet."

Gabe let out a low moan, but amazingly he obeyed. One foot lifted awkwardly, then another.

"There you go. That's it." The steps quickened, nearly matching his own.

Then, before he realized what was happening, another soldier approached from behind. Without a word, he took Gabe's free arm and swung it over his own shoulders.

Dan glanced over to see a stocky man with black hair. He looked Italian, and his ruddy skin looked healthier than any Dan had seen for months.

Dan shook his head in a warning. "You better not. They'll—"

The dark-haired man shrugged his shoulders. "I'm fine. They're not paying attention." Their steps quickened—even Gabe's, who nearly carried his own weight between them.

"I'm Tony. What's your friend's name?"

"Gabe Lincoln. I'm Dan Lukens."

"It's a good thing you've done here—helping your friend. When I saw you, I knew I wanted a pal like that."

Dan smiled—the first one he'd attempted since the siege began. "Welcome, Tony. I'd be honored to be considered your friend."

Twenty

DECIDES SETTLING OF COAST EVACUEES: WAR RELOCATION AUTHORITY TO PLACE 105,000 JAPANESE ON FEDERAL-OWNED LANDS

San Francisco, April 14—West Coast Japanese, numbering 105,000, who have waited to be moved from military area No. 1 under Army supervision, are to be settled in communities of 5,000 or more population on lands now owned or to be purchased by the federal government, under a policy announced today by Milton S. Eisenhower, director of the War Relocation Authority.

The evacuation of Los Angeles zones was completed during the day. The 2,500 evacuees went to the Santa Anita assembly center.

Lawrence E. Davies
Excerpt from the *New York Times,* April 15, 1942

Libby borrowed the small Interstate Cadet for the short flight down to the Los Angeles area. For weeks she'd remained holed up in her father's house, granting some interviews, but mostly keeping to herself, trying to decide what part she could play for the war effort. Since she was too late to participate with the fliers in England, Libby hoped the United States would soon develop its own program.

Yet when the phone call came from Mrs. Lukens, Libby knew a trip to southern California was in order.

"It's only for one day," she told her father. "I'll be back tomorrow." Yet as she flew into the small airfield at Redondo Beach, the sight of the ocean caressing the shore brought it all back, and nothing sounded better than walking the shoreline and feeling the waves lap against her feet. *Maybe two days would be okay.*

The small plane touched down, then taxied down the runway lined with palm trees. She parked the plane, grabbed her small satchel from the passenger's seat, and searched her flight suit for the directions to Dan's house. His parents had assured her that she'd be able to catch a taxi from the airfield. So after seeing that the plane was taken care of, Libby made her way to the front of the building, her eyes scouring the parking area.

"Can I help you with something?"

Libby turned and looked into the face of a handsome man with hazel eyes and a broad smile. He was dressed in tan slacks and a white shirt buttoned at the collar. A greasy set of coveralls was thrown over his arm, and he held a metal lunch pail in the opposite hand.

"Pardon?" Libby combed her fingers through her hair.

"Just wondering if you needed a ride somewhere. You're looking kinda lost."

"Not lost, but I am looking for a taxi." Her eyes scanned the parking lot once more. "It seems there isn't one."

"Where you headed?" He nodded his chin toward an old truck in the lot. "Just got off work. I can give you a ride."

"I don't think that's a good idea, Mr. . . ."

"Struthers." He bowed low and pretended to tip a hat. "Sam Struthers, at your service."

"I don't think that's a good idea, Mr. Struthers. I'll just see if I can telephone a taxi. But thank you very much."

Libby strode back into the small airport office and approached the counter. An elderly gentleman sat behind the desk, flipping through an old flight manual. From the looks of him, Libby was sure he must've flown with the Wright brothers.

"Go ahead, ask him." Sam's voice startled Libby.

She turned to see that he'd followed her inside.

"Ask him to vouch for me," Sam repeated.

"Sam's okay, little lady." The gray-haired man lifted his head and winked. "One of my best mechanics and a gentleman too. He's safe to give you a ride to town."

"Well, okay then." Libby tightened her grip around the satchel. "Do you know where Rivera Street is?"

"Know the place exactly." Sam took the satchel from her hand, then waved his arm toward the office door. "After you."

❧ ❧ ❧

Ima Jean was as warm and friendly as Libby had imagined. Sam had dropped her off in front of the house; and before Libby could make it up the front steps, she found herself wrapped in the woman's embrace.

"Come in, dear; we're so happy to have you. Aren't we, Alex?"

Her husband, who looked like an older version of Dan, smiled from the kitchen, where he was pouring Libby a cup of tea.

"Yes." He grinned with an enthusiastic nod of his head. "Yes, we are."

Libby looked around the cozy house and tried to imagine Dan growing up here. She glanced out the window at the two palm trees centered on the front lawn and the similar houses lining the block.

"He used to play in those two trees." Ima Jean lifted a teacup to her lips and nodded toward the lawn. "One summer he and his buddies made an airplane out of scraps of lumber. They figured out a pulley system between the trees that allowed them to raise and lower it."

"Do you have any photographs? Of when Dan was a boy?"

Ima Jean led her to the living room wall. "We always wanted more children, but it wasn't in God's plan." She pointed to a photo of a chubby toddler sitting on the back of a wooden rocking horse.

"It didn't matter, though." Dan's father peered through his glasses. "He made us proud enough for a dozen sons."

"Have you heard anything more?" Libby looked to the next photo of Dan in elementary school, flashing a wide grin, minus two front teeth, at the camera.

Alex's voice was thick with emotion. "Not since the newspaper article. But it sure made me proud reading that."

Ima Jean brought out a small album. "Here's one of him on the UCLA football team." She ran a finger down the page. "He got a full scholarship." She flipped to the next one. "And this is the day he received his pilot's license. Have you ever seen a bigger smile?"

Libby placed a hand over her mouth, unable to answer.

Ima Jean patted Libby's cheek. "Now, don't you worry. It's okay to shed a few tears. Lord knows I have. Daniel's a fighter. He'll make it. And you know why?"

Libby pressed her lips together and shook her head.

"Because he has you to think of. The prettiest, kindest, sweetest, smartest girl he's ever met . . . and those are his words exactly."

Her eyes moved to the ring on Libby's hand. "May I see?"

Libby held up her hand with the gold band for Ima Jean's inspection.

"Yes, my son always did have good taste . . . and

I'm not just meaning the ring." She gave Libby's hand a gentle squeeze. "Let me tell you what we need to do."

Her light blue eyes reminded Libby of Dan even more.

"We need to pray like we've never prayed before. We don't know what he's going through right now, but God knows. And we'll pray that God will shower upon Daniel an abundance of strength, wisdom, and whatever else he needs at this moment."

❧ ❧ ❧

The screaming monkeys mingled with the hooting of the owls, stirring Dan from his heavy sleep. Above him the sky was clear with brilliant stars. It reminded Dan of the sky he and Libby had walked under during one of their last nights together. Was she looking at the same sky, thinking of him?

These thoughts were soon pushed out of his mind as the shouts grew louder, and Dan was suddenly aware of a stinging feeling all over his back—like the bites of a thousand fire ants.

"Gabe, check my back, will you?" By the end of the day Gabe's energy had rallied, and he had carried his own tattered body without help.

"Blisters everywhere." Gabe winced. "Some have already split open."

Dan realized they must be the same puffy water blisters he'd found under his arms and sides the previous day.

"I've heard they're called Guam blisters." Tony rose to his feet. "Just don't scratch them, or they'll get infected."

Dan didn't have time to worry about scratching. Before he could speak another word, the Japanese soldiers urged them to their feet, and the march began once more.

Before long, the sun blasted down on them, and Dan thought back to the salty waves of Ewa Beach. He remembered Libby and the fresh mangos they had picked during a walk to her apartment from John Rodgers Airport. He smiled to himself, remembering the laughter of those carefree summer months.

Gabe and Tony trudged along beside him, but neither said a word. It was easier that way. Easier to bear up alone, lost in one's own thoughts. Living in the world of memory rather than reality.

Dan stumbled on something in his path and landed hard on one knee. A Japanese voice sounded behind him, and he struggled back to his feet. But before Tony or Gabe could reach down to help him, another pair of arms hooked under his armpits from behind and hoisted him to his feet. As he righted himself, Dan glanced over to see the familiar face of the Philippine scout.

"Paulo!" Dan embraced his friend.

"You doing good now?" Paulo's eyes were filled with concern.

Dan nodded and glanced back over his shoulder, quickening his pace.

"Here. This make you stronger." Before Dan could

object, the scout pushed half a can of meat into Dan's hand. "It's good. I have some for friends too."

Dan's jaw dropped as Gabe and Tony also received a can to share.

"I'll be back later." And before Dan could object, Paulo moved on, helping other weary soldiers down the line.

Trucks continued to move past, stirring up the dust. It was all Dan could breathe, all he could taste. Americans drove some trucks at bayonet point. The guards punctuated the marching with slapped faces, kicked shins, and brutal shoves that sent men sprawling to the ground. Each sadistic prank brought more laughter.

As they staggered on, the rains finally began. Dan stared upward in amazement, noticing clouds that had not been there before. He lifted his face to the sky and opened his mouth wide, accepting its offering. Then he opened his canteen and lifted it, thankful for fresh water to drink. In less than a minute, they were soaked to the skin. They continued on, feet sloshing in the muddy road, but the cool refreshment renewed Dan's vigor.

Libby awoke to the sound of Ima Jean's voice in the kitchen singing "Amazing Grace." She pulled the yellow-and-blue quilt tightly to her chest and snuggled in deeper.

She was sleeping in Dan's old room and loved being surrounded by his football trophies, Benny Goodman records, and, of course, model airplanes. *How many hours did you spend playing make-believe with those?*

It had been a wonderful visit, except for missing out on the beach. Last night they'd driven down to San Pedro Beach Park only to discover the streets packed. Army men were erecting sandbag-and-barbed-wire defenses along the waterfront. Cars and trucks filled with families crammed the streets. Taking a closer look, Libby had noticed that the families leaving were all Japanese.

"They're being sent away to internment camps," Alex Lukens had explained. "Over three thousand Japanese aliens and their children. It'll make it safer. We can't let what happened to Pearl Harbor happen here."

Libby didn't want to think about Pearl Harbor or the memories of caring for the injured after the attack. She threw back the covers and slid a robe over her nightgown. She scanned the walls of Dan's childhood room. On the bookshelf sat paperback war pulps. On the wall, posters of flying aces Red Baron and Eddie Rickenbacker.

"You stay where you are." Ima Jean entered with a tray. "A lady needs breakfast in bed once in a while."

"Will you join me?"

"I'd be delighted." She set down the tray and pulled up a chair. "I hope you like your bacon crisp and your toast dark. That's the way Dan liked it."

Libby laughed and lifted a slice of toasted bread from the tray. "Around our house, the only prerequisite is that it's edible."

❧ ❧ ❧

The sun cast a golden mist over Hong Kong. Spring had come to the hills, and light yellow flowers filled the countryside surrounding Stanley with a terrific fragrance, sweet like nectar. Emerald trees set against the clear blue sky made it seem that all was well in the world.

But Natsuo knew it wasn't. He'd been given the weekend off and was able to entertain himself by driving around the conquered countryside, but he found no leisure witnessing the smoldering houses and stray, starving animals. The main streets were filled with hawkers. As soon as the town was overrun, the Chinese—those who hadn't been rounded up—had looted the houses and shops, and Natsuo was sure that anything was available for a price.

Hong Kong was in a stage of transition. Workmen continued to clean up roadways. In a matter of months, the debris would be cleared from Central Market along Queen's Road, and the island would appear as it had before—only under a different rule.

Yet even as he took in the countryside, a certain prisoner's face refused to leave his thoughts. And Natsuo knew what he had to do.

Entering the camp, he strode through the open-air courtyard. Heat radiated from the dirt roads under his boots, but a soft ocean breeze cooled his face. Natsuo moved through the streets, noting that the roofs of houses and corners of buildings and roads were still marked by shrapnel. Finally, outside a small bungalow, he spotted her. She sat in the grass with her two youngsters, reading from a large children's book. Her eyes filled with fear as Natsuo approached; then they softened.

"I would like a word with you." He nodded in the direction of a fallen log now used for seating.

"It's you. You're the one who saved me."

Natsuo noticed she still wore the same dress, but the ripped collar had been stitched up with thick brown thread.

"I wanted to see how you fared." He looked closely at her. "Is there anything I can help you with?"

Dark circles sagged under her eyes, and her thin, nervous hands worked in her lap. "Actually." She let her breath out in a low sigh. "Some of us mothers have created a list of requests, but we're afraid to submit it."

"Do you have this list with you?"

The woman nodded, rose, and slipped into the bungalow. In a moment she was back and handed him a slip of paper. Handwritten words had been written around the title page of a book.

Natsuo scanned the list. "No promises, but I'll see what I can do."

"Thank you, sir." The woman grasped his hands, then quickly pulled away. She glanced around the compound to see if the guards had noticed her actions.

Natsuo's eyes did the same. Strangely, he felt both fear and excitement. "No promises," he said again. Then he turned and strode away.

⁂

A smile curled on the lips of the camp commander as Natsuo approached with the list of requests.

"Sir, the prisoners. Well, they are in need of some items and have prepared a list of requests. It is not much." He lowered his gaze, showing he was still the ever-dedicated servant of the emperor.

"Go ahead." The commander offered a wave of his hand. "Humor me."

Natsuo cleared his throat and began. "Permission is sought for each prisoner to write next of kin a simple statement that he or she is alive.

"Request is made that at least one item of European food be included in the rations.

"Request for a Roman Catholic priest to enter camp.

"Request for drugs and medicines for those seriously ill and dying from dysentery.

"Permission to bury in a cemetery those who have already died.

"And they have a request for toilet articles and bedding. That is all." Natsuo stood silent, his eyes still fixed on the paper in his hands.

"Is it all?" The commander steepled his fingers and placed them before him on his desk. "Permission denied. You are excused." He cleared his throat.

Natsuo dared to lift his gaze, his eyes meeting the commander's stone-cold glare.

"And next time you are asked . . . know that the emperor judges how his prisoners are cared for—not you."

Natsuo bowed low. "Thank you, sir. Long live the emperor." He turned and hurried from the room as fast as his legs would take him.

Then he knew. He wasn't adept at playing his charade after all. He'd seen it in the commander's eyes. Natsuo teetered on the fine line between honor . . . and disgrace. His concern for the prisoners had cost him the respect of his superior.

What have I done? Why do I not learn?

Dan scanned the faces of the Filipinos who gathered along the roadsides offering cups and pitchers of water. Some handed out cigarettes and ice cream. Others kind words. The faces of the Japanese soldiers reddened with anger, and they swung at the crowds, knocking many to the ground with cries of pain. Yet the faithful pushed forward, attempting to provide what they could for the captured GIs.

Ahead a road sign read SAN FERNANDO. Could this be their destination?

The Filipinos seemed in shock to see the tiny Japanese driving the Americans along. The GIs, after all, had driven the Spanish out of the Philippine Islands. The United States had reigned over the islands for forty years and had promised the Filipinos their independence if they helped them defend the islands from the Japanese. Still, though most couldn't offer more, the compassion in their gazes was like balm to Dan's soul.

Behind them, an American soldier's cries filled the air. Dan turned.

The GI's eyes were wild, and Dan knew he'd lost his mind. The soldier shouted at the top of his lungs and alternated between hitting the ground and knocking his helmet against his head. Japanese soldiers hovered around him, jeering in words Dan couldn't understand.

"Poor man has gone mad." Gabe hobbled away from the crowd, shaking his head and refusing to watch.

"Surprised? I can't believe we all haven't. These Japs. I wish I could—" Dan didn't finish. Instead, he let the murderous thoughts fill his head.

The roar of the crowd intensified. Dan covered his ears and then watched as the man paused. Wide-eyed, he turned in a slow circle as if seeing his captors for the first time.

With a shriek that sliced the air, the man lunged at the Japs and swung his helmet full force. With a sickening thud, it connected with the head of a jeering soldier. The Jap's head jerked back and his cheek split open.

The voices were silenced, and Dan sucked in a breath as a half dozen bayonets were thrust into the GI's body.

The American soldier straightened, as if in slow motion, then let out a moan. He peered at his stomach, covered the weeping wounds with his hands, and then folded onto the ground.

More cheers. More laughter.

And Dan turned away, his aching chest making it hard for him to breathe.

Twenty-One

60,000 CAPTURED BY FOE ON BATAAN: 35,000 COMBAT TROOPS AND 16 GENERALS TAKEN WITH 25,000 CIVILIANS, STIMSON REPORTS

Washington, April 17—While beleaguered Corregidor continued today to nick the edges of sustained Japanese aerial attacks, the War Department announced that approximately 35,000 United States and Filipino "combatant troops" on Bataan Peninsula were presumably in the hands of the enemy.

In addition, it was stated, the Japanese captured "several thousand noncombatant and supply troops and about 25,000 civilians." The civilians were refugees who had followed the armies into Bataan from cities and villages of Luzon Island.

Charles Hurd
Excerpt from the *New York Times,* April 18, 1942

Inside the small office, the commandant was seated behind his desk. Next to him a thick-waisted man stood with a uniform that matched Natsuo's—an interpreter's uniform.

Upon Natsuo's entrance the commandant rose. "I am punishing you in order to set an example for others who dare to show kindness to the prisoners of the emperor."

Natsuo blinked his eyes, uncertain if he'd heard correctly.

The commandant stepped in front of Natsuo, then proceeded to strike his hand across both of Natsuo's cheeks several dozen times. The intensity of each slap built upon the one prior, until Natsuo was certain he'd collapse under the pain. Though he tried to remain erect, he felt his body swaying back and forth. It was all he could do to withstand the blows.

"Forgive me! Forgive me!" Natsuo finally called out. Only then did the blows cease.

The commandant took a step backward, panting from the effort. "You are no longer head interpreter. You will report to Iku Yamamoto. Is that clear?"

Natsuo bowed low, feeling as if his head would fall off his shoulders. "Thank you, sir. Thank you." With low bows he exited the room, daring not to turn his back on the commandant.

Only outside was he able to catch his breath. He deserved this. He'd been a fool, allowing his weakness to stand in the way of what was best for his country.

Natsuo strode away, refusing to allow himself the

relief of rubbing his stinging cheeks. What would Father think? What shame if the news ever arrived home.

I will not fail again. He strode with more determined steps. *I will not.*

❧ ❧ ❧

The one helping of rice they'd been given sat heavy in Dan's stomach. They'd been loaded into boxcars—over fifty in a car—for the next trek of the journey from the town of San Fernando to the prison camp ahead. Dan felt short of breath, light-headed, and it seemed there wouldn't be enough air for the trip.

"If we work together, I think we can sit."

Dan sank to the ground with his back against Tony's chest and Gabe's back wedged between his legs. The doors closed, and the car began to hurtle through the darkness.

Dan wished he could sleep, but the heat was suffocating. Except for a lone, whispered prayer, no one had energy to talk. Some even lost the will to live.

Finally the train stopped at Capas. Dan resisted the urge to push his way out of the car, willing his cramped legs to cooperate. From the village of Capas, they walked the remaining seven miles to Camp O'Donnell. When it seemed as if he had no strength to continue, the faint outline of barbed wire and nipa-thatched huts built on stilts loomed in the distance.

Again Filipinos lined the roads outside the gates. Many young girls with babies on their hips searched the faces of the men, eager for a glimpse of their missing husbands or lovers.

Dan was thankful Libby didn't have to see him in such a state. She was at home, among Americans, safe—at least he hoped she was. Even in the suffering and tears, it brought a smile to his lips thinking of her soaring above the clouds—maybe even with the U.S. civilian workers.

As they shuffled through the gates, Gabe leaned in close. "Welcome to Hell Hole Number One."

"I heard of O'Donnell," Tony commented. "Some of the guys trained here before the war. The water was bad and couldn't supply eight thousand men."

"So what does that say for the tens of thousands, half-starved, mostly dead ones here now?" Gabe wiped the sweat from his brow.

A small Japanese guard ran up and down the lines and waved a baton. Dan couldn't understand his words, but from his wild arm motions it was clear he wanted them to line up in rows.

"What now?"

From there they were pushed into an open marching field and told to place all their possessions on the ground in front of them. Officers walked up and down the rows of men.

Dan watched as the men in line were stripped of all personal possessions—nail files, razors, matches, blankets—anything of value. Anyone who was found with a Japanese souvenir was killed, beheaded by a swift arc of a samurai sword.

Afraid his helmet would be taken, Dan removed the photo of Libby from the liner and stuck it in his sock next to his boot. "Sorry about the smell, Libby girl."

After the last man had turned over his possessions, a small captain climbed onto a platform before them. The pint-sized Japanese officer wore riding breeches, a pith helmet, white shirt, and highly polished black boots. A sword hung on the left side of his belt, and medals draped his uniform.

"You no honorable soldiers," he said in heavily accented English. He knocked the side of his head with his fist. "You deserve to die. Cowards! All of you! Your lives are spared by the benevolence of the emperor!" He ranted on for twenty minutes, waving his arms and throwing punches in the air. "Your dead comrades are lucky ones!"

Dan felt his knees weakening under the heat of the sun, and the man's voice seemed to fade into an echo.

"The Japanese warriors will enslave all Americans. Be prepared! We will start here. Know, cowards, that you must obey all orders, immediately, without question! You don't deserve to live. Japan will destroy your country, even if we fight a hundred-year-war to bring your defeat!"

When the speech was done, they were marched to a wire-enclosed stockade and turned over to the administration of their own officers. Next, they found themselves led to several dozen billets, which consisted of four bamboo walls, a dirt floor, and a thatched roof.

A room designed for sixteen men was now packed

with forty ill soldiers. Cogon-grass mats had been arranged for sleeping, but just as Dan and the others prepared to lie upon them, Japanese soldiers ordered them to be turned in.

"It seems even the smallest comfort will be denied." Dan sighed. His whole body ached. As the last of the daylight faded, he and the others finally settled on the bamboo floor, overlapping their legs in order to lie down.

"Boys, welcome to our hotel," the officer in charge called out. "Enjoy a good night's sleep."

But sleep was impossible. The sick and dying in neighboring billets cried through the night. For food. For water. For relief from their misery.

❧ ❧ ❧

Dan rose from his place on the floor, eyeing the others in the room. The roof consisted of grass matting, and the windows were no more than openings, letting in the reek of decay that hung in the air. Bodies continued to pile up by the day, faster than they could be buried.

It had only been a week since Dan had arrived at Camp O'Donnell. In that time, the prisoners had grown weaker, but the guards seemed to have grown stronger. And they relished tall GIs on bended knee.

The food at the camp consisted of *lagao,* a watery gruel made from rice, twice a day. It was half rotted before the soldiers received it. They also ate putrid camotes, a type of root barely fit for animal fodder. There was no salt. No water to wash the kettles. No soap.

To obtain drinking water, it was standard procedure to stand in line for six to eight hours a day for a canteen from the single pump. Additional water was also obtained from a river about a mile away. The river was four inches deep—slimy mud into which the overflow of the pit latrines seeped, with only a scum of water on top, which had to be boiled.

"We must do something about the water," Dan told their group as they finished their breakfast. "We need volunteers—groups of ten men to guard the river and to keep order. We also need to prevent the men from drinking the water before it is boiled. Hundreds are getting diseases."

"It is the young ones who are sick and dying," Gabe interjected. "They don't know or care about the importance of clean water." He leaned against the bamboo wall. "Some were sent here with only a few weeks of basic training, so they don't know that it's the stuff you can't see that will kill you."

"Let's do something about it. We can get the other groups to work together." Dan's hand trembled as he returned his spoon to his empty bowl, but he tried to ignore it.

"Why us?" Gabe's head seemed to flop on his shoulders as he turned to look at Dan. "Let someone else organize things."

"And let more people die? Come on. It's better than

just sitting around all day listening to the growl of our hungry stomachs. Besides, it's either water duty or corpse duty. Your choice."

Dan strode outside the building, hoping that others would follow. He scanned the enclosed area, actually missing their time in the foxholes under the trees. Although Camp O'Donnell sat in the middle of a lush jungle, it was treeless. In fact, the only sign of vegetation were the weeds that grew everywhere.

Dan covered his mouth and gagged as a horrid stench overpowered him. He willed his rice to stay down, at the same time standing at attention.

Four fellow prisoners passed Dan, carrying bodies in blankets that had been strung over a pole. A Jap guard followed close behind these stretcher bearers. "Speedo! Speedo!"

Humming along with the funeral procession were black and blue blowflies. Dan swatted as one buzzed around his face, and wished he could swat so easily at the menacing guards.

Twenty-Two

AT OUR ENEMY'S HEART

Tokyo bombed! Yokohama bombed! Kobe bombed! After four months of defeats in the Pacific War these words have abruptly electrified the pulse of America and started a chain of repercussions throughout the world. Up to the moment of this writing, to be sure, all the news has come from Tokyo itself; there is not a word of confirmation from any American, Chinese, or Australian source.

The important thing is that the battle is being carried to the very heart of the enemy. He is literally being "hit where he lives."

Excerpt from the *Washington Post,* April 19, 1942

The group of Brits and Australians squatted in a vast semicircle in the dusty main square of their camp as they did every Sunday morning, chattering as they waited. It had been two months since they were brought here, and their European fashions, once crisp with starch, were now brown, clinging to their bodies like used dishrags.

Natsuo watched as a mother tickled her small toddler, and his innocent laughter carried among the voices. *How can he laugh in this place?*

The day was bright and clear, the sun casting golden rays on the small huts surrounding the square, but a storm cloud filled Natsuo's thoughts.

After everyone had assembled, one thin Englishman, Charles Hayward, wearing a tattered, double-breasted suit, stood to speak. "America has bombed Japan."

Excited gasps sounded from the dusty group.

"A group of planes has attacked Tokyo in retaliation to the bombing of Pearl Harbor. That is all I know." He returned to his seat on the ground and lifted his hands, fending off questions.

Though no one dared cheer the announcement, Natsuo clearly noted pleasure in their eyes. A woman next to Natsuo nodded to her neighbor with a slight smile. She turned, expecting to see another prisoner behind her, and spotted Natsuo. The woman's eyes grew wide, and the color drained from her face.

Natsuo lifted an eyebrow, and though his chest constricted with the news, he would not let these English see his rage. He offered a small smile in return, and the woman quickly looked away.

Most had grown used to seeing Natsuo among

them. They'd heard rumors of his offered help to Anna, which, Natsuo had learned, was the name of the young Englishwoman. They'd become at ease in his presence, and it was exactly what Natsuo wanted. Like a weasel being welcomed into the chicken coop. It was a brilliant idea, if he thought so himself.

"I can hear more—learn of planned escapes or uprisings." Natsuo had bowed low before his superior. "They'll speak more freely to a friend than under a hundred lashes of the whip."

At first the commandant hesitated; then he finally agreed. "Yes. But alert us quickly when trouble arises! I'd hate to think your motives were anything less than a complete commitment to our emperor. Your honor is at stake."

"Yes, sir. Of course."

That was weeks ago, and his plan was working even better than he'd imagined. He was their friend. He knew their names.

When the excitement settled, they continued with their church service. Throughout the English prayers and sermon, Natsuo remained seated with his arms crossed over his chest. He paid no attention to their beliefs. Instead, he sat remembering an old Japanese saying: "After victory, tighten your helmet strings."

He wondered if perhaps his country had not tightened them enough.

"Why don't we close our service in a song?" said Dr. Bell, a well-respected physician, as he stood before the group.

"I fear no foe, with Thee at hand to bless," they sang. "Ills have no weight, and tears no bitterness. Where is death's sting? Where, grave, thy victory? I triumph still, if Thou abide with me."

Many rose and stood, their mouths belting out traitorous words. "Hold Thou Thy cross before my closing eyes; shine through the gloom and point me to the skies. Heaven's morning breaks, and earth's vain shadows flee; in life, in death, O Lord, abide with me."

Natsuo rose. *Point me to the skies.* He laughed to himself. *The only thing they will see coming in the sky is their demise.*

For even if this one American victory were true, it would be the imperial army who would dominate the air. Children of the emperor, offspring of the Rising Sun.

❧ ❧ ❧

"May is the rainy season." Tony peered up at the darkening sky as he helped Dan carry buckets of water to the billets. "Surely, the sky will open soon."

Finally, around nine o'clock, the sun did release its scorching grasp upon the earth, and the rain fell in torrents. It came as a gentle roar across the jungle, gaining momentum, building into a crescendo.

"Thank God for rain!" Dan watched the water flow outside his hut, turning the aisles between their billets into rivers. "Tell someone to put out the buckets!"

But soon he realized the rain was both a blessing

and a curse. With it came the cold. The prisoners huddled together under pieces of tin, ponchos—anything in an attempt to protect themselves.

"You okay, buddy?"

Gabe shivered next to Dan. His teeth chattered. "Never th–thought it'd be cold in this place."

Clouds covered the sky, and now the only lights came from the spotlights sprayed across the barbed-wire fences. Dan's only consolation was that at least they had a roof over their heads, while outside the night guards slouched in muddy shadows, receiving the full brunt of the rain. *Let them suffer for once.*

Dan ran a hand over his matted hair and turned to his side, avoiding the open sore on his left hip. He had another one on his right butt cheek. Sleeping on the bamboo had given him and most of the others these sores, which made finding a comfortable position almost impossible.

When they awoke the next day, the sun had returned high in the sky, blistering hot. It seemed as if last night's cold spell had been a dream. Dan curved two fingers and spooned rice gruel into his mouth, slurping the tasteless paste and licking it with his tongue.

"Sometimes I think of my mother's pumpkin pie, the crust just lightly golden and the bottom slightly undercooked, almost doughy." Dan took another bite. "She always said she should cook it longer, but she never did. She was always so afraid of burning it. Now I kinda like my pie that way."

"Pie can't beat my mama's spaghetti." Tony closed

his eyes, his fingers stopping midway to his mouth. "She simmers the sauce for two days, adding a little of this and a little of that until she considers it done."

Dan scanned their billet. There were no longer forty men filling their quarters. In fact, their numbers throughout the camp dwindled by the day, especially from the Zero ward, where sick soldiers were taken but never returned.

"I see that Baker and Evans are missing." Dan placed his empty bowl on the floor. "I'm going to miss their help with the water detail."

"We took them over to Zero. I don't think either of them had one conscious moment yesterday. But getting them across camp was quite a feat." Gabe attempted to brush clumps of mud from his ragged pant legs. "You should see the grounds. It's like a war zone. The gravediggers have only been going down three feet deep because of groundwater, and the rain last night washed mounds of bodies back up. And the blowflies crawling in and out of their mouths . . . I swear, if I ever get time alone with a Jap—" Gabe clenched his hands as if strangling an invisible neck, shaking it. "They will never know who did it."

Dan glanced at Gabe's thin arms and knew that even if his buddy had the chance, he wouldn't have the strength. Still, the same rage flowed through his own veins.

When they'd first arrived, shock and fear had occupied every thought. But hatred had taken fear's place. He wished there was a way to kill them. Every last Jap.

“I’ll be back soon.” Tony rose from the ground. “I’ll help with the water when I get back.”

Gratitude and worry fought for a place in Dan’s mind as he watched Tony leave. No one said it out loud, but they all knew. Tony had made a connection with someone on the outside. He often showed up with a few eggs or a small bunch of bananas. No one dared ask specifics.

“Be careful out there. You don’t want to slip up,” Gabe called after him.

“Heck. I’ll be fine.” Tony offered a wave. “The Lord only takes the good.”

The Lord only takes the good.

The words continued circling Dan’s mind as he led water detail. They sloshed around like the water in the buckets he carried back to camp, mocking him.

The path was slick, but he urged himself on, trudging as fast as he could back to their billet. It led him past the cemetery, called Boot Hill. Dan had managed to keep his eyes fixed ahead, focused on the back of Tony’s head, during the walk there. He’d seen enough death. Didn’t need another glimpse. But on the way back, he thought he heard movement from the tangled mass of recently buried bodies that had now resurfaced. By instinct he looked, only to see two vultures skittering from body to body.

“Get outta here!” Dan shooed them from the thin skeletal frames of naked American GIs tangled with Filipino soldiers.

They’d been buried naked because their clothes and

boots were too valuable to plant beneath the earth. Many bodies bore evidence of beatings on their backs, their shoulders, and even their faces. Dan paused, looking closer. One Filipino soldier appeared to have been beaten so severely that only half of his face was distinguishable. But the other half looked as if he slept.

Dan looked closer and realized it was Paulo's half face that stared up from the tangle.

"Oh, no." Dan legs faltered, and he sank to one knee. The buckets of precious water tipped and spilt into the dark earth.

Dan thought back to the last time he'd seen his friend. It had been on the march. Paulo had brought Dan food. Then he'd quickly moved on to help others.

Shouts erupted behind Dan. Curses due to the water Dan had spilt. But he didn't care. His gut ached. He knelt to the ground, smothered in the stench of death. And he knew Tony's words were true. *The Lord only takes the good.*

What Lord?

Surely, if there were a God, He wouldn't let things like this happen to His own.

Dan's shoulders shook, and he covered his face with filthy hands.

℞ ℞ ℞

Dan slowly trudged toward their billets at their new "home," Cabanatuan. Camp O' Donnell was behind him now. July 4th had been an independence day of sorts for him and fifteen hundred other men. Dan had to line up with others who seemed to be in the best condition and be checked and prodded for diseases such as dysentery and malaria. Dan was grateful he hadn't had a spell of yellow fever for the last couple of weeks.

After the inspections, the head Jap guard asked for volunteers for work detail in another camp. Dan, Gabe, and Tony had stepped forward in unison as the Jap guards eyed them. They'd discussed it before, knowing that survival meant finding a way out of O'Donnell. In Dan's mind, a worker would be worthy of food, and though the Japanese had been overwhelmed with the sheer number of ill prisoners at first, things could only get better.

And things had—slightly. At Cabanatuan, located on a hill on the other side of island, there was clean water, rice three times a day, adequate latrines, and a small hospital—never mind that they had no medicines or supplies. They were also under their own command. American officers took charge and divided the nine thousand men into platoons. Dan noticed the thin cheeks and saggy eyelids of those he worked with and wondered if he looked the same.

The sun was setting behind the lush, green mountains as he slowly trekked across camp toward his bamboo billet. Each building had a wide catwalk down the center. Two levels of sleeping bays, upper and lower, ran the length of the building.

Dan spotted Gabe leaning his scarecrow body against the opening of the doorway and hurried to his friend. Gabe grasped Dan's arm and led him to the corner of the building.

"I've been checking things out." Gabe's voice was raspy from lack of nourishment. "We could escape anytime. The perimeter isn't as closely watched as the Japs would like us to think. At some points they've even posted American sentries."

Tony approached, overhearing. "That's nuts." He shook his head. "It would be like escaping into the Everglades. Do you know how to survive in the jungle? Besides, the Filipinos get a hundred-pound bag of rice for every American they turn in, and they're as hungry as we are."

"But they love us. Did you see them waving the V for victory as we were trucked through Manila?" Gabe raised two fingers in the air.

"Most of them would help. Like Paulo, God rest his soul." Tony made the sign of the cross. "But as my mother always told me, it only takes one bad apple to ruin the whole bunch."

"What about Japan?" Dan leaned against the building and wiped a layer of sweat from his forehead. "I heard Doc say they'll be choosing crews to work in factories over there."

"Heck, if you think I'm going to help the Nips with their war production, you've got another think coming." Tony flicked a cockroach from the wall and stomped it.

"Not war production—normal factories," Dan insisted. "Besides, even if we could escape, we wouldn't be able to run. We don't have the strength, and where would we hide?"

Gabe nodded. "Guess you're right. Don't know how we'd find our way off the island anyway. Can't really swim to Hawaii." He grinned. "Although, I wouldn't mind stealing a Jap plane and—"

Dan gave him a firm glare.

"Okay, okay. Japan it is, then—if they will take us. Anything sounds better than this heat. But enough talk —we'd better get back to work. Gotta mend those fences. Can't let the prisoners get out."

As they turned to head back to the perimeter of the camp, shouts split the air.

Dan turned to see three men from their billet being jerked into the roll-call area at gunpoint by four Jap guards. Their hands were raised, and blood trickled down their faces. One man's eyes were swollen shut. Dan grimaced, remembering Paulo's face. More Jap guards ran up and down the rows of billets, motioning for the GIs to form a single line. Dan and the others had no choice but to oblige.

"This is what happens to those who try to escape," the Japanese translator called out in English.

"You!" One of the guards pulled an American from the line of spectators. He thrust his bayonet into the short, dark-haired private's hands. The guard made a jabbing motion with his hands toward the first escapee. The private froze, then shook his head.

The guard's face reddened, and his eyes bulged in anger. He motioned again, in jerking movements, obviously wanting the soldier to plunge the bayonet into the escapee's stomach.

"I–I can't!" the private wailed. "I won't." He shook his head, the bayonet shuddering in his shaky hands. The guard grabbed the bayonet, pulled out his pistol, and aimed it between the private's eyes.

"Please! No!" the man screamed. The guard casually pulled the trigger, and the soldier slumped to the ground.

The guard then tossed the bayonet to the next person in line, a man in his thirties with sergeant's stripes on his collar. Dan knew this man, had heard him talk about his wife and three boys. The Jap made the same thrusting motion toward the escapee's stomach. The soldier closed his eyes and with shaking hands stepped forward and thrust. A cry erupted from the escapee, and then a thud as he hit the ground. Still alive, the man moaned in pain. Dan looked away.

Another gunshot sounded as the next soldier made his choice—then another cry from the escapee as they moved down the line, growing ever closer to where Dan stood.

The next guy refused to even touch the bayonet. The gun was raised to his chest. "God bless America!" he cried as he hit the ground.

Dan turned away—staring instead at his worn boots and his toes sticking from the end. More alternating gunshots and cries from the escapees followed as they moved down the line.

Dan's heart pounded as a tall man only ten feet away leaned down in order for the Jap to get a better aim at his head.

"Go ahead, Nip. You can kill me before I'll hurt another American." The shot rang out, and the man slumped forward.

Dan knew what his decision would be. He'd never be able to live with himself if he took the bayonet into his hands and thrust it into a dying man.

Then he thought of her. *Libby.* He wanted to see her again. Be with her. He'd made a promise to return.

The guards were only a few men away when Japanese shouts filled the air. One of the officers strode across the compound, screaming words Dan couldn't understand.

Gabe leaned close to Dan's ear. "I think I recognize the word for 'work.' He's telling them to stop killing his workers."

With a wave of the officer's hand, they were disbanded. Dan moved as fast as he could past the two dozen bodies that now littered the ground. He raced toward the slit trench as bile surged up his throat.

How close he'd come to making one of the worst decisions of his life. He wiped his chin and chest, feeling ashamed.

Later that night, the sky was pitch-black when Dan felt Gabe's hand upon his shoulder. "You're shaking like a sapling in a hurricane. We have to get you to the doctor."

At first Dan believed it was the day's events that had made him so ill. Instead, the malaria had returned—full force. The heat that Dan remembered from earlier that day had been replaced with an icy chill that caused his teeth to chatter.

"What good will it do?" he moaned, shaking off Gabe's hand. "There's no medicine."

"Maybe in Japan things will be better." Gabe glanced into the eyes of Tony, who also hovered over Dan. "Doc says they might have more supplies, medicine too. He thinks the prisoners will be better taken care of."

Dan wrapped his arms tighter around himself and nodded, his cheek rubbing against the grass mat.

"Japan," he whispered. The thought both horrified him and gave him hope. Hope that dared to rise up, even in the darkest point of the night.

Twenty-Three

JAPANESE SEEK WORLD RULE
BY "DIVINE APPOINTMENT"

R*io de Janeiro, Brazil, Aug. 10—According to the propaganda fed to the Japanese people by the military clique that has seized control of the Japanese government, Japan is prepared to wage war for a hundred years and will not stop till the United States and Britain are crushed, till Japanese troops parade down Piccadilly and the Japanese Navy holds a victory review off New York.*

Though they are willing to concede the establishment of this divine rule may take some time and trouble, their doctrine is that Japan can never rest till that rule becomes an actuality, till every nation receives its "proper place," according to the principle of Hakko Ichiu, *which is to make the whole world one household under the paternal sway of the Japanese emperor.*

Today the Japanese "war gods" themselves are apparently prisoners of their own war propaganda and their own success.

Otto D. Tolischus
Excerpt from the *New York Times,* August 11, 1942

Dan attempted to calculate the days he'd been held captive. Including the march, his time in Camp O'Donnell, and Cabanatuan, he'd been a prisoner for four months.

Now he found himself in a new home. Bilibid Prison was an old Spanish penitentiary in the heart of Manila that had been condemned and shut down before the war. Deeming it fit for enemy prisoners, the Japanese had reopened it, filling it to capacity.

During daytime hours, Dan, Gabe, Tony, and the other prisoners toiled on the famous million-dollar Pier Seven, jutting out on the Manila waterfront. Their job was to load cargo ships for the Japanese, including the officers' trunks, crates, and satchels bound for southern outposts of the island via inter-island ferries.

Dan received more quinine for the malaria, and his strength rallied during his work on the pier. Perhaps the renewed vigor was due to the better rations of two rice balls a day. Or maybe it was the guards' "vitamin sticks" —thin rods cut from mahogany or coconut trees, which caused an awful sting to the head or back of one moving too slow.

"I'm tired of hauling all these crates. Let's try that trunk." Tony tightened the cord holding up his baggy trousers and hurried over to the large metal trunk.

Dan groaned but obliged. He approached one end of the trunk. Gabe took the other end, and Tony the face. Under the scrutiny of a Japanese guard who watched in the distance, they hoisted the trunk and muscled it up the plank, and then down a narrow flight of steps into the hold. Dan's frayed boots twisted on his feet, pushing his bare toes through the splits in the leather. He glanced across the trunk to see Gabe's face reddening under the exertion.

Dan chuckled. "You doing okay there, Gabe? You look more strained than you did last night at the slit trench." Dan felt the pull of the weight on his own arms and clenched his teeth as they moved into the underbelly of the steamer.

"Ha, ha. Very funny. I've got the heavy end of the load. What does this guy have in here anyway? Gold bars?"

Then Dan noticed that Tony wasn't carrying any of the load, but was jimmying the trunk's lock with a small pocketknife.

Tony's eyes darted from side to side. "Keep watch, will you?"

"Are you nuts? Stop—stop *now.*" Dan's heart pounded. He shifted his weight, and the trunk sank a few inches.

Tony's voice was harsh. "Ease up, will ya? I've almost got it. Come on, are you a soldier or a pansy?"

"I'm a pilot, remember?"

Having possession of a knife would be cause for Tony's execution. But breaking into an officer's baggage? It was enough to get them all killed.

They turned one last corner, and Dan heard a small click.

A grin filled Tony's gaunt face. "Thank you, darlin'." He slid the knife into a pocket.

They turned the corner, and a Jap guard leaned against the wall, lighting a cigarette. Dan paused briefly, but Tony had already resumed his hold on the trunk. They moved past the guard, and he glanced at them, unimpressed. Thankfully he hadn't noticed that the trunk was no longer latched, with the lid actually bouncing slightly as they walked.

"Do you want to get us killed?" Gabe hissed when the Jap was out of earshot. His eyes narrowed. "Close that thing!"

They entered the hull, and Tony nodded toward a large pile of crates. They carried the trunk around the corner, and in less than ten seconds, Tony had sifted through the top layer of items, removed a few small packages, and returned the lid with a click. Dan watched in amazement as Tony slid the items into a pocket sewn into the inside of his baggy trousers and trudged out of the hold, past the Jap guard, and back into the radiating sunlight as if nothing had happened.

Dan and Gabe followed him back to the dock. They watched as Tony bypassed a few small, boarded-up crates and again moved to a heavier trunk. They repeated the previous scene, Tony unearthing more items to stash in his pocket.

When they returned to the dock the third time that day, Gabe led them to another officer's trunk. "I was wrong. Tony's not trying to get us killed." Gabe hoisted one end. "He's trying to save our butts. I knew I liked this guy."

That night, holed up in their small prison cell, they spread their loot out on the scratchy gray blanket on Tony's mat and examined it by the light of the one bulb that shone down the hall. Three field-ration kits with compressed rice, dried fish, and other packages that weren't marked. But as long as it was food, they didn't care. There were also a few packages of pickled radishes and a dozen rice cakes. Tony divided the food among them, and they hungrily devoured it, depositing the packaging in the filthy slit trenches.

Dan lay on his mat, trying to block out the sound of shrews scampering down the hall, and smiled. Thanks to a good friend—and some Japanese officers—for the first time in months, his stomach didn't ache with hunger as he drifted off to sleep.

It was with eager steps that they hurried to the docks the next day. A Jap guard greeted them at the end of the pier, but instead of forming them into their typical work crews, he ordered them to the far end of the dock.

Dan instinctively bowed low as a Jap officer dressed in a white, starched uniform approached them.

"*Kirei!* Attention!"

He saluted. The rest followed suit.

A beautiful Filipino woman stood by the officer's side. She wore a colorful kimono, a perfect shade of cocoa that matched her eyes. It was the closest Dan had been to a female in months. His gaze moved up her body till their eyes met. Dan knew he should look away, but he couldn't.

The woman followed the officer with slow steps, lagging behind. As she passed Dan, she leaned close and whispered into his ear, "Don't hate me, Joe. I have children to think of. I do what I can to save them." Her perfume lingered as Dan watched her board the steamer, and a warm sensation stirred in the pit of his stomach.

Tony leaned close. "That was a sweet piece of heaven. Too bad she's not sticking around. I bet she'd be willing to help us."

Dan dragged his gaze from her parting steps and forced himself to scan the docks and large buildings framed against the azure Manila skyline.

"Yeah, I bet she would. But I'm sure there are others around too who are sympathetic to American Joes."

A few hours later, Dan watched a Filipino fisherman strain to lift a large bucket of fish from his boat onto the dock. Seeing that the guard was occupied farther down, Dan hurried over, grabbed the handle of the bucket, and hoisted it for the fisherman.

The Filipino's big smile revealed his mostly missing front teeth. "Thank you, sir."

Dan spotted the silver chain with a crucifix hanging over the Filipino's shirt, and it reminded him of Paulo. "You a Christian?" Dan pointed to the jewelry.

"Me Christian." The man nodded. He pointed to Dan. "You Christian?"

Dan made the sign of the cross as he'd seen Paulo do on numerous occasions.

"Yes, you Christian." The fisherman's grin broadened; then he shifted his eyes and looked both directions. He stealthily reached into his pocket and pulled out a ball of cooked rice with one hand and a handful of sugar candy with the other.

"Thank you." Dan glanced over his shoulder and winked at Tony. The guards hadn't seen the little exchange. They were too busy watching more women board the steamer farther down the dock.

Dan motioned to Tony, then palmed him the rice ball and candy. Tony slid them inside his pocket, and together they returned to loading cargo.

"Forget hitching a ride to Japan." Dan kept his voice low. "We need to stay here. The weather's no better, but I think we can find help. That officer's lady, the fisherman—if we can befriend a few people, maybe we can make it home after all."

Visions of Libby's warm smile filled Dan's head, and an aching filled the pit of his stomach. *Home.*

Dan let his mind wander as he continued to load more crates. He thought about the Filipino woman, who was only trying to keep her children alive. Of fellow soldiers at Cabanatuan being forced to choose between a comrade's life or their own. And he was starting to understand all too well how one's conscience took a backseat to the desire for food—for life. Yeah, he might make it back. But would he be the same person Libby had known and loved?

ঌ ঌ ঌ

Natsuo looked at his spread—fish, barley rice, dried figs, and a cup of green tea—yet his stomach turned, and he couldn't take a bite. This was his last evening meal at the guards' kitchen at Stanley. Tomorrow, the ship *Shi Maru* would be sailing from Hong Kong back to Japan, and he had a ticket to ride along.

Natsuo had a new assignment. Groups of American prisoners would be arriving by the thousands to work in the imperial homeland. His services were needed for communication with the GIs.

Natsuo blamed himself for the transfer. He'd done well, informing the commandant of men who stirred trouble within the barbed-wire fencing of Stanley. Now those men, and six hundred more from other camps all over Hong Kong, would be joining the voyage. They'd be transported in the ship's hold. Locked up like freight, while Natsuo reclined in his own cabin on the upper decks.

Natsuo lifted the cup of steaming green tea to his lips, taking it in slowly, feeling its warmth travel to his tense stomach. It wasn't leaving the English that bothered him—although he had to admit he'd miss seeing Anna. Rather, it was the idea of once again being in the presence of Americans.

How his memories loved them. How his mind hated them. He'd found friends in their ranks, but that was years ago. Now they'd imprisoned his sister, along with all Japanese on the West Coast. They'd locked up his niece and nephew too.

One thing was certain. They must pay. Pay for the

way they'd twisted his heart to their ways. Pay for any harm done to his beloved family.

Natsuo picked at the food on his plate, knowing he must eat to be strong. He needed strength for what he was about to face.

❧ ❧ ❧

The wind lashed Natsuo's words as he stood before the English prisoners the next morning, some arrived from Stanley, but most from the main POW camp Shamshuipo.

"You will be taken away from Hong Kong." He clasped his hands firmly behind his back. "To a beautiful country where you will be well looked after, well treated."

He scanned the faces before him. Some stared blankly, as if expecting this. Others wore wide-eyed expressions of shock. Had they really believed the rumors that they'd be released or exchanged? Didn't they realize no rescuers dared oppose the imperial army? Singapore and the Philippines had already fallen under their sword, and the news from the European Theatre was that England held on by a mere thread.

In a weary line, the thin prisoners boarded the ship —up the gangplank, then down into the hold. After the last hatch was locked in place, Natsuo stepped onto the deck. Soon the boat left the docks, and Natsuo watched the fragrant harbor fade into the distance. And though he was journeying back to Japan, he did not return as the warrior-god he'd hope to be.

❧ ❧ ❧

Rays of pink dawn and the buzzing of a dozen blue flies filtered through the small, barred window above their bed. Dan rubbed his eyes with the back of his hand, rising from Tony's side. His muscles ached from weariness as he stretched. It had been a long night.

Tony had tossed and turned from a high fever. When the headaches, vomiting, and full-body rash made their appearance, Dan knew it was dengue fever —a virus transmitted by mosquitoes. He'd witnessed its effects before.

Most healthy men took four weeks to recover. Would Tony last that long? Though their "extra rations" had helped them during the last month, the hard work and intense heat were taking their toll.

"We'll be back in a few hours. Keep your chin up." Dan patted Tony's sweat-drenched forehead.

Tony's eyes opened slightly, and he nodded. "I'm not going anywhere." He reached inside his pocket and pulled out the small pocketknife, handing it to Dan. "You might need this. Bring me back somethin' decent to eat. Preferably not those soup sticks." Then his eyes fluttered shut once more.

Dan slid the knife into the top of his boot. "I'll see what I can do."

Guards escorted him and the others to the courtyard in front of the prison, now packed with men. A new group of GIs must have arrived in the night. He scanned them, looking for familiar faces. They all looked like old men in tattered uniforms, tired and ill. Would he even recognize a friend's face? Would they recognize him?

As they lined up, Japanese officers in white uniforms with gold braid and combat medals strode down the lines, inspecting the group. They studied the rows, then stopped before Dan and Gabe.

Dan's body swayed, thinking that his end had come. Had someone noticed the missing rations? He wanted to look to Gabe for a reassuring gaze, but doing so would implicate them both. Instead he stared intently at the officer's shined boots and waited.

Nonchalantly, the officer before him lit a cigarette and blew the smoke in his face. Dan breathed in slow breaths, refusing to cough or brush it away.

The officer continued on, and Dan let out a slow sigh. The officer spoke in hurried Japanese to the interpreter, then quickly strode away.

The interpreter climbed to a small platform in front of the group. "You Americans are to be taken to Japan at the request of the emperor. We will leave at once!"

Guards circled them and motioned in sign language to line up two abreast. As the morning sun blazed, they marched through town, down the pier, and toward a small freighter. Dan read the words on the ship's side: *Toro Maru.*

Around him, the docks bustled with activity. Some prisoners loaded the gray ship with scrap metal, others with bags of rice. When they stopped, Dan's entire group was ordered to turn away from the ship, looking instead to the harbor. Dan's shoulders pressed tight on the right side to Gabe and to another prisoner on the left.

He dared to turn his head slightly and watch the commotion behind him. A long line of Japanese soldiers were passing hundreds of small, white cardboard boxes down the docks and into the ship's hold. Each one was labeled in Japanese.

"What's up with the boxes?" Dan turned his attention back to the waves rolling in the harbor.

The GI on Dan's left spoke. "They're remains of Jap soldiers. Each box supposedly contains a soldier's ashes. They're being sent home to shrines where they'll be worshiped as war gods."

Dan wiped his brow. "And just think. If we were killed we might get a write-up in the hometown newspaper."

"I'm already in there today." Gabe's voice was solemn. "It's my birthday, September fifth. They always run photos and stories about soldiers on their birthdays. I wonder what they have to say—or if they even know I'm alive."

"I'm sure your wife misses you. Your boys too." Dan rarely brought the subject up, seeing how it pained Gabe so.

"I loved being a dad." Gabe's shoulders quivered. "Coming home at night and seeing their smiling faces. Hearing their cries for 'Daddy' as I strode up the walk. I bet they baked a cake and—"

The sound of officers' footsteps approached, cutting off Gabe's words. For another hour, they stood in silence as the Japanese loaded the small boxes into the ship's hold. Out of the corner of his eye, Dan watched the thousands of boxes being passed down the line, each one representing a Japanese soldier . . . and a family back home.

Finally, when the last box was loaded, the guards hurried their prisoners up the wooden gangways.

"What about Tony?" Dan dared to look to Gabe as they boarded the ship. "I told him we'd be back. Who's going to take care of him?" The pocketknife in Dan's boot burned his ankle, and he regretted taking it.

Gabe didn't respond but only looked ahead. They knew too well what happened to weak soldiers left to fend for themselves. Even if Tony was lucky enough to be transported to the prison hospital, there was little food and no medicine. Dan's heart ached for his friend.

As the Americans boarded the ship in stunned silence, the guards motioned to a cargo area accessible by ladder. Dan and the hundreds of others climbed down into a compartment with gray metal walls and wooden planks over a steel floor. As he shuffled to one corner, Dan gagged as the stench of baking horse waste hit him. *The previous passengers.*

The heat in that steel "oven" was like being in the inside of a roasting pan. Within minutes, sweat dripped from his face and neck. With a loud *clang*, the hatch was closed and bolted, and all was dark.

Dan heard the sound of a lighter clicking, and the warm glow from a cigarette lit up the face of a weary soldier in a back corner.

"Four hundred ninety of us cusses, packed in here." He flicked his ashes to the ground, and low moans rose from those settling in. "Give or take a few."

"Tony is better off where he is. It will be at least a week's journey by ship." Gabe settled onto the planks, covering his nose and mouth against the stench. He glanced around. "As it is, I have a feeling some of us won't make it out of here alive."

Twenty-Four

WAFS IS LATEST WOMEN'S UNIT

Established on an experimental basis and without benefit of special legislation, the Women's Auxiliary Ferrying Squadron will consist initially of about fifty women, all of whom will be recruited on a civil service basis.

They will be used to ferry planes inside this country and, eventually, it is conceivable, may ferry bombers to bases overseas—although such action is not now contemplated.

The WAFS will be commanded by Mrs. Nancy Harkness Love, a beautiful 28-year-old blonde.

Christine Sadler, Staff Writer
Excerpt from the *Washington Post,* September 11, 1942

Libby's cheek touched the cool airplane window as she peered down at her first view of New Castle Army Air Force Base. The base itself sat on Delaware Bay, not far from downtown Wilmington. Five days ago she was cooking rubbery eggs and burnt toast for her father, wondering when she'd get a chance to fly for the army. Today—as the small prop plane taxied on the runway and as she pressed her hands over her brown herringbone tweed suit to remove the wrinkles—she knew.

Just a few days ago she'd opened the door to a delivery boy with a telegram. Her hands had trembled, and Dan's face had filled her thoughts. Instead, she'd been pleasantly surprised.

> AIR TRANSPORT COMMAND IS ESTABLISHING GROUP OF WOMEN PILOTS FOR DOMESTIC FERRYING STOP NECESSARY QUALIFICATIONS ARE COMMERCIAL LICENSE STOP 500 HOURS 200 HORSEPOWER RATING STOP ADVISE IF YOU ARE IMMEDIATELY AVAILABLE AND CAN REPORT AT ONCE AT WILMINGTON AT YOUR OWN EXPENSE FOR INTERVIEW AND FLIGHT CHECK STOP BRING TWO LETTERS OF RECOMMENDATION PROOF OF EDUCATION AND FLYING TIME STOP GEORGE ARNOLD COMMANDING GENERAL ARMY AIR FORCE WASHINGTON STOP

Libby took in a deep breath of cool, salty air as she stepped off the chartered airplane and viewed the base.

Construction progressed in all directions as asphalt swallowed up the cornfields around the perimeter.

"This place can accommodate ten thousand men." The narrow-faced pilot waited at the bottom of the narrow steps and raised his hand, offering it to Libby as she climbed down, satchel in hand. "But I have no idea where they're going to put the little ladies. Never imagined the army'd need to."

"I understand we're staying at a boardinghouse downtown." Libby released his grasp.

A petite blonde, no taller than shoulder-height to Libby, strode forward from a waiting car and stretched out her hand. "Betty Blake. And you must be Libby Conners. I read about you in the papers—your little rendezvous with the Japs. Come on, we've got a car waiting."

The chauffeured car carried them past the rows of buildings—supply depots, mess halls, administrative offices, and then a row of military barracks crowded with men. The organized chaos reminded Libby of how Wheeler Field used to be.

"Soon you'll meet Nancy Love." Betty's perfectly manicured fingers rolled down the window a crack, letting in the waft of musty sea air. "She's the one organizing this whole thing." Betty was dressed in a simple, light blue traveling suit, with short hair reminiscent of movie star Barbara Stanwyck's latest bobbed style.

Libby tucked a strand of hair behind her ear. "Nancy? I thought Jackie was in charge."

Betty winked. "That's a subject we don't want to

bring up in front of Nance. Last I heard Jackie Cochran was still in England, ferrying planes for the British. But of course I don't get into the politics of this organization. I'm only here for the flying.

"Oh, and a few other taboo subjects you don't want to bring up." Betty punctuated with a finger. "Plumbing in the barracks, and the fact that the finance office hasn't actually put us on the payroll yet. I've been here a few days helping out in the office. Nancy's about ready to blow her top."

"Anything else I need to know?" Peering outside the car window, Libby spotted a formation of P-40s in the air. *Oh, Dan. I wish you could see me now.* She imagined his huge grin, displaying that sweet dimple on his left cheek.

That's my girl, he'd say when he heard the news.

My girl. She touched the ring on her finger.

"Well, tomorrow you're up before the examination board." Betty jarred her from her pondering. "They'll check your flight log. Ask about your experience. They may even throw in a few questions about different kinds of aircraft. A piece of cake. Before you know it, you'll be part of WAFS."

"WAFS?"

"Women's Auxiliary Ferrying Squadron. Try saying that ten times fast."

Libby chuckled. "Hmm . . . maybe, after I'm certain I'm in."

❧ ❧ ❧

That afternoon, the other female pilots trickled into the boardinghouse one by one. Ruth Bennington arrived in a short-sleeved summer dress, with a big purse and a car full of trunks and satchels.

July Alexander, on the other hand, had one large duffel slung carelessly over her shoulder and a wide, easy smile. July, who introduced herself as "just a farm girl from Tennessee," was as sunny as her name.

"I've been running an airfield for five years, and I have to go up in front of an examination board?" Ginger Thomas's black hair fell straight to her shoulders, and her gray suit was tailored to fit her equally straight figure. "They've got to be kidding!"

In the end, eight female pilots circled the dining table at the boardinghouse that evening. The conversation began with polite questions about family and homes, but picked up in fervor when the subject shifted to planes.

Betty sat on Libby's right, Ruth on her left.

"So what got you flying, Ruth?" Libby asked.

Ruth's shoulders shook with laughter. She took a sip from her water glass and delicately placed her fork on the side of her plate. "Oh, that's easy. I knew my father just hated women who insisted on doing men's work. I signed up for a few weeks of flying lessons as a practical joke, but it turned into a passion I couldn't shake." She brushed her blonde hair off her shoulders. "I mean, what's better than having lunch with Mother and Father in New York, then flying down for dinner with friends in Philadelphia?"

The young woman across the table spoke up. "My husband, Jeffrey, was the first to take me up in a plane. I'm Annabelle, by the way."

"Your husband?" Libby didn't mean to sound so shocked, but the tall, thin girl with braids didn't look much older than sixteen.

Annabelle smiled. "Oh, yes, and I have two kids, Howie and Elizabeth. They're five and six and are staying with my mother while I'm away." Annabelle's voice quavered despite her smile. "With Jeff in England, I had to find a way to support the war effort."

Libby felt an instant connection with Annabelle, seeing the tenderness in her eyes when she mentioned her husband. "I'd love to hear more about Jeff. It must be hard."

The door opened then, and every head turned to watch Nancy Love, in a tailored suit and pillbox hat, stride into the room as if she owned the place. Her hair was prematurely gray, but her wide-set gray eyes showed a warmth Libby had not expected. She waved to the group, then leaned down to give Ginger a quick hug. Libby suddenly felt as if she were in the eighth grade again, vying for the attention of the most popular girl.

"Welcome, ladies." Nancy spread her arms wide. "You may have heard there's a war in Europe. England, France, Poland, Finland—they're all in trouble. In the South Pacific, things are no better. Island nations have fallen to the Japanese one by one."

She glanced at each woman seated around the table.

"That's where we come in. I told the War Department I could come up with fifty amazing women pilots. It's a small start, of course. But with your help, we're going to prove that women pilots can be a valuable asset to the war effort. Are you ready to knock them dead?"

The room burst into applause. Libby clapped the loudest.

Nancy pulled up a seat, and dinner continued. Laughter and conversation swirled in the air as they discussed ways to find more pilots and the types of planes they might possibly be flying. The women agreed that flying was not only a mental and physical challenge but also a spiritual experience.

Libby looked around the table and grinned. This time she didn't see competition. She recognized sisters.

Rose has to meet these women, Libby thought. *She would absolutely love this . . .*

Dan crawled to the overflowing waste bucket, his body convulsing as the little rice and fish he'd managed to choke down now forced itself back up. He wiped his face, moaned, then crawled over to where Gabe slept on the dirty floor. The man next to Gabe screamed out in pain. He suffered from beriberi, a deficiency of vitamin B1. The man jumped to his feet and stomped on the ground, attempting to stop the tingling of electric shocks in his feet and legs.

Mercifully, the hatch had been opened to let in fresh

air and light. Dan looked around, cursing the Japs for turning them into animals whose every waking thought centered around the food and water lowered to them twice a day.

Dan attempted to ignore the stomping man. Tried to ignore the sounds of five hundred men breathing. It grated on his nerves to the point that sometimes he wondered if he could stand it one more night.

He curled onto his side and instead tried to focus on the footsteps of Jap soldiers moving above him, letting last night's dream replay one more time.

He'd been healthy and strong once more, and to his captors' surprise, he'd climbed out of the hold, grabbed the neck of the guard, and squeezed until the Jap stopped breathing. As he did, cheers rose from the weak and dying below. Joining in were the cheers of the dead—Oliver, José, Paulo—the friends he'd lost. Then their voices rose in one huge cry for vengeance.

If it weren't for the hatch being opened for a few hours during the day, the men would have completely lost track of time. The hold was twenty feet high with no electricity; their eyes, now used to the darkness, were blinded every time the metal door above creaked open.

Seasickness added to their misery. The ship never ceased rocking. It sometimes creaked so loudly Dan was certain it would break apart. And with less than five square feet per man, soon the entire floor of the hold was covered in filth.

A week ago there'd been the sky, trees, ground, the

fence surrounding the perimeter of the camp, bodies continuously buried and clouds that seem to weep for them. Now no air, no sky, no ground to bury the bodies. Instead, the strong among them handed their dead up to the Japs, who tossed them into the sea, like the rest of the trash on the ship.

Shouts burst forth in Japanese. "*Sensuikan!* Submarine." A siren shrilled through the air. The ship's engines revved even harder and waited.

Panic seized the faces of the men around him, and some fell to their knees in prayer. They were locked inside a ship that sailed alone under the Japanese flag, with no life jackets, no chance.

It might be over soon. One direct hit and they'd be at the bottom of the sea, never to suffer again.

I'm sorry, Libby. Dan pulled the tattered photo from his sock and caressed her smile. *I tried. I did all I could to make it home.*

Twenty-Five

JACQUELINE COCHRAN TO HEAD TRAINING OF WOMEN PILOTS

Miss Cochran, long an outstanding flier, will be in charge of a program designed to create a pool of trained women pilots from which will be drawn, as needed, personnel for noncombatant flying purposes, to release as many men pilots as possible for combat and other important duties.

Formation of the Women's Auxiliary Ferrying Squadron, under the command of Mrs. Nancy Harkness Love, which was announced September 10, is part of the program for the utilization of this additional reservoir of trained pilots, it was explained.

Excerpt from the *Washington Post,* September 15, 1942

Libby scanned the room, noting the gray filing cabinets and bookshelves lined with aviation books and manuals. Eight groggy women pilots had walked across the airfield in the cool predawn hours, and now they were packed into Nancy's office like sardines in a can.

When Libby walked in, she noticed a bouquet of tulips on Nancy's neat desk centered between a black, three-line telephone and a blotter. Nancy stood behind her desk, but Libby could barely see her through the heads of the women.

Nancy began in a businesslike tone. "More pilots will be arriving throughout the week, and you'll all be starting out the same—from ground zero.

"In addition to meeting with the examination board, each of you will have to do a flight check with the instructor. They'll grill you on things like the stick, pedals, rudder, gauges, the concept of lift—kindergarten stuff. Any questions?"

"I have a question." Annabelle raised her hand. "When's lunch?"

Laughter filled the room. Libby had discovered that Annabelle, though tall and slender, had an even bigger appetite than her own.

Nancy's voice held a hint of amusement. "Ladies, there's a lot of work before lunch. In fact, within the hour, reporters will be arriving to interview all of you." She held up a blue flight suit that looked like a circus tent in comparison to the size of the women. "You'll change into these for photos. *Life* wants you to look as 'pilotlike' as possible."

"But those are men's flight suits," Ginger complained. "We'll look like a bunch of apes with our sleeves hanging to the ground."

"Well, there will be no official uniforms until we prove we can pull this off," Nancy said. "And . . . if you haven't heard, it's just been announced that Jackie Cochran will begin a new program to *train* new women fliers. But the first step will be proving the current pilots—you ladies—can pull it off. If all goes as planned, hundreds of trainees will be looking up to you as examples—literally." Nancy passed the uniforms around the room.

"One size fits all." July held hers to her shoulders. "Texas-size."

The women lined up to use the latrines situated behind the main office to slip into the flight suits. Betty was the first to go in.

"Oh, ladies." They could hear Betty's voice through the closed door. "How thoughtful . . . special sinks to hand-wash our undergarments."

Laughter filled the hall.

When they were all dressed in their flight suits, with sleeves and legs rolled up, the line of women walked out to the tarmac where a small group of reporters and photographers waited.

For the next several hours, they posed. Mostly they stood rigid in front of airplanes, trying to look like the tough pilots they were. For one shot, a cigarette-wielding photographer placed a map on the silver fuselage of the PT-19A trainer and had Libby pose as if studying it.

And, of course, they took several pictures of the girls circled admiringly around their mentor, Nancy Love.

Libby rubbed her cheeks, realizing they were actually sore from smiling.

"Miss Conners." A young female reporter strode up, tucking her pencil behind her ear. "I read about your exploits in Pearl Harbor. Any way we can get a few photos of you alone . . . inside one of those planes?"

Libby glanced at Nancy, who waved her on. She climbed into the plane.

"Okay, Miss Conners. Lean out and smile."

She did the best she could, sitting up on one knee to peek out of the cockpit.

"Great. Now wave at your fellow pilots," the photographer instructed.

Libby grinned and waved at the group. All of them waved back, except Ginger. Instead she tilted her face to the sky and checked out a formation of bombers passing overhead without so much as a glance in Libby's direction.

Later that day, the eight women were led one by one into the colonel's office for interviews with the examination board.

"Miss Conners, please enter. I'm Colonel Baker."

In addition to the colonel, several flight instructors and Nancy Love sat around the light-colored wooden table. They flipped through her flight log and asked a few questions. Libby smiled politely and answered. It was easy to see this was a mere formality.

"Well, Miss Conners, I'm pleased to say that as long as you pass your flight examination, you're in. Your four weeks of WAFS training will begin shortly."

"Thank you, Colonel Baker, Mrs. Love." She took the hand of each and gave it a warm handshake.

I'm in! Libby felt as if she were once more soaring over Oahu as she walked to the ready room where the other women waited. There was no need for them to ask how it had gone when they spotted the grin on her face.

Annabelle leapt from her seat and grabbed up Libby in a warm hug. "I'm so excited. I knew you'd make it. I'm in too. Just think—we'll be flying planes for the military! My kids are going to be thrilled, and my parents, too. I have extra paper, if you want to write to your family."

Libby felt her smile fade. "My mom's dead. But my dad would love to hear from me."

She hated lying to Annabelle, but it was easier than answering the hundred questions the truth always brought up.

Annabelle covered her mouth with her hand. "I'm sorry, Libby; I didn't know."

"Of course you didn't." Libby gave Annabelle's shoulder a reassuring squeeze. "It was a long time ago."

After the last of the interviews was complete, the jeeps arrived to take them across the airfield to the hangars. Libby's eyes widened as she spotted the rows of aircraft, from trainers to bombers and everything in between. She glanced at the B-17 on the runway and estimated that half a dozen cadets could fit inside it. Her mind immediately went back to the last time she'd been in a B-17. It had been cracked open on the airstrip at John Rodgers—fire, smoke, and men pouring from its side.

A few wolf whistles met the fliers as they approached the hangars. A group of pilots-in-training marched past, and Libby felt their eyes pursuing her, even with the baggy flight suit hanging on her frame.

"Ignore them, gals." Betty tossed her blonde hair. "The men on this base are off-limits. Not that we're interested in measly privates anyway."

The warm air was on their backs as they approached the hangar filled with Fairchild PT-19A trainers, painted in shiny silver. A new crop of journalists and photographers awaited their group.

"Now I know how Judy Garland feels with all the press attention." Annabelle twirled her braid. "Wait till my kids get a load of their ol' mom on the front page of the *New York Times*."

As the group circled the trainer, a stocky bald man wandered up to them. "I'm Jim Cook, one of your instructors. We're going to do a short flight test today. I'm aware that most of you have been instructors before, so it should be easy. Who wants to start?"

Ginger raised her hand, but the photographer turned to Libby.

"Miss Conners. What about you?"

Libby glanced at Ginger. "No, really. Why don't we give someone else a chance. I think Ginger—"

Ginger shrugged. "No, go ahead. It's obvious your fame precedes you."

The cameras flashed as Libby grabbed the parachute pack and slid on the helmet and goggles. With quick steps, she circled the plane for inspection. The PT-19 had two open-air cockpits. The student sat in the front cockpit and the instructor in the back. The instructor's job was to help with the controls and give advice through the headset.

Libby climbed onto the hard seat, buckling in, as the instructor climbed in behind her. Libby plugged in the headset. "Can you hear me, Mr. Cook?"

"Loud and clear. And please call me Jim," the male voice answered. "The plane's all yours. Take 'er up."

She moved through the motions as she'd taught her students a hundred times. *Remove control lock. Flip master switch to check fuel gauges and run flaps down to full extension. Turn fuel selector to ON position.*

As her sweaty hands readied the controls, Libby realized it had been over a year since she'd flown one of these larger planes.

Just like riding a bike. It all comes back once you get on.

When Libby gave the thumbs-up, one of the other WAFS cranked the propeller and pulled the wheel chocks away. Soon Libby was guiding the plane down the runway, then maneuvering it flawlessly into the air.

"Good work, Miss Libby. Can you do a few forty-five-degree turns?"

Libby followed his instructions; then she worked through some additional turns, climbs, and descents. It felt strange to be the student once more, knowing her every move was being critiqued. And it wasn't only *her* flying being judged. From now on, her every move would be representative of the WAFS program.

Jim's voice crackled through the headset. "Not bad. Women don't have as much upper body strength. I'm actually surprised by how well you are able to maneuver the plane."

"Really?" Libby turned the plane in a slow figure eight. "I'm not sure why. An airplane responds the same whether a man or a woman is flying it, don't you think?"

The instructor chuckled. "I suppose you have a point there. Go ahead and take her down. Let's see if you can land as well as you fly. And take it slow . . . I'm sure those newspaper people would like to take your photo coming in."

Annabelle stood at the door of the boardinghouse, acting as housemother, welcoming the girls as they entered.

"Just think. Ladies flyin' for the army. Yes, ma'am." She laid a hand on Libby's shoulder. "I think your face is frozen into a permanent smile." She grinned. "Hurry now, ladies. Freshen up. We need to get over to the officers' dining hall."

In the officers' mess, the ladies ate at a separate table, under the watchful eyes of dozens of men.

"I feel like a caged tiger at the zoo," Libby muttered to Betty.

"Worse than that." Betty peeked over the rim of her coffee mug. "I feel like I'm the one who will be pounced on, if they had the chance. I'm ready to get back and relax. How 'bout you?"

After a long soak in the blue-painted bathroom of the boardinghouse, Libby threw on her flannel pajamas and sank onto the sofa in the common area. Betty sat in a recliner, painting her nails the brightest shade of pink Libby had ever seen.

They chatted about the type of training they'd receive and the uniforms they'd be issued, and wondered if they'd be forced to make their beds the "army way" once they got into barracks.

Annabelle unbraided her chestnut hair and brushed it out. "Do you think we'll really move on base? I can't imagine bathrooms with—"

"The undergarment sinks?" July finished.

The girls laughed.

"There's a lot to write home about—that's for sure," Betty said.

"It's no use writing my folks." Ruth's silk pajamas fit her curvaceous frame like a glove, and a satin eye mask was propped on her head.

Libby hadn't realized one could look so glamorous for bed.

"Daddy refuses to answer my calls. Mother says he swears he's sending the chauffeur for me. I told her I'm not leaving, and Dad can't make me. I'm twenty-four, for goodness' sake—not a little girl."

"Golly, my dad thinks this is the cat's meow." July's face was scrubbed clean, and though her hair was pinned up in the same way as Ruth's, on July it looked frumpy rather than chic. "I called him this afternoon. He scrimped and saved and sold extra cows to get me my lessons. He's thrilled it's paying off."

Ginger had come in during the last exchange, and she ambled into the center of the room, puffed out her chest, and held an imaginary cigar to her lips. "No daughter of mine is going to take part in a women's ferrying unit . . . unescorted."

Laughter filled the room.

"I'm with Ruth," Ginger said. "My dad thinks this is about the dumbest thing I've ever done."

"What about you, Libby? What does your father think?" Annabelle lay on the carpet on her stomach with her chin propped on her fists.

"My dad's a crop duster in northern California. I was flying with him from the time I could say 'up.' He always let me turn the key to the ignition." Libby chuckled. "I used to think there was a sleeping dragon that stirred to life under the cowl."

Libby pulled her legs to her chest and leaned her head back against the sofa. "He's going to be real proud.

Every time we'd go up, he'd always say the same thing: 'This is the future, Libby-girl. Let your dreams soar.' "

There was silence for a moment; then Ginger spoke. "That's a sweet story, Libby, really it is, but we'd better get some shut-eye. Morning's going to come early, and if there are more photos planned, some of us better get our beauty sleep."

Libby didn't respond, but like the others she rose and went to her room.

Twenty-Six

CURVES IN COVERALLS:
WAFS WON'T HAVE NATTY UNIFORMS,
SAYS DIRECTOR; THEY'RE STILL AN "EXPERIMENT"

An East Coast Army Air Base, Sept. 16. Sorry, girls —if you join the WAFS, you won't get any beautiful uniforms. It's going to be coveralls for flying and "standardized" skirts for the classroom.

However, there won't be any curfew, and when the day's work is done, you can dress as you please.

You will get to bunk in brand-new quarters, originally designed for bachelor officers, and there will be full-length mirrors in the bathrooms, Venetian blinds at the windows, and a few scattered rugs to "feminize" the place.

Mrs. Nancy Harkness Love, director of the WAFS, related these facts today in announcing that some 25 women pilots are expected to start training here Monday as qualified members of the newly organized Women's Auxiliary Ferrying Squadron.

In addition to Mrs. Love, five women pilots already have qualified, and it is expected about 20 more will be recruited this week.

Jane Eads
Excerpt from the *Washington Post,* September 17, 1942

"They have got to be joking." Ginger rose from the desk in the small classroom and placed her hands on her hips.

Nancy and the instructor had just left the room, and the black-haired pilot wasted no time expressing her thoughts.

"We're only qualified for cadets and trainers? I've heard that in Britain the ATA girls are flying more than a hundred types of planes, and all we're going to be doing is shuttling these small potatoes?"

July joined in, but without Ginger's penchant for drama. "It's bad enough we have to spend every morning going over course work that we once taught."

"Yes, but in the afternoons, we *will* begin to ferry planes from factories to the bases where they're needed." Libby tapped the pencil to her lips. "It's a start anyway."

"Correction. We get to ferry only every other day." Ginger paced to the front of the small classroom, glancing at the bulletin board with pinups of the recent articles about the WAFS. "We still have flight instruction on the odd days. It's just not fair. They're spreading out over a month the same training that male pilots finish in nine days. Sometimes I just wonder if this whole thing was one big publicity stunt to make women feel they're valuable in the war effort."

Ruth raised her hands, attempting to calm Ginger. "Just because we won't be ferrying pursuits and bombers now doesn't mean it won't happen eventually. We're under a three-month probation. From there, who knows? And as for the training . . ." Ruth sighed. "We all know the stuff. Why don't we just grin and bear it?"

"Besides," Betty interjected, a twinkle in her eyes, "I overheard the colonel telling Nancy that our barracks are ready. After today's class we get to move in."

Later that afternoon, the passel of women pilots descended upon Bachelor Officer Quarters 14, like sorority girls newly arrived at college. Libby climbed from the jeep, and her heart sank as she took in the pea green structure that looked like a two-story railway car derailed in a muddy, treeless field. It was a long way from the tropical beauty of Hawaii.

She dropped the satchel to her feet and turned to Annabelle. "Home sweet home."

Annabelle lowered her chin and gazed at the structure with cocked eyebrows. "We're paying $4.50 a week for this?"

The women quickly toured their new home. The large bathroom featured toilets and shower stalls without doors. There was also a line of urinals.

"Great, just what we need." Ruth scrunched up her nose.

There was a large main common area, dozens of small rooms with two beds in each, and two phones—one upstairs, one down.

Libby and Annabelle soon found a room to share. Annabelle stuck her pinky through a crack in the pine-studded walls. "Libby, look. I can see through these gaps. Can you imagine what it will be like when it rains? Or wait. When it snows?"

Libby settled onto an iron cot with a sagging mattress. She looked around, noting the two dressers and a rod for hanging clothes. "Let's just hope they hand out snowsuits with our uniforms."

Betty entered, pinching her lips together in a perfect imitation of the colonel. "If the WAFS are to succeed, your personal conduct must be above reproach. No male visitors inside the barracks." She shook her finger and deepened her voice. "There will be no rumors that my pilots are 'playing house' in government property."

Libby cast a sidelong glance at Annabelle, and they burst into laughter. Libby jumped to her feet and saluted. "Yes, sir. You can count on me."

Annabelle followed suit. "Me too." She lowered her salute and leaned in close. "If you haven't heard, we're spoken for, sir. *Our* men are off winning this war."

"Very good. Carry on." With a salute and an about-face, Betty left the room.

Libby instantly sobered. "I hope that Dan is still fighting. At least in spirit."

Annabelle crossed the room and sat down beside Libby. "We are going to win this war, you know. And as for our guys, they're going to make it back just fine."

"Do you hear from Jeff much?" Libby leaned back against the wall, feeling a cool breeze from outside hit her neck.

"Last I heard he was in London. He's been over there for nearly two years—joined the Eagle Squadron even before we were in the war. But as of last month they were incorporated into the Army Air Corps."

"It must be hard—being apart for so long. It's already been a year since I've seen Dan. I'm not sure how much longer I can take."

Annabelle fiddled with the hem of her blouse. "Harder than I ever thought. At least I hear from Jeff—he's good about sending letters and v-mail. It would be worse not knowing."

"You want to see some photos of Dan?" Libby got her satchel and pulled out her snapshots from Hawaii. She spread them before Annabelle on the thin army blanket. "Here's one of us on the beach. And one of Dan in his uniform." Libby peered over Annabelle's shoulder. "Doesn't he have the best smile?"

"Yes, very handsome indeed. You two look so happy." She handed the pictures back to Libby. "He looks like a nice guy. Tell me why you fell in love with him."

Libby laughed as she took some thumbtacks from among her things and tacked a photo of Dan to the wall. Then she sank down onto the bed.

"You mean besides the fact that he's a handsome flier?" She took a strand of brown hair and twirled it between her fingers. "Dan made me feel admired and appreciated. I didn't have to prove myself. He encouraged me without making me feel pressured." Libby paused and closed her eyes. "I've never felt safer than when I was with him."

Annabelle's eyes filled with sympathetic tears.

"I wish I knew for sure that he was . . . okay."

Her friend rose and pulled a handkerchief from her suitcase. "Oh, Libby. I'm glad to know there's someone else who understands. I'll remember to pray for your Dan when I pray for Jeff."

Libby flopped backward onto her pillow and spread her arms wide. "I'd give anything to know how Dan was doing. To let him know I still love him, and I'm waiting for his safe return."

❧ ❧ ❧

Dan's pocketknife, the one from Tony, had carved fourteen marks on one of the wooden beams on the floor, representing the days they'd been in the hold of the *Toko Maru*. Unable to see them in the dark, he caressed the last line with his fingers, realizing that perhaps it might be the final mark.

The engines felt different; they had slowed almost to a gentle purr.

From the stir of bodies, Dan knew the others sensed it too.

"Charlie," a voice called out, "what's the news?"

A few days into the trip, they'd discovered that one of the men, Charlie Patrickson, knew how to speak

Japanese—or at least could understand it. Since then, Charlie had been their connection to the world outside the hold, creeping up the ladder to listen to the Japanese sailors at work.

Even though Dan couldn't see Charlie in the dark, he could hear the sound of his boots on the ladder. Japanese voices called out, as orders were passed around the ship. The GIs in the hold were silent, waiting for the interpretation.

"Gosh dang, we aren't in Japan. We're at a place called Takao, Formosa. We're docking here to make repairs."

Formosa! Formosa was only six hundred miles from Manila —a day's flight in his pursuit. And it had taken them fourteen days to get this far? Dan cursed under his breath and banged the back of his head against the wall.

They could hear Charlie's descent on the ladder. "And a good thing we're stopping too," he declared. "I think the only thing binding this piece of rust together is the coat of paint they applied before leaving Manila."

The engines quieted, and voices around the hold rose in disgust.

"Wait. There's more," Charlie called out. "We'll be getting out. They need workers while the ship's getting fixed." He stopped talking as the hatch opened.

Bright sunlight flooded in. Dan shielded his eyes against the sudden glare, stood, and stretched his legs. "Anything. I'll do any type of work to get out of this place."

He reached a hand toward Gabe, pulling him up.

"Me too," Gabe groaned. "Especially if they add in a bath."

Dan shuffled forward, feeling pressed on all sides by foul-smelling bodies. "Since you're dreaming, you might as well wish for hot water and soap."

With as much strength as they could muster, the men shuffled forward, chins lifted, eyes eager for a view of the outside world.

Libby sat in the ready room and stared at the forms spread before her on the table. One thing she learned was all AAF planes had a pocket on the right side of the cockpit for Form 1. It listed each plane's takeoff point, landing point, and duration of flight. The other side of Form 1 was Form 1-A. A red diagonal line anywhere on the page meant the plane had a defect. If there was a red X, then the plane was unfit to fly. She flipped over a few pages, then looked at her notes, trying to remember which exact information went into each form.

"Having fun?" Annabelle peeked over Libby's shoulder.

Libby craned her neck, trying to loosen up the stiff muscles. "Just trying to figure this out. There are all these mysterious blanks . . . for the serial number, altitude, wind direction."

Annabelle took the seat next to Libby and spread out her forms. "Not counting the forms for weather delays. Or the RONS—remain overnight forms."

Ruth walked over from where she'd been sitting cross-legged in a chair, her nose stuck in a thick romance novel. "Ron? Oh, I remember him." She pressed the novel to her chest. "Yeah, he did want me to stay overnight on more than one occasion. But I told him absolutely not. I have standards."

The women were laughing as Ginger strode into the room and settled into a chair. "Just like high school," she said. "Are we talking about boys again?"

Ruth placed a hand on her hip. "How did you guess?"

"Did you hear about the new officers' club that's supposed to open next month? They'll have a bar, and tables for cards, and dances once a month. I've been dying for a drink. This place is dryer than my granny's house on the Sabbath."

"The dances sound fun." Annabelle stacked her forms into a neat pile. "But I really don't drink."

Ginger kicked her feet up on the table. "That's right; you're one of those religious types. I saw you with your Good Book the other morning." She pulled a cigarette from the pack in her flight suit.

Libby felt heat rising to her cheeks. "Ginger, what was that for? Annabelle doesn't act like she's any better than the rest of us. We're all in this together."

Ginger flicked the cigarette to the table, rose, and pointed her finger directly in Libby's face. "You should talk. Just because you happened to be in the right place at the wrong time, now you're the glory girl of the whole unit." She moved toward the doorway, then turned to look back at the others. "I want to fly, that's it. I'm not here for slumber parties and girl talk."

Ginger slammed the door behind her, and no one moved as they listened to her stomp down the hall.

Ruth placed a hand on Libby's shoulder. "Don't take it personally. I think she's afraid to get too close to anyone. She doesn't want to get hurt again."

"Hurt again?" Annabelle said. "What happened?"

"Don't you know?" Ruth glanced toward the door. "Ginger's husband and little girl were killed in an automobile accident just a few months before she got her WAF telegram in the mail. She was in the truck with them, but she hardly got a scratch. Someone told me she wasn't planning on coming, but she couldn't handle living in her empty home."

Annabelle picked up the flattened cigarette and plopped it in the trash. "Poor Ginger." She crossed her arms tight to her chest. "I can't imagine losing one of my little ones. Knowing I'd never see their smile—or hold them in my arms again."

Libby sank down into the chair, angry with herself for letting her mouth run loose. "All I can see is Dan's face. His smile. Boy, do I feel like a jerk."

"Just when you think you've got someone figured out, you discover things aren't as they seem at all . . ." Annabelle stood behind Libby and placed a hand on her shoulder. "All of us have hurts, some of us deep ones. Poor Ginger."

"I guess it's easier to try to pretend the pain never happened," Ruth added.

“But it never goes away.” Libby patted Annabelle’s hand. “The pain has a way of resurrecting itself when you aren’t looking.”

Twenty-Seven

AXIS GOALS: THE UNKNOWN FACTORS

For the Axis this is a war of expansion. Our enemies have made no secret of that fact. Germany and Japan, densely populated industrial nations, set out with brutal frankness toward the conquest of (1) essential raw materials needed for industrial and military self-sufficiency and (2) manpower to furnish not only crude labor but also markets for industrial products.

At the Japanese end of the Axis, the raw material and population conquest seems to have been put through to a degree even greater than Germany has attained. Japan now has everything needed for self-sufficiency, including oil. Territorial and political expansion has been sufficient to set up a great empire, provided Japan can go over to the defensive and gain the time needed to organize and consolidate the gains.

Japan is potentially a tremendous mass producer, but at this moment lacks the plant to compete on even output terms with Britain, America, or Germany.

Paul Schubert
Excerpt from the *Washington Post,* October 14, 1942

A lone seagull landed a few feet from Natsuo as he stood at the dock, watching the blindfolded American GIs stagger off the small ship, awed that almost five hundred of them had been packed in the hold. They tottered like cripples and stank worse than barn animals. It was hard for Natsuo to believe they were the same people he'd once lived amongst.

Then he reminded himself of the truth. These soldiers were the sewage runoff from a filthy nation. Scum from a country of impurities. Natsuo had heard that phrase often during training. He turned his back and covered his nose at the sour scent of their bodies.

In contrast, his own men, the guards escorting these prisoners, looked beautiful in their pressed green uniforms. Their black hair and golden skin were examples of the purity of the Japanese race.

We are pure. We are untainted by intermarriage, uncontaminated by immigration. Natsuo puffed out his chest, proud to be Japanese. *Our land is the Land of the Gods, which His Majesty the emperor so graciously rules. A land to be protected from such filth as this.*

The words of a warrior's song ran through his mind, and he hummed along.

Even if the enemy comes in the millions,
They're all a pack of fools,
And even if they're not a pack of fools,
We've got justice on our side.

Natsuo squared his shoulders, ready to return to work. He'd been allowed to return home to his father's noodle shop for three days upon his arrival on the mainland. Everyone rejoiced over his work for the emperor, and many neighbors asked the same question. "Have you seen the *Kichiku Bei-Ei,* the American-English devils?"

Their question was a test. The entire neighborhood had been aware of his schooling in America and knew that his sister still lived there. Natsuo said what he had to. Said what would soon be true.

"I haven't yet, but when I see them I promise this: I will kill the American animal. After all, who better to hunt prey than one who knows their habits?"

❧ ❧ ❧

Dan's head lifted, and he fought the fog that clouded his mind, hearing the ship's horn blare two short and one long blast. The shrill was followed by loud Japanese voices giving commands.

In addition to the voices, they heard more motors and horns from other ships. They felt the jarring of a pilot boat leading them into the harbor. Finally, the rolling motion of the water ceased.

Voices and movements grew louder as the hatch opened. Dan pushed to the front, hoping Gabe was behind him. He blinked against the sun as he climbed to the top of the ladder. A Japanese guard pressed on his shoulders, keeping him from climbing completely onto the deck. Dan took a breath of clean air, exhaling the foulness from the hole. The guard slipped a blindfold over his eyes. Dan struggled onto the deck the best he could, his movements sluggish.

The first time they exited from the ship's hold had been on Formosa. There they'd worked for nearly two weeks on a detail picking bananas, loading them into another of the ship's cargo bins—one that was far cleaner than the hold they were locked in. The worst part had been the constant eyes upon them as they worked. Dan hadn't been able to take one bite of the delicious fruit.

Another three weeks of transport, and this was the real thing. Japan. If Dan's calculations were correct, it was October 14. Less than one year ago he'd arrived in Manila; now—according to Charlie—they were at a place called Moji, Japan.

Dan instinctively stretched out his arms as the guard led him off the ship. He felt the downward slope of the gangplank and reached for a rail to steady him. There was no railing, but his fingers caught on the tattered shirt of a man walking beside him.

"Steady there."

The voice was Gabe's. They were still together.

The damp coolness of the coastal valley surprised

him. As they walked, Dan's ears perked up to the sounds of the harbor. He could hear the rumble of large ships—perhaps even aircraft carriers and destroyers. Now he understood why the Japs had blindfolded them. He also heard the whispers of female Japanese voices. He tried to imagine what their pitiful group looked like to the women—emaciated bodies, tattered clothes, filthy and stinking.

When the blindfold was finally removed, Dan looked around, taking in the streets of the Japanese neighborhood. The small houses were bamboo with thatched roofs. A few municipal-type brick buildings intermingled with the houses. Automobiles were parked along the paved streets, and red-and-white flags lined the roadway, whipping in the wind like snake tongues.

The guards motioned for them to line up in rows of three and march. But their marching was more like a stagger. The ground seemed to sway under Dan's clumsy attempts at keeping step.

As they walked through the streets, huge crowds of Japanese gathered. Civilians gawked and pointed. Women muffled laughs. Old men and children swung heavy sticks, striking those who wobbled along the sides or in the rear.

"Hayaku, hayaku!" the guards shouted. "Faster, faster!" Hustling as quickly as they could, they finally reached their destination. One-story cinder-block barracks stood in neat lines. Surrounding the barracks was a six-foot-tall wooden fence, topped with two feet of

barbed wire. Behind that, beautiful green hills jutted from the earth.

So this is Japan.

In the open courtyard, they were ordered to undress. Dan did so, making sure the pocketknife and photo of Libby were safely tucked in his socks.

As soon as they undressed, a group of jabbering Japanese women hurried out to spray them from head to toe with disinfectant. The women wore coveralls with masks over their faces and gloves on their hands. In spite of the masks, Dan got the gist of their lively chatter. He felt his face redden, and he attempted to cover his genitals.

He cleared his throat and turned to Gabe. "How nice! The last woman to see me naked was my mother when she changed my diapers . . . I wish I could thank these ladies for a good time."

When they were finished being sprayed, Dan grasped his thin arms around his equally thin body and hopped from foot to foot, shivering in the crisp air. Bits of gravel had stuck to his swollen feet, causing him to wince in pain.

Finally, they were handed clean clothes and told to dress. Dan and Gabe glanced at each other, then back to the Japanese-style clothing. They held up the shirts and pants—all one size. Dan slid it on, amazed that the clothing fit around the waist and chest. It was far too short in the arms and legs, of course, but it was clean.

The last piece of clothing was a strip of white cloth, nearly two feet long and a foot wide with a string at one end. Dan turned to Gabe. "What's this? A turban?"

Gabe chuckled, unbuttoning his pants. "Dan. It's like a loincloth. You tie the string around your waist and pull the other end of the cloth up. Then through and over."

Dan undressed and tried again, this time finishing his outfit off with the typical Japanese rubber-and-canvas work shoes that buttoned on the side and had a split section for the big toe. His heels hung off the back.

Dan ran a hand down his bearded face, then spread his arms out, turning to Gabe. "Well, how do I look?"

"Honest?" Gabe cocked an eyebrow and blew into his hands for warmth. "Like a piece of crap."

"Yeah." Dan smirked, taking in Gabe's long tangled hair, thick black beard, and sunken cheeks. "You too."

When everyone had dressed, the group was herded to an enclosed area. Dan paused, wanting to shout a hallelujah as he saw the spread of food awaiting them. Hot rice, fresh water, bowls, chopsticks, and hot tea in tin cups. He was sure he'd never seen a more beautiful sight in his life—except for Libby, of course. Although after so many nights apart, the memory of her was beginning to fade.

After they finished their meal, they were led into the barracks, where three men were forced to share each bunk. Gabe and Dan shared with another soldier they didn't know. They slept head to foot to make more room.

"How long did you know Libby?" Gabe's voice whispered in the dark.

Dan turned to glimpse his friend's face over the pair of feet between them. The question didn't surprise Dan.

Seeing the Japanese women, getting clean and fed, had made the men feel as though they were back in the land of the living.

"It's been over a year since we met, and we only had four months together. But it seemed like I'd known her forever. Being with her—" He broke off.

"What?"

"Never mind. It's corny."

"Tell me."

"Well . . . she reminded me of Thanksgiving."

"Thanksgiving?"

He could hear the smirk in his friend's voice.

"Yeah, you know that feeling when you glance around the table, with a full stomach, and see all the happy faces of your family? I used to think, *It can't get any better than this.*"

Gabe chuckled. "Actually, with my brothers, their wives, and all our kids, Thanksgiving was like a Ringling Brothers three-ring circus—only without the tent, or sawdust, or elephants, for that matter."

"But you know what I mean, right? It's like contentment, comfort, and expectation all wrapped into one."

"Yeah, I know that feeling. But it's been so long. Sometimes I think Joyce is only an illusion. I wonder if she's still out there, thinking about me like I'm thinking of her."

Dan's throat tightened. "I don't wonder. I know Libby's out there—up there—tearing up the sky. I just hope I make it out of here."

Tomorrow he'd face reality again and hide any hint

of his feelings. The Japs could sense weakness. They feasted on GI emotions like a bird of prey flipping over its kill to reach its soft underbelly.

"'Night, Gabe," Dan finally said.

"Good night. Sweet dreams."

Dan closed his eyes. "I sure hope so."

❧ ❧ ❧

Dan had been dreaming of a kiss, but it was a strong hand across his face that woke him to another dark morning. His breath misted before him, and his heels stung from the cold of the stone floor as the guards prodded them through the long, windowless room, screaming and waving their fists. No matter how many mornings he'd faced such awakenings, he'd never gotten used to these human alarm clocks.

After a breakfast of slushy brown rice and tea, they were hurried onto a waiting train. Dan thought how ridiculous this group of hundreds of Americans must look with bony legs sticking out the ends of their too-short pants. By the light of the rising sun, the guards motioned for them to board—not in the cattle cars in back, but in the regular coaches. Dan sat down, sinking his aching body into the red, cushioned seat near the aisle. The soldier near the window lifted his thin hand to the blackout curtains hung in front of the glass.

"Uh, I don't think you should—" Dan warned, but before he could get the words out, a guard was upon them, jamming the butt of his rifle into the man's fingers. When the guard hurried away, Dan leaned over. "I think those curtains are there for intelligence reasons. They don't want us to spy on them."

The man held his fingers to his chest, blood staining his light green shirt. "Thanks for saying so. A little late, don't you think?"

"Sorry." Dan leaned his head back, and his body relaxed as the train pulled out, speeding from the station with a gentle sway.

He must have drifted off, because in what seemed like only minutes later, bento boxes were handed out to each man. Dan opened his meal box made out of balsa wood. Inside he found rice, pickled seaweed, pickled cherries, and even a pickled miniature bird. He hungrily ate every bit, especially relishing the pure, white rice—not the slop they'd been living on for so many months.

Even though they couldn't see outside, Dan knew from the slow, upward chugging of the train that they were heading into the mountains. Every so often, he'd hear a loud hissing noise as the train stopped to pick up civilian passengers, loading them into other cars.

Six hours later the train whistle blew, and they disembarked. He found Gabe, and they joined the masses of GIs lining up, three abreast. As they began marching through the village nestled into the hillside, Gabe let out a couple of raspy coughs.

"You okay, man?"

"I'm fine, I guess." Gabe pointed toward the village. "Reminds me of photos in one of my sons' storybooks." He scratched his dark beard. "Andy and William loved that story." He coughed again, then quieted and stared out at the miniature bamboo homes with their curved-up roofs and gnarled trees dotting the roadside.

In the green rolling hills, squatting people dropped their hoes and scurried from fields and yards to investigate the Americans. A little boy ran up, his eyes almost closed as he snickered. He rolled up his pants and rubbed his face as if feeling a beard. Then he started marching alongside, slumped, limping. Dan ignored him and kept walking. The air was frigid. He rubbed his hands up and down his arms for warmth. After an hour of hiking the increasingly stony road in ill-fitting shoes, his feet ached. How much farther before reaching their new "home"?

Gabe hacked like a barking seal as they marched. His face had turned pasty white.

"Are you okay?" Dan slowed down.

Gabe's shoulders shook in another fit of coughing. "I don't know if I can make it."

"Sure you can." Dan slung his friend's arm over his shoulders and helped support his weight. "We've made it this far. It's no time to give up now. Besides, after that train ride I'm thinking things will get better."

After a five-mile march, they approached a large compound. Gray clouds replaced the crystal blue sky, and the Japanese guards hurried them inside barbed-wire gates with shouts and waves of their bamboo sticks.

Gabe limped along, and Dan pulled on his arm. "Come on, we don't want to get stuck in back."

Too late. With a swing of his stick, a guard slammed

the rod into Gabe's back. The force knocked him to the ground. Gabe sprawled, hitting his face on the packed dirt, and cried out in pain. The guard stood over him, screaming words of Japanese they couldn't understand. Dan rushed over and helped Gabe to his feet. Amazingly, the guard allowed it. Dan hurried, nearly dragging Gabe through the gates.

A barbed-wire fence circled the camp with guard towers. Three dozen barracks were arranged in neat, straight rows. The camp was clean, but a chill traveled down Dan's back as the gates closed behind them, locking them in once more.

Once inside the gates, the guards motioned for them to circle a small platform. A Japanese officer mounted the wooden block with an interpreter at his side.

The officer spoke in Japanese, and the interpreter repeated his words. "We will win the war against the Americans. Your country has broken off trade with our people, causing a great suffering. You also have our countrymen interned in your camps. Your country cages our women and children like animals."

A hot wave washed over Dan as he listened to the interpreter's voice, and he leaned forward to get a closer look. *Natty.* He shook his head. "It can't be."

He turned to Gabe, whispering. "I know that interpreter." His knees grew weak, and an upsurge of hope rushed through him. "It's my friend. I know him!"

Gabe turned to Dan, wide-eyed. "Shhh." He covered a cough, then angled his chin toward a guard who weaved through the crowd, heading their direction. "No talking."

The guard stopped just behind Dan as a warning, and Dan turned his eyes to the platform, focusing on the face of the man speaking, willing Natsuo to look his way.

"You will work hard for the emperor," he continued. "Your job is in the coal mines. You will salute or bow to any Japanese you see. If you do not, you will receive severe punishment."

The interpreter's voice—Natty's voice—droned on, and Dan's mind was transported back to UCLA.

❧ ❧ ❧

They had met in an English literature class. Dan was having a hard time, but for Natsuo the course was nearly impossible. The eager student had mastered the English language, but the nature of English poetry was a mystery to him.

"In Japan," he had explained, "poetry follows certain patterns, like haiku. Once you understand the pattern, the message is easy to grasp. But here, sometimes you use words literally and other times symbolically. Every one has a different form. Why make it so hard?"

Natsuo asked many questions in class and was eager to learn, but other students soon grew weary of his constant interruptions.

"Why don't you just go back to your own country?" another student commented as they exited class one day.

"Ah, don't mind him." Dan strode up and patted the Japanese student's shoulder. "I have a hard time with it too, and I grew up speaking this language. Why don't we meet for lunch sometime? We can work on our assignments together."

"I'd like that." Out of habit, Natsuo offered a quick bow.

Dan straightened the other fellow's shoulders. "On one condition . . . no more of that bowing stuff. Deal?" He stretched out his hand.

Natsuo vigorously shook his hand. "Deal."

They decided to study Emily Dickinson for their class project and made plans to meet the next day.

"I'm Natsuo," the Japanese student said as they parted. "But you can call me Natty. It's a more American-sounding name, don't you agree?"

"Yeah, and you can call me D.J. There were two other Daniels on my block growing up, so I was called by my initials."

Natty smiled, his white teeth shining in contrast to his dark face. "Okay, as your friend, I will call you D.J. See you tomorrow."

PART THREE

"Because of the Lord's great love we are not consumed,
for his compassions never fail.
They are new every morning; great is your faithfulness.
I say to myself, 'The Lord is my portion; therefore I will wait for him.'
The Lord is good to those whose hope is in him, to the one who seeks him."

Lamentations 3:22–25 NIV

Twenty-Eight

MOTHERS WITH WINGS: HANDS THAT ROCK THE CRADLE NOW WIELD WAF CONTROL STICKS

An Eastern Army Air Base—Now eight American boys and girls can brag: "My mama flies Army planes, too. She's ferrying PT-19-As and L4-Bs."

I just spent a day at a ferrying division of the Air Transport Command to watch these first feminine ferry fliers fit their civilian flight experience into the precision of the Army air program.

Although only experienced pilots, with at least 50 hours in the air in the past year and at least 500 altogether, can be considered for ferrying, about 40 letters come to Washington daily from women who want to learn how to fly.

Margaret Kernodle
Excerpt from the *Washington Post,* October 17, 1942

After yesterday's confrontation with Ginger, Libby was glad to get back to work. It was too bad "work" meant sitting around. She flipped through the pages of a flight manual as she waited in the ready room for her next lesson. With a limited number of instructors, the women spent more time waiting for lessons than actually flying.

Betty poked her head into the room. "Libby, you're wanted at the main office. Someone from the government, and a lady who says she's a relative."

Libby rose and placed the manual on the table. "That's odd. I don't know of any relatives from the East Coast." Her stomach churned as one face came to mind. *No, it's been too long. It can't be.*

Annabelle stood and stretched. She finished off her coffee and set her ceramic mug to the side. "Most likely an adoring fan trying to meet you. I'm finished for today; mind some company?"

"Love some."

The trees in the distance displayed autumn leaves as the two women strode across the tarmac. A yellow convertible sat parked in front of the office. Libby glanced at the driver—a gray-haired man with a handlebar mustache. He smiled at her—a bit too friendly—and Libby looked away. Guys like that gave her the creeps.

The secretary waited at the door. "A representative from the War Department is in the office to the right." She gave a sly smile. "And your other guest stepped into the restroom. When she's finished, should I tell her to wait?"

"Uh, sure." Libby turned to Annabelle and shrugged. Then she tugged her friend's arm. "Come on; you're sticking with me until we get to the bottom of this."

Libby entered the office, where a young gentleman in a navy blue business suit waited. He jumped to his feet as she entered. "Miss Conners, it's an honor to meet you. I'm Darnell Dennis with the State Department."

"Nice to meet you, Mr. Dennis. And this is my friend Annabelle Hopkins. I hope it's okay for her to join us today."

"Sure thing. Annabelle, pull up a chair. I'm sure you're mighty proud of your friend here."

Annabelle sat down and crossed her legs demurely. "Yes, of course."

Darnell tilted his hat back from his forehead. "I'm here, Miss Conners, because I have a proposition for you. I'm sure you're aware that the War Department has recruited talent from all over the United States to help us sell war bonds. We've signed up folks like James Cagney, Lucille Ball, and Bing Crosby to help. Would you be interested in joining our ranks?"

"Me?" Libby placed a hand to her chest. "I hardly think I'm anyone special. I mean, me and Mr. Cagney? We're not exactly in the same league."

"I'm not so sure about that." Mr. Dennis leaned closer. "Lady fliers are all the buzz around the capital."

"In that case, I'd love to help . . . as long as you're interested in *all* the lady fliers." Libby placed a hand on her friend's back. "Take Annabelle here. Her husband's a pilot stationed in England, and she has two young children at home. I think that makes her more of a hero than I am. I mean, all I did was run away from the Japs as they attacked."

"Sure thing then—good idea." Darnell Dennis rose from his seat. "We'll get some photographers out here right away."

Libby stood and walked him to the door. "After you get Mrs. Love's approval, of course. Last I heard she was getting pretty tired of all the media fuss—feels it's taking too much time away from our flying."

He bowed and donned his hat. "Yes, of course. I'll check with Mrs. Love."

Darnell Dennis gave them each a strong handshake and strode away.

The two women followed him out into the main office, where a row of windows faced the small parking lot and the airfield beyond.

"Imagine that," Libby said. "I never dreamed being a female pilot would be so—"

"Libby?"

The voice caused Libby's words to catch in her throat. She turned, feeling the color drain from her face. "Mother?"

She studied her face, as if remembering it from a distant dream. Libby took two steps, then paused as joy and anger fought for top billing.

Hazel Conners was exactly as Libby remembered. Her brown locks curled around her face in a similar fashion to Libby's, and her figure was as trim as the day she had walked out of her daughter's life. It was only as

Libby looked closer that she noted deep sadness in her mother's eyes.

"My little girl, just look at you." Hazel smiled and opened her arms.

Annabelle nudged Libby's shoulder. "Oh my gosh, you look just like her. But I thought you said your mother was dead."

"She was to me." Libby took a step back. "Mother, what in the world are you doing here? How did you find me?"

Hazel pulled a copy of *Life* magazine from her purse and flipped it open. "I found this on the newsstands. I knew my little girl would be a pilot someday. You always loved to fly. But I never imagined you'd be such a famous one." Hazel took Libby's hands in her own.

Libby shook them free. "Mother, you're joking, right? You walked out twenty years ago. You think you can just stroll back in because you saw my photo in a magazine?"

"Well, Delaware is fairly close to New York. That's where I've been all these years, New York City." Hazel took a cigarette out of her purse but didn't light it. It bounced on her lips as she talked. "I went there to sing. Remember, your father used to call me his little songbird? He always thought I had potential. Well, he was right. I'd like for you to come and hear me sometime."

Libby walked over to the window. "That man in the car. Is that the guy you left with?"

"Oh, no. Hank vanished long ago. He was just a

friend who urged me to follow my dreams. That's Wilbur. He's a piano player—and a good one at that. We've been together on and off for the last few years. But enough about me . . ." She returned the unlit cigarette to her purse.

Libby turned to Annabelle, unsure of what to say or do. The gray walls of the office seemed to close in. She sank into a cold metal chair.

Compassion filled Annabelle's gaze, but Libby knew this was not something her friend could help her with.

"I'll wait outside," Annabelle mouthed, moving toward the door. She placed a soft hand on Libby's shoulder. "I'll be praying."

A rush of nausea overcame Libby, and she placed a hand over her mouth, staring at the black-and-white diamond pattern on the floor. She was sure if she moved one muscle she'd lose it all—her composure, her temper . . . her lunch.

Hazel squatted on one knee before her daughter. Her small hands brushed the wayward curls from Libby's face. "I know this is hard. It must be a shock after all these years." Her voice was tender. "But I want you to know it's always been my intention to return to you. Your father and I had lots of problems. You were just the one stuck in the middle."

Libby's voice caught in her throat. "All those years I thought I'd done something wrong. You said you'd be there in the morning. You said we'd make pancakes. You never called or even wrote." Libby sat straighter and pulled her face away from her mother's touch.

"Surely you must know what it's like to want to follow a dream, Libby. To believe in yourself even when those around you don't. I had to do it. Had to try."

"At the expense of your daughter? Of missing me grow up?" She studied her mother's gaze, looking deep into her eyes, as she'd wanted to do for the past twenty years. And although there was sadness, Libby also saw self-justification in the set of her mother's chin. She hadn't come for reconciliation but to tout Libby as a prize.

"I'm sorry, Mother." Libby stood and swept her arm toward the front door. "I can't do this right now. You're alive. At least I know that now. You've found your dream. That's all I really need to know." She opened the glass door, hearing the little jingle of the bell. Libby could feel Wilbur's gaze upon her, but refused him the pleasure of an acknowledgment.

"So that's it? You want me to leave. Just like that?" Hazel straightened her blue jacket.

"Yes, I do, Mother. And I don't think it will be a problem for you. In fact, you do it quite well."

Hazel hurried from the room without a parting glance. Libby closed the door and leaned her head back against the wall, waiting for the sound of the car's engine to fade into the distance.

Then she returned to the office chairs, sat down, and covered her face with her hands. There was no way to count the number of tears she'd spilt over the woman, and she refused to release one more. The ticking of the clock was her only evidence that this wasn't some horrible dream.

The door jingled, and Annabelle reappeared.

"Libby?" She curled into the next chair and placed an arm around her shoulder. "Are you okay?"

Libby glanced up into her friend's face. "I'm sorry I lied."

Annabelle brushed a strand of hair from Libby's face just as her mother had done. "I understand. You don't have to explain."

Libby rose and crossed the room, her fists balled and pressed against her hips, the anger inside her finally winning out. "I just don't understand how someone can do that. I mean, *nothing* is worth abandoning your child. No dream. No calling—" Libby looked at Annabelle and paused.

Watery tears filled her friend's eyes. Then Libby remembered. Annabelle had two children at home. A ton of bricks fell in Libby's gut.

She hurried over and kneeled before her friend. "I'm sorry. I didn't mean it like that. I wasn't talking about you. Your situation is different. Completely different."

"Is it?" The tears broke forth and rolled down Annabelle's cheeks. "Sometimes I wonder. Am I really doing the right thing?"

Libby didn't answer. She didn't need to. Annabelle glanced at Libby's face and started to cry even harder.

Twenty-Nine

D.C. FLIER, 249 OTHERS GET VALOR AWARDS

Approximately 250 American air heroes, including Maj. Felix M. Hardison of Washington, yesterday received a total of 386 medals for feats of valor performed during the United States Army's brief but colorful history in the southwest Pacific.

All of yesterday's awards could not be presented—some of the recipients were dead, some were hospitalized, others were away on war duty.

Excerpt from the *Washington Post,* October 18, 1942

Dan had been working in the coal mines nine days now, and he wondered how many more they'd have to face before their liberation.

After using the small shack that was their restroom, he trudged into the barracks, which was divided into seven rooms, and hung his number on the pegboard. His number was his identity now. It was to be worn around his neck like a dog tag and had to be hung on the wall of any room he entered. To be found in a room without it would bring on a severe beating.

He walked through the narrow corridor down to their small sleeping room, knowing the stench of the barracks was only staggering when one first came in from the fresh air. By morning he wouldn't notice it. His weary legs stepped onto the platform as he slid open the wood-framed door, covered with rice paper. Beyond, eight thin mattresses lay on the floor side by side. Seven weary men still slept on them under threadbare blankets. It had been cold lately, and they'd pushed them together for added warmth.

"Rise and shine, boys. Time to head back to the pit." They'd been divided into three complete shifts so that work in the mines continued day and night. Their actual "shift" lasted eight hours, but marching, organizing, and cleanup took up half of their day.

They dressed, ate, and lined up in the dark for a three-mile walk to the underground shaft mine. Except for large spotlights that guarded the perimeter, the camp was under blackout conditions. From rumors circulating around camp, Dan learned that American bombers had already hit mainland Japan, and as the months passed, worries arose that they'd strike again.

Dan scanned every face they passed, hoping to find Natty once more. That first day, he'd pushed his way through the crowds of milling GIs, trying to reach the platform, but by the time he'd arrived it was empty.

Every day after that, Dan continued to look for his friend, searching each Japanese face he passed. But he didn't see him again. Natsuo was gone.

Their first night at Camp 17, Dan told Gabe the whole story as they lay in their small room with six others.

"I can even remember the poem we memorized together." Dan recited it slowly, barely louder than a whisper.

> *"He ate and drank the precious Words—*
> *His Spirit grew robust—*
> *He knew no more that he was poor,*
> *Nor that his frame was Dust—*
>
> *"He danced along the dingy Days*
> *And this Bequest of Wings*
> *Was but a Book—What Liberty*
> *A loosened spirit brings—"*

"I like it." Gabe looked to him with tired eyes. "It's a great poem about the Bible."

"You think so?"

"Yeah. What other book can loosen someone's spirit and bring liberty?"

Dan had folded his hands behind his head. There had been many in his poetry class who had made the same assumption, but he didn't feel like getting into that now. "It's not the poem I'm concerned about, but finding Natsuo. I just know if I can find him, he would help us."

The thought that Natsuo was somewhere near gave Dan hope as he trudged to the mines day after day. It was the brightest his outlook had been in a while.

He'd been so sure that the army would provide support and supplies as they fought on in the Philippines. When that didn't happen, Dan still had a glimmer of hope that MacArthur would keep his word and regain control of the island. But during the dark voyage across the sea, he wondered if there was any hope of being rescued at all. Each mile the ship sailed through dark waters, his resolve faded.

Surely their country had not forgotten them. Perhaps somewhere the government officials plotted to find a way for their safe return. The bombers now hitting Japan proved that, didn't they? Also, maybe somewhere across the ocean, the American people prayed. Maybe they remembered their boys in the hands of the enemy.

These hopes were doubled with the knowledge that Dan had a friend in the ranks of the imperial army—someone who might be willing to offer him and his buddies assistance. Perhaps they'd be able to leave Japan after all.

If we survive the mines.

On the first week there, Dan discovered the Mitsui mines had been abandoned for a reason. They'd been closed down before the war due to the number of worker deaths. In their first week of work, the rumored dangers proved true. They witnessed cave-ins causing crushed limbs, internal injuries, and even the death of one GI.

Today Dan's group trudged through the forest trail to the mines just as another group ventured out. The men emerged filthy, and they didn't even lift their eyes to acknowledge the new shift. They were the exploration group. Their job was to look for new veins of coal in the hard rock.

Dan's group, the construction team, were to shore up the ceilings and make them as stable as possible for the extraction team to follow. It was that last team's job to blast and dig out the coal.

Just outside the opening to the mines sat a large gold statue of Buddha. Dan approached the massive image, took off his hat, and bowed as required.

Stupid Japs, bowing to a carved image made of gold. As if bowing to a metal statue could really make a difference.

Inside, the ground slanted sharply with a single track leading into the darkness. If they were lucky, there was room inside the railcars, and they'd receive a free ride to the sixth level where they worked. Today was not one of those days; and instead Gabe, Dan, and the others scurried down the steep incline, their arms filled with jackhammers, shovels, and their bento boxes, which held that day's lunch.

As the light from the opening faded, Dan clicked on the light attached to his cloth cap. His feet slid on the loose dirt, and he wished he had a free hand to help brace himself against the walls.

At Dan's side, Gabe coughed, and his chest made a wheezing sound. The air grew hot and stuffy the farther down they got, and the walls seemed to close in. Even Dan's breathing was labored as his lungs worked hard, longing for clean air.

They arrived at the coal area, dropped their tools, and immediately stripped down to their loincloths. Sweat already glistened on Dan's thin body.

Two civilian workers were assigned to oversee them. One of the men, Tumato San, refused to speak to them, instead screaming his orders and waving his arms as if they were oxen. The other, Kiyoko San, had a kind face; and though he didn't speak much, Dan noted hints of compassion in his gaze.

They worked in a hunched-over position for the next eight hours, building a wall strong enough to keep the tunnel from crumbling under excavation. Together Dan and Gabe struggled to lift boulders that either of the men could have easily tackled alone before.

Piece by piece, their group built a support wall. Every few hours they'd hear a cry echoing through the chambers, and they knew someone else had gotten hurt. Dan suspected that some of these injuries were deliberate. *Anything to leave this hole.*

By the end of the day, Dan's neck and back ached. His arms throbbed, and Gabe looked even worse. Finally, Kiyoko motioned for them to stop. Dan glanced back and studied the long wall they'd managed to build. It would be there tomorrow for them to continue. And the day after that.

The railcars carried them to the top of the hill, and daylight greeted them. Dan's eyes adjusted to the light as they were herded into the large bathroom outside the mines. Three tubs measured at least twenty feet long, with a seat around the inside rim. Since all three shifts used the same tub, it was always a murky brown. Still, the water was hot, and there was soap for them to scrub their bodies.

Dan climbed in. He dunked his whole body in the water, then pushed his hair back from his face and turned to his friend. "Well, you got your wish. Hot bathwater and soap."

Gabe cast Dan a sideways glance. "After digging in the depths of hell, they let you dip in a little hot water." He stood and began lathering his body. "Yet somehow I never feel clean." Gabe shivered despite the heat of the water. "There is a darkness down there that even the strongest soap can't scrub away."

Thirty

GREAT FAITH HELD WORLD'S NEED NOW:
IT CAN BE PRODUCED ONLY BY A GREAT WORD,
CHRIST, THE REV. F. R. TIFFANY ASSERTS

Declaring "this is the beginning of a new age," and "Christ is the great word for this hour," the Rev. Fred Robert Tiffany, in a sermon yesterday morning at the Richmond Hill Baptist Church, 114th Street and Ninety-first Avenue, Queens, described today's need of "a great faith produced by a great word."

"The Bible declares that in the beginning was the Word. And so history validates that biblical statement. In the beginning of every great movement is a great word. Guiding every humanitarian enterprise is a great word.

"Let it be noted that Christ is the Great Word of the Bible. Old Testament poetry sang Him; ancient

prophecies foreshadowed Him; old seers longed for this Great Word."

Excerpt from the *New York Times*, October 19, 1942

Libby opened one eye and moaned when she realized it was morning. It had been announced last night that today would be their first ferrying assignment. She'd tossed and turned with excitement . . . and she worried that she'd somehow mess up and forget to follow procedure.

"Good morning, sunshine."

Libby rolled to her stomach and eyed Annabelle sitting on her bed, wrapped in a white cotton robe. An open book was in her hands.

"How can you be so chipper?" Libby propped herself up on one arm.

"Morning is my favorite time of day. The whole base is quiet. It's a nice time to think and read and pray." She played with the edges of her worn leather Bible. "When I was little, I loved to stay overnight at my grandmother's house. When I'd come down to the kitchen each morning, I'd always find Grandma at the kitchen table with a cup of coffee and the Bible opened before her." Annabelle sighed and looked to Libby. "I'm reading from Psalms this morning. Would you like to hear something?"

Annabelle's expression reminded Libby of Dan's mother as she hummed her favorite hymns. "Sure."

"This is from Psalm 139. The whole chapter is about how God made us, knows us, and will never leave us.

"If I ascend up into heaven, thou art there: if I make my bed in hell, behold, thou art there." Annabelle read the words slowly, emphasizing each one. "If I take the wings of the morning, and dwell in the uttermost parts of the sea; even there shall thy hand lead me, and thy right hand shall hold me."

Libby sat up and pulled her blankets around her. "When you read that, I pictured us flying in the heavens. Sometimes it does seem like I'm completely alone up there. And the second part . . . Dan, and your Jeff, they're over the 'uttermost parts of the sea,' that's for sure." She pulled the blanket tighter. "But if God can see Dan even . . . even when I have no idea where he is . . ."

Annabelle crossed the room and scooted next to Libby's side. "That's exactly what I was thinking. I'm glad God chose to share that with us today." She squeezed Libby's hand. "Uh-oh, I think I hear Betty rustling around next door."

She jumped up. "I guess these paper-thin walls are good for something. We'd better hurry, because if that group gets to the showers first, we won't have a chance for hot water."

Libby rose from the bed and straightened the sheets. "Go ahead. I'll be there in a minute."

Annabelle swept up her towel and shuffled to the shower.

When Libby heard the water turn on, she moved toward her friend's open Bible. She found the verses Annabelle had read, then moved down the page: *The darkness hideth not from thee,* she read, *but the night shineth as the day: the darkness and the light are both alike to thee.* She closed the book, thinking about what Annabelle had said. *"I'm glad God chose to share that with us today."*

Was that really how it worked? All her life, Libby had believed the Bible was God's Holy Word. But could He really use it to speak to real people about the real situations they faced every day?

Libby went to her dresser and pulled out her clothes. Dan's photo on the wall greeted her with a huge grin.

"God's with you, Dan." She leaned close to the photo for a better look. "I know we didn't talk much about Him, but I hope that no matter what darkness you face today, you'll know that it's not too dark for God's light."

Libby heard a sound in the hallway, and turned to see Ginger standing outside the open door. Her face reddened at the thought of being caught talking to a photo, and she squared her shoulders.

Ginger turned away without speaking, but not before Libby saw the tears that streaked her face.

Four women in flight coveralls carried their parachutes as they climbed out of the Boeing twin-engine, which had just arrived at the airfield of the Piper Cub factory in Lock Haven. Libby jutted out her chin and added a little extra sway of her hips as she noticed the stares from the ground crew and other pilots who were just arriving for the day's work.

Yes, we're the female pilots you've heard about.

After checking in with the ground crew, the women found the correct planes by the tail numbers. Libby inspected her plane, climbed in, and figured her airspeed and flying time in her little, round-wheeled flight calculator. Then she waited for the line crews to crank the props.

Within a matter of minutes all four planes were lined up, ready for takeoff. Libby noted the white star on the wing—the symbol of the U.S. Army. This is what she'd been dreaming about. Finally, her time had arrived.

Then her eyes spotted something across the field. P-40s lined up in a neat row. She blew them a kiss.

I'm doing this for you, Dan. Look at me, sweetheart.

As the navigator, Ginger ascended into the sky first. July, assigned to the number two position, followed. Once in the air, July moved to the navigator's right and back slightly.

Annabelle, the third in line, took off behind the others, moving to the left of Ginger. Libby was last. And as the flight leader she had responsibility for all other pilots, keeping an eye on them from the rear position.

It was a system they'd studied during those long days in the classroom, and each knew her part. They knew that when Ginger had navigated their group within ten miles from their destination airport, she'd throttle back. Then Libby would move forward and lead the group in.

At first, Libby had been pleased to be assigned flight

leader. Now the responsibility weighed heavily on her shoulders. *What if something goes wrong? Can I handle it?*

It didn't help that it seemed as if the whole country was watching and waiting to see if these lady pilots would succeed.

Since they didn't have radios to communicate, Libby rehearsed their signals in her mind.

If someone has engine trouble, she dips her nose a few times before she goes down.

If the navigator is off-course, the flight leader should come forward and take over.

The flight leader must dip her right wing if the navigator is headed too far left.

Lifting the plane's nose means pilots should fly to a higher altitude, where they might find it easier to cruise.

Despite Libby's worries, a few hours later the planes were safely deposited at an airfield in New York—all before most military workers were breaking for lunch. And since they were flying the smaller planes, with hardly any power, it took about the same amount of time to fly the course as it would to get there by train.

Libby climbed down from the plane and shuffled through her paperwork. She met the airport manager inside the main office. "Please sign here, sir. Then these planes are yours."

"It's about time. I needed them three weeks ago."

Libby shrugged and handed him a pen. "Sorry, we just got the orders today. Please sign."

The airfield manager cocked one eyebrow but did as

he was told. "Do any of you dames want to stick around for a drink after work?" He slid a grease-covered hand down his unshaved face and glanced toward the group of women who waited outside.

Libby smiled, debating whether or not to inform him that he'd left a large grease mark on his cheek.

"Sorry. We have a six thirty train to catch. And the girls are wanting to catch a glimpse of the Statue of Liberty before heading for a bite to eat downtown."

When the women returned to the base later that night, they strode into their barracks as if they'd been ferrying all their lives. It was only after they closed the door that hoots and hollers rose, echoing down the narrow hallway.

Annabelle dropped her flight jacket and gyrated her hips in a victory dance.

July was much more subtle, grasping Libby's hands and leading her in an impromptu waltz down the corridor. Ginger simply stood there and grinned.

Betty's face poked out from the third room. "I was wondering when y'all would return. I suppose it went well? But come quick; presents arrived while you were away."

The women crammed into the small room that Betty and Ginger shared. On the floor were two large B-4 canvas sacks, double-stitched for strength.

Betty awkwardly lifted one and shook out its contents onto the concrete floor. "Winter flying suit, navigation case, leather jacket and pants." She held up a leather helmet with a chin strap. "There's one of these and a face mask. Oh, and boots and gloves. Golly. It feels like Christmas!"

"Goodness gracious." Annabelle lifted the other bag. "This thing must weigh a hundred pounds." She dropped it back to the floor with a *plunk*.

"Ninety, actually." Betty stuffed the gear back inside hers. "Nancy and I weighed them."

"Well, let's see how they look!" Ruth unfastened her skirt and dropped it to the floor, showing off her bright white undergarments. She slipped on the heavy wool stockings, followed by the woolen underwear and leather pants. Then she strode over to the floor-length mirror, shaking her head.

"Tell me the truth now, girls," she said, striking a pose. "Does this outfit make my butt look big?"

Thirty-One

MESSAGES SENT TO JAPAN: RECORDINGS TO AMERICANS GIVE PROMISE OF EARLY RELEASE

We'll have you back home soon! Hold on and God bless you!"

That confident prediction was the keynote of numerous messages sent yesterday by New Yorkers to Americans who are prisoners of war in Japan. . . . The sponsors explained that they hoped to get the record to the Americans in Japan before Christmas.

Excerpt from the *New York Times*, November 8, 1942

Friday morning Libby staggered into the barracks with her large brown B-4 bag and sifted through her things, forming a pile of clothes to haul to the army Laundromat. She held up the white blouse she'd worn for three days in a row and noticed a coffee stain from the 6:00 a.m. rush in El Paso. Then she pulled out a pair of army-issue long underwear—definitely made for a man.

Who cares? Kept me warm in Montana.

She'd already been gone a full week, washing her blouses in hotel sinks and drying them on the radiators—and she was sure she'd be leaving again tomorrow.

Emptying her bag, Libby found her notepad with a letter she'd started to Dan's mother.

November 1, 1942

Dear Ima Jean,

Greetings! I'm sending this letter as an official member of the WAFS. Thank you for the letters you've continued to send. They always brighten my day. Between you and my dear father, I always seem to have a note waiting for me in the mail—which is the most excitement I've had lately.

The weather has been dreadful, and there have been more articles written about our work than the number of planes we've actually ferried. I spend most of my time on the Link Trainers, which are flight simulators we call the "Maytag Merrerschmitts." We've also taken part in a review for the ATC commander. We WAFS looked quite the sight marching with all the male troops. And you should have seen the guys' faces when the general took time to speak to each one of us ladies, while the men waited at attention.

We hope things will pick up soon, and Novem-

ber turns up more work than October did. As the holidays near, my mind and heart turn to Dan. Have you heard anything? I was so thrilled when you wrote to tell me that he'd been awarded the Silver Star for his service in the Philippines. I only wish we could hear something of his status. Like you, I refuse to believe he is dead. (I'm having a hard time even writing that word!) He's out there somewhere. I know it.

I'm sure you would let me know if you had any news. It's hard to believe this will be my second Thanksgiving and Christmas without him.

The letter had ended abruptly when they'd been called up to work. Libby chuckled and realized she'd have to start over completely. Things had picked up—boy, had they. For the last two weeks, she'd been halfway across the country and back more than once, as had most of the other girls.

Libby had just returned from New Orleans, where she'd sampled jambalaya for the first time. She had a hard time understanding the waitress's thick accent, but the food was great. She hadn't been over to check out the Ready Room yet, but she knew the map on the pegboard filled with colored golf tees would show where the other WAFS were. Some of the ladies were at the Piper factory, others at Lake Charles, Louisiana.

Wonder where I'll be tomorrow. . . .

Laughter erupted from the sitting room. "Come on, gals, are you ready to boogie?" July called.

Then Libby heard the crackle of the record player, followed by "He Wears a Pair of Silver Wings" by Kay Kyser. She stuffed the letter into her drawer and took out a pencil to start a new one.

The door opened, letting in the blaring music.

"Libby, you're back!" July rushed in, her face flushed from jitterbugging. "Did you hear about Ginger and Betty?"

"What happened? Were they hurt?"

July threw back her head and laughed. "Just their pride. When they landed in Charlottesville, it had been raining on the airfield, and their front wheels sank. Slam, they landed right onto their noses, breaking the propellers!"

"You'll have to tell me all about it, but first"—Libby stood and slipped her shoes on—"I need to dance." She grabbed July's hand. "Let's go."

As Libby headed toward the door, she suddenly realized what was missing in the room. She'd been so preoccupied with her laundry and her letter that she hadn't noticed that the photos of Jeff and the kids were missing from Annabelle's dresser, as was her Bible. Annabelle's pink chenille bedspread was also gone. Libby looked at July.

"Where are Annabelle's things?" Her heart pounded in her chest. "Where's Annabelle?"

"Sleep Lagoon" wafted down the hall as she hurried to her friend's dresser and slid open the drawers.

Libby felt a hand on her back.

The humor in July's voice was gone. "She went home.

Said that as much as she loved being a part of the WAFS, her kids needed her."

"She didn't tell me. I had no idea . . ." Yet even as loneliness for her friend overcame her, Libby realized she'd known all along. She'd seen Annabelle's reaction after the incident with Libby's mom.

"You're getting a new roommate. I heard Nancy saying that she'll be here in the morning."

The music in the other room seemed to kick up a notch, and more laughter erupted. July squeezed Libby's shoulder. "I know it's hard. But, c'mon, dance it out. It'll make you feel better."

Libby kicked off her shoes. "Go ahead. Have some fun. I'll be okay, really."

July gave her a quick hug, then hurried out the door, her stocking feet padding down the hall to the tempo of Jimmy Dorsey's "Tangerine."

Libby stepped out of her flight suit and let it fall to the floor. A cold winter wind hit the barracks with force, and bits of rain found their way through the cracks in the walls.

"Not a new roommate," she complained to Dan's photo.

Every time she came back, Libby was pleasantly surprised to find more female pilots—all previously licensed—who'd finished their training and now boasted shiny pairs of silver wings pinned to their blouses. But she hated the thought of starting from ground one with someone new. All the awkward small talk. And who could be as understanding as Annabelle?

Libby rubbed her arms and hurried to her dresser to find her warmest pajamas. She opened the top drawer and paused. There, on top of her clothes, was Annabelle's Bible.

Libby quickly pulled on her pajamas, then slid under the covers and curled onto her side, Bible in hand. She rubbed the smooth cover and pressed it to her cheek, breathing in the leather smell. *Oh, Annabelle. Thank you . . .*

She opened the front cover, and a slip of paper fell out.

Dear Libby,

I'm sorry I had to leave without a formal goodbye. Know that I'll be back to visit, and I'll bring the kids for you to meet. You should have heard the excitement in their voices when I told them Mommy was coming home.

I'm leaving you this Bible with promises that I will also keep you in my prayers. May you continue to soar, and may Dan soon be home with you.

Time to go. I must finish packing so I can catch the train.

Always your friend,
Annabelle

Libby refolded the paper and saw that Annabelle had also written an inscription on the inside front page.

May you discover Truth within these pages, and may you trust Him all your days. John 14:6.

Love, Annabelle

Libby found the book of John and read the verse out loud. "Jesus saith unto him, I am the way, the truth, and the life: no man cometh unto the Father, but by me."

May you discover Truth.

Jesus saith, I am the truth. . . .

Libby understood Annabelle's message as plainly as if she were here explaining it. Libby had believed in religion for many years, but she realized that Annabelle wanted more for her friend. She wanted Libby to discover Jesus. To know Him on a level she'd never dreamed of before.

Libby closed the Bible and set it on the floor. The jazz still blared from down the hall, but a different melody danced in Libby's heart. Sadness for the loss of her friend, but joy over the new friend she'd been given.

I want to know You, Jesus; I really do. Help me to know You better.

And just before Libby drifted off to sleep, she added a postscript to her prayer.

And please let me like this new girl. Help us to hit it off from the start. Amen.

Libby awoke to the sound of footsteps entering the room. She smiled to herself, hearing the female chatter from down the hall and remembering she was "home." Then her smile faded as she realized that those weren't Annabelle's footsteps that had awakened her.

The footsteps stopped just inches away from her bed.

How dare she . . . crowding in without a chance to get to know each other first. Libby pulled the blankets around her, sat erect, and looked up into a familiar pair of pale blue eyes. Her hand flew to her mouth, and she held back a squeal.

"Rose!" Libby swung the covers off and nearly dove into her friend's arms.

Rose laughed. Oh, how wonderful it was to hear that laugh.

Libby held her at arm's length, noticing the WAFS flight suit on her friend. "It's you. You're here. And you're one of us?"

"Yes, it's me. I'm here—although not officially a WAFS yet. I still have to earn this uniform."

Libby did squeal then and bounced on the concrete floor. Other faces peeked through the open doorway to see what all the excitement was about.

Libby spun Rose around to face the others. "Everyone, this is Rose. My best friend in the world. We were flight instructors together in Hawaii." Libby swept her arm toward the group. "And Rose, this is . . . everyone. Ginger, Betty—"

Suddenly Libby realized the others were already dressed in their uniforms, ready for the day's flights.

"Oh, man." She swept up her blouse, trousers, and

undergarments. "Oh, man. You just got here, but I have to hurry. I need to go."

Rose laughed and grasped Libby's arms. "Go. I'll be here when you get back. I'm your new roommate."

"My new roommate? Yes, you're my new roommate!" She gave Rose a quick kiss on the cheek, then covered her mouth. "Ew, sorry. Haven't brushed my teeth yet. Oh, I have so much to tell you. It'll have to wait until I get back tonight . . . or next week. I'm not sure; I haven't checked my schedule yet." She scurried down the hall to the bathroom.

"Yeah, and don't worry. We'll fill Rose in," Betty chirped. "We have plenty of dirt on you. Just wait until she hears what you've been up to."

* * *

Nancy peered up at the group over the top of her reading glasses. "Your assignment today is to fly the first PT-19s from Hagerstown, Maryland. The planes are to be delivered to a training base in Chattanooga, Tennessee, a 650-mile flight. Unlike the L4s that have closed cabins, these have open cockpits . . . so make good use of that winter gear that just arrived."

The WAFS nodded, then headed outside to the transport that would fly them the hour's trip to Hagerstown. As they made their way toward the plane, Libby couldn't help but laugh at the waddling group. "I feel like one of those big Sumo wrestlers. And you all look ridiculous."

"At least we'll be warm," July commented. "And if you want to laugh, take a look in the mirror, Libs."

Once they arrived in Hagerstown, they waited inside the smoke-filled Alert Room for the chilling cloud cover to lift. They watched from a window, and as soon as they could see clear skies above the nearby mountains, they knew it was time to take off.

Libby climbed into the new PT-19, straight off the assembly line. "Just like breaking in a new colt." She wished she had a large pen to autograph the cockpit. "First flown by Libby Conners—female pilot." She even imagined drawing a little heart over the "i" in her name, just for fun. Then she wondered if women—Rosie the Riveters—had made the plane. *We should all sign them.*

Within a matter of minutes, the group of six planes was heading southwest toward Chattanooga. As the designated navigator for the trip, it was Libby's job to keep track of their position on the series of maps called sectionals. They were pleated like an accordion and tied to her leg so they wouldn't get blown out of the cockpit.

On the sectionals, Libby had drawn a line from their origin to destination. The line passed between checkpoints on the map—roadways, a cluster of power lines, the bend in a river, a small town.

I guess this is one way to see the country.

Libby's PT-19 ascended to three thousand feet, and the Appalachian Mountains appeared beneath her like thick wrinkles in a quilt that need to be smoothed. Farther on, the ground was patchworked, the squares and rectangles varying in shades to make a colorful pattern —with the farmers' windmills like pins in the seams.

While it had been cold on the ground, the wind rushing past the cockpit at over a hundred miles an hour instantly chilled Libby to the bone.

Lotta good this long underwear is doing now. She was sure the temperature was below ten degrees.

"Aloha, oye' " she sang with a smile, remembering that Rose awaited her return. She thought of Ewa Beach and the hot sand. Thought of the picnics on the lawn, under the palms trees, engulfed by the smell of papayas . . . but it only made her colder.

As she glanced at the other primary trainers dotting the sky around her, Libby wondered how the other pilots fared. It seemed to be getting even colder. Her face felt numb. Her jaw chattered, and she couldn't even sing anymore.

Libby's heart began to race, and for the first time, she wondered if she could really do this. All she wanted was to touch down at their first destination to warm up. But the trip had only begun.

Libby looked down at the highway they followed. Bucking a headwind, the light and underpowered trainers actually seemed to be moving slower than the vehicles on the road beneath them.

Her teeth clattered, and she tried to keep her mind occupied, thinking of all the things she wanted to tell Rose. The news, or rather lack of news, about Dan. The media blitz about the WAFS. Her mother's visit.

The trip to Chattanooga took eight hours, and the

light had nearly faded from the sky by the time they arrived. Libby was too tired to look around. The scenery mattered little compared to getting warm.

As soon as she landed, Libby tied down the plane and used the seat belt to hold the stick so the wing surfaces wouldn't move. As a group, they closed the flight plans, watched the line boys fill the tanks, and checked their parachutes into a locker.

It was a slow, tired group who finally found a Western Union office to send their RONs back to New Castle.

"The whole time I was flying, all I could think about was fried chicken, mashed potatoes, and a hot, hot cup of coffee," said July.

"I've been thinking about a pig roast and mango-guava juice."

All eyes turned to Libby.

"Hey, remember, I used to live in Hawaii! Days like this make me ready to return."

Libby, July, and four of the newer pilots staggered to a bus that had been reserved to pick them up. With numb fingers they pushed their B-4 bags down the aisle, slumping onto the frigid seats.

As the bus taxied them around town, six sets of eyes eagerly looked for a nice place to eat, but it was too late. Everything was closed.

"There goes my chicken and mashed potatoes. Let's hope the hotel will at least serve breakfast in the morning."

Libby was grateful when they finally found their hotel.

"Hey, are y'all those lady pilots? Well, I'll be." The desk clerk handed out their keys.

"Yes, we are." July's voice quavered. "The famous, tired, cold, hungry women pilots."

Libby was too tired to talk. She thanked the boy and labored up the stairs to her room.

The first thing she did was crank on the radiator. Her teeth chattered as she tackled the cold zipper on her flight jacket. Tomorrow they'd be taking the train back to New Castle. Tomorrow she'd see Rose. But tonight all she could think about was a hot bath.

⁂

The train ride was uneventful, and with each passing mile Libby's excitement about getting back to New Castle grew.

As she tramped into the barracks that night, she stopped short at the doorway, tossing her bag inside. Her wide smile faded when she saw Rose and Ginger sprawled on Rose's bed, lying side by side. Photos were spread before them, and a box of tissues was snuggled between their shoulders. Two heads of black hair were twinlike from behind, and when they turned toward her, Libby saw two sets of red, puffy eyes.

"Hey, welcome back." Rose dabbed her face with the tissue. "We were just swapping stories, although Ginger has a lot more to share. She was married to Josiah for nine years, and look."

Rose held up a photo of a little girl in a white dress

with a swishy skirt. The curly haired youngster smiled into the camera with a wide grin. Her two front teeth were missing.

Libby's throat tightened, and she kneeled on the floor next to the bed.

"They died in a car accident. Our truck was struck by another vehicle going too fast. Just like that—"

Libby took the photo in her hand. "What was her name?"

"Lillian," Ginger said in the softest voice. "She was eight."

Libby handed it back. "I'm sorry I never asked. I—"

Ginger wiped her face, then waved a hand in Libby's direction. "You really didn't have a chance to ask, the way I was acting." She glanced toward the photo of Dan on the wall. "I never asked you either."

Ginger patted Rose's hands. "I'm glad for Rose. She told me about your fiancé and about Jack. And she forced me to spill my guts about the accident. It was hard but healing in a way."

Libby unzipped her leather jacket and hung it on the hook on the back of the door. "I guess we all have stuff we need to deal with." She sat on her bed, pulling her legs to her chest and wrapping her arms around them. "I don't know why we try to be so strong all the time."

"I think it's because we're women pilots." Ginger tucked a strand of black hair behind her ear. "We have to prove ourselves, show that we can do a man's job. But I think sometimes . . ." She sighed. "Sometimes we forget what being female is all about. We miss out on the close friendships that women do so well."

"So why don't we make a pact?" said Rose. "That we'll be tough when we need to be tough, and weak when we need to be weak. That we'll laugh but not be afraid to cry. Deal?"

"Deal," said Libby and Ginger together.

Thirty-Two

CARRIER TOOK FLIERS TO WITHIN 800 MILES OF JAPANESE CAPITAL: NONE OF 16 PLANES RETURNS; 64 OF 80 MEN CAME THROUGH

Telling at last the story of the daring American raid on Tokyo a year ago last Sunday, the War Department revealed last night that the intrepid United States airmen took off from the aircraft carrier Hornet *and bailed out or crash-landed in Asia.*

The long-withheld account of the devastating attack was made public with an official warning to the Japanese homeland that further "attacks still lie ahead."

Of the 80 Army Air Force men taking part, five were interned in Russia, eight are prisoners of Japan or are presumed to be, one was killed, two are missing, and the rest made their way safely into Chinese territory. Seven were injured in landing but survived.

John G. Norris, Staff Writer
Excerpt from the *Washington Post,* April 21, 1943

Natsuo spoke low. Low enough that the pilot before him had to strain to hear his every word. And somehow his voice seemed detached, as if it wasn't his own.

"Are you telling me you dropped bombs over our country, and yet you know nothing?"

Natsuo slapped the red-haired pilot's freckled face, sending him crashing against the bamboo walls of the interrogation room. The afternoon sun crept in through slits in the bamboo, casting striped shadows on the brawny American.

"Where did you take off from? Who was your commanding officer?"

The man struggled to a kneeling position. His bloodied, swollen lip turned up in a defiant smirk, but he said nothing. Natsuo turned his back. It was strange to see such a strong, healthy American again. It was easy to think of the skin-and-bones, filthy prisoners as less than human, but this man reminded him of—

No. He wouldn't let his thoughts go there. He slammed his hand against the wall next to the prisoner.

"Fine, so you will not tell me." He turned to the guards by the door. "Go ahead. Hang him up!"

The two guards snapped handcuffs on the American pilot's wrists. Dragging him, they twisted his arms upward, wrapped their arms around his waist, and lifted him, dangling him from a peg on the wall. Though the pilot was tall, his toes barely touched the floor.

Natsuo marched from the room, knowing that the longer the man hung there, the sooner he'd give in. Natsuo smiled. And if this didn't work, something else would. While the Americans often proved strong in body—lasting beyond his perceived limits—they were weak in spirit.

He walked down the hall to his private office, opened the top drawer of his wicker desk, and pulled out a slip of paper with Red Cross letterhead.

Dear Mr. Johnson, he typed. *I'm sorry to inform you that your wife, Abigail, has been killed in an automobile accident. Your children were injured but are expected to survive. We are arranging for your transfer. With much regret, General Arnold, Army Air Corps.*

Natsuo pulled the slip of paper from the typewriter.

He'd wait at least eight hours. Then, when Lt. Solomon Johnson's body was twisted in pain, Natsuo would read the letter "just in." He'd also agree to the transfer home, on one condition—that Lieutenant Johnson provide a few minor details of the American aircraft carriers he'd been assigned to. A simple exchange—the life of a father who was needed by his children for air corps information that was mostly likely outdated.

It was plans such as these that had moved Natsuo so quickly through the ranks. He had worked at the Mitsui coal mines in Omuta for only a few weeks before being transferred to Shinagawaku, recently renamed Tokyo

POW Main. Natsuo discovered he "worked" best with the captured American pilots.

Who better to hunt prey than one who knows their habits?

Natsuo's best hours of work happened in the still halls of the prison. Hidden, alert, like an owl in the night, he quietly listened to the secrets they shared in the dark. Stories of families and home helped Natsuo to discover their weaknesses. Still, there was one pilot Natsuo couldn't wait to meet up with face-to-face. Daniel John Lukens. Or D.J., as Natsuo had once called him. It had been his luck to find his old friend's name in the American paper, listed among the recipients of the Silver Star. The words behind D.J.'s name had said, "Location unknown. Assumed dead or missing in action." But Natsuo knew exactly where he was.

He had used the information from the newspaper as a starting point. The group who'd received the Silver Stars had taken part in the defense of the Philippines. And, he knew, the strongest of those survivors were now on mainland Japan. Natsuo had used his position to make a few calls, and his wit brought him success once again.

Natsuo's old pal was listed among the prisoners at Omuta. Working in the mines. In fact, Dan Lukens had arrived during the first day Natsuo had been stationed there. If only Natsuo had known that amongst that mass of filthy humanity was a man he'd once considered a friend.

Had Dan seen him upon that platform?

Did he see me in my uniform? See me in my glory?

Natsuo had put in a request to return to Omuta. To Camp 17. He'd told the truth—there were pilots there who'd not yet been interrogated. Natsuo did not mention that these pilots hadn't flown for nearly two years. He didn't let on that the interrogation was of a personal nature only.

Will you remember me, D.J.? As I remember you?

❧ ❧ ❧

The sound echoed in Libby's mind again, the droning filling her ears, vibrating through her brain and catching a ride on her nerves until every part from her toes to fingertips trembled. It was the noise of a thousand planes filling up the Pacific sky over Hawaii. An endless sea of metal hornets, sucking away Libby's breath with their dominance, until she knew none of those on the ground would outlive the planes' destruction.

Dear Jesus, save us all.

"Libby?"

A voice called to her, yet the droning grew louder, blocking out the voice.

"Libby," the voice called again. A female voice.

Libby's body shuddered. She opened her eyes and dared to look up. Instead of the Jap planes over Pearl Harbor, Rose stood over her. Her hair was tucked into her pilot's turban, her eyes bright. Then Libby remembered. She and Rose were hitching a ride in a B-17, heading to Long Beach, California, for their permanent assignments with the 6th Ferrying Group.

It had been a busy few months with Libby sometimes traveling two weeks straight without making it back to New Castle. Some mornings she'd have to ask the hotel clerk what city they were in. Hotel rooms, airports, restaurants—it was a blur.

They'd boarded the larger bomber, and Libby had thrown her parachute and bag into the waist gunner's area behind the bomb bay, using the parachute as a lumpy pillow. She must have been tired, because she didn't even remember the large gray beast lifting off.

Rose stood above her, her body taking on the natural sway of the plane.

"Do you still want to check out the cockpit?" Rose laughed. "You've been out for hours, but I understand. The purr of the larger engines always makes me sleepy too."

Libby stretched. "Yeah, I want to see what flying one of these big babies is all about. After all, you'll be piloting one soon." Libby brushed a hand over her face, smacking her lips. Sleep had deposited a wad of cotton in her mouth.

Still her dream wouldn't leave her.

It was just a dream. The Japs are far, far away. We're safe. They won't make it this far.

"Libby?"

She opened her eyes and wondered how she had managed to fall back asleep again.

"On second thought, maybe you'd better keep sleeping. I'll tell the pilots you'll catch it next time."

Libby tightened her lips, then raised her voice over

the engines once more. "Sorry. No, I really want to see. I'll be at the controls in a quick minute. Just need a drink to wash away this cotton mouth."

Rose nodded, then moved forward toward the flight cabin.

Libby was thankful for this time spent with her friend, and the chance to be roommates—although she knew that might be changing soon. Rumor had it they'd soon be allowed to ferry almost every plane available, which meant more training schools scattered over the United States. Rose had let Nancy know that she was interested in piloting the big bombers, such as the one they now rode in. But as for Libby, her mind was set on the pursuits.

"The faster the better," she told the other WAFS, although secretly her motivation wasn't the speed. She hoped instead to find a connection with Dan. To know what he'd experienced over the skies of Hawaii and the Philippines. To soar as he once did with the screams of the big Allison engines in her ears.

Libby took a long drink of lukewarm water from her canteen. Then she stretched her body, despite its complaints, and planted her feet on the aluminum floorboards of the B-17. Yet, even when she stood, something inside told her not to go to the cockpit—not yet. A consistent inner nagging told her she needed to pray. The dream wasn't just a coincidence. It continued to tussle with inner stirrings that Annabelle called the voice of the Spirit.

I might not be in danger, but maybe Dan is.

A year after the U.S. had surrendered the Philippines, they hadn't received one word from him. In fact, the only news was that one newspaper clipping. Yet she knew—she believed—he was out there somewhere.

Pray for him. The thought would not leave her. *Pray.*

Libby inclined her back against the wall and felt the rumble of the engines. She pulled a slip of paper from the chest pocket of her flight jacket.

Read these verses from Psalm 91 before you fly, Annabelle had written on a slip of paper. *Use them as a prayer of protection. And know that I'm praying for you.*

Libby unfolded the paper, but it was Dan she now prayed these words for.

He that dwelleth in the secret place of the most High
shall abide under the shadow of the Almighty.
I will say of the Lord, He is my refuge and my fortress:
my God; in him will I trust.
Surely he shall deliver thee from the snare of the fowler,
and from the noisome pestilence.
He shall cover thee with his feathers, and under his
wings shalt thou trust:
his truth shall be thy shield and buckler.
Thou shalt not be afraid for the terror by night;
nor for the arrow that flieth by day;
Nor for the pestilence that walketh in darkness;
nor for the destruction that wasteth at noonday.
A thousand shall fall at thy side, and ten thousand
at thy right hand;
but it shall not come nigh thee.

She refolded the paper and slipped it into her pocket.

Dan, I'm not sure what's happening. But I wish you could know I'm praying for you. I hope you also understand that God is always with you . . . no matter what darkness you face.

Feeling a new sense of peace, Libby stood and made her way to the cockpit. She eyed the mass of gauges and meters. The pilot and co-pilot sat in the front seats with a beaming Rose watching their every move.

"Okay, guys." Libby offered them a wide grin. "Show me what this big bird is all about."

❧ ❧ ❧

The short trip to Omuta had been quickly granted once Natsuo informed his superiors that there was an important prisoner he needed to interrogate. He'd purchased one ticket for the trip there, but planned on two returning. Knowing Dan as he did, Natsuo had no doubt his old pal would follow this plan as choreographed. *Let the games begin.*

Natsuo approached the civilian overseers, asking around until he found the man he was looking for. Noting the evil gleam in the overseer's eyes, Natsuo knew there wouldn't be a problem with his request. And when he showed the overseer twenty packages of cigarettes, the man was all too eager to comply.

After Natsuo gave the man his orders, he moved to a dark corner and waited for D.J. to stagger into the tunnels. Natsuo's eyes widened as he spotted him. Dan looked about fifty pounds leaner than he remembered, yet his face didn't wear the look of defeat he'd witnessed on so many prisoners.

Good for you. Natsuo pulled a cigarette from his pocket and lit it. The smoke seeped from his lips as he smiled. *It is an honorable thing to be strong under such conditions.*

❧ ❧ ❧

Dan and Gabe walked side by side down the long, dark tunnel, the flashlights on their heads bouncing against the scarred tunnel walls.

"I'm glad to see the daylight getting longer." Dan swung the large pick to his opposite shoulder. "It will be good to spend more time in the fresh air of the courtyards, rather than huddled together in the cold, drafty rooms with the tiny spindly tails." Dan clicked his nails against his helmet.

"Hey, some of those shrews are my friends." Gabe chuckled.

They arrived in the new section of tunnel they'd been shoring up, and Gabe placed their bento boxes on top of a large boulder. The two civilian overseers were already there, in addition to the six other workers on their team. "Spring has always been my favorite time of year. I remember my boys, as soon as the grass started turning green—" Gabe's words cut off short when a loud crack filled the tunnel.

Dan turned, watching in horror as Gabe's body shot

back against the tunnel wall. Gabe let out a cry of pain, holding his ribs. The larger overseer, Tumato San, stood above him with a board in his hand.

Dan lunged for his friend, covering Gabe's body with his. "What do you think you're doing? Are you crazy?"

Tumato San dropped the board and lunged at Dan, throwing him into the wall. Dan slid down the rough surface, feeling the jagged pieces of rock tearing into his back. The room grew dim, and he wondered if he was blacking out, but then he realized it was only the lamp knocked off his head.

Gabe cried out even louder, the sickening sounds of punches drawing an even larger crowd.

Dan jumped up and saw Tumato bearing down on Gabe, swinging punches, one after another, causing Gabe's head to whiplash from side to side.

"Stop!" Dan tugged at Tumato's shoulders, but the large man didn't budge. Dan then kicked the aggressor in the kidneys. Tumato winced slightly but refused to turn. Dan looked to the other workers who hovered in the corner. "We have to stop him! He's going to kill Gabe."

No one dared stand up to the overseer. Fear filled their faces.

Then Dan spotted it—the board Tumato had dropped. He lunged for it and gave it a mighty swing. The board connected with the side of Tumato's head, making a horrific cracking sound. The overseer's punches stopped, and he toppled over, nearly landing on top of Gabe. Dan panted heavily as he looked at the two men lying side by side, slumped against the wall. The attacker and the victim both bloody, both appearing dead.

"Gabe, open your eyes. Gabe, please." Dan kneeled before him. His trembling hands wiped his friend's bloody face. Dan let out a sigh of relief when he heard the smallest moan escape from Gabe's lips. He cradled Gabe's head in his arms and lowered it to the ground. Footsteps grew louder behind him; then strong arms wrapped around Dan, pulling him back. He kicked and fought with all his strength as they dragged him upward toward the entrance of the mines.

"Gabe!" Dan screamed. "Don't die! Please, Gabe. Don't die!"

Outside, sunlight hit his face. Dan felt a strong fist to his jaw, and his body was thrown to the ground. He shook his head, attempting to clear the fog, and noticed two shiny boots on the ground before his face. He froze, panting, knowing today would be his last.

I'm sorry, Libby. I tried.

"Get this prisoner to his feet," the man before him hissed.

Dan was jerked to his feet by a guard on each side, then felt a fierce slap against his cheek. Dan's eyes widened as he looked into the face of Natsuo.

Natsuo stuck a finger in Dan's face, breathing heavily. "How dare you lift a hand to a servant of the great emperor? You deserve death for such an act."

"But, I—"

"You dare speak to me? You dare look me in the eyes?"

Dan lowered his gaze.

"Take him to my office!" Natsuo screamed. "I will deal with the *gaijin* there." He spoke the words in English, for Dan's benefit. Then he motioned to the guards and repeated the words in Japanese.

Moans of despair tore from Dan's lips. Gabe. Poor Gabe. And now this.

Dan's body ached from the fight, but his heart throbbed even more.

Thirty-Three

GOVERNMENT GIRL PLANES PURCHASED:
ARMY MUSTANG AND NAVY CORSAIR
TO BE CHRISTENED SUNDAY

Two grim Scythian ladies—manicured and bristling with the weapons of their profession—will make their bow to thousands of admiring federal workers in an impressive ceremony Sunday, May 9, at 3 p.m.

They are an Army P-51 Mustang and a Navy F4U1 Chance Vought Corsair—otherwise, the two "Government Girls," bought and paid for by dollar contributions in an amazing two-week campaign carried on by the Council of Personnel Administration and the Washington Post.

Each of these Amazons will be appropriately christened "Government Girl." They will be completely equipped for combat duty and ready to roll down the ramp on speedy hard-hitting missions, carrying with them the prayers of approximately 150,000 federal employees.

The warplanes selected are undoubtedly the finest of their respective types of any nation on earth. Of the Mustang, Capt. Eddie Rickenbacker recently said:

"In my travels throughout the hell holes of the world and my associations with the boys that are flying and maintain them, I find that it is the outstanding fighter plane anywhere in the world. I saw comparative tests with the German Focke-Wulf, their latest fighter type, and frankly the Mustang outperformed it."

Excerpt from the *Washington Post,* May 4, 1943

Libby slipped the cloth helmet over her head and adjusted her goggles. The California sun was just rising, tinting the sky with a soft shade of pink. Behind her the mechanics swung open hangar doors, their greetings splitting the warm morning air.

She slowly walked around the P-51 Mustang, doing a detailed flight check and feeling a little awed by the Hamilton Steele eleven-foot propeller. When all checked out, she climbed onto the wing and scrambled into the cockpit.

July and Ginger thought she was crazy for tackling this plane. It had three times the accident rate of other pursuits, and in order to keep the engine running smoothly, it was necessary to leave the runway at full throttle. Even then, sometimes the plane would stall and have to be restarted midair. She'd even heard of engines catching fire.

But it's fast. Dan would've loved it.

So Libby had studied the flight manual in detail, especially the long section on handling emergencies. Underneath the enormous cowling was a 1,400-horsepower engine. Behind the engine was the Plexiglas cockpit and underneath that an air scoop as big as Libby's room at the barracks. From there the fuselage narrowed until it finally flared at the tail.

Here goes nothing.

She held the canopy and stepped into the cockpit one leg at a time. In the smaller planes, she could reach the canopies from a sitting position; here she had to step lightly on the edge of the seat. She then grasped the lid with both hands and slid it forward. The canopy shut, and her body sank into the seat. She scooted the seat a few inches forward until she could reach the rudder pedals with ease.

She started the engine and it roared to life, pulling against her hands like a lioness struggling to escape from her cage. Because of the tilt of the plane, Libby could see nothing of the runway before her. She saw only the plane's large nose and the sky above.

She cleared her throat, then spoke loudly into the microphone. "Tower, this is P-51-210347. I'm on runway three requesting clearance for takeoff."

Even with the canopy closed she could barely hear herself over the engine. There was a second of static, and then through the earphones she heard the voice respond.

"P-51-210347, this is Tower. You are cleared for takeoff."

Libby gently pushed the throttle until the pressure gauge read 61 inches and the tachometer 3,000 rpm. The engine roared even louder, and the Mustang rumbled down the runway. She watched the speed increase. 45, 50, 60, 65.

As promised, the rear wheel lifted until the tail was level with the nose, and for the first time she could see the airstrip straight ahead. The speed increased. 75. 80. 90. At 100 mph she pulled gently on the stick and held her breath. The vibrations stopped as the plane lifted itself from the runway, and the ground fell away. Libby was at a loss to say whether she flew the plane or it flew her.

"Whoo-wheee!"

Laughter sounded through the earphones.

"Sorry about that, Tower."

"That's okay, young lady. I guarantee if I was flying one of those planes I'd be doing the same."

Libby checked the navigational map she'd strapped to her leg. It was only a short trip from Long Beach to March Army Air Base in Riverside, so she cherished every second.

I wish you could see me now, Dan. I know you'd have the biggest smile on your face.

"Enough of that." She spoke over the roar of the engine. "He will see me flying these babies one day. He *will.*"

The trip went too quickly, and Libby soon found the airfield and circled it, preparing to land. She tuned into the correct frequency. "Tower, is it okay to come in now?"

She didn't get a response, so she continued in the holding pattern.

"Tower. Is it okay to land?"

"Lady, would you please get off the airwaves? I have a P-51 I'm trying to make contact with."

Libby banked the plane and turned toward the tower, giving the operator a wave. "I'm sorry, sir, but I *am* the P-51."

"Uh, P-51 cleared to land on runway one . . ."

"Thank you, Tower. P-51 touching down."

A grin filled Libby's face as she sauntered into the airport office.

The man from the tower now stood by the front desk. "See, Chuck. I told you it was one of those lady pilots."

A man entered from an adjoining room, wiping his greasy hands on his coveralls. Libby approached the desk and began filling out the correct forms, ignoring the men's gawking stares.

"Didn't realize the government allowed girls to fly such powerful aircraft." Chuck strode to the waiting area and poured himself a cup of coffee. "Want some?"

"No, thanks." Libby focused on her paperwork.

"Yeah, I just heard about that other lady flier this morning, poor thing." Chuck took a sip of his coffee.

Libby lifted her head. "What do you mean?"

"Didn't you hear? One of them was killed yesterday in a crash over Tennessee. I heard it on the radio. She had a weird name too, like one of the months or sumthin'."

A twinge of pain shot through Libby's chest, and she sank into the nearest chair. "July? July Alexander?"

"Yup, that would be it." The mechanic pushed his cap back from his head. "Now, what kind of name is that?"

A sob erupted before Libby could stop it. The tears flowed next, and she covered her face with both hands.

"Now look what you've gone and done," the other man said. "You made her cry."

Libby didn't wait for the rest of the conversation. She threw the paperwork onto the office desk and hurried from the office. *July? Dead?* She wished it wasn't true, yet the risk was a reality they lived with every day.

Libby grabbed her B-4 bag and parachute and hurried outside to find a ride to the train station.

The pale sunlight and light blue sky blinded her briefly as she stepped along the walkway. Only five steps outside the flight office door, Libby's leg began to quiver, and she plopped down, using her parachute pack as a seat.

It had only been two days since she'd seen July. She'd been in town and had come bursting into Libby's room, inviting her to a movie. Libby pressed her fingers harder against her eyes.

Oh, July. I miss you already, but I know you're soaring now—higher than any of us.

"Are you okay?" a voice asked.

Libby turned, expecting one of the men from the office. Instead it was a tall man she faintly recognized, hat in hand. She wiped the tears from her face. "I'll be fine. I'm just trying to find a ride to the train station."

The man smiled, his friendly eyes crinkling at the corners. "Hmmm, you need a ride. How come that sounds so familiar?"

Libby wrapped her arms around her stomach. "I know you, don't I? We met before in Redondo Beach."

"Yeah, I gave you a ride to your friend's house. You're Libby, right?"

"Yes, and I'm sorry. What was your name?"

"Sam. Sam Struthers." He pointed to her uniform. "And I see you're part of the WAFS now. Where are you catching the train to?" He picked up Libby's bags and swung them over his shoulders as if they were filled with cotton. "I'd be happy to give you a lift to the station."

"Long Beach. I just transferred there a few weeks ago."

They walked to the parking lot where a brown army jeep, emblazoned with a large white star on the door, waited.

"Is that so? I spend a lot of time in Long Beach. I just happened to be called to these parts today, checking out the engine of a bomber that's giving them fits." Sam set Libby's bags in the backseat of the jeep. "That wasn't you coming in that P-51, was it?" He slid in and patted the seat beside him.

Libby stood by the door, glancing back at the office. "Actually, it was."

Sam let out a low whistle. "I'm mighty impressed.

And I'd be happy to give you a ride all the way back to the base. It's not too far from my next job."

Libby bit her lip. A ride to the base would be easier than waiting at the station, loading and unloading her things from the train, and catching another ride back to the base.

At first the WAFS had been under strict orders not to hitch plane rides with male pilots, but over the last few months things had become more lax, especially with male and female pilots now ferrying the big bombers together. And if it was okay in the planes, then . . .

"I'd love a ride, and if possible a cup of coffee. I need something to clear my mind. I just received some terrible news."

Sam glanced at his watch. "I think we can squeeze that in. And if you're interested, I'm a pretty good listener."

They stopped at Rhonda's, a small café not far from the base. It was filled with military and civilian workers —soldiers in uniform mingling with Rosie-the-Riveter-type gals who chatted over breakfast before heading to work. Libby felt more at ease.

Just two more workers stopping off for coffee, she thought as they slid into a booth.

Sitting across from him, Libby felt like one of those munchkins in Judy Garland's new movie. Sam had to be at least six foot six, and his striking gray green eyes always seemed to smile when he looked at her.

As they sipped their coffee, Libby told him about July.

"I'm so sorry. I hadn't heard about that. She sounds like a fine woman."

"All the women pilots are wonderful. Some more challenging than others, but they really have a passion for flying and serving their country."

"Sometimes I wish I was over in the fighting." Sam put sugar into his cup, stirring it quickly. "I didn't realize it would be a curse to be so dang good at what I do. There's too many planes around here that need fixin'. At least that's what they tell me."

Libby glanced at his hand, observing that he didn't wear a ring. "But I'm sure that makes your family happy. They at least know where you are. That you're safe."

"Sometimes I think that's why I'm still here." He cracked a grin. "My mom's the most godly woman I know. I think her prayers are working, and God won't dare defy one of His most faithful by sending her son into danger."

Libby chuckled, finished her coffee, and waved off the waitress when she offered a refill. "We'd better get going, don't you think?"

Sam reluctantly rose from the chair. "Yes, but only if you promise we'll do this again. I love hearing about your flying adventures. It makes me feel as if my work is even more important."

It was only a fifty-mile drive between Riverside and Long Beach, but by the time they arrived back at the base Libby felt as if she'd known Sam all her life. He'd told her about growing up in a small community and always being taller than everyone else—even his third-grade teacher—and never really fitting in.

She, in turn, shared what it was like to be the only one without a mom at home, and feeling as if she had the cooties—never being invited to sleepovers or the other silly things that truly matter when you're twelve. She also told him about Dan and the newspaper article about him, which was the last news she'd heard. The jeep pulled up at the barracks in front of the base, and Libby almost felt sad to have the conversation end.

"Do you need a hand with those bags?" Sam jumped from the jeep.

"Are you kidding? If you stepped into the barracks, that would be the end of my military career—not to mention you might be mauled by dozens of lonely female fliers." She took the bags from him. "Besides, I'm used to hauling these monsters around."

Sam nodded, then waited as she walked to the door. Libby turned and waved, and only when she crossed the threshold did he climb back into the jeep and drive away.

Libby sighed, then dropped her bags and kicked them down the lime green hall. *I like him.*

She opened the door to her room, and the heat hit her full in the face. She left the door open and hoisted open one window. On her bed she noticed a newspaper clipping about July's accident.

At first Libby felt horrible for letting the tragedy slip her mind, but as she unpacked and prepared her wash for the next day, she realized it had been refreshing to have a conversation with a new friend. Libby glanced at the photo of Dan, smiling from the wall. *What would he think if he knew I'd spent the afternoon with a handsome mechanic?*

She sniffed her blouse and put it in the "to be washed" pile. *Still, it wasn't as if I planned it. It was only a simple ride.*

"Oh, no. It was anything but simple," Libby told herself as she glanced into the mirror and ran a brush through her thick, dark hair. Nothing had happened except small talk, but Libby knew it was not a good idea. She'd been lonely without Dan.

I won't be seeing any more of Sam Struthers. And that's a good thing.

Being one of the original pilots, Libby was thankful for her "in" with Nancy Love, especially when the lead WAF chose Long Beach for Rose's training in the big bombers, making her and Libby roomies once more.

Their barracks room was similar to the one in New Castle, except now their biggest problem was the heat, instead of the snow drifting through the cracks. Tonight was no exception. Warm air blew in from the open window, and as Libby lounged in her underwear, she challenged herself to guess the make and model of the roaring engines of the planes taking off and landing.

Down the hall a radio played "Don't Sit Under the Apple Tree," and Libby tuned out the words. *It was only coffee,* she thought as she studied the newest flight manual.

When Rose came in that evening, the two friends wordlessly embraced.

"How did you hear about July?" Rose asked, and Libby told her of the mechanic's careless comment.

"Oh, Libby. It was so horrible being there when it happened. Did you know that since we aren't 'officially' considered military, they wouldn't even pay for the transport of . . . of her body back?" Rose's voice trembled. "So we pitched in. All the WAFs that were there. Betty even volunteered to ride back with the coffin, just to make sure it got safely home to July's parents."

Libby focused on Rose's words. "Do we know how it happened?"

"They said July got too close to a plane with a male pilot and accidentally clipped *his* wing, sending her plane spiraling to the ground, but I've seen that type of carelessness before. Those guys fly too close. They play around with those planes, trying to spook us." Rose took a deep breath. "Sometimes I wonder why I came at all. Maybe I should've just stayed in Hawaii."

"I know what you mean. But at least we're getting a chance. We may get all the wrong type of attention, but we get to fly these planes."

Rose didn't respond but instead lay down on her bed and opened a magazine.

Lord, help me to remember all things are in Your hands . . . even the hard, painful things.

Especially the hard, painful things.

She wanted to share her growing faith with Rose. Share the hope she found even in the midst of all the hard stuff. But the words didn't come. Instead, Libby retrieved her Bible from her dresser, praying Rose would ask.

Libby opened to the Psalms and quietly read verses that she'd found a few days earlier. *Remember the word unto thy servant, upon which thou hast caused me to hope. This is my comfort in my affliction: for thy word hath quickened me. Psalm 119:49–50.*

But Rose didn't ask, and Libby finally put the Bible away. Before she went to sleep, she prayed one final prayer.

Help me to be strong. And use my weakness to learn to trust You more. Give me the right words for the right time, and give me hope that things will turn out okay.

No matter what new challenges the morning brings.

Thirty-Four

JAPS REPORT PRISONERS'
TREATMENT: THEY'RE FED RICE

The Berlin radio asserted yesterday that Vatican authorities have received Japanese assurances that Japan's war prisoners are receiving "satisfactory" treatment but also having been told that "the way of living by the Japanese people differs so greatly from that of western Europeans and this fact must be taken into consideration in judging the problem of the treatment of war prisoners in Japan."

Associated Press
Excerpt from the *Washington Post,* May 8, 1943

Libby was thankful for the day off as she lay around on the creaky, iron-framed bed, wanting more than anything to spend the rest of the day on top of its covers.

She'd found a picture of herself with July and Annabelle early in training and pinned it onto the wall next to Dan's photo. She thought about her prayer for strength the night before. And after the mail arrived with a letter from Dan's mom, she needed it more than ever.

Dear Libby,

First, thank you for letting me know that you've been reassigned to Long Beach. It's wonderful to know that you're so close. Please try to get up to see us as soon as you can. Or maybe we can meet in the middle for dinner.

Also, I wanted to send this letter from the War Department. It arrived last night, and although I've lived with not knowing Dan's whereabouts for so long, it was difficult for me to see these words on paper. I wanted more than anything to hear that Dan was alive and doing well. I'm praying for you, knowing that you will face the same pain. And I know we'll both be keeping Dan in our prayers, especially on his upcoming birthday.

In the Lord's hands,
Ima Jean Lukens

Libby unfolded the letter and took a deep breath. A news clipping also fell out of the envelope, and she pushed it to the side. A lump already formed in her throat, and she hadn't even read the first word.

May 7, 1943

The records of the War Department show your son, Daniel J. Lukens, as missing in action in the Philippine Islands since May 7, 1942, presumed either dead or a prisoner of the Japanese.

I deeply regret that it is impossible for me to give you more information than is contained in this letter. In the last days before the surrender of Bataan there were casualties that were not reported to the War Department. All available information concerning your son has been carefully considered, and under the provision of Public Law 490, 77th Congress, as amended, an official determination has been made concerning him on the records of the War Department in a missing status. The law cited provides that pay and allowances are to be credited to the missing person's account and payment of allotments to authorized allottees are to be continued during the absence of such person in a missing status.

It is to be hoped that the Japanese government will communicate a list of prisoners of war at an early date. At that time you will be notified by this office in the event his name is contained in the list of prisoners of war. In the case of persons known to have been present in the Philippines and who are not reported to be prisoners of war by the Japanese government, the War Department will continue to carry them as "missing in action," in the absence of information to the contrary, until twelve months have expired. At the expiration of twelve months and in the absence of other information, the War Department is authorized to make a final determination.

I fully appreciate your concern and deep interest. You will, without further request on your part, receive immediate notification of any change in your son's status. I regret that the far-flung operations of the present war, the ebb and flow of combat over great distances in isolated areas, and the characteristics of our enemies impose upon some of us the heavy burden of uncertainty with respect to the safety of our loved ones.

Very truly yours,
J. A. Ulio
Major General

Libby wiped a tear and opened the newspaper clipping. It was from the *Washington Post,* dated April 22, and was headed "Doolittle Raid."

Just last month President Roosevelt had announced over the radio the execution of members of the flight crews who'd been the first to bomb Japan, now referred to as the Doolittle Raiders. But what did an article about these raiders have to do with Dan?

Why the American people have to wait for anniversaries in order to be told the full facts about certain episodes in this war is known only to the White House. The habit started with Pearl Harbor. Not till the first anniversary of that disaster, or long after the damage had been repaired, were the American people taken into the Government's confidence. The full story of what happened to the airplanes in the Philippines is still withheld in the official bosom. But the marvelous tale of the Doolittle Raid on April 18, 1942, is vouchsafed exactly a year after it happened. . . .

Libby stopped reading, her mind focusing on the sentence Ima Jean had underlined. Then her eyes moved to Ima Jean's handwriting on the margin.

Just what did happen in the Philippines? Lord, protect my son. Psalm 91:1.

A chill swept up Libby's back as she noted the Scripture reference. It was the same one Annabelle had sent her.

Libby pulled out the slip of paper from where she'd tucked it between the pages of her Bible and read the words once more. *He that dwelleth in the secret place of the most High shall abide under the shadow of the Almighty.*

Then she hurried to her dresser to find a piece of paper and pen, knowing that she had to tell Ima Jean that God had led them both to the same Scripture.

Lord, surely it's a sign that Dan is in Your hands. Surely it's a sign he's not dead.

And somewhere deep inside, the glimmer of hope brightened.

Despite the miles that separated them, Dan knew his parents' thoughts were with him even more than usual today. *Happy Birthday.* Since he didn't smoke, he bribed a guard with one of the rationed cigarettes he'd swapped for an extra portion of rice.

He scooped the rice ball into his hand, ignoring the grains that wriggled in his fingers—maggots camouflaged in the rice. *Protein,* he convinced himself. *Should consider it a blessing.*

He placed the rice ball on his lap, remembering the way his mother always mixed the ingredients for his cake slowly. He wanted to tell her to hurry, to work faster, even though he knew he wouldn't get a piece till after supper—after the song harmonized by a dozen voices, mostly off-key. He closed his eyes and lifted the rice ball to his mouth. The refrain of "Happy Birthday" floated through his thoughts.

Dan bit into the rice ball and, for an instant, was certain he tasted the fluffy softness of sweet chocolate cake.

It had been one month since he'd been transferred from Camp 17 to the Tokyo Main Camp, traveling by train with blackout windows for most of the trip. He was then driven by jeep across a narrow wooden bridge to an artificial island on Tokyo Bay. The whole man-made island, now a miniature fortress, appeared to be no more than 250 feet long and 200 feet wide. A tall bamboo fence with barbed wire strung along the top enclosed the perimeter. The prisoners' barracks sat in the middle of the island surrounded by the administration buildings, the soldiers' quarters, and antiaircraft guns.

Dan had plenty of time to study this view over the days and weeks. He was confined alone in one of three small rooms in a far corner. Even though he could hear the voices that carried across the island, his only actual contact with another person was the taps of Morse code that came from a man on an adjoining wall, also in solitary confinement.

From his small, square window, Dan peeked out at the bright sunlight curving over the horizon, sending a thermal ripple of light over the wooden buildings where the other American soldiers were housed. It was from here he watched the prisoners in work crews, wishing he were one of them.

With shouts and the pounding of their canes against the walls, guards awakened the workers. A few minutes later, he watched as the GIs were led to the dusty courtyard where guards used large wooden ladles to scoop their morning rice into bowls. Then the prisoners circled in small groups, hungrily devouring their meal.

Dan's eyes were drawn to one man as he tucked his hand into his shirt, drawing it out and pushing something into his mouth. Once, when the men were loading a truck just outside the solitary confinement cells, he had heard them speak of their work unloading supplies from the docks and railway cars around Tokyo. They no doubt stole extra food in an effort to remain alive one more day, just as he, Gabe, and Tony had done so many months ago in Manila.

Guards paced amongst the prisoners, wearing their familiar caps, khaki green uniforms with baggy pants, belted coats, and wooden-handled swords that hung from their waists.

From behind the barred window, Dan gasped as one guard approached the lone prisoner. The GI glanced up, a handful of smuggled bread nearly to his mouth when he spotted the guard. The man's fingers dropped the food, and he winced and covered his head in anticipation of the blow to come.

Raising the stick, the guard brought it down upon the man's skull with a horrible whack that echoed across the island. The man flopped forward, and Dan forced himself to look away. Still, he could hear the dull thuds of the stick hitting the man's body, until there was only silence.

Next Dan heard the loading of prisoners and the rumble of trucks as they were driven to their work details.

Dan slumped to the dirt floor. His chest ached, and he remembered the ache of being driven away, not knowing if the friend he'd left behind was dead or alive. He wondered if the man's body still lay beside the barracks. But he refused to look, remembering . . .

Forcing Gabe's face out of his mind, Dan tidied his tatami mat, paper blankets, and straw pillow. The morning was warm, so he removed his outer jacket—his most cherished possession. He thought about the brave Englishman who had stripped it from an American who'd succumbed to illness, then smuggled it over to Dan's prison cage.

“Keep your head up, ol’ chap. I heard U.S. bombers in the distance last night. Surely this bloody madness will end soon.”

The few sentences could barely be considered intimate conversation, yet it was enough for that one night. Hearing others’ stories—sharing his own thoughts—that was what Dan missed most. How he longed for the days when he and Gabe would talk late into the night. He even looked back with fond memories at the darkest places they’d been, remembering the thoughts they’d shared.

Gabe. It was useless trying to ignore the scene that never left the forefront of Dan’s thoughts. And this morning, he let the events of his last day in the coal mine replay.

After the attack. After being taken to the mine entrance. After being thrown at Natsuo’s feet . . . he’d been dragged to an office in the main building. Two guards held his arms as he faced his old friend.

“Don’t speak, Mr. Lukens.” Natsuo’s gaze bore into Dan’s eyes. “It is a dishonor to say a word unless I give you permission.” Natsuo fumbled with some papers on his desk, then cleared his throat. “You are a flier. The American newspapers also report that you were a hero, shooting down many enemy planes. Fliers are not considered prisoners of the imperial army, but rather criminals. Many who have been captured have already been put to death.”

Natsuo’s fingers trembled as he turned to the next page. “Now you have attacked an imperial workman in the mines.”

"I was defending a friend—" Dan reached a hand toward Natsuo. "Surely you can understand that."

Natsuo dropped the papers, his fists pounding the desk. His eyes met Dan's. "These marks on your record are enough for you to be put to death. Don't you understand? Instead, you will be taken to Tokyo Main Prison and held there in solitary confinement!" He leaned across the desk, and for the briefest second Dan saw the Natty he knew. Natsuo's voice lowered. "My decision is merciful."

That was the last time Dan saw him.

"Merciful?" he mumbled now. "Being locked away, alone? Not knowing if Gabe or the others lived or died?"

Dan leaned his head against the wall and studied two names carved there. *Jonathan Winthrop. Bruce Evans.* Names of other men who had lived in this hole —no more than four feet by four feet—yet had not found their freedom. Under the others, Dan had used his pocketknife that he had somehow managed to keep hidden to carve his own name. *D.J. Lukens.*

Dan closed his eyes. How could he make it one more day?

Thirty-Five

WOMEN TAKE BOMBER ON WAY
TO FRONT LINE: FLIGHT OF TWO WAFS
FROM WEST COAST SETS A MARK

Cincinnati, June 26 (AP)—A B-25 medium bomber, racing in from the West on June 23, circled a Midwestern airport, nosed into the wind, and landed, writing another chapter in the history of women in aviation, according to an announcement tonight by the Army Air Corps ferrying division headquarters here.

It marked the first time in American military aviation that a woman pilot and co-pilot flew a bombing plane on part of the trip from the factory to the front line.

Excerpt from the *New York Times*, June 27, 1943

Libby and Rose sat on the picnic table in front of their barracks, watching the newest batch of pilot trainees practice their night flying. Although the sun had passed over the ocean, the temperature still stayed at 90 degrees. They sipped warm Cokes from small glass bottles and stirred up the air with fans made from the torn covers of army flight manuals.

It had taken nearly a month to arrange a day off together. Libby finally got the chance to tell Rose about the letter from Dan's mom, the news clipping, and the Scriptures Annabelle had written out for her.

"Don't you see?" Libby slipped off the yellow-and-blue scarf holding back her hair and patted the perspiration that dripped down her neck. "I think this is from God. It's His way of telling me He's taking care of Dan, watching over him."

The barracks' porch light cast a shadow over Rose's face as she cocked one eyebrow. She swished the last of the dark liquid in the bottom of the bottle, then finished it off. "So God is talking to you now? Libby, please. With all that's going on in the world, you think that God really takes the time to send you secret codes about a boyfriend you dated, what, two years ago?"

Libby shrank back as if she'd been slapped. "I don't believe you just said that. I love Dan. We're going to get married when he returns." Libby touched the ring on her hand.

Rose leaned forward and looked squarely at Libby. "I have to ask you, Libby. Do you love Dan, or do you love the *idea* of him?"

"I don't know what you're talking about."

"You know. The idea of your dreamy California fly-boy, who is struggling to survive in order to make it back to you. The idea of someone being in love with you as much as you love him." A breeze blew a strand of dark hair into Rose's eyes, and she tucked it behind her ear.

"I mean, how much did you really know him? Your relationship was just getting warmed up when the big, bad war got in the way. Do you think your feelings would still be the same if you had both stayed on the island? If the Japs hadn't gotten in the way of your romance? Do you think you'd still be heading down the same path to married-ever-after if Dan had stuck around?"

Libby stood and turned her back to Rose. "I can't believe you would say that. Of all people. I mean, the other girls never met him, and maybe he does seem a bit too good to be true. But you were there. You knew him. You saw us together. You said yourself that we were made for each other."

Libby remembered the four of them laughing around the table at Lau Yee Chai's, she and Dan, Rose and—

Rose didn't reply.

Libby turned back to her friend and lowered her voice. "I know it's hard for you, Rose. It was horrible what happened to Jack, but I need you to remind me again of my time with Dan. To offer me hope that we'll be together again."

"Hope? Libby, you're wishing for something against all odds. Things have changed, can't you see? We expected to join this war and have it over in six months.

Sometimes our image of how things should be blocks our view of how they really are."

Libby reached over and took her friend's hand. "Rose, what's gotten into you? I don't understand. Ever since . . ."

Rose stood and folded her arms across her chest. "Ever since July died? You're right. July's accident just woke me up to the truth. At first I thought being in the WAFS was wonderful. I loved all the women and really felt a connection. But if you could have seen her body—" Rose shook her head. "No, I wouldn't wish that on anyone. Sometimes not knowing is much easier."

Rose walked away, leaving her parting comment to replay in Libby's mind.

Sometimes not knowing is much easier.

Maybe not knowing what Dan faced right now *was* easier. *But God knows.*

Libby lifted her chin and watched the final trainer descend. She kept her eyes on its path until it finally touched down.

It wasn't that she didn't worry. Thoughts of losing Dan and never finding love again haunted her. When she was tired or weak, those thoughts hovered over her like an oppressive darkness. Yet, despite all those things, she'd found something greater. Something she could hardly understand herself.

All she knew was the truth had a voice different from those nagging worries. She'd discovered this truth in God's Word, and the more she let it in—the more she meditated on it—the more this voice of truth silenced her fears.

"I will say of the Lord, He is my refuge and my fortress: my God; in him will I trust," Libby said aloud.

This was the voice she wanted to listen to. Yet even her closest friend thought she was a fool for doing so.

❧ ❧ ❧

"Lord, get me out of this darkness. I need to feel light and heat. I need to touch the flesh of another person."

Dan curled into a ball in a corner of his small cell. It was the last corner that hadn't turned to mud due to the overflowing waste bucket.

His cheek rested on the cool ground, and he tried to imagine a time when stench did not fill his nostrils. He thought of the azaleas that used to bloom on Oahu. Of the salty ocean air. Of the pine trees and mossy soil of the California mountains near his home.

The memories of these scents stirred within Dan a knowing that someplace on this earth, all was well.

He recalled the smell of plane fuel and oil, letting the memories take him back to Clark Field, where thousands of men had lived and worked together. And the scent of fried fish. He tried to remember it, thinking of crowded restaurants in Honolulu. The loud, playful banter of young soldiers, and the harbor, busy with the movement of men and machines.

Freedom had been displayed in a happy rhythm of bodies at work and play. So different from this place where touch was nonexistent, and the only sounds of life filtered through walls that caged him.

Man wasn't made to be alone. Didn't the Bible say something about that? He was sure he'd heard those words before. Men were created to live together and interact. To share joys and sorrows. To lend a hand to those in need, and to hold the hands of those dying.

As the long days in the cell slipped into longer nights, Dan thought back to the times he had felt part of a community of people. And to other times when he'd failed to offer a touch to those who needed it. Images of men crumpled on the side of the road during the march in Bataan haunted him. He hadn't known their names, but their faces, young and old, now radiated in his mind as heavily as the Philippine sun had borne down on his head.

Dying, the men had stretched out their hands to those who passed. At the time Dan had thought they sought assistance—food, water, strong arms to pull them to their feet. But the more time Dan spent alone, the more he realized their outstretched hands simply longed for human touch. As they felt their souls slipping from this life to the next, perhaps they just wanted someone to hold them, to speak words of comfort, and to remind them they mattered and would be missed.

Perhaps the greatest tragedy of this war so far was that so many men had to die alone.

A faint tapping vibrated on the wall near his head. Dan's eyes opened and he scooted closer. He missed the first letters, but soon caught on. . . .

. . . S-o-n o-f m-a-n i-s c-o-m-e t-o s-e-e-k a-n-d s-a-v-e t-h-a-t w-h-i-c-h w-a-s l-o-s-t. L-u-k-e 19 10.

The message stopped there, and Dan pondered those words. He'd memorized lots of verses in Sunday school when he was a kid . . . but the prizes for memorization had meant more to him than the words themselves.

It was different now, thanks to the patient communication of the prisoner on the other side of the wall. Ben Morgan, Dan had gradually learned, was a flier from Omaha, captured by the Japs after a bombing raid over New Guinea. He'd already faced more days in solitary confinement than Dan had spent in the hell ship and the coal mines put together. Ben had tapped out verses to Dan, encouraging him to put his trust in God.

Dan wondered why he hadn't clung to these truths earlier. As a kid he'd liked the idea of God, but as he grew older he'd taken more comfort in God's remoteness. Since Dan couldn't see Him and didn't hear a loud booming voice from heaven, he'd figured that even if there was a God, He wasn't too interested in communicating with His people.

To believe was to trust, but what about his questions? Maybe questions were allowed . . . even if he didn't know the answers.

He'd heard many men cry out for God's help. Those same men had died horrible deaths. Paulo came to mind. His disfigured face, lying in the pile of bodies.

For Dan, it had been easier to keep pushing the thoughts of God away than to try and figure out why He would let these things happen. Only here there was no place to hide from the examination of eternity. Here, his every thought was exposed. In this place, there was nothing else to do except think.

And pray.

Dan opened his eyes and peered into the pitch-blackness, focusing on the thin thread of light where the moon dared to squeeze through the cloud cover and his window. He tapped to Ben a message he'd received from him a week before.

I o-n-c-e w-a-s l-o-s-t b-u-t n-o-w I a-m f-o-u-n-d w-a-s b-l-i-n-d b-u-t n-o-w I s-e-e.

That would make old Ben smile. Dan's heart felt a strange peace because of those words—even in this hellhole.

Thirty-Six

GRACE BEFORE MEAT

Every nation has its feast of thanksgiving, but the American Thanksgiving will not be confused with any of the others.

The feast is not the food. What could be drearier than the traditional menu eaten alone and in silence? The biblical dinner of herbs eaten in the company of those we love would be better. Thanksgiving is a day of reunion. More important than what is on the table are the friends gathered about it. This is, for those who celebrate it properly, a day of forgiveness, of quarrels forgotten, a new recognition of the value of a friend.

Excerpt from the *New York Times*, November 25, 1943

Natsuo paced the small office at the Tokyo Main POW complex. His eyes darted toward the isolated barracks at the far end of the island. It was his greatest test, and thus far he'd succeeded. His will for his country was stronger than his love of a friend.

Beware of those who stand in the way of clear victory. The time has come for those born in the imperial land to repay with decisive action. The imperial benevolence should not be confused with mercy. Honor is granted to those who obey with stern countenance. Who unite as one, ready for death. Who fight bravely until our long-cherished desire is achieved—all the world under the imperial roof.

"No, I cannot do it. I cannot continue." Natsuo's voice was no more than a whisper, but the words that had torn at his heart for months now escaped his lips. Ever since the day D.J. was thrown at his feet, the same dream had met him during the night.

⁂

He was in California walking home after a late night of study. His feet quickened as he heard a group of rowdy students exiting a bar. The group of young men circled, taunting him.

"We know what you people have been up to," one young man slurred. "Think it's okay killing all those women and children in China? Huh, Nip?"

Before he realized what was happening, Natsuo found himself on the ground. He curled into a ball on the cold sidewalk, wincing as they kicked him.

Then one voice rose above the others.

"Leave him alone, will ya? What's he done to you?"

Natsuo opened his eyes, and Dan's face met his gaze. "D.J.?"

"Come on." Dan offered his hand. "They won't bother you anymore."

Dan helped Natsuo to his feet. He was amazed at how the other boys scattered. Then he saw that a couple of other guys from the football team also backed Dan up.

"Natty, these are my friends. As long as we're around, nothing's going to happen to you."

❧ ❧ ❧

The same scene, same words visited Natsuo every night. It wasn't just a dream. It was a memory.

"I'm sorry, Great Emperor." Natsuo ran his fingers through his hair, feeling the debt of his inner soul. "The emotions are too great. I'm doomed to fail."

Once a noodle boy, always a noodle boy.

Natsuo sat on his metal chair and leaned over his desk. The morning sunlight glared in his eyes, and he reached over to close the bamboo shades. He attempted to concentrate on paperwork, but every few minutes he'd look up, eagerly watching for Yashimo to arrive for work. When he finally did, exactly on time, Natsuo called him into his office. The young guard bowed low before him, then fixed his eyes on Natsuo, eager to serve.

"Bring to me the prisoner in solitary confinement,

cell three. But first, give him a meal. Take him to the shower and make him put on the worker's warmer clothes. Get him a haircut and shave. Then, when he no longer stinks, bring him to me."

Yashimo nodded, and a secret smile filled his face. "It is a very Christian thing to do. To love your enemies."

Natsuo glanced at the cross that hung around Yashimo's neck, then turned his back to the man. "I am not Christian. And you'd better tuck that cross under your shirt. Go and do as I say. And mention it to no one. I could have you turned in for wearing that, as a soldier of the emperor."

"Yes, sir."

❧ ❧ ❧

Libby awoke to a piece of paper being placed on the pillow by her head. The scent of Rose's perfume wafted through the room. She scratched her nose and studied the note.

Dinner tonight? Call me. Sam.

"Libby, please. The guy's going to drive me crazy. He just wants a friendship. Honestly, Dan would understand."

Libby crumbled the piece of paper and dropped it to the floor. "I told you I'm not interested. He wants me to go to his house for Thanksgiving—it sounds too close to 'bringing the girl home to show the parents.' "

Rose nudged against Libby's hips until she scooted over; then she sat on the bed. "How about I join you?

Then it wouldn't be like that at all. I don't have any plans."

Libby rubbed the sleep from her eyes. "Fine. I'll call him. We'll go to Thanksgiving dinner, but that's it. And if he keeps asking me out after that . . . I swear, you're going to pay."

Rose stood and zipped her flight suit over her white blouse, and for the first time in ages, a smile played on her lips. "Yes, I'll pay. Now just go make the call." Rose sauntered out of the room. "Oh, and tell him we'll need a ride," she called back over her shoulder. "I don't think the army will let us travel by our normal mode of transportation."

❧ ❧ ❧

Cottonwood trees clapped their hands happily in the wind as Libby climbed out of Sam's pickup truck after Rose. The ride to his house had looked strangely familiar —the rows of sky-reaching palms, the brown rolling hills, even Roy's Fruit Stand. The farther north they drove, the more she realized that Sam lived amazingly close to Dan's parents. *I wonder if he'd swing me by to see them?*

Libby quickly pushed that thought out of her mind. How strange would that be, to show up with another man—no matter how innocent it was.

Libby playfully punched Sam on the shoulder, noticing the passel of kids running around the white picket-fenced yard. "Why didn't you tell me you were married and had so many kids?"

Sam raised an eyebrow as a little boy on a tricycle zoomed in front of them, ringing his bell and waving. "Hey, Stevie," he called. Then he turned to Libby. "Well, I thought if you knew, you wouldn't come."

Libby's jaw dropped.

"Nah, those are just my nieces and nephews. Goodness, you *are* trouble." He wrapped an arm around Libby's shoulders and led her toward the small yellow house.

This isn't right. But I have to admit, his touch is nice . . .

A girl about three years old with long, wavy brown hair ran up and lifted her arms to Sam. "Up. Up. I wanna touch the sky."

Sam pulled his arm away and lifted the girl to his shoulders, then began spinning in slow circles. "Here we go. Liftoff. Can you touch yet?"

The youngster squealed, and Libby couldn't help but laugh.

Rose sidled up to Libby. "Now tell me that doesn't just warm your heart."

Libby nudged Rose in the ribs. "Stop that. We've already had this conversation."

By the time he placed the girl back on her wobbly feet, a line of youngsters had formed in front of Sam. He turned to Libby and shrugged.

"I'll leave you to your fun," she said. "Rose and I will introduce ourselves and see if your mom needs any help."

Sam rapped her chin with a soft curl of his finger.

"There you go, being great. I'm sure she'll appreciate it."

Rose slid her arm into Libby's as they walked toward the house. She cleared her throat. "A-hem. Did Sam just have his arm around you?"

Libby forced a grin. "I knew I should have left you at home."

❧ ❧ ❧

Dan felt alive again. His stomach bulged with his small dinner of fresh fish and clean white rice. His pink skin still stung from the scrubbing that had peeled off layers of dirt, and the sensation of his new clothes against his skin was almost foreign. He rubbed a clean hand against his shaven face. How long had it been?

With a smile, he tucked the faded photo of Libby and the pocketknife into his trousers. "Okay, I'm ready."

The guard, Yashimo, led him to the main office. "When you enter the room there will be a man sitting behind the desk. You bow, stand at attention, and wait for orders. Understand?"

Dan didn't have to ask who the man would be. So many nights within that solitary cell his mind had played a game of tug-of-war, yanking his thoughts between love and hatred. When he couldn't stand the conflicted emotions, he prayed for Natty, though at first it was hard.

Now he found it was even harder to hate someone when he placed him at the feet of Jesus in prayer.

"Yes, of course. I will honor him." Dan paused and

placed his hands over his face, overcome with emotion. He swallowed hard, then breathed out slowly. "I'm ready."

The room was lit only by the afternoon sun, and at the desk sat Dan's former classmate. Fatigue marked Natsuo's overall expression, and his once-glittering eyes sat as dark pieces of coal in his head, devoid of life. Natsuo waved the guard away, who closed the door.

"Sit, D.J."

Dan bowed low, then did as ordered.

"Do you remember how, even as I lived in the United States, I would work very hard and send money home?" Natsuo spoke to Dan, but his gaze was somewhere else, at another place and time.

Dan nodded.

"Japan is a very poor country. There are too many people. They need so much. Remember how you'd even help me save the lead foil from gum and cigarette wrappers? You did not know, but when the Japanese freighters came to San Pedro to buy American scrap metal, I would take them the foil. In a small way it was my contribution."

Dan watched as Natsuo's eyes finally scanned his thin frame, then looked away.

Natsuo's voice was solemn. "I miss breakfast from the student union, the ham and eggs, bacon, sausage, coffee." He folded his hands and placed them on his desk. "So many breakfasts and lunches spent together. Hamburgers and fries were my favorite." He paused as if searching for words.

"I remember buying you your first chocolate malt." Dan's voice was low, guarded.

"Yes. Now we find ourselves on opposite sides of this desk and this war." Natsuo lowered his head, and when he lifted it again, his eyes were red.

"You are my enemy, and I must treat you as such." His voice was raspy. He stood and paced. "You think the place I have put you is harsh. But you are safe." Natsuo leaned forward, pressing his hands onto his desk. "My comrades are angry. Many have lost their wives and children. Prisoners are slaughtered every day for the smallest offense. Do you understand?"

Dan nodded.

Natsuo returned to his chair. "I just wanted to ask you, is there anything you need? Anything I can get you?"

Dan bowed his head, and he couldn't control the shaking of his shoulders. "A Bible. In English. And medicine for Benjamin? I don't think he's doing too well."

Natsuo steepled his fingers and placed them to his lips. "Your request does not surprise me. Always thinking of the needs of a friend first. You will have as asked."

"Thank you . . . Natty."

Natsuo walked to the door and signaled to the waiting Yashimo to take Dan away.

❧ ❧ ❧

The kitchen bustled with activity. Children ran in and out, snatching cookies that cooled on the counter.

Sam's three sisters were busy shooing the children away and setting up long tables that had been butted up against one another.

After introducing herself to Sam's mother, Rose grabbed up a large pile of silverware and started setting it out on the white tablecloth.

Libby noticed the scents of cinnamon and cooked turkey as she was squished into Glenda's warm embrace.

"I'm Glenda. And it's so wonderful to meet you."

Glenda's plump hands threw an apron over Libby's head and set her to work mashing potatoes.

"Sam has said so many things about the wonderful lady pilot."

"He has?" Libby pushed the masher up and down, watching the steam rise off the hot spuds.

Glenda's smile faded, and she shook her head. "Honey, you're being too gentle. Like this." She took the potato masher from Libby's hands and vigorously plunged it into the boiled potatoes. "You have to be rough with them or they won't turn out fluffy."

Libby took the masher back and plunged it up and down with a vengeance.

Glenda's round face smiled approval; then she continued cutting corn from the cobs. "I'm sorry to hear about your fiancé. Sam said you lost him in the war."

Libby felt the masher slip from her grasp, clattering to the floor. Glenda continued her steady stream of chatter, never noticing Libby's stunned expression.

"What were the odds of Sam's being there twice

when you needed a ride? I don't believe in coincidences. I told him it could be the Good Lord's way of putting you two together. Since you didn't get the hint the first time, He gave you a second."

With shaking hands, Libby picked up the masher and rinsed it off at the sink.

"Sam warned me not to say anything to you," Glenda said, shaking her head. "But I've been praying for the perfect wife for my son. It's probably not my place to say, but I saw the look on your face when you two first arrived. I thought maybe you felt the same about my Sam."

Libby felt the color rush to her cheeks, then mashed harder, tightening her jaw.

Glenda turned to Libby and frowned. "Oh, dear, it looks like you're getting more potatoes on the counter than in the bowl." She took the masher away again, cocking one eyebrow. "Honey, why don't you just go find Sam and see if he needs any help with the kids?"

Libby forced a smile onto her face. "Sounds good."

She let the screen door slam behind her and found Sam under the cottonwood tree. She didn't stop, didn't talk to anyone until she reached him.

He waved, but his smile disappeared as she grew closer.

"How could you do this to me? Tell your mother that I 'lost' my fiancé. There's no evidence that Dan's dead. No proof, don't you understand that?" Libby placed her hands on her hips and peered down at him. "I thought I'd made it clear that I can offer you no more than friendship. And . . . and although I like you, I really do, I just can't give up on Dan. I made a promise." Libby turned and hurried across the yard, desperate to find a place to be alone.

"Libby, please. Wait." Sam jumped up from the ground, and she could hear his footsteps quickening behind her.

She paused, feeling her chest heave with pent-up emotion.

"I'm sorry. I shouldn't have said anything to my mother. You're right; you haven't received official word yet. But really, Libby. You need to consider the facts. Libby, please."

Desperation clouded Sam's voice.

She turned and looked up into his eyes.

He reached out his hand as if to caress her cheek, then thought better of it and dropped it to his side once more. "I need you to give me another chance. I want to explain."

Libby placed a hand over her eyes and told herself not to break down. Not here.

"I'll give you your space, if that's what you need," he whispered.

"Yes, that's what I need. I can't do this without knowing for sure. I mean, Dan could be out there. And . . . and how would you feel if you were in his position, wondering if the girl you loved was being wooed by some other guy?"

Sam's smile faded. "It's not like I tried to break you guys up. Dan's dead, Libby. We all know what happened on those islands. We know how the guys were treated, especially the fliers. There's no reason to feel like a louse when we both know he's not coming back."

The words hit Libby like a fist to her gut. She turned and made her way back to Sam's truck. Her knees felt weak, and she paused, realizing she had nowhere to run. Sam approached and placed his hands on her shoulders. "Don't be mad. I didn't expect things to turn out like this. I didn't expect to fall in love with you."

She pulled away from his touch. "Dan is not dead. I know—" The words cut off, because the truth was, she didn't know. Maybe she was just trying to fool herself. Maybe Rose and Sam were right after all.

"Can you take me to the train station, please? I need to get back to the barracks. You can give Rose a ride home later. I don't want to ruin her Thanksgiving. I'm sure she'll understand." Libby climbed into Sam's truck. Her whole body trembled.

Lord, please. Find a way. Anything. Let me know Dan still lives.

❧ ❧ ❧

Dan awoke in the night, knowing he needed to pray. His first thoughts were of Libby. The last time he'd heard from her had been a batch of letters he received right before the bombing of Pearl Harbor. Who knew what had been happening in her life since then? Who knew what, exactly, he should pray for?

God knows, Dan realized. He'd read just that morning that God's Holy Spirit would pray the right words for him even when he didn't know how.

Things had been better lately. He'd been given extra food, although his arms still looked like flesh stretched over bones. He'd also been given a Bible. And he devoured it, sitting under the window reading by the light from dawn to dusk.

But as Dan lay there he realized that it wasn't only Libby that God was asking him to pray for. Someone else needed his prayers tonight too.

The world keeps changing, and I'm still trapped inside these same walls. O God, even when I don't know when dawn is coming for my freedom from this place, please help me to be faithful in the dark.

Dan turned to his side and pulled the dirty coat over him like a blanket. Then he heard the sound of footsteps outside his window, and he cocked his head. He crawled toward the wall with the window, leaning against it. This wasn't the first time. The visitor came in the middle of the night, when the other guards on the island were fast asleep. And while his visitor was silent, Dan had carried on one-sided conversations, sharing all kinds of memories with the listener.

"I remember the first day my friend played football with me. We were at the beach, just goofing off, a whole group of us. My friend got the ball, and he was so afraid of the big guys tackling him that he wouldn't stop running. Even after he passed the goal line, he kept going. I had to run down the beach to get him."

Dan listened for a moment to the steady breathing.

"And I remember the first dance we went to together. He was so nervous that no one would want to dance with him . . . Then a pretty blonde came up to him, and he was on the dance floor so fast I had whiplash." Dan chuckled. "Yeah, those were the days.

"And in a college English class, the same friend and I were once asked to critique a poem by Emily Dickinson." Dan paused, sure he heard breathing, then continued.

"We picked a certain poem, mainly because it was short." He sighed, then pulled the coat tight around his shoulders. "The poem was about a Book with a capital B, but my friend and I argued that the poet didn't necessarily mean the Bible. Dickinson always capitalized nouns she felt were important.

"We analyzed the poem and presented our ideas to the class. I said that the 'precious Words' in the poem loosen the reader's spirit, breathing life into the weary soul. He sees life differently because of the joy inside."

Dan cleared his throat. "At the time I was sure the poem talked about the journey we take when we open the pages of a book. But if I could talk to my friend again, I would tell him that not just any book can bring such liberty. Though my body is caged, my spirit is loosened by the greatest gift ever given to me—this Bible." He began to recite the poem aloud.

"He ate and drank the precious Words—
His Spirit grew robust—
He knew no more that he was poor,
Nor that his frame was Dust—"

And as he spoke the poem, the person on the outside of the window joined in. It was no more than a whisper, but Dan's lips curled in a smile.

> *"He danced along the dingy Days*
> *And this Bequest of Wings*
> *Was but a Book—What Liberty*
> *A loosened spirit brings—"*

Thirty-Seven

END OF WASP TRAINING PLAN
RECOMMEND BY COMMITTEE

The House Civil Service Committee yesterday recommended termination of further recruiting and training of Wasps (Women's Air Service Pilots) for noncombat civilian duty with the Army Air Forces and urged use instead of "several surpluses of experienced pilot personnel."

The report, which condemned the program as costly, "experimental," and unjustified in the light of large untapped polls of trained pilots, recommended continued use only "of Wasps already trained and in training."

To handle the faster and heavier ships, a woman pilot must receive $20,000 worth of training, the committee said.

Excerpt from the *Washington Post,* June 6, 1944

It had been seven months since Libby's conversation with Sam, but his words wouldn't leave her alone.

Dan's dead, Libby. We all know what happened on those islands. We know how the guys were treated, especially the fliers.

Libby scanned the blue sky as the engine of the P-51 roared beneath her. She made a right turn, following the winding river she'd mapped, and wished she could steer her thoughts so easily.

Lord, please. Give me the faith I once had. I want to trust You. I want to escape these worries. But it's been another year and still no word.

Libby spotted the airfield ahead of her and prepared to land.

Once she had signed the plane over to the correct person, Libby hurried out of the office and found a familiar face waiting for her.

"Ginger! It's been so long. How are you doing?"

Ginger lifted her hand, and Libby noticed a ring.

"I'm engaged to a wonderful man named Quincy. He's an engineer working on new military planes, and believe it or not, he enjoys my input!"

Libby gave Ginger a quick hug. "Congratulations. Are you still ferrying?"

"Yes. And I know I was the one who put up the stink about flying the small trainers, but in order to stay close to Quin, I've taken a gig ferrying Cubs from the factory to a nearby military base. Which leads to my asking a favor."

"Anything." Libby plopped her bag to the floor.

"Well, I'm pretty sure you've heard, but the House Civil Service Committee is bent on stopping our training. Quin and I worry this is just the first step to cutting the WAFS off completely. Anyway, he pulled some strings, and I have an invitation to a hearing on the subject—if I can get someone to cover for me. I've already talked to Nancy, and she can relieve you of your duties for a few days if you can help."

Libby wrapped an arm around Ginger's shoulders. "Ferrying Cubs? That should be interesting after flying these metal monsters. Sure, why not? It'll be good to know someone's going to speak up for our program."

Ginger gave Libby a thumbs-up. "Great. The first batch of Cubs needs to be delivered tomorrow morning. Looks like you'll be staying with me tonight. I'm in a great boardinghouse downtown, and my car's outside."

"Sounds great." Libby grabbed her bags and hoisted them over her shoulder. "That will give us tonight to catch up on old times. Rose has been asking about you. I can't wait to tell her about your new love."

Ginger wrapped a fuchsia scarf over her black hair and led Libby to a small gray Buick. "I hope Rose can find someone else as wonderful as Jack," she said, placing the key in the ignition. "There were many nights we cried on each other's shoulders."

"Rose is a trouper; she always pulls through." Libby brushed the blowing hair back from her face. "And she has fallen in love . . . with those big bombers. Imagine, that little wisp of a girl flying those big planes. You've gotta love it."

❧ ❧ ❧

The door opened with a clang, and a flood of white light poured in. Dan waited for the sound of his rice ball dropping to the floor. Waited for the door to slam shut as quickly as it opened. But the light remained. Dan lifted his head, shielding his eyes. It took a few seconds for them to adjust. The thin, short figure of a man came into view.

"Yashimo!" Dan clawed against the wall and pulled himself onto his shaky feet.

"Come closer; I have news for you." Yashimo placed his palm downward as if he were swatting a fly, and motioned to Dan. "I come to tell you the interpreter worries about American bombers hitting island. He says a work crew is to go to hills. They say to round up ten healthy men. The interpreter say to get you—if you are well enough to work."

Dan took a step forward, lifting his face to the light and allowing it to cascade over him like a waterfall of warmth and brightness.

He reached for Yashimo's hand and could clearly see concern in the young soldier's face.

"Do *you* think I'm well enough?" Dan tried to study his eyes, but Yashimo quickly lowered his gaze.

Yashimo's voice lowered, hinting of deep sadness. "I see what they do to the weak. Overseers are cruel. They find more ease to kill than to wait, than to help their workers."

Dan leaned against the wall, feeling his shoulders

quiver. *If only God would give me the strength. Please, God.* Yet instead of feeling energy surge through his muscles, they screamed at him for even attempting to walk across the small cell.

"What about Benjamin? Is he well enough to go?"

Yashimo shook his head. "No, your friend is sick. Medicine no work. He cannot rise from ground. He not be a good choice."

"But that can't be. The medicine *was* helping. He was fine. Besides." Dan ran his hand down the cool wall. "His verses. Every hour, he shares them with me. I share others in return."

Yashimo's voice was no more than a whisper. "How do you say, 'His heart is willing, but body weak.'"

Dan pressed a hand to his temple. "It can't be. What about the others? Are . . . are the men on the other sides of Ben leaving?"

Yashimo reached for Dan's hand and pulled him forward, deeper into the light. Dan breathed in a huge breath of warm, fresh air.

"Yes, they already going to storeroom for boots."

"Boots." Dan spoke the word in a whisper. He glanced down at his sore-covered feet. His eyes darted to the corner where his tattered shoes still hid the knife and the photo.

Yashimo finally lifted his eyes to Dan. It was clear from his furrowed eyebrows what he hoped Dan's answer would be. "And you? What do you like me to tell Natsuo San?"

Dan took three steps when he heard the slightest

tapping on the wall. He stopped. "Tell him that I am staying. I can't leave my friend alone. Who would be here to share the Holy Scriptures with him? To give him hope?" Dan bowed low before Yashimo. "Thank you for bringing me the Word. Thank you for offering light and life. Tell Natsuo San thank you too."

Dan moved back into his dry corner.

"That is kind of you. Sharing God's Word with your friend. Benjamin will be grateful."

Dan tightened his lips into a thin line, realizing Yashimo's assumption was also true. Yet Dan did not confess that he was actually speaking of another friend—of his night visitor.

The sound of a truck roaring to life flooded the small room, making Dan realize how muted his world had become inside these walls.

Yashimo glanced back over his shoulder. "I must go. But I will pray you can be strong." He bowed low and stepped from the doorway, allowing the door to slam with a clang. "The Lord I also serve will be with you."

A deep sense of loss flooded Dan's chest. He scurried to the door and fell against it. He wanted to call out, to tell Yashimo to wait, that he'd changed his mind. That it would be worth a try—even if his strength failed him, it would be worth at least stepping into fresh air one last time.

Dan touched his face, remembering the momentary warmth of the uninhibited sunlight. He turned his back to the door and slid to the ground. "Lord, have I made a terrible mistake? Should I have gone?"

Yet, even as Dan prayed, he knew it was not to be. Even in the darkness, a sense of peace settled over him. His time of darkness wasn't over. The final night had not passed.

His ear perked to the Morse code being tapped against the wall.

Dan crawled back to his corner and curled against the cool wood. *P-l-e-a-s-e b-e-g-i-n a-g-a-i-n,* he tapped, then pressed his ear to listen.

T-h-r-o-u-g-h t-h-e t-e-n-d-e-r m-e-r-c-y o-f o-u-r G-o-d w-h-e-r-e-b-y t-h-e d-a-y-s-p-r-i-n-g f-r-o-m o-n h-i-g-h h-a-t-h v-i-s-i-t-e-d u-s t-o g-i-v-e l-i-g-h-t t-o t-h-e-m t-h-a-t s-i-t i-n d-a-r-k-n-e-s-s a-n-d i-n t-h-e s-h-a-d-o-w o-f d-e-a-t-h, t-o g-u-i-d-e o-u-r f-e-e-t i-n-t-o t-h-e w-a-y o-f p-e-a-c-e L-u-k-e 1 78 79.

Dan considered those words. "To give light to them that sit in darkness." He said the words slowly as if digesting each one. "To guide our feet into the way of peace."

Peace. Could it be around the corner? More bombers roared overhead by the day. American bombers. The Japanese had completely lost control of their own sky.

Lord, I've discovered eternal liberation within these walls. Will it be from here my body is also liberated?

Dan pulled out the photo of Libby. So many years. And he was a different man from the one she'd fallen in love with. Did she still wait?

Can she accept me for the broken man I've become?

⁂

The airstream acted similar to waves of a choppy sea, tossing Libby's Cub about.

It's like riding a log raft in the rapids.

Finally she spotted the airfield. "We're here." She patted the seat. "I don't know how Ginger does it, flying you toys all day."

Since the Cub didn't have a radio to communicate with the tower, Libby put the small flier in a holding pattern and waited for the red light on the runway to turn green.

She nearly laughed as the plane bounced upon landing. She could land a large, fully armed pursuit with ease, but it would take a few times to remember how to land the little trainers.

Libby felt a strong crosswind as she taxied to the parking area in front of the hangar. She cut her engine. But, as if not willing for the trip to be over, the Cub bucked under the mercy of the wind, its wings wobbling.

"Whoa, Nelly. Easy gal." Libby jumped out, her boots landing on the pavement, and grabbed the plane's strut, but the wind pulled harder.

Suddenly the plane began to spin. Its wing passed over her, and before she knew what was happening, the propeller struck Libby's forehead full force. She flew backward, sprawling on the tarmac.

"Ugh." She heard footsteps and opened her eyes to see a man grabbing the lightweight Cub and pushing it to a better spot.

"Are you okay, miss?"

Libby moaned. "I think so. Do you see any blood?"

"No blood, but a nasty bump. Let's get you inside and put some ice on that."

The man pulled Libby to her feet, but a rush of nausea came over her. "Uh, you better set me down. I think I need a few minutes."

Her head throbbed, and Libby moaned, imagining the news story. *Lady Pilot Wrangled Large Pursuits, Shown Her Match by Bucking Cub.*

Thirty-Eight

"LET OUR HEARTS BE STOUT": A PRAYER BY THE PRESIDENT OF THE UNITED STATES

Almighty God: *Our sons, pride of our nation, this day have set upon a mighty endeavor, a struggle to preserve our Republic, our religion, and our civilization, and to set free a suffering humanity.*

Lead them straight and true: Give strength to their arms, stoutness to their hearts, steadfastness in their faith.

Many people have urged that I call the nation into a single day of special prayer. But because the road is long and the desire is great, I ask that our people devote themselves in a continuance of prayer. As we rise to each new day, and again when each day is spent, let words of prayer be on our lips invoking Thy help to our efforts.

Thy will be done, Almighty God.
Amen.

Excerpt from the *New York Times,* June 7, 1944

The small community of Hanson, Kentucky, had no hospital, so Dr. Brown made a house call, checking on Libby at the boardinghouse where Ginger had a room.

The elderly, gray-haired doctor examined Libby's eyes with a penlight.

"Yup, that's one nasty bump. I'm sure you'll have black eyes tomorrow." He gently pressed on the area around her nose.

Libby winced and pulled back.

"Tender, yes. But the thing that's got me worried is your nausea. Could be sign of a concussion. But even then, you should be fine. We'll just keep an eye on you. The worst case would be trauma to your optic nerve."

"Is that serious?"

He flipped off the penlight, sliding it back into his shirt pocket. "Could be. My suggestion is that you stay down for a few days. Mrs. McMurphy said she'd take care of you. Keep the ice pack fresh for that bump."

"But I told Ginger I'd ferry the planes for her. I—"

Dr. Brown scowled. "Now listen here. The last thing you want is to be piloting a plane with a head injury. It's not like walking around, you know. If you black out, that will be the end of you. I'll be back in a few days to check in."

"So I have to lie here and rest for two or three days? What else can I do, you know, to speed up my recovery?"

The doctor moved to the window and lowered the shade. "Are you a religious woman?"

Libby nodded, then winced from the throbbing in her temple.

"Our boys are fighting a mighty battle as we speak, storming the beaches at Normandy. It might be a good time to send up some prayers. It seems the tide of the war can turn to our favor if we succeed today."

Libby let her eyelids flutter shut. "Of course, I'll pray. And I guess in the scheme of things, a bump on the head isn't that bad."

Dr. Brown patted her leg. "That's a good girl. I'll be back to check on you; and if anything changes or things get worse, just let Mrs. McMurphy know. She's a saint, that woman. You're in good hands."

Ginger arrived home two days later. "You poor thing. Just look at you." Her hand covered her mouth, holding back a giggle. "Libby, I'm sorry, but you look like a raccoon."

"I look like a raccoon, but I feel like a donkey. What was I thinking, trying to hold down a spinning Cub?"

"Have you tried to get up?" Ginger sat in the chair next to Libby's bed.

"Just to the bathroom and back. Mrs. McMurphy has been a doll. I wish I could take her home. She even made blueberry muffins."

"And the doctor. What does he think?"

"He's supposed to drop by tomorrow, but I'm sure everything will be fine. I think my body's just using this time as an excuse to get some extra sleep. I hadn't realized how exhausted I was." Libby sat up in bed. For an instant the room seemed to blur, but she ignored it, choosing instead to focus on Ginger's concerned smile. "And what about you? How were the hearings?"

Ginger rose and moved to the nightstand, fiddling with the bouquet of white roses Mrs. McMurphy had brought in from her garden. "I—I was hoping you wouldn't ask." She took a rose from the vase and lifted it to her nose. "Honestly, things aren't looking good. There are a whole bunch of stuffed-shirt bureaucrats who consider the WAFS simply a pet project. I'm really worried. The training program has been shut down for good, and they still don't want to give us military status. Just between us . . . I'm afraid the whole program might wash out."

"You can't be serious." A sharp pain shot through Libby's head. She let out a low moan, and the room faded into fuzz. She quickly closed her eyes, pressing her fingers to her eyelids.

"I'm so sorry. I shouldn't have said anything."

"No, I'm glad to know—but, my head. I think I've tried to do too much."

"Of course." Ginger's voice faded, but Libby didn't open her eyes. "I'll be back to check on you later."

The door closed, and Libby felt her stomach turn. "Dear God, no. Please no." She turned to her side, grabbing the bucket Mrs. McMurphy had left for her.

Her stomach retched, and she heaved into the bucket. "God, please help me."

She tried to muffle her sobs into her pillow. The worst part was, Libby didn't know which she was crying harder about—the thought of the WAFS being disbanded or fear about her future. What did "trauma to the optic nerve" mean, exactly?

Libby wiped her eyes, daring to open them. "Please, Lord. Please." But it was no use. The room faded just as it had before, and even turning her head on her pillow caused the room to black out completely.

She curled onto her side and tucked the blankets around her, wanting more than anything to have someone there to brush back the hair from her face and tell her everything would be okay. But it wasn't just anyone she wanted. It was Dan. And more tears flowed as she considered the reality that he might not be coming back.

"Remember, there are men fighting and dying at this very moment," she tried to tell herself. "In comparison, I don't have it so bad."

But even as she whispered the words in the fading light, her heart told her otherwise. It seemed that everything she cared for and loved was being stripped away.

Thirty-Nine

PRAYER FOR ARMED FORCES

To the Editor:

It may interest your readers to have the following, a prayer for this crisis. It is taken from one of seven leaflets for the armed forces and their friends at home. This is shortened a little from the original.

"Jesus Christ, our Savior, King of Kings, in Whose pierced Hands are held the destiny of nations, we ask You for a just victory and lasting peace for our dearly beloved native land. Protect the souls and bodies of all in the armed forces, and bring them back safely to their dear ones. Guard and comfort those who must wait at home, and move their hearts to prayer and confidence in You, Who live and reign, almighty and all-loving God, forever and ever, Amen."

Edward F. Garesche, Catholic Medical Mission Board, Inc.
Excerpt from the *New York Times*, June 17, 1944

Libby turned her face to the footsteps nearing the door and squinted, trying to decipher the face of the man who entered. The one she hoped would give a better second opinion.

"It's okay, Miss Conners. You don't have to open your eyes for me. I'm no Jimmy Stewart, if you know what I mean."

Dr. Anderson laughed, but Libby didn't join in.

She closed her eyes again, and her eyelids shined red from the light of the examination room. But even as she lay upon the table, the room seemed to sway around her, like the rocking of a life raft on a gentle wave.

"I'm afraid it does look like traumatic optic neuropathy, which is just a fancy way of saying that you got a bad knock to the bones protecting your eyes. Unfortunately, this is one of the worst cases I've seen." He turned to his chart. "The impact has caused a buildup of blood from the injury. It's putting pressure on the optic nerve. That accounts for the blurriness you're experiencing."

"But you can do something about it, right? Surgery? Or is there something I can do? I'm a pilot, you know. I—I've already spent too much time away."

He didn't answer for a few seconds. "Surgery won't work. Even if we're able to relieve the pressure, the scar tissue could cause the same type of pressure. I'm afraid all I can say is to wait." He took her hand in his.

Libby opened her eyes and saw sympathy in his gaze.

"Wait for the pressure to go down. Sometimes it happens, and other times . . ."

Libby didn't need for him to say the words. A pain shot through her chest, making her breathing labored, as she realized that her whole world was collapsing around her.

I don't think I can do it, Lord. I can't be this strong . . . be strong for me.

Rose's laughter filled the railroad passenger car as she chatted with a group of reserves on the way home for weekend leave. This was their second day on board together, and Libby had thanked Rose a dozen times for taking time off to join her on the train ride home.

Rose shrugged. "That's what friends are for."

The rumbling of the engines and the gentle rocking of the train had lulled Libby into a state of numbness. "Last time I returned home a hero. This time, what do I have to show for myself?" She touched the bandages over her eyes. "I can't even read the newspaper without feeling sick, let alone wash my own laundry or cook."

Rose rested her head on Libby's shoulder. "Not that you were much of a cook to begin with."

Libby reached over and pinched her friend's arm. "Thanks a lot. I can always count on you to make me feel better." She could hear the smile in Rose's voice.

"I aim to please." Rose sighed. "Besides, if things continue sliding downhill the way they are, none of us will be flying soon."

"Flying for the military, that is. But even if you have

to go back to commercial work, you can still race through the sky."

The train began to slow, finally pulling to a stop. The noises of men and women adjusting in their seats, or standing to stretch, filled Libby's ears.

Rose lifted her head. "I think this is it. We're here. Oh, look, there's your dad. I recognize him from his picture."

"Oh, *look*?" Libby's bottom lip pouted.

"Sorry. Here. Let me get that for you."

Libby felt the satchel lifted from her grasp. She stretched her hand forward, keeping her hand on Rose's shoulder.

Rose's hand curled on her elbow. "Careful, there's a step here. That's it. One more."

As soon as they stepped from the train, down onto the platform, she felt strong arms encircling her.

"Oh, Daddy." Libby wrapped her arms around his neck, feeling the scratch of his whiskers against her cheek. His hand brushed back her hair, and Libby wondered why she'd stayed away so long.

"Daddy." Libby took a step back and turned to where Rose stood beside her. "This is my best friend, Rose. The one I've told you about."

"Rose, nice to meet you. I was wondering if the train would be on time today. There was a shipment of coffee rations and such that came in yesterday. It was fifteen minutes late. It seems they can't keep on schedule anymore."

"Well, we may be a few minutes late, but I'll be

around for quite a while." Libby shuffled as she took small steps forward.

Her father grasped her other arm, and Libby heard him sniffle beside her. He released his grasp and blew his nose into his handkerchief.

"Well, one thing's for sure." Libby tried to make her tone light. "You always said I do everything with gusto, and when I hit my head, I did it up right."

Her father led her to his old truck, and they squeezed into the cab—Libby in the middle. It smelled of old vinyl and dust. It also smelled of her father's favorite soap.

I'm home.

She didn't need her eyes to know what streets they were turning down. She could almost anticipate every pothole.

Her dad patted Libby's knee. "I swear, every time you're set to come home, the phone is ringing off the hook. A few of your pilot friends have called to check on you. And your boyfriend's mother. Is it Ima Jean?"

"Yes, Ima Jean. It will be great to hear from her."

"Oh, and someone named Anna-Lou called and said she was heading out West to visit some distant relatives, and she'd stop by to see you."

"Anna-Lou. Do you mean Annabelle?"

"Yes, Annabelle, that's right."

"She's really coming?" Libby took Rose's hand and squeezed. "Anyone else call?"

Her father was silent as he turned on the final road and parked on the gravel patch in front of their house.

"Only your mother, but I remembered how your last meeting went, and I told her not to bother you again."

Rose climbed from the truck and helped Libby do the same.

"Did you get a number where I could reach her?"

"Now, girl, why would I take a number?"

"Just wondering." The truck door made a loud slam. "There's a whole lot of reconsidering I've been doing lately."

❧ ❧ ❧

Libby lay in her childhood bed, and outside the window a songbird sang. She had returned. And the same feelings of aloneness and abandonment stirred within. She felt five again, waiting for the sun to come up in hopes the next day would be brighter. Only this time, even with eyes wide open, there was no brightness to look forward to.

To make matters worse, Annabelle had called to say she couldn't make it after all.

"Howie broke his leg. Of all things! I'm so sorry, Libby."

Instead, her friend had sent a set of Scripture cards, and Libby forced her father to read them repeatedly until she'd memorized every word.

"Come, behold the works of the Lord, what desolations he hath made in the earth," Libby whispered. "He maketh wars to cease unto the end of the earth; he breaketh the bow, and cutteth the spear in sunder; he burneth the chariot in the fire. Be still, and know that I am God: I will be exalted among the heathen, I will be exalted in the earth."

But oh, how hard it was to be still! And confusing too. Hadn't her part in the war effort mattered to God? Wasn't she doing the right thing by freeing a pilot to fight?

"Lord." She let her hands smooth the quilt around her bed. "I can't get much lower than this. I feel useless just lying here."

Be still and know.

Be still and pray.

Those were the messages that continued to stir inside her.

Libby lifted the bandages from her eyes and looked around the room. It was clear for a moment. But as soon as she lifted her head to find the bird in the trees, the room around her spun, and she felt a rush of nausea.

"No!" Libby punched the mattress beneath her. "I can't do this. I can't."

But no matter how frustrated she was, the tears wouldn't come. Because deep down she knew that her work wasn't done . . . she'd just changed occupations.

Be still and know.

Be still and pray.

Forty

WOMEN UNAFRAID

Tomorrow the Wasps (Women's Air Force Service Pilots) will become history. Twenty-five years from now Americans will look at faded photographs of these daring young women in their "teddy-bear" flying suits, their goggles, their oversize helmets, and their parachutes, and will smile as we smile today at pictures of 1918 yeomanettes.

The Wasps are not needed, says the Army, because there is a surplus of veteran men pilots to do their work—to ferry planes on non-combat assignments. So the 1000 or more young women who participated in one of the most venturesome jobs of the war will receive certificates of service and return to more traditional and possibly "ladylike" pursuits.

No more will they tramp through mud to hangars,

take out planes and soar into the clouds, riding alone for hours, often facing, from open cockpits, blasts of rain and snow and biting winds. No more will a slight, weary girl deliver at an airfield a bomber or fighter. No more will timorous citizens shudder at the thought of a chit of a girl at the stick of a roaring plane overhead.

Malvina Lindsay
Excerpt from the *Washington Post,* December 19, 1944

Her father's voice trembled as he read the news article. She could hear the paper rustling as he folded it and placed it on the dining room table.

Libby sat in her usual spot at the kitchen table, feeling better, feeling stronger. She'd discovered she could do almost anything as long as she kept her eyes bandaged. Everything but fly a plane, of course. *Not that I'd be able to do that as a WAF or WASP, or whatever they want to call us . . .*

Libby could see without the bandages—sometimes as long as thirty minutes at a time—without getting dizzy, but then the room would spin and the nausea would come.

For a gift, Betty had sent a pink satin mask similar to the one she wore to sleep. Libby had been so excited, she'd asked for a few more in different colors. Betty had been happy to oblige. Libby only wore those at night, of course. During the day she covered her bandages with the sunglasses she'd worn in Hawaii.

Over the past few days, Libby had even ventured out for walks around the neighborhood on her father's arm or with a cane. Miss Evelyn Mead always came to the fence for a chat, her ear cocked to the radio playing in the background. The neighborhood girls knew Libby too. At first they were shy of the "nearly blind pilot" until she invited them to sit on her front porch and listen to her stories about Hawaii, the Jap bombing of Pearl Harbor, her training, and her flights across the United States in the powerful fighter planes that now helped the Allies to win the war.

"I want to be a pilot when I grow up," said Rosemary.

"Me too! Me first," her older sister, Susan, had declared.

Libby took a sip of her tea, remembering their enthusiasm—so similar to hers once—and imagined what type of planes these girls would be able to fly someday.

"Are you okay?" Her father set down a plate of French toast on the table before her.

"Thanks, Dad. I can't believe it's over. Just like that." Her throat tightened, and she slumped in her chair. "All the others—I can't imagine what they're facing. Having to pack up, saying good-bye." She wiped a tear. "But I think it would've been harder to face if I hadn't left earlier. Six months has been a long time to get used to the idea."

She pushed the plate away.

"I've had time to think and to pray. And I guess it shouldn't surprise me that we face suffering in this life. I mean, Jesus went all the way to the cross."

She could hear her father's chair scooting back and his footsteps walking to the window.

"It looks cold out there. A winter storm might be heading our way. I'd best get out and see how Evelyn is getting along with your Christmas present."

"My present?" Libby turned her face to his voice.

"Well, it was something we started when you first were in Hawaii, and for a while I wondered if it would be worth giving to you at all, but . . . well, you'll see. I'll be back in a few minutes."

The door opened, then shut again.

If anything, Lord, you've brought Dad and me closer together. Or maybe showed me a closeness I was too busy to appreciate before.

Natsuo stood outside the small cell, listening to Dan's labored breaths. The sky was clear tonight. And the air ice cold. Stars hung on the velvet darkness like a thousand lanterns decorating the emperor's palace—or at least the way they had before the bombing raids.

The moon hung in the center of it all, and Natsuo reached up a hand as if he could touch it. Around the man-made island, waves crashed over the compacted dirt and rocks, eroding a little of it away with every swipe.

Just as the Americans are eating away at our island. Piece by piece.

His gloved hands still trembled as he remembered the sky filled with enemy bombers. A few Zeros had risen to meet them, but they looked like hummingbirds rising to fight a squad of eagles. The bombers had flown slowly and close to the ground, picking off targets with ease.

Today, they first hit a hundred miles away at Nagoya. Natsuo heard they'd wiped out a great airplane plant, leaving nothing but fires in their wake. Then the bombers moved into Tokyo from the west, swarming the industrial areas. Two had even flown directly overhead, buzzing inland and dropping their load perilously close to the emperor's palace.

Natsuo pulled a cigarette from the pocket of his thick coat and lit it. He usually did not smoke during his night watches, but whom did he fool? Dan knew he was there.

And what if the bomb *had* struck the palace? What if their emperor was killed? Could their god really die?

The radio warned of more raids to come. Swarms of people packed the roads leaving the city.

Natsuo had known this would happen. He'd given Dan the chance to head to the hills. Yet he was not surprised when D.J. had chosen to provide comfort to a dying friend, rather than to save himself.

To save your life you must lose it, Dan had said one night through the small window.

The emperor believed the same. Many soldiers gave their lives for their god. Yet something was different about the Christian way.

And that was what troubled him. Dan's God gave His life for His people. Not the other way around.

"D.J., can you do something for me? When your country wins this war?" Natsuo took the butt of his cigarette and tossed it to the ground. It glowed on the cold, hard gravel.

"I'll do my best." It was a muffled voice. A tired voice.

"My sister. She lives in California, remember? When you make it home, can you find her and help? I do not know what type of condition she will be in . . . after."

"And if I don't make it?"

"I have done all I could to ensure you do." Natsuo pulled his fur collar tight around his face. "For the sake of my sister, of course."

"And for the sake of a friendship?"

"I cannot do it all. The rest I leave to your God—to see you through. If He is able."

Dan coughed, and Natsuo heard his voice grow in strength as he neared the window.

"He is able." Dan's voice held no fear. "But no matter if I live or die, I will still trust Him. I hope you can come to understand that same hope someday."

Natsuo placed his hand against the wooden wall. "I understand you have found great strength, although you are no better than dead."

Then he strode away, not giving Dan the chance to hear his last words. "I also understand that even though I am free, I am dead inside."

Forty-One

JAPS QUIT UNCONDITIONALLY:
GUNS STILLED

President Truman last night dispatched through Secretary of State Byrnes an order for the Japanese government to stop the war on all fronts.

The war's over!

President Truman proclaimed the end at 7 o'clock last night.

He said that Japan had accepted the Allied surrender terms without qualification.

Edward T. Folliard
Excerpt from the *Washington Post,* August 15, 1945

Libby sat in the sunshine and lifted her hands, praising God that she had gone one hour without bandages over her eyes. Lying back in the soft grass, she'd watched a baby bird on its flight and laughed at the awkward movements of its body.

She plucked a blade of grass, studying the simple beauty. “I have new eyes,” she often told her father. “I see things differently these days.”

In a strange way, this new way of seeing was a gift from the darkness. With her physical eyes closed, her focus turned to what her heart needed most—namely, connecting with God in prayer.

Praying had become her sole service to her country. She cried out to God for His assistance to their fighting soldiers—in France, Belgium, and as they pushed their way through Germany. She prayed for those in the South Pacific, who reclaimed lost islands and destroyed enemy fortifications.

Libby prayed especially hard after reports came in about captives who’d been in the hands of the Japanese. Some were saved when Japanese ships carrying prisoners were bombed, and they were picked up by American subs. Others were rescued when the U.S. regained control of the Philippines. They all told about the horror of Bataan, the camps, the ships.

She prayed in sorrow when she heard that President Roosevelt had died, not living to see the victory for which he’d often prayed over the airwaves, fortifying the resolve of a fearful nation.

She’d rejoiced through tearful prayers when V-E Day was announced—*Victory in Europe!* And she prayed for a final peace after two atomic bombs flattened Japanese cities.

That's not to say she didn't worry too. What if Dan was on one of those ships but didn't get pulled from the waves? What if he was imprisoned in one of the destroyed cities? Or what if he did not make it at all? What if he had died four years ago on Bataan?

What if?

But Libby had discovered the one thing to combat these fears. "Perfect love casts out all fear," she'd tell herself. And that's how Jesus' love had become to her . . . perfect.

Libby turned onto her stomach and opened the cover of her Christmas present. It was a scrapbook her father had put together for her with the help of Evelyn. She scanned the headlines:

U.S. Sending Scores of Pilots to Hawaii and Philippines

Bataan Falls After Epic Struggle

Japanese Seek World Rule by "Divine Appointment"

It was like reading one's own story within the words of news headlines. And in the eight months since receiving the book, Libby had added her own headlines:

Rangers Rescue 513 "Death March" Captives on Luzon—February 2, 1945

800 Yanks Die in Sinking of Jap Prison Ship—February 23, 1945

B-29s Rain Fire on Tokyo, Hit Kawasaki Hard—April 16, 1945

Victory in Europe—May 8, 1945

Jap Prisons Treat Americans Better—July 10, 1945

Now there was a new clipping to add to her book

from today's paper. *Japs Quit Unconditionally: Guns Stilled—August 15, 1945.* Which could only mean one thing.

If Dan's alive, he's coming home!

ꝶ ꝶ ꝶ

Dan shielded his eyes and raised his face to the sun. A wide grin spread over his face at the sight of the American planes. He stood on the wooden roof of the barracks, leaning over to finish his message.

He'd painted three letters on the roof. *P.O.W.* Then underneath, he'd written a longer message. *What took you so long?*

With a flourish of his brush, he hunkered down on the peak in the warm sunshine. To watch. To wait. The hymn "Great Is Thy Faithfulness" escaped from his lips.

The night that Natsuo asked Dan to care for his sister was the last Dan had spoken with him. Rumor had it that the interpreter had requested a transfer closer to Kobe in order to care for his aging father and mother. Some said he had gone mad after that, taking off the heads of a half dozen captive pilots in a single day.

Dan had witnessed a beheading once. The pilot kneeling on the ground, and the heavy blade making a downward arc, slashing through the man's neck in one clean sweep. The pilot's head fell forward and then there was a gurgling sound, then only silence.

Impossible. Not Natty.

Others claimed Natsuo had softened and was actually helping those in the camps. Dan hoped the latter was true. All he knew was that the day Natsuo walked away, his solitary confinement had been over. Dan's prison doors were opened. So were Benjamin's.

It was a gift actually; Dan was able to meet his friend face-to-face, sitting by Ben's side during his last hours. How different this death was from the others Dan had seen during his days in captivity. As Dan held Ben's hand and recited the Scripture verses that his friend loved so much, he witnessed not a prisoner dying in bondage, but a child of God peacefully leaving this world to enter into an eternity with Jesus.

And after that, Dan was once again able to live and work with the other prisoners. It was hard work but satisfying to be connected with people once more.

Then, a few weeks ago, as the bombings increased, the guards turned away from violence and instead began showing kindness. Only the commandant and a few guards remained, attempting to keep order.

Dan looked to the ground and noticed the commandant approaching. He no longer wore his crisp white uniform or carried his samurai sword with the beautiful gold-and-emerald scabbard. Instead he was dressed in the olive drab uniform of the average soldier.

Dan scooted to the edge of the roof and climbed down, joining with the seventy-five others to circle the small man. The commandant's hands shook as he lifted the proclamation to his face.

"His Imperial Majesty, in an effort to put an end to

the death and bloodshed, has agreed to an unconditional surrender and cessation of war. All hostilities have been terminated. His Majesty and your General MacArthur will sign the terms of surrender on 2 September 1945. I have been ordered to inform you that, as of this moment, you are no longer prisoners of war. You are free. I have also been instructed to ask that you all remain here until your authorities come for you, after the surrender has been signed."

"Free! Did y'all hear that?" one soldier called. He removed his cap and tossed it into the air. Then almost all at once, the men became a sentimental mob, laughing, crying, embracing.

One man approached Dan and placed a large kiss on his cheek. "We're going home! Sweetheart, here I come! I can't wait to see my woman again."

"What about the Nips?" Another soldier, Harvey, rolled up his sleeves. "They deserve to pay for what they've done."

By this time the commandant was scurrying across the island, running for a waiting jeep. The soldier took two steps toward him.

Dan hurried over, placing a hand on Harvey's chest. "Let him go. He's not worth it." Dan raised his shoulders and peered directly into the soldier's eyes. "I don't know about you, but I can't go home feeling completely innocent for what I've done. It's war. And in war horrible things happen."

"But what they did. You didn't see—" The man's words stopped short as he studied Dan's face.

"I was there. In the thick of it." Dan nodded. "Justice will catch up to them someday."

"The kitchen!" another man called. "Food."

They rushed like hungry animals to the food stores, opening up the small warehouse. Then the commotion paused as their wide eyes took in Red Cross packages stacked to the ceiling.

"Can you believe this? All this time it was right here."

Dan began handing out packages. "Sometimes we don't realize what we have . . . right under our noses. Feed up, boys!" He grabbed a few packages and headed to the far solitary cells, settling down where Natsuo had stood in the dark so many times before. He opened a package to find canned meat, chocolate, and crackers, but limited himself, knowing too much too soon would make him sick.

Harvey approached, settling down beside Dan.

"Do you believe that you can truly forgive them, Dan? Can you leave this place with anything but pure hatred for this whole race of people?"

Dan took a bite of chocolate. It was thicker than the small Hershey bars back home, and he let the sweetness melt on his lips. "I'm going to try."

"Well, I'm not. And I'll tell you why." Harvey took a cigarette out of his shirt pocket, lit it, and took a long drag, flicking away the ashes. "Nobody wants to forgive. Those who say they do just don't want to deal with the truth. They're delusional. You aren't going to be able to shrug off those memories.

"I see it in your eyes," Harvey continued. "You want to say things are okay, but you're haunted. There's something bothering you, even if you don't want to admit it."

"Yeah, there is something bothering me." Dan placed the food package to his side. "I'm worried I will forget. That I'll get home and get on with life too easily." Dan cleared his throat. "I don't want to do that. When I get home, I want to find a way to share the stories of the men who can no longer speak for themselves. It's a hard story to hear, but those who haven't experienced war need to know."

"All of it? About the march? The ships? A story about seeing your buddy's stomach spilled open right before your eyes?"

"For some of us, it's also a story of hope. A story of the dawn that comes after darkness."

Both heads turned at the sound of a jeep rumbling up to the locked gates.

Then came the call of an American voice. "Where is everybody? Get your lazy butts out here. Don't you guys know you're free?"

"Some of us *can* be free." Dan rose and offered a hand to his friend. "If we're willing to accept it."

Forty-Two

3 PLANES ARRIVE WITH
80 SURVIVORS OF "DEATH MARCH"

Hamilton Field, Calif., Sept 25 (U.P.)—Three transport planes carrying 80 survivors of the Bataan death march and Wake Island . . . landed here today.

The roar of the planes failed to drown out the happy shouts of relatives as they watched the craft land. Many of the liberated prisoners were weeping as they stepped from the ramps.

Excerpt from the *Washington Post,* September 26, 1945

Dan struggled to choke back tears when his booted feet climbed the metal steps of the airplane. He took his seat next to a window and waited for the rumble of the engines to tell him they would soon take off. He'd made it. He was leaving Manila, going home. He could hardly believe it.

As each minute in the sky brought him closer, he found himself wiping his face with the back of his hand, blotting out the tears from his clean, shaven cheeks.

Memories filled his mind of saying good-bye to Libby on that rainy morning, the bombings at Clark Field, the death march, the hell ships, the mines. He caught his breath—Gabe.

Oh, buddy. I wouldn't have made it without you.

He remembered the months in solitary and his final conversation with Natty. *Lord, please take care of him.*

Dan looked at his thin, weak hands. Would they ever be strong again? *Will I ever be the man I used to be?* His jailers had broken his body—memories plagued him of beatings, hunger, and the malaria that still weakened him. But his body would heal. Good food, rest, the army's best medicine. He was already on the mend.

The years imprisoned had also broken his heart. The verbal abuse, being treated as less than human. And so many friends gone. *Tex, José, Paulo, Tony.* His chest tightened.

Dan stared out the window at the sun breaking away from the velvet darkness, rising over the pink and orange clouds. His *heart*? Well, that was being healed too.

He opened his Bible and took out the old, crinkled, faded picture of Libby. Along with that silly pocketknife, it had been his only possession for so many months. *Libby.*

How many tears had he cried over that photo? Was the image real? Could it be that in just a few hours he'd come face-to-face with the person his heart had longed for most?

❧ ❧ ❧

Dan exited the airplane into the cool California morning and gazed out over the crowds amassed on the tarmac of Hamilton Field, the tears returning again. They flooded down Dan's cheeks and dripped off his chin. Home. After all that darkness.

His knees felt weak, and he gripped the handrail to steady himself. *C'mon, legs, don't fail me now.* The warm sunshine kissed his face, and all he could do was whisper, "Thank You. Thank You . . ."

He took in the sounds of the crowd of mothers, fathers, wives, sons, daughters on the tarmac—all waving, cheering, most weeping.

He waved and scanned the faces, noticing a woman and three young boys screaming, "Daddy! Daddy!"

The oldest one pointed. "I see him! My dad! Look!" He grabbed the youngest into his arms and pointed again. "That's your daddy."

Dan turned away as the woman ran into the soldier's arms.

He scanned the crowds. *Where is she? Where's Libby?*

He finally caught sight of his mother's frantically waving arms and beaming face. His father stood behind her, and Dan could clearly make out his voice over the crowd. "My son. He's home. My son!"

Flashbulbs and voices blurred as Dan rushed into his mother's embrace.

"You're home, oh, Daniel." Her body shook; whether from laughter or tears, he couldn't tell, maybe both. She squeezed his neck so tightly he didn't know if he'd ever escape. When she finally did release him, she held him at arm's length. "Oh, you're so thin." She wiped his tears with her trembling hands. "But we'll fix that."

He placed a warm kiss on her cheek. "Mom, I missed you so much."

"Enough, woman!" Dan's dad interrupted. He grabbed Dan into a hug even tighter than his mom's. "I'm so proud of you, Son. I couldn't be prouder."

"Thanks, Dad," Dan managed to say. "Now, where's Libby? Isn't she here?"

His mother's eyebrows creased. "Dan, dear. She's waiting in her father's truck. She's having a bad day, headaches again. I think it's all the excitement. Did you get my letter?"

"Yeah, yeah. She has a little vision problem. But she's alive and breathing, right? Come on. I need to hold my girl."

Dan hurried through the crowd, hoping his parents trailed behind. He tugged on his pants, wishing he'd gotten a smaller size or he had another notch to tighten his belt. Even after the weeks spent at the hospital in Manila, he was fifty pounds lighter than when he'd entered the service. But he was alive. He was home, and that's all the mattered.

He moved past the first row of vehicles, looking into truck windows. His heart pounded.

"What took you so long, soldier?" said a voice from behind him. "What's it been, a thousand nights, at least?"

Dan turned. Years of welled-up emotions flooded him, and instead of whisking her into his arms as he'd imagined a thousand times, he froze. Stared. Her eyes were so beautiful, brown and warm. Her lips looked so soft, warm, kissable. And in her hair she wore an orchid.

He pulled her into his embrace.

"Libby. It's you." He breathed in the scent of her. Kissed her hair. Then he set her down and traced the outline of her face. "It's really you."

❧ ❧ ❧

Two weeks after their quiet wedding in Dan's parents' backyard and a romantic honeymoon on the Oregon coast, Libby awoke to the sound of Dan's mother singing from the kitchen. They decided it would be best to stay with his parents awhile—until Dan finished his classes on the GI bill and they could get on their feet.

The smells of pancakes sizzling on a grill brought a smile to Libby's face.

Sunlight sifted in through the white curtains as she snuggled in closer to Dan. She pressed her cheek against his chest and ran a finger over his muscular arm.

She glanced up at Dan's model airplanes that she'd

seen on her first visit to Ima Jean's house. At that time Libby hadn't been sure she'd ever see Dan again. Now . . . she sighed and sank back into her pillow.

"You awake?" he whispered, brushing the hair from her face.

"Mm-hm."

"Did you hear that?"

"You mean how your heartbeat quickened as I pulled myself closer?"

He kissed her forehead. "Not only that. The words of the song my mom's singing."

"'Amazing Grace'?"

"Yeah. I mean, I've heard them hundreds of times, but . . ."

"I once was lost, but now I'm found. Was blind but now I see," Libby whispered.

He pulled her tighter against him. "Yeah, that part. Amazing, isn't it?"

Epilogue

Libby slid the sunglasses over her eyes and reached into the backseat of the car. She lifted one model airplane off the seat and groaned softly as her expanding girth refused to let her bend to retrieve the other one off the floor.

"Dan, can you reach the Cub for me? It slid down next to the bags of clothes."

"Junior getting in your way again?" He rubbed her stomach as he scooted past her, his left hand already holding two airplanes of his own.

"Yes, *she's* growing so big I'm not even sure if I'm wearing two matching shoes today."

"It's a boy, I'm telling you." Dan placed a hand on the small of Libby's back and led her toward the rolling waves of the Pacific Ocean.

Libby wasn't even sure of the name of this beach, but it was a beautiful spot. They were somewhere near

Santa Cruz on their way to visit Natsuo's family. The bags of clothes in the backseat were those their church had collected for Hoshiko's children, and for other families trying to start a new life after the relocation camps.

Libby breathed in the scent of salty air and lifted her face to the sun already beginning to fade in the western horizon. They'd been driving most of the day along the California coast looking for the perfect spot. And they'd found it. A small beach of sand, with a parking area right off the road. Though the beach was peaceful, large waves crashed against jagged rocks in the harbor. *Perfect.*

Dan's grip tightened around her side, steadying her as she climbed over a few rocks that lined the shore. "Doing okay, doll face?"

"Mm-hm, doing great."

It had been two days since Libby's last headache, and as long as she lay down every few hours to rest her eyes, she pretty much lived life as normal—or as normal as it could be without flying.

Beginning on the day he arrived home, and every day since, Dan found a moment to stop and pray for Libby's eyes. And his prayers were being answered. The doctor told them that the healing was simply her body doing its work, relieving the swelling around the optic nerve, but they knew better. It was a miracle.

Libby lined up her three planes on the sand next to Dan's models, out of reach of the waves, and watched as he slid off his shoes, then rolled up his pant legs to his knees. She was thankful for this man of strength, of faith, of prayer. Thankful that instead of holding on to the pain of his war years, he was sharing his memories with church congregations and civic groups—ensuring that the lives of his friends would not be forgotten and encouraging his listeners to forgive. His was a much-needed message for soldiers and civilians alike, as they attempted to begin new lives of peace after years of war.

After every meeting, audience members sought him out—to share their stories, show pictures of their sons or husbands or friends, and to seek prayer. There was one person who had refused to wait until the end of the service to speak with Dan.

It was during a visit to Sacramento that a young, dark-haired fellow hurriedly entered through the back of the church. "Excuse me, Mr. Lukens, sir." He jogged up the aisle. "But I believe you have my pocketknife."

Dan had rushed from the platform, pulling Tony into a tight embrace. Then with a wide grin he'd pulled the knife from his pocket. "I've been holding it for you, just keeping it safe."

Even now the memory of their joyful reunion brought a smile to Libby's face.

When Dan finished rolling up his pant legs, he did the same for Libby.

She wiggled her bare toes in the wet sand, pushed her sunglasses to the top of her head, and glanced into the waves. "It's strange to think Rose is back across that ocean on that little island again. Who knows, maybe one of these planes will wash up on Ewa Beach."

"Could happen." Dan lifted the model of the small Cub off the sand and handed it toward Libby. "Want to go first?"

"Sure." She looked down at the miniature replica of the plane. It was just like the one she'd flown at John Rodgers Airport. Across the plane's body she had written *In memory of George Abel—start with what you know.*

Libby lowered her head and whispered a prayer. A few tears escaped as she cocked back her hand and then let the plane sail into the waves.

"What a throw." Dan kissed her forehead. "That's the girl I love."

Dan was next, picking up a P-40 that he'd dedicated to his friends who lost their lives in the Philippines, launching it into the waves.

With another silent prayer, Libby followed with the model of July's trainer. And after that, Dan launched the plane he'd crafted especially for Gabe.

After each throw, they'd watch the plane soar, then hit the water, becoming lost in the white foam and mounting waves.

"There are two left." Libby looked to the matching P-51s. One had *Libby* written in script on the side, the other *D.J.* Libby's chest constricted as Dan handed her the model with her name. She let her fingers trail the cockpit, remembering what it was like climbing in, starting the engine, and soaring into the clouds.

"I don't know if I can do this, Dan." She let her hand drop to her side. "The others were our way of saying good-bye. But . . . but what if God does a miracle? What if we both find ourselves able to fly again?"

Dan plucked his plane from the sand, walked behind Libby, and wrapped his arms around her shoulders. "Letting them sail is not the same as saying 'never,' Libby. Only God knows what's in store for us. Just think of it as releasing our future into God's hands."

Libby turned her head and kissed his arm swung over her shoulder. "That I can do."

Dan released his embrace and strode into the waves, cocking his arm back in a perfect football player pose.

"Wait!" she called over the sound of gulls approaching from the sea. "Together, on the count of three."

She wobbled to his side and then cocked her plane back. "One, two, three . . ."

Their planes sailed through the air side by side, finally crashing into the waves.

As they stood there a few more minutes, feeling the cold water swirling around their legs, Libby knew they had done the right thing. Releasing their future to God. Placing their hope in His plan. It was all anyone could do on this earth. It was the one thing that brought true hope.

Libby placed one hand on her growing stomach and slid her other hand into Dan's larger one. Then she lifted her face to the setting sun, a prayer of thanksgiving in her heart.

Start with what you know.

Acknowledgments

It takes a village to support a writer. My gratitude for help with this project goes to:

John, my amazing husband. I wouldn't be able to do this without you. You are forever loved.
Cory, Leslie, and Nathan, my three great kids. Thanks for supporting me and understanding when I'm glued to my computer chair.
Linda Martin and Dolores Coulter, my mom and grandma, whose prayers and encouragement I depend on.
John and Darlyne Goyer, my parents-in-law. Thanks for your love and support!
My best friends, Tara Norick, Twyla Klundt, and Cindy Martinusen. Your cheers make my day!
Janet Holm McHenry, writer, teacher, and friend. Thanks for the poetry lesson!

My prayer friends and writer-groups, especially One Heart and Blessed Hope. What would I do without you?

My agent, Janet Kobobel Grant. Thanks for believing in me!

My editors, Andy McGuire and LB Norton. I'm thrilled to work with such a great team.

My "unofficial" editors, Ocieanna Fleiss, Mike Yorkey, Bruce and Suzan Robertson, Jim Thompson, and Amy Lathrop. Your input is so appreciated!

Finally, this book wouldn't be written if not for the wonderful men and women who help with my research:

Tony Banham, Hong Kong Historian and author. I'm forever grateful for the day I stumbled across www.hongkongwardiary.com. Thanks for answering all my questions!

Wally Scragg, policeman who was interned at Stanley.

Barbara Anslow, former prisoner of Stanley and member of ARP (Air Raid Precautions).

Reed Lamb, master mechanic extraordinaire. Thanks for letting me sit in the planes!

My ACRW friends who assisted my Hawaiian research.

Paul Inzer, WWII Veteran and ex-POW of three and a half years of the Japanese.

Lester Tenney, Bataan Survivor, ex-POW of the Japanese, and author.

Federico Baldassarre, Bataan researcher.

Clarence Graham, Bataan survivor and author.

Nick Gaynos, Pearl Harbor survivor.

Earl Williams, Pearl Harbor survivor.

Millie Dalrymple, former member of WASP (Women Air Service Pilots).

Bernice Haydu, former member of WASP (Women Air Service Pilots).

Lorraine Z. Rodgers, former member of WASP (Women Air Service Pilots).

AJ Starr, former member of WASP (Women Air Service Pilots).

Shutsy Reynold, former member of WASP (Women Air Service Pilots).

May your stories live on through these pages!

More from Tricia Goyer & Moody Publishers!

A Story of Liberation

Nazis flee under cover of darkness as American troops approach the town of St. Georgen. A terrible surprise awaits the unsuspecting GIs, and three people—the wife of an SS guard, an American soldier, and a concentration camp survivor—will never be the same. Inspired by actual events surrounding the liberation of a Nazi concentration camp.

From Dust and Ashes
ISBN: 0-8024-1554-7

A Story of Sacrifice

Young Jakub finds himself in the prisoner-led orchestra of Hitler's Mauthausen death camp. Engulfed by evil and weakened by starvation, he learns more than music from the world-renowned conductor imprisoned with him. Meanwhile, outside the camp, the beautiful daughter of an Austrian diplomat aids the resistance movement while her brave American fiance risks everything to find her. Will they be able to survive the Nazi evil that hunts them?

Night Song
ISBN: 0-8024-1555-5